STEALING FIRE

Accipiter War

Book Two

The Fort Brazos Saga

Patrick & Blake Seaman

STEALING FIRE
Accipiter War # 2

by Patrick Seaman & Blake Seaman

Printed in the United States of America
Copyright © Patrick Seaman: June 2020

3RD Edition, January 2023

First Paperback Printing: June 2020
Amazon Paperback ISBN 979-8-6559438-5-8
Amazon Hardcover ISBN 979-8-5185659-3-7
Milstar Books Paperback ISBN 979-8-9873243-4-9
Milstar Books Hardcover ISBN 979-8-9873243-3-2

Cover Art by Ron Miller
MilStar Books
MILSTARBOOKS.COM

Printed in the United States of America

This work is dedicated to the men and
women who selflessly defend freedom
and civilization every day.

- Patrick and Blake Seaman

Thomas Harding

TopSide: New London

August 30th, New London Day (NLD) 0, 6:00 PM.
Fort Brazos Day (FBD) 28

Commander Thomas James Harding's eyes bulged as he awakened, spasmodically gulping breaths of cold, still, frigid air. He sat up on the bed, blinking at the unfamiliar hotel room around him. Reflexively he reached for the slight bulge of the thumb drive sewn into his undress Navy uniform jacket.

Still there!

Then an uncontrollable wave of nausea and dizziness washed over him, and he swung his legs over the side of the bed and spotted the small trash can just in time to retch into it. Sweat burst from his forehead, and in moments his uniform felt damp and chill against his heaving chest.

He set the trash can down, folding the plastic liner over the former contents of his stomach.

Where the hell am I?

He bent over, clutching his pounding head in his hands. There was a bathroom across from the bed. He stood up but found that his legs were rubbery and the spinning in his head nearly forced him to his knees as the memory, dream, or nightmare of falling stars briefly flashed through his mind. He steeled himself and lurched dizzily to the bathroom, his shoulder colliding painfully with the door frame. He staggered to the sink, removed his oversized glasses, clumsily dropped them to the counter, bent over and washed his mouth out, and splashed the icy water on his face, staring at his reflection in the mirror.

Dizziness, nausea, headache, muscle control…. He sucked a breath in. I'm drugged. I've been drugged. They caught me! Maybe I'm not even here, and I'm strapped to a chair in some black site somewhere far from hope….

He shakily grabbed his glasses and nearly dropped them as he struggled to put them on, then turned and bolted out of the bathroom, his heart racing as his eyes darted this way and that, looking around the generic hotel room.

The cold tang of ozone mixed bitterly with the smell of his vomit. Opposite the hotel room door was a floor-to-ceiling sliding glass door visible behind the curtains. He straightened himself up and forced himself to walk calmly and deliberately to the curtains and pull them aside.

Looking out the sliding door, he saw that his room appeared to be many stories up in a tower, facing other buildings with similar balconies. The buildings were pastel-colored with no weather stains, laundry, or personal items on any of them. They all looked brand new.

He swallowed, ground his teeth, and slid the door open. The air outside was just as cold as the air inside, but it did not smell right. It did not smell like a city. There were none of the typical smells of auto exhaust or food or grime and decay. It smelled fresh, clean, and… sterile.

Something is wrong. Either the drugs are affecting my sense of smell too, or I really am strapped into a chair, and they've messed up trying to fool me.

He stepped onto the balcony and grasped the smooth, polished railing. All around him, other uniformed personnel and civilians were emerging onto their balconies, looking confused, upset, or both. Others seemed to be in shock, staring gape-mouthed at the sky or gesturing wildly.

A petty officer on the balcony next to him called out, "Sir, do you know what is happening?"

He stared blankly at the man, then shook his head.

His dizziness was fading. The biting cold air helped, but nothing made sense. He clearly was not in New London, Connecticut, anymore. There was no faint ocean smell at all. The pale buildings almost reminded him of Hong Kong, but they were too new and pristine.

He looked up to see what many of the people were pointing at. Eventually, he realized that his own jaw had dropped. He blinked and shut it with deliberate effort. The blue sky was not a sky. It was… It was a roof of some kind. Only it had to be at least a mile high or more, inlaid with what, from this distance, appeared to be a delicate circuit-like pattern.

He shook his head. This only confirms it. I must be hallucinating. It's the drugs. Maybe I really am strapped to a chair somewhere….

Or, in a glimmer of what he knew was false hope, *Maybe I escaped, and they are hunting me.*

He frowned, or they let me go to see if I would incriminate myself.

Swallowing, he decided. Whatever is happening to me, I cannot stay here. If I am in that chair, nothing I do will matter. So I might as well try to do something. If not, maybe I'm already free, and the drugs are making me hallucinate. If I move fast, perhaps I can make a run for it, and the drugs will wear off. If I am free, I will not let them retake me. I won't go out that way… not like John Walker, rotting in prison, probably as someone's bitch.

He turned back inside, closed the door and curtains behind him, and walked calmly to the door. He checked his pockets. Everything seemed to be there, including the small, polymer-framed Kahr P380 pocket pistol he had started carrying when, recently, he had seen the same face in the crowd one too many times.

He stopped for a moment, thinking. *Yesterday?* When was *Yesterday?* Pulling out his cellphone, he checked the date and sighed in relief. Then he noticed that there were no signal strength bars. The display read 'no service.'

He returned to the bathroom and dropped the cellphone into the water in the toilet. Checking his face in the mirror, he straightened his uniform and hair and walked to the exit door. Looking out the peephole, he saw that the hallway was filled with servicemen and women standing and talking animatedly to each other. He took a deep breath and exited the room.

Several people tried to ask him questions, but he ignored them and found the nearest stairwell without even looking for an elevator.

The stairwell was crowded with nervous, confused people. Most seemed more intent on escaping the building than talking.

In the lobby, he bodily pushed through the crowd and out into a street full of people. Outside, there were no cars, busses, or trains, only the cacophony of agitated, bewildered people. Something else about the scene bothered him, but he couldn't put a finger on it. Then it hit him. There was no commercial signage, street vendors, random trash, or, looking down, even tire marks on the pristine concrete street.

He walked and walked until the randomly spreading throngs converged along the only path available. He passed by several small parks and numerous empty storefronts with no signage whatsoever, as though the spaces had never been occupied. It struck him that this was an empty model city, like a model home in a new subdivision. Or a blank movie set. It was as though it had been built from the ground up, from scratch, and then all these people were dumped into it.

★ ★ ★

Brian Kupe had awoken in a room identical to Thomas Harding's. Like Thomas, Brian was taken aback by the impossible things he had seen around him, except that Brian did not think that he'd been drugged or was hallucinating. Brian had a well-earned reputation for being calm and calculating in a crisis. He was an exceptional chess player who never entered into a situation without being dangerously well prepared.

At the moment, though, Brian was as utterly clueless as everyone else. Still, a lifetime of discipline allowed him at least some degree of calm as he walked down the increasingly crowded and noisy but completely sterile and clean streets. He listened to the questions and conversations around him, alert for some kind of clue or insight, processing everything with the careful, methodical, and analytical mind that had led to him becoming one of the top counter-espionage agents in the FBI.

Brian was of medium height and medium build. His hair was somewhere between brown and black and cut in a European style. He was tanned with light olive skin and was often mistaken for being Latin American, Middle Eastern, or Mediterranean, depending on what he wore and how he behaved. He ruthlessly leveraged this and the language skills that went with it to his benefit.

Today, however, he was dressed like any ordinary civilian office worker or contractor, inexpensively but professionally. He blended into the surging, half-panicked crowd that was aimlessly headed to where no one knew. For the hundredth time, he glanced up at the impossible not-sky, or dome or ceiling, or whatever it was, with those delicate patterns and shapes overhead. There did not seem to be any immediately apparent physical danger. Still, the sky, and the obviously brand-new *everything* around him, was simply too much for him to not be profoundly affected by it.

Then, in a moment of professional weakness he would never forgive himself for, he stumbled in his tracks, causing people to bump into and flow around him like a rock in a stream. Standing twenty feet in front of him was the first familiar face he had seen thus far. Thomas Harding.

✪ ✪ ✪

Four years earlier, when the investigation into the leak of classified Navy documents had begun, Thomas Harding had not been on the radar. He was third-generation Navy, and while competent at his job, he did not unduly draw attention to himself or overly impress his superiors. He was one of the silent majority – people reasonably good at their jobs and reasonably happy doing them.

Eventually, his name had shown up on one too many lists, once too often, and the magnifying glass had turned in his direction. Nothing had stood out about him, his bank accounts, or the usual tells. Over time, though, the lists his name was on grew shorter and shorter by process of elimination.

In the last six months, his behavior had begun to show glimmers of paranoia. Warrants were obtained, his house bugged, and his calls monitored. The case was still circumstantial, but the accretion of coincidence had convinced Brian that Commander Thomas Harding was the mole.

✪ ✪ ✪

Thomas did not like what was happening around him. The crowd, whether it was real or not, became increasingly agitated. He kept telling himself that the sights around him could not be any more real than the crowd, that they were, at the very least, heavily altered by his hallucination. The surging mass of people were clearly looking for something or someone.

There were still no cars anywhere, but hundreds of golf carts lined the road as the streets widened. He thought about taking one of them but worried it might make him more conspicuous, especially if he ran over someone, and with this many people, that seemed more and more likely. His panic grew, and his breath quickened as the crowd swelled. He looked for an escape. All the roads, though, seemed to ultimately lead to the same place.

As he turned a corner and his street merged with another, he suddenly saw a familiar face. At first, he recognized it as one of the omnipresent civilian workers in his building, but… no. He knew that face. It was a face he had seen enough to cause an itch. And now, the other man's reaction was not one of ordinary recognition.

At that moment, amidst the familiar and disturbing otherworldliness around them, both men stopped in the streaming crowd of people and stared at each other with masks forgotten. Thomas's heart hammered in his chest, and his eyes widened in surprise. He knew once and for all that it was over. The other man, whoever he was, was the hunter and Thomas the prey.

He bolted in the only direction the crowd allowed. Forward. He did not need to turn to look and see if the other man pursued. Ahead, the streets had converged on a massive colonnaded building. It was the Pentagon, but it wasn't the Pentagon. He had been tricked and fooled into going there. He raced up the long steps toward the entrance, dashing ahead of the crowd, and seized the doors.

A short, wiry young woman with short sandy-blonde hair, a Navy rating, caught up with him, grabbed his arm, and asked breathily, "Sir, do you know what is happening?"

Thomas turned to face her, then looked at the crowd of excited people running up the steps. They were chasing him! He reached into his pocket, retrieved the pistol with one hand, and wrapped his arm around the woman's neck, holding the gun to her head.

She shrieked angrily and struggled hard, her cover knocked to the ground, but he out-massed her almost two to one and jerked her off her feet entirely. She lost one shoe but tried to kick him in the knees until he pressed the gun harder into her head.

He shouted to the crowd, "Stop! Stop, or I'll shoot her! Back off! You won't get me this way!"

The crowd was either confused, did not hear him, or both. Propelled by their mass and momentum, they did not slow down. He pointed the gun up into the air and fired a shot.

Just then, Master Sergeant Julian Dąbrowski emerged from the building behind Thomas. Julian was a massive, bear-like man. He scowled at the unfolding scene. The man with the gun had not heard him approach over the noise of the crowd. As the man raised the gun and fired, Julian swiftly and brutally disarmed him, broke his grip on the young woman, and tossed him bodily down the marble steps.

Apocalypse

Lieutenant David Garreth was just 24 years old, but worry lines creased his forehead. His green eyes were heavy with responsibility and the weight of survivor's guilt from a world lost and gone. That, and the discovery that he and everyone else had been abducted and deposited inside a hollow alien world.

If that wasn't enough, he and his men had been captured and cocooned by an alien creature. Corpsman Mendez and Sheriff's Deputy Grayson Miles had been vivisected and consumed by the alien. They haunted his dreams.

Despite all of that, he could not entirely suppress the hint of a smile on his face. Everyone seemed to have known before he had that he'd fallen head over heels for young Sandra Hoffman, the dairy farmer's daughter whose whole family had been similarly cocooned. Her parents and brother had not survived. However, Sandra, her sisters, and her toddler brother had lived, and in the hospital quarantine afterward, Garreth had been unable to take his eyes off the irrepressible blonde-haired, blue-eyed Sandra Hoffman, and nor had she, him.

Now, Garreth found himself looking at his second impossible sky in less than a month. High above the pristine new cityscape was a delicately patterned, sky-blue, clearly artificial roof of some kind. Without an object of scale, it was hard to make out just how high it was. However, the laser rangefinder they had aimed at earlier indicated something close to 6 km, but he wasn't sure he believed it.

He rode in the third Humvee in the column, with two Bradley Fighting Vehicles in the lead and Sergeant Garvesh Bahun's comm's trucks, formerly of the 29th Queen's Gurkha Signals Regiment, in the middle. Two more Bradleys had been left behind as rearguards at the massive three-hundred-foot square elevator that had carried them all "up" from the interior of the hollow world.

Ahead of them flew a small, hand-launched Puma UAV, which sent back stunning live video, which left Garreth and his men speechless. The video showed thousands of people… men, women, and even children. More survivors!

Many were in U.S. Navy or Marine uniforms, walking along roads that converged on a massive colonnaded building that seemed to be in the center of the entire area. The feed was also being streamed back downside to the Fort Brazos Joint Reserve Base and the City of Fort Brazos, both of which had apparently been scooped up whole and kidnapped or, alternatively, rescued, depending on whose interpretation you chose, by the aliens everyone was calling 'the Gardeners.' The base and the city were hours away, via the elevator, on the inside of the four-thousand-mile-long hollow world.

The city ahead of them appeared to be organized into three sections that encircled a central zone. One of the surrounding areas seemed to be a primarily residential collection of dozens of tall, multistory balconied apartment buildings. The second section was an equally large group of office towers. The third was an open-air stadium complex. In the center of it all was a massive, sprawling twelve-story white marble building surrounded by parks and lakes.

Nearly three hundred miles away, down the elevator system, in a command center inside a former dirigible hanger on the outskirts of the Fort Brazos Joint Reserve Base, a crowd of people breathlessly watched the drone footage on a bank of computer monitors. Most were in uniform, including U.S. Air Force Major General Alexander Marcus, staff officers, specialists, and marine guards in full battle rattle.

Despite her business suit, one of the two civilians, Gail Finley, still looked every inch the Air Force Major and fighter pilot that she had been before becoming the newly elected Vice President. The other, John Austin, formerly the Fort Brazos county Sheriff, still managed to look uncomfortable in his new role as President of all that remained of humanity. Now, though, there were yet more survivors than anyone had dared dream was possible.

John's eyes widened, and he asked excitedly, "Look at all those people! And that city? Another one kidnapped like ours? What city is that?"

Gail shook her head, "I don't recognize it. The architecture is modern western, and look at all those parks."

Alexander ordered, "See if you can zoom in on some of those people." As the image grew on one of the monitors, he continued, "…Looks like most of them are wearing U.S. Navy and Marine uniforms."

Gail pursed her lips, "Whoever they are, wherever they are from, maybe they have answers!"

Alexander radioed orders for Garreth to find out what he could.

They watched the drone footage as Garreth's column worked its way through streets increasingly crowded with people and lots and lots of golf carts. They slowed to walking speed and fruitlessly asked questions, but it was quickly evident from Garreth's reports that no one in the crowd had any idea what was happening or where they were.

Alexander nodded approvingly when Garreth's column of vehicles paused, and they raised small American flags that his men had evidently fished out of their various pockets and packs.

The reports from the column quickly painted a painfully familiar picture. The people here had only been awake for a few hours, and all reported the same unpleasant Awakening Day symptoms. From the reported timing of things, apparently, these new survivors had been brought back to life the moment Garreth's men had started their elevator journey from the interior of the hollow world.

Alexander, Gail, and John retreated to the lecture hall meeting room where John and Gail had anxiously waited out the long elevator ride.

John kicked off the discussion, "General, those people are going to have questions, and they're going to be scared and confused. Just like we were. Do you think they might try and mob your men?"

Alexander worriedly thought for a moment, looking at the large screen above the stage where the feed from the drone was mirrored. "It was good thinking for Garreth to have them raise American Flags. That should reassure people. Also, they all appear to be unarmed, and the column is very obviously heavily armed, so let's hope nobody gets stupid."

Gail sat down and shook her head. "They're going to want answers, and they're not going to like anything we tell them."

Alexander nodded at the screen, "Since so many are in uniform, they may all be coming from an American base somewhere. We should prioritize finding the senior officer present."

John sighed, "And hope he or she has a level head."

Garreth and his men eventually arrived at the steps of the central structure, which, if not for its pristine newness, would not have looked out of place in Washington, D.C. An enormous crowd engulfed their vehicles, but there was no hint of violence so far. He climbed onto the nearest Bradley Fighting Vehicle and clambered up to the top of the turret amid the crowd's cacophony of questions and noise. The Bradley's commander handed him the mic for the loudspeakers. He spoke into the microphone, and his amplified voice boomed, "Stand clear! Everyone, please stand back before someone gets hurt! Stand clear!"

The crowd quieted a little, and some people tried to comply, but more and more people were arriving behind them. "I say again, STAND BACK! I need to talk to the senior officer present!"

A small wedge of marines, surrounding a Navy admiral, worked their way down the steps through the crowd towards Garreth, who hopped down off the turret and climbed down to the pavement. The marines arrived and formed a semicircle around Garreth and Vice Admiral Preston Milner III.

Garreth saluted, and a visibly angry Preston returned the Salute. Both men were cut from the same mold. They stood eye to eye at five foot eleven inches, but Preston's close-cropped hair was grey to Garreth's deep brown.

Preston demanded with a forced smile, "Lieutenant, where did you come from, and do you know what the hell is going on?"

Garreth stiffened, "Sir, Admiral, we're from Joint Reserve Base Fort Brazos, and what is going on, well, Sir, that is a very long story. Sir."

Preston took a half step back, stunned, "Fort Brazos? Texas? How is that possible? I repeat, what the hell is going on here?"

Garreth swallowed, "Sir, Admiral, my orders are to connect you to… higher, so they can debrief you and answer your questions."

Preston glared at Garreth, "Son, do you have any idea what we've been going through here? We've all been kidnapped and woken up in this strange place, we can't contact our families or command, there seems to be no way out of here, and some people are beginning to panic. We even had a hostage situation. Now I want answers, and I want them right goddamned now!"

Garreth nodded stiffly, "Yes, Sir, I understand, and I sympathize, but I have my orders. If you will please follow me, Sir, you can talk to people who can better explain things than I can."

Preston glowered and frowned, "Very well, Lieutenant, lead the way."

✪ ✪ ✪

Preston entered the comms truck but insisted that the door be left open so that the crowd could still see him.

The Comm Specialist was a petite, attractive olive-skinned woman with a nametag that read Balaska, who could not be more than twenty-one. She ushered him to a small seat in front of a monitor with a webcam and handed Milner a headset with a microphone. With a rolling English accent, she apologized, "Sir, we're running the signal through relays, so it's a bit shaky."

On the screen was a dark-skinned, uniformed Air Force Major General and other Air Force officers and civilians, none of whom Preston recognized. As a Vice Admiral, he outranked a Major General. Preston took an aggressive tone, "To whom am I speaking with? General? What the hell is happening?"

Alexander frowned, "Admiral, I am Major General Alexander Marcus, and to my left, on your screen, while it will take some explaining, is your new Commander in Chief, President John Austin, and the Vice President, Gail Finley."

Preston blinked. *What?* "Is this a joke, General? I am Vice Admiral Preston Milner, Deputy Chief of Naval Operations, and I've never heard of any of you."

His mind raced, "…and if this is a succession situation, I personally know most of the senior Senate and House members as well as all of the Cabinet members. My wife Livia and I had the Attorney General over for dinner just last week."

He almost blanched as he shamelessly name-dropped. *That's not me… that's Livia talking….* His heart skipped a beat as he thought again about not being able to reach his daughter Helena on the phone or by text. He was used to not being able to contact Livia.

The General and everyone on the screen looked at him with haunted eyes. Their pained expressions gave him pause. Milner swallowed as realization began to sink in. "My God. How…. H-How far down the succession line?"

The man who the General had identified as the new President shook his head. "Admiral, my name is John Austin. I would be amazed if you had ever heard of me and the reason for that is far, far worse than you think. You see, just about a month ago, we woke up just like you did today. Since then, we have learned that… that we have all been kidnaped and relocated inside an alien world. An artificial world created by those who took us. They took us from the Earth at the moment we all would have been incinerated by an invasion of the planet by a massive alien fleet of over sixty thousand starships. The invading aliens have since… have since wiped out humanity, and…." He looked down for a moment, swallowing, "… and we are all that is left. Our abductors have tested us by sending alien creatures to attack and kill both civilians and soldiers. I myself have seen and fought one of them. As for politics, Admiral, I'm afraid that the truth is that there was no succession possible. No one was left alive in the line of succession to take up that responsibility. After meetings between the General and the Fort Brazos City Council, it was agreed that we should have an election and plebiscite to vote on whether the people would agree to the Alien's demands to fight for them and elect a President and Vice President. Major Finley and I were… volunteered as candidates for the job, and we were the unfortunate winners."

The man on the screen was talking, but Milner wasn't hearing what he was saying. He could feel his blood pressure spiking, and his ears were ringing. Blood pounded in his ears. Dizzy, angry and confused, he was about to rip the headset off when he looked up at the Comm Specialist and locked eyes with her. Tears streamed down from her lovely dark eyes. He stopped himself. She was trembling, but not with fear. He could see that. No, it wasn't fear. It was sadness and loss and hopelessness.

Specialist Balaska blinked the tears away, sniffed and wiped her nose, and whispered, "Sir… it's true—all of it. God help us. It's all true."

As he looked into her eyes, he tasted her anguish and pain. He wasn't sure why, but he believed her. Maybe it was the impossible dome or roof or whatever it was overhead and the impossibly clean, sparkling new city around them. Perhaps it was the thousands of other clueless people gathering outside. Or maybe it was something he already knew from a barely remembered dream. When he had awakened hours ago, he'd hastily pushed the thought, the memory, of some kind of endless limbo from his mind. Dread realization washed over him. Yes, he knew in his heart that it was true. Milner slumped in the chair and took a breath. He swallowed and looked at the screen in front of him again. Apparently, the people on the other end of the call had been waiting for him.

President Austin continued, "Admiral, until now, we thought we were the only survivors. The city of Fort Brazos and the adjacent Joint Reserve Base were preserved… mostly… and deposited inside a hollow alien world. Our total combined population is around one hundred and twenty-one thousand. Do you know how many survivors are in your location?"

Milner answered mechanically, his words tasting of metal… he had bitten his tongue. "I… I don't know. I don't know where we are, and all the buildings appear to be brand new. The people I've seen all seemed to be from New London and Groton Submarine Base, where I was visiting… There are thousands of people here that I could see, and the base population was around twenty-one thousand. I was here for meetings and events this week…."

President Austin's eyes flashed with hope and surprise, and he sucked in a breath. His expression was mirrored by those around him. "My God…So many people…. It's a miracle."

Vice President Finley leaned forward, "Admiral, you say everything is new. Are there any buildings or structures or anything there that you recognize, even as new versions of something familiar?"

Milner shook his head, "No. No Ms… Vice President… Everything here is new. There is no wear and tear anywhere and no trash or even skid marks on the roads. Even so, it all looks very ordinary, very… human, except…." He glanced upwards at the vehicle's roof, "Except the sky here isn't a sky. There's some kind of ceiling very high up, and it's like nothing I've ever seen."

Alexander shook his head, "Admiral, it gets stranger. We are, we think, about three hundred miles, well, beneath you. Your new city, we think, is near the surface of a hollow cylindrical world. We're on the inside, and we reached you via a huge elevator system. The world's interior is nearly four thousand miles long and has its own set of oceans and continents, and weather systems. It's a world in a bottle. The Joint Reserve Base and the City of Fort Brazos were… brought here almost in their entirety and deposited intact. Indeed, it was hours before anyone realized that we were no longer on Earth anymore."

Milner asked in a low voice, "Where… no, why are we here?"

Everyone shifted uncomfortably on the other end of the call. Vice President Finley answered, her voice hard and cold, "Admiral, we're here for one reason and one reason only. The aliens who rescued us did so for the purpose of recruiting us to fight the aliens, different aliens, who attacked Earth. It seems they're a galactic scourge, and we've been shanghaied to balance the equation, and, Admiral, if we refuse, our rescuers have already demonstrated that they will kill us all and start over. The day we arrived, they murdered five percent of the surviving civilian population just to make sure we took them seriously. In effect, they rescued thousands and then killed them all…." She grimaced, "Just to make a point."

Milner's head spun, and he tasted bile rising in his throat. He swallowed hard and looked up at Specialist Balaska's grim expression and out the door to Lieutenant Garreth. The Lieutenant looked back at him with hooded eyes. He turned back to the screen. Decades of duty and experience in command and under pressure helped him get control of himself. Some. He swallowed hard again, "I see…. Mr… President, Ms. Vice President… I have some questions…."

An hour and a half later, Preston disconnected the call and slumped back, sitting limply in the chair. He could not decide whether to curse, scream, pray or cry. In his heart, he knew he would likely soon be doing all four, probably at the same time. Now, though, having learned that his planet and probably everyone he knew was dead and gone, his family, wife, and daughter Helena…. and aliens and a hollow world, and they were all copies of their former selves, and, and, and….

The noise from the crowd outside shook him from his funk. He turned to Specialist Balaska, "Thank you, Specialist." He took her hand and held it for a moment. Hers was hot and moist in his own dry, cold, suddenly much older hand. He forced a small smile, "Thank you."

She nodded quickly, her eyes red and swollen. Watching the conference call had forced her to experience, all over again, the pain, despair, and sorrow of the past month that she had hidden away in her mind and heart.

She thought to herself, and He handled it surprisingly well.

Milner turned and shakily walked to the exit of the truck. He shivered as he exited. As he did, his legs went rubbery, and he stumbled. Garreth caught his elbow and steadied him. Preston looked into Garreth's eyes and saw the truth of it all and the young man's uncompromising professionalism.

"Thank you, Lieutenant. I… I apologize for being angry with you earlier. I think that had I been in your shoes, I wouldn't have known how to tell me what has happened either, and, thank God, there have been no alien attacks on our people here, but I'm grateful General Marcus is sending men and equipment to begin patrols, just in case."

Garreth nodded, "Thank you, Sir, but we've had weeks to digest all that has happened, and even that was in bits and pieces over time. We at least had some time to begin to absorb and cope with it all." He glanced at the crowd of anxious faces, "Sir… your people…. What will you tell them?"

Preston took a deep breath, collecting himself. He swallowed, "Lieutenant…."

Garreth waited. He could see the weight of their lost world suddenly thrust upon the Admiral's shoulders. The man seemed smaller and years older than when he had entered the truck.

Preston blinked and looked out over the noisy crowd. He pursed his lips, gathered himself up, and swallowed, "First things first, Lieutenant. There is no food here that we've been able to find."

Garreth's eyes widened. He glanced out at the crowd. *And this will give people something else to think about, won't it?* "Yes, Sir, I understand. We'll distribute what we have immediately and coordinate to bring up as much as possible as fast as possible. May I ask if you intend to go down to Fort Brazos, Sir?"

"No, Lieutenant, I need to stay here and organize. I'm told a delegation will be coming here instead."

Livia

Livia Milner gasped as she lurched upright on the bed, her large jade green eyes bulging as she clutched her empty stomach, the sudden movement straining the rich fabric of her long, green-black Chanel gown. Her body spasmed so hard that her red bottom Christian Louboutin heels fell off her clenched feet. Her bone-pale translucent skin faded even more, and her long, lustrous black hair spilled loose about her shoulders as she blinked hard and cried out in pain and terror.

Karl Johansson, nearly twenty years her junior at 20, was beside her on the bed. His awakening was less fortunate. Unlike Livia, who was used to not eating to maintain her size four-figure, He was an All-State linebacker and had the vigorous appetite to match. He promptly threw up his heavy meal into his tuxedoed lap before shouting a string of unlikely obscenities, then leaped from the bed, splashing vomitus across the floor. He landed in a crouch, searching for enemies.

Livia remained where she was, taking in the room as her eyes came into focus. *My God, what is this? Some pedestrian hotel? How the hell did we get here?* Her nose wrinkled, "Clean yourself up, Karl." Despite the smell, she allowed herself a moment to drink in his broad neck and shoulders and how he filled out the tux.

Karl relaxed slightly, grunted, and frowned at his ruined pants, "What's going on? Where are we, Livy?"

Livia paused, struggling to remember. She had been at the charity event long enough to be seen and then snuck away with Karl to go to a very discrete bed and breakfast next to the base. However, she could not remember what had happened next. She had a brief, vivid memory of her clutching and digging her nails into Karl's muscled back… and then… and then there was a memory or perhaps a dream… of falling stars…. She shook her head and snapped herself out of her reverie.

She'd known Karl and his father, Andre, recently promoted Rear Admiral Lower Half Andre Johansson for years. For the last several months, her intimate relationship with Karl had quietly, secretly blossomed, and Livia had discovered in him a seemingly endless ability to satiate her passions and thus vent her growing frustration. So, she affectionately used and taught him, and she was reasonably confident that he understood the boundaries of their relationship.

Likewise, she knew her husband was aware of her appetites and that as they mainly led separate lives, she at least had the pride and dignity to keep her dalliances discrete. Their relationship had not always been this way, but Preston had grown increasingly distant over the years, and the marriage had evolved into something more akin to a business partnership.

Now, however, she and Karl had awakened in a strange hotel room, and she had no idea how they had gotten there. In her circles, she knew perfectly well that some would actually be jealous of her choice of boy toy. On the other hand, the ugly possibility that this could lead to public embarrassment and potentially derail her plans for her husband's career and future far outweighed the scandal of mere discovery.

Livia edged off the bed, retrieved and donned her lost shoe, found her vintage Gucci clutch bag next to the bed, and carefully made her way around Karl's mess to the bathroom. She took a moment to straighten her gown and hair, then briskly walked to the door. She paused and briefly stroked Karl's hair.

"It will be OK, Karl. Obviously, we must have had too much to drink at the Gala and ended up… here, wherever here is. So, call the concierge, have your clothes laundered, and have housekeeping clean up."

She fished a credit card out of her bag. It was from one of her many private, personal accounts. She raised her eyebrows, looked around the room disapprovingly, and sighed, "Perhaps they can switch you to a better room."

She smiled sadly and handed it to him, "My treat. Stay here, watch some TV, and order room service. I'll call and check on you later." She smiled, "I might even join you again. I'm not done with you yet."

Karl swallowed and shook his head as the smell began to permeate the room. "I don't blame you, Livy. Get out of here before the smell gets in your dress."

Livia flashed a perfect smile, "I'll see you soon, lover."

Then she stepped out the door into a hallway full of frightened, confused servicemen and women in uniform who had been talking animatedly to each other. She froze as the door shut behind her with a clunk. Everyone turned and stared at her in surprise.

Blood Phoenix

There were supposed to be protocols for how a President is first introduced to his top military officers. For one thing, there was a formal election cycle, an inauguration, and the auspices of the Oval Office to help cement both the legality and the perception of power and authority.

Vice Admiral Preston Milner III was afforded none of this. All he had was an insane conference call that had left everyone he knew and loved raped and murdered, and his world chewed up and spat out. For him, it was a fait accompli.

After the call, things began to get more organized. The New London survivors, now confirmed to be upwards of twenty thousand men, women, and children, gathered in the park around the fountains and reflecting pool bordering the massive administrative building.

What food Lt. Garreth's men had brought, the convoy supplies, and even the paltry selection of power bars and miscellaneous snacks they carried on their persons did not go far, but to everyone's credit, it had all gone to children. Garreth, in particular, seemed particularly concerned about the children and the women with babies and had radioed back an urgent request for baby food and supplies.

When the call came for Preston to leave and go to the warehouse area, he did not immediately respond. Preston had not been stationed in New London. He'd only been visiting. He would not leave them. However, his shared fate with them and, being senior, made them his people.

His emotions raged. Some small-town sheriff now claimed to be President, and a woman who had only been an Air Force Major a mere four weeks ago was now Vice President!? Intellectually, abstractly, he understood the circumstances, but the rest of him screamed Junta or Coup or God knew what. And to be held hostage with *food?* And now, to be summoned by them was just too much to take.

"Sir? Admiral?" Lt. Garreth talked to him or tried to, but Preston had not been listening. Garreth motioned that he would like to speak with him away from the crowd.

Preston ground his teeth, hesitated, then nodded and followed the Lieutenant.

When they were a discreet distance from the noisy crowd and the boisterous children playing a game of chase, Garreth asked, "Sir, permission to speak freely, Sir?"

Preston sighed and nodded curtly.

Garreth's expression was sympathetic, "Sir, like I said earlier, the rest of us have had weeks to get a handle on everything that's happened. With your permission, I'd like to tell you what I've observed about our current… leadership," he looked furtively around him, "…but I will deny ever saying any of this. Sir."

Preston's eyes widened, his brow furrowed, and he nodded, "OK, Lieutenant, I did not hear what you are about to say."

Garreth took a deep breath, "Sir, I'd never met General Marcus, President Austin, or Vice President Finley before all this happened, and when it did happen, well, Sir, things very nearly went to hell. The General had just taken command of the base a few days before Awakening Day. Then, in addition to the chaos of our first day, we discovered that forces from 19 other countries, some of whom are enemies of the United States, had also been abducted and deposited on the base."

Preston raised his eyebrows.

Garreth continued, "Sir, we almost had a small war, but General Marcus defused that situation, and then we found out that the aliens had killed thousands of civilians in the city, in Fort Brazos, and General Marcus took it hard. When the city government realized that we were basically all alone, they were afraid that General Marcus would roll in and take over and that he wouldn't be willing to take orders from a small city government."

Preston shook his head, "I suppose that's understandable on both sides."

"Sir, nobody trusted each other, and the city was piled high with bodies. I know. I was first on the scene."

"You were?"

"Yes, Sir, a flyover of the city had shown us that an alien structure had been placed in the middle of town, and there were reports on the radio of chaos. General Marcus feared that there was an attack taking place."

"I see."

"Sir, the city leaders somehow kept their cool, for the most part. They met with General Marcus and, well, I think they realized that they needed to figure out how to go forward, and that's when they drafted Sherriff Austin and Major Finley."

Preston blinked, "Drafted?"

Garreth nodded, "Yes, Sir, kicking and screaming. It was a compromise. Under the circumstances and with the population imbalance between the reserve base and the city, they decided that one person from the civilian government and someone from the military would be elected. That and the alien ultimatum."

Preston's face fell as his eyes gazed into the distance, and he shrunk back, "My God."

"Yes, Sir, so we had an election and voted to go along with the ultimatum and elect Austin and Finley, oh, and to have a constitutional convention in a few months. Sir, if I may, please cut us some slack. We've all got a gun to our heads, and, well, I have to say that I've really come to admire the General as well as President Austin and Vice President Finley. I know that I sure as hell would not have held up as well as they have if I were in their shoes. Sir. Vice President Finley, well, she's tough and as smart as they come. Oh, and Austin was the first person to kill an alien."

"He what?" Preston cocked his head.

"Yes, Sir, Sheriff Austin gunned down one of the alien creatures. It's all on video…. Sir, he personally killed the alien who killed one of my men and several civilians and nearly killed me. Sir…" Garreth swallowed, "President Austin, he saved my life. Also, you should know that he was already quite popular before the Aliens came. People say he would have run for Governor of Texas and won."

Despite the cool temperature, Garreth was sweating.

Preston swallowed and began to reevaluate Garreth and many other things. "Thank you for your candor, Lieutenant…."

Garreth waited pensively.

"It's too bad I never heard you say any of it."

Garreth closed his eyes briefly and sighed. "Thank you, Sir."

✪ ✪ ✪

THE HANGER

The three-hundred-foot square elevator system that connected New London to Fort Brazos on the interior of the hollow world terminated inside a large warehouse. Inside was a control room identical to the one on the Fort Brazos side, which had been discovered inside an old dirigible hanger turned junk warehouse on the outskirts of the Fort Brazos Joint Reserve Base.

Outside the warehouse stood a long row of enormous blast doors. When first discovered, only one of them had been open, and a long, winding, pristine highway led through it to the city beyond. Now, however, another blast door had opened.

A patrol had been sent to investigate, which led to the decision to summon Preston here – instead of following the original plan for John, Gail, and company to go to the city.

Preston's anger at being yanked away from the city evaporated when he learned why.

The metallic-smelling air was pungent with ozone. Lt. Garreth's platoon escorted Preston, John, Gail, and their details to the open blast doors and the enormous hangar bay beyond them on foot, where Lt. Pendleton and his men waited. They decided they wanted to see everything on foot and that the vehicles would follow behind them, providing video coverage and, if needed, support or evacuation.

John marveled, "Even this… hangar bay… must be bigger than anything man has ever built…. How tall is this place?"

Gail shook her head, "I don't know, but look at the equipment on the ground… you could fit a skyscraper in here."

John shook his head, "A whole bunch of skyscrapers."

The entire far end of the bay was a titanic, caution-striped blast door that dwarfed the contents of the bay itself. In the middle of the bay stood what could only be a spacecraft, although it was bizarre, to say the least.

The outer shell of the craft appeared to be at least eight hundred feet tall. Enormous elliptical rings with a very alien and vaguely blue-green organic hue wrapped around a long, black, cylindrical object. Beneath it, a large rectangular section was attached that looked different from everything else. A central spindle impaled the whole thing.

John muttered, "It's like some misshapen Christmas ornament…., the kind with a cage around an object inside. What *is* that thing inside it? Is that…?"

Preston stopped and stared. "I don't know about that thing tacked on beneath it, but, my God, it looks like… maybe the Montana with her propulsion section missing and the sail looks… odd." He heaved a sigh, "That's why the aliens picked New London!"

John raised his eyebrows, and Gail answered, "New London is, or was, a nuclear submarine base in Connecticut."

John objected, "A submarine? What? Why a submarine? Why not the ISS or something?"

Gale shook her head, "Of course! It would be the logical thing for us to do if we were to try and merge human technology with a working alien propulsion drive. A submarine is a closed environment that already has a life support system. It is already a warship designed to operate underwater without resupply for months or longer. The ISS is paper-thin and fragile and can only carry a handful of people, and it is not a warship. The gardeners have merged our technology with something alien to create a hybrid ship with at least some systems we can understand. It's… training wheels."

Preston turned to John, "And the Navy has the training and traditions for operating a long way from home, independently, for extended periods." He nodded to Gail, "And no offense to the Air Force, but Air Force missions are generally measured in hours and operate from fixed locations."

Gail smiled softly, "No offense taken, Admiral. It appears that the Gardeners have studied us more closely than I had imagined."

They started walking towards the spacecraft again. The hangar bay was too large for an echo and seemed to swallow the noise from their conversations. Even the noise from the Bradleys seemed muted.

John turned to Gail and Preston, "You noticed how strange it sounds in here?"

Gail thought for a moment, exchanged knowing looks with Preston, and smiled, "Flight decks can be brutally loud. You need hearing protection. I suspect that when things get busy in here, the noise would be deafening, so the Gardeners have some sort of active noise abatement going on."

John nodded, "That's what I was thinking. On an oil rig, the noise can make it hard to communicate, and that can lead to accidents."

As they approached the base of the ship, Gail frowned, "There's nothing that looks like an engine or nozzle or anything. I suppose those rings could be some kind of warp drive, but if they are, they're really weird. Those concept designs that NASA did a while back of what a warp drive ship might look like had a couple of simple fat rings that were parallel to each other around a central hull."

John asked Preston, "Admiral, is there anything else you can deduce from looking at the submarine portion of this thing and what the big box underneath it is?"

Preston nodded, "From here, it looks like the engine room and propulsion sections are gone, but I believe the reactor section is still there, assuming that's what is still inside. Maybe they want us to use our own power systems and separate them from the external alien part? As for that large section underneath, I would guess that that would contain controls and instrumentation to navigate and operate the spacecraft portion of the vessel."

John nodded, "I suppose that keeping as much of our own technology intact means there is less complexity to deal with, and we already know how to use and maintain those systems."

John stopped in front of one of the blue-green rings. The surface was glassy and smooth. He reached out and touched the cold and nearly frictionless surface. He swallowed and ground his teeth for a moment.

He looked up at the vessel that towered above him and whispered,

"Though much is taken, much abides; and though
We are not now that strength which in old days
Moved earth and heaven, that which we are, we are;
One equal temper of heroic hearts,
Made weak by time and fate, but strong in will
To strive, to seek, to find, and not to yield."

Gail blinked and looked at John in surprise, as though for the first time, *Who are you?*

Preston stopped and reached out to touch the ring himself, "One of my earliest memories was my dad taking me to see the ship he commanded at the time. It seemed so vast, and I was so small I had to be carried across the gangplank lest I were to fall into the water. I wanted to see everything, but I was so small that dad had to carry me everywhere…." His voice fell to a hush, "I feel small."

Gail traced her hand across the surface of the ring, not even leaving a smudge. "My father… the Colonel, he took me flying when I was little." She looked at Preston, "We are children again… but this time, we've been left on the gangplank alone to fend for ourselves, and our fathers and everyone else has been murdered."

She swallowed and let her arms fall to her sides, her hands clenched into fists. Her lips tightened as she gazed up and up at the craft. She took several steps back until both John and Preston were in front of her.

Her eyes glinted as her anger grew, "Admiral… John…. I believe we should name this ship the Blood Phoenix…. She is risen from the pyres of our dead… the blood of our fathers and our world."

Preston's eyes widened, and he slowly nodded.

John smiled thinly, "And may her flight be terrible and true."

The eight-hundred-foot-tall spheroidal starship was composed of twenty rings that converged at the top and bottom of the comparatively slender spindle that intersected the hull aft of the odd-looking sail, what people used to call a conning tower. The rings appeared to be about twenty feet wide and were more or less torus-shaped, with a flattened interior side. They were somewhat squashed and canted in the same direction as the submarine hull suspended within. On closer examination, the spindle did not appear to actually pierce the hull, but rather it widened and wrapped around it in a fat, nearly translucent ribbon.

At the rings' interior top and bottom apex, squat bulbous structures filled perhaps a tenth of the upper and lower space. The spindle between the upper and lower 'nodes' formed a thin column. The rest of the interior space was empty, save the spindle and the submarine hull.

The submarine itself appeared to be… incomplete. The aft section was missing, which would have contained the drive shafts, dive planes, rudders, and screw (propeller). Judging by the flat, unfinished bulkhead that truncated the hull, it appeared as though it would be possible to attach something else in its place. Similarly, the bow section that should have contained the Sonar was sheared off. Attached to the bottom of the former submarine was a large rectangular structure.

Surrounding the starship were dozens of lift trucks, scaffolding, construction elevators, cranes, ladders, storage bins, rows of shelving, tool bins, storage tanks, generators, forklifts, fire suppression tanks, and other assorted equipment. Massive overhead cranes spanned the width and breadth of the hangar bay and could be moved on tracks anywhere along its length. Heavy cables with padded cradles looped around several of the rings, ensuring the ship remained upright and did not roll along the deck.

A row of lines ran parallel down the length of the hangar bay deck, leading to the colossal airlock doors. Caution stripes marked where panels could be removed to reveal what had to be a track system to move ships or large objects in and out of the bay. Large sliding doors were labeled as "Fab" shops, "Machine" shops, and numerous warehouse and parts storage areas along the hanger walls.

Gail turned to the nearest member of her ever-present security detail, reached out her hand, and asked, "Corporal Hopper, a knife, please."

Corporal Nathanial "Nate" Hopper towered over Gail at 6'3" plus his cover. He grinned, quickly fished a Spyderco pocketknife out of a side pocket, and handed it over. On Awakening Day, there had been a single detachment of Marine Embassy Security Guards in Fort Brazos: Seven Corporals plus their Sergeant NCO, Jesse Roberts. They had been passing through.

Before Awakening day, back on Earth, Marine Security Guards had been tasked with providing security at U.S. embassies and consulates. After the alien Stalker and Wardog attacks, General Marcus had decided that the new President, Vice President, and the city council members should each have a personal security detail, whether they liked it or not.

Sergeant Robert's team was divided up and augmented with selected Marines who were given a crash course, an on-the-job training version of the MSG school. Nate commanded Gail's detail, which included Corporals Jose Cruz and Jermal Dixon. As was required of an E-5 MSG, all of the men, like Nate, were single with no dependents.

As President, John's detail was one man larger. Sergeant Roberts commanded two Corporals, Jorge Diego and Antoine "Tony" Bouchard, and their MSG NCO commander-in-training, Sergeant Benjamin "Benny" Jenkins.

Gail expertly flicked the knife open without looking and vainly tried to scratch even the slightest mark on one of the rings. She shook her head. "Thanks." She folded it closed and handed it back, then looked over at John and wondered aloud, "If this is indeed some form of warp drive that the Gardeners married to our submarine, you have to wonder what was replaced? The interior section does not look like something is so much missing, as though it were actually meant to have something removable in its center…. Look how the spindle thing wraps around the ship so tightly. I cannot imagine that whatever was originally there just happened to be the same dimensions."

John nodded, "The Gardeners can build a 4,000-mile-long hollow, inside-out planet, Xerox us off of Earth the instant before we would have been incinerated and put us here. Somehow, engineering an existing starship to hybridize it with one of our submarines doesn't sound like much of a stretch."

Gail nodded, "Or just maybe the Gardeners picked something that would be easier and simpler to work with, so they wouldn't have to rip out the guts of an integrally designed main hull…."

At ground level, scaffolding and boards covered the rings' frictionless surface, so it was possible to walk over them. Preston made his way up a conveniently placed ramp and headed toward the mutilated Montana. As he got closer, he paused, "That's odd. The acoustic coating is … wrong."

The ex-submarine was suspended within the rings a few hundred feet above them. Ramps and caged freight elevators rose from the floor of the hanger to the deck of the ship. Without waiting for anyone else, he trotted over and entered one of the construction elevators, punched the button, rode it up, and abruptly stopped it when it was closest to the hull.

He reached out to gingerly touch the strange material that covered the hull. It was soot-black colored and was both needle-sharp and spongy at the same time and threaded with vein-like structures.

Gail called up to him, "What do you see, Admiral?"

Preston shook his head, "I have no idea." As he looked down and along the hull, he noticed another feature not apparent from the ground. Every ten feet or so was a black embedded half dome that appeared to be a foot or two in diameter. The domes were utterly smooth but not glossy. *Sensors? Weapons?* He shook his head in wonderment and pushed the elevator button to finish the ride to the deck entrance level.

John followed the same ramp that Preston had used and instead walked over to the flat inner surface of one of the rings, where he noticed the color was different. It was not uniform. He reached out and could feel a slight tingling sensation pushing back just above the surface. He traced the edges of the resistance. As he did, the color darkened slightly behind his fingers. It formed a roughly ten-foot-wide oval that he could barely reach the top of. When he completed tracing the pattern, the oval darkened to a depthless black. It then burst into a three-dimensional riot of colors that took the form of various shapes, waveforms, and alien text that was very different from the Accipiter glyphs the Gardeners had been showing them.

He took several steps back, "Whoa! I'm guessing this is some kind of diagnostic interface for drydock maintenance and calibration."

Gail wandered over to him and stared at the rapidly changing 3D display. After a moment, she cracked her first smile since entering the hangar, "I think those are their equivalent of bar charts and graphs. Congratulations, John, you've discovered the first-ever alien Key Performance Indicator display. You'd better get your patent filed quick."

John started to snap a reply but stopped as a sound no one had heard since coming 'TopSide' startled everyone. It took a moment for him to realize that it was his cellphone. He pulled it from his jacket pocket. It was Dr. Nakamura.

Gail blinked, "How are you getting a signal here?"

John shook his head, "I have no idea." He put the phone on speakerphone and answered, "Dr. Nakamura, how in the world are you getting a signal to me here?"

Dr. Takumi Nakamura, Ph.D., Dean of the School of Science and Technology, Bonham State University, and newly the President of the University, after his predecessor had not survived Awakening Day, hesitated before answering. "Mr. President, my apologies. I overheard one of the technicians here saying that they thought cellular service had started working. How did he put it? Ah yes, 'cellular service has spontaneously started working TopSide.' Personally, I hope that term doesn't take hold."

Gail closed her eyes and sighed. Dr. Nakamura had a well-earned reputation for preambling.

John shook his head, "Yes, Dr. Nakamura, that's... that's quite remarkable and surprising. However, I expect that's not why you decided to call?"

Dr. Nakamura continued, "Of course, of course. You see, Mr. President, something extraordinary has happened! We've been watching the video of your discovery, and we believe it may be some form of warp drive, so we did a quick search to pull up the latest scientific papers on the subject. What we found was... well, it was astounding."

John and Gail traded worried glances. Since Awakening Day, using a phrase like "something astounding has happened" tended to conjure up feelings of fear and dread.

John grimaced, "Dr. Nakamura, what have you found?"

Dr. Nakamura seemed to be talking to someone else, then resumed, "Oh, yes, you see, what we found was that all the papers we've examined so far have been changed. Certain assumptions have been redlined, and new information has been put in its place. Values for physical constants have been… altered, and much of the, well, the physics have been changed. Some of the changes are subtle, but many are, well… astounding."

Gail and John exchanged sharp looks. Gail stepped closer to the phone and asked, "You mean the Gardeners have corrected our math? They've told us what we did wrong and showed us how it really works?"

John slowly nodded, "That could mean that they have advanced our knowledge decades, maybe generations ahead."

Dr. Nakamura added, "Mr. President, Ms. Vice President, of all the sciences, Mathematics is humankind's most advanced field. In many ways, our understanding of Mathematics far exceeds our understanding of the other sciences. The Gardeners didn't change our Math. It wasn't that our math was wrong at all. The assumptions we put into the theories we used math to model were wrong. The Gardeners have made corrections to our assumptions and, in doing so, adjusted our math to fit. As a result, we should now be able to rapidly move forward with practical engineering solutions."

John nodded, "So, they didn't plan for us to wait tens or maybe hundreds of years to figure everything out on our own. After all, if we can't build *and* understand starships, how could we possibly be expected to go out and fight a galactic war?"

Dr. Nakamura asked, "But why? Everything they've done so far has been on an epic scale. It will take a great many generations to populate this artificial world. The fleet of ships that attacked Earth reportedly had over 60,000 starships. How can they expect us to accomplish anything of significance with a single hybrid starship, partly built from a submarine, of all things?"

Gail frowned and nearly spat the words out, "Because, Doctor Nakamura, we're being tested. Again. This world they've built is obviously an investment. The Gardeners either refuse to fight themselves or they can't. They don't want to wait for generations to find out if humans will play their game or not, or whether or not we can play it well enough to satisfy them."

John looked at Gail. Her face was tight and pale. Despite the sharpness of her tone, her eyes were not baleful. They were hooded and damp. In the past few weeks, they had spent a lot of time working together. The very first time they had met, on Awakening Day, he'd seen actinic fury in her eyes. Her wingman had clipped her plane, and she'd just barely managed to avoid crashing into the High School and ejected only a fraction of a second before impact. Her ejection seat rockets had slammed her into the framework of a large billboard, severely fracturing her leg. Since then, he had seen many sides of her, from anger and resentment to icy coolness, thoughtfulness, and weary, exhausted, dangerous brilliance.

Above all, he knew how much she resented him and the fact that it was he who had pulled her from that billboard and carried her to safety moments before it collapsed. She resented that he was there with her and that she was forced to work with a former country Sheriff to lead the survivors of Earth. She resented being injured and losing her flight status. She resented that Awakening Day had utterly destroyed all her carefully laid plans and ambitions. She resented being shanghaied into becoming, of all things, Vice President.

Her hatred of the Gardeners was incandescent, only a close second to that of the Accipiters themselves. She was a ball of fury wrapped up in the wiry body of a 5' 9" auburn-haired fighter pilot call-signed "Banshee." He knew painfully well how much she resented him and that were it not for her fondness for John's vivacious 8-year-old daughter Matti, he was certain Gail would not even bother to tolerate him at all.

So very much had happened to Gail and what remained of humanity. He had marveled at how strong and determined she remained. Now, standing there, as the dark implications of the starship sank in, he saw something new.

For a fleeting moment, he saw pleading in her eyes. He knew the feeling well. Pleading that they would all wake up from this nightmare. That somehow, some way, none of this had happened. And now, he could see the shared weight of humankind's very existence on her slim shoulders. He was shocked to see that she was trembling, even if ever so slightly, and that she allowed herself to show some level of weakness and reach out for support in that brief moment. To him.

He held her gaze and nodded slightly, and without even realizing it, he reached out and rested his hand on her shoulder, not in superiority or condescension but in the solidarity of shared pain and struggle. And perhaps something more.

When two people truly see each other for the first time, when the massive bandwidth of the human gaze is fully exceeded by minds racing with new thoughts and awareness, time itself can seem to dilate. The entire moment lasted no more than two, perhaps three breaths. John disengaged his hand from her shoulder as both their eyes widened.

Dr. Nakamura had been saying something on the phone, but neither John nor Gail had any idea what that might have been.

Gail took a step back and stammered, "Th-Thank-you, Doctor Nakamura." She quickly averted her gaze, turned, and started walking back toward the perimeter of the starship rings. She waived her detail on, "Come on, boys, let's see what else there is to see."

John took a deep breath, "Dr. Nakamura, please work with General Marcus and start putting together a list of anybody and everybody with math, physics, and engineering expertise down in, well…. DownSide. We'll have the folks up here do the same."

Dr. Nakamura's voice brightened, "Yes, Mr. President, I'll also work on identifying people with backgrounds that may be useful in life support and atmospheric processing. I believe nuclear submarines use part of their power budget to convert seawater into air. We'll need to figure out an alternative. Among other specialties, we'll need astronomers to help figure out navigation. Also…"

John sucked in a breath, "Thank you, Dr. Nakamura, I'm sure the list will be long, and you're the right man to start working on it. This will be something of a

Manhattan project, with both military and scientific teams working under stressful conditions. I don't need to tell you that we cannot afford to get it wrong."

There was silence as Dr. Nakamura considered John's words, "Of course, Mr. President. As my students are fond of saying before finals,… *no pressure.*"

John ended the call and put the phone on silent. Gail and her detail were already halfway around the rings. She was busy pointing at things while Corporal Dixon hurriedly took notes. John chuckled. He squared his shoulders and hastily brushed aside the half-realized thoughts of their brief encounter.

He looked around for Admiral Milner and did not see him and realized that Milner must have already entered the former submarine while Gail and John had been on the phone. He flushed with resentment that the Admiral had done so not only without asking… but first.

John shook his head, *and would you have a clue what you were looking at if you went in there first?* He avoided the thought that there was no way in Hell that Sergeant Roberts would have *allowed* John to enter the craft without it being searched and checked out beforehand.

John nodded to Sergeant Roberts, "Roberts, have someone go up and check on the Admiral."

Sergeant Jesse Roberts, the overall commander of all the protection details and lead on John's personal detail, spoke quietly into his comm as he pointed upwards.

Gail shouted from a distance, pointing upwards at the rectangular 'addition' to the submarine hull. It was as long as the submarine itself and at least twice as wide. "John, I don't think that is a control room. It has doors!"

John and Gail boarded the construction elevator, bracketed by their details, and arrived at the exterior deck level, where a gangplank extended to the elevator entrance. As they arrived, it was apparent that significant changes had been made. The sail was now… an airlock.

Preston stood next to it, waiting. He motioned inside, "Mr. President, Ms. Vice President, it seems your aliens have been quite busy making changes to the Montana."

They stopped and waited for the Admiral to continue.

"As you can see, the sail has been converted into an airlock, so things like the mast, sensors, and laser are all gone. I also checked the main hatch, and it has also been altered somewhat but can still be used to load and unload equipment. Inside, however, some things appear perfectly normal, and some are completely changed. The sonar control room and aux diesel rooms are empty, and… the torpedoes, missiles, and related equipment have all been removed." He swallowed, "And there are no obvious weapons that replaced them."

John snorted, "What, they don't trust us to put guns on our tricycle?"

Gail shook her head and gestured wildly, "John, the Accipiters attacked Earth with a fleet of sixty thousand starships. Sixty Thousand! We don't even know how to fly the damned thing yet, so I think it makes a certain amount of sense for us not to go off halfcocked and think we can take the Accipiters head-on just yet, so, yeah, no guns on the tricycle."

John shrugged, "I get it. I do. Besides," he looked up at the rings that towered above them, "anything that has the power to travel to the stars is, itself, ultimately, a weapon. Maybe there's really no such thing as an unarmed starship."

Gail asked, "Admiral, and about that big box underneath with those doors?"

Preston's face brightened, "That, Ma'am, is a sight to behold."

The airlock was only large enough on the inside for three or four people at a time. It took Sergeant Roberts several minutes to organize who went on each trip, but eventually, two-thirds of the details went inside, and a third remained behind as rear guard.

The CIC was beneath the sail airlock. There were lots of monitors and controls, and other than a conspicuously non-submarine-looking large wall monitor, nothing looked to be of alien origin.

Preston shook his head as they gathered, "This is all wrong. I have not tried to turn anything on, but this layout has been completely changed, and while that is both interesting and troubling, what I expect you are going to want to see is this way."

Preston led the group down, past the middle deck and the crew mess, to the lower deck with the now empty auxiliary diesel engine room, to another set of doors. This led to a hatch leading into the large, added-on, rectangular box underneath the hull, which was larger than it had seemed due to the height above the hangar deck.

Once inside, it was clear what its purpose was. It was its own large hangar bay. The interior walls looked very human in construction, but the thing strapped down in the middle of the deck was most emphatically not human-looking. While it had slick, almost organic-looking rings like the big ones outside, these were vastly scaled-down and were wrapped snuggly around a bulbous, almost frog-like craft.

Gail gasped as she climbed down the ladder into the compartment, "It's a ship!"

Preston nodded, "Even though it is bigger than most human cargo planes, I suspect this is their version of a shuttle or landing craft of some kind, but it's at least a hundred and thirty or forty feet long, and the beam is maybe 80 or ninety feet, about the size of a Navy LCU, but wider."

John pointed at the rings around it, "It has rings. Does that mean it is warp capable?"

Gail darted around the shuttle, her remaining detail struggling to keep up with her, "From what I remember, warp doesn't necessarily mean faster than light…. And look at the size of the airlock doors on it. They're big. Proportionally bigger than I would expect for something this size…."

Preston nodded, "I noticed that. Maybe the people who built this were bigger than we are? Or maybe it's big so they can load cargo."

Gail completed her circuit of the craft and asked, "Have you gone inside?"

Preston shook his head sharply, "No, Ma'am, absolutely not. As a nuclear submariner, you learn things like not to push buttons that you don't already know what they do."

Corporal Nate Hopper silently positioned himself between Gail and the shuttle airlock. His expression was carefully neutral, but it was blindingly obvious that nothing she could do or say would convince him to allow her to go inside herself.

Gail sighed, "Very well. Let's set up a live video feed to document every square inch of the ship before we start… touching things."

Descent

John, Gail, Preston, their escorts, and a growing collection of officers and aides exited their vehicles and paused outside the warehouse. Soldiers with lighted batons guided a caravan of relief vehicles and 18-wheelers unspooling off the elevator. They shepherded them into a line that slowly rolled out the warehouse doors, preparing to head into the city.

Despite the vehicle noise, a hubbub of conversations broke out. John turned and looked past the city blast door "gate." On the other side of the gate, it had grown dark. Streetlights from the highway, and the city beyond, shone through. He blinked, "It's dark."

Sergeant Roberts nodded soberly, "Yes, Mr. President, the city has begun its first night cycle. It's after 20:30, Sir, and if I may, Sir, you've been up for over forty-eight hours straight."

John rubbed his eyes and smiled tiredly. He answered sharply, "Thank you, Sergeant. I think we're all painfully aware of that." He shook his head and softened his tone, "But you know, it's not every day you get to walk the deck of mankind's first starship… and reach out and physically touch the instrument of our fate."

Roberts pursed his lips. He was worried about more than just John's health, "Yes, Sir. Big day Sir, and I pray it's not a dark one."

John started to answer, but Gail interrupted. She stepped forward, raised her hands, and whistled over the vehicle noise to get everyone's attention. The caravan finished exiting the warehouse, the drivers gunned their engines, and the column rumbled past, leaving a sudden quiet in its wake.

Gail inhaled deeply, then spoke in her best command voice, "In case you couldn't hear him, Sergeant Roberts just commented on how big a day this has been. He's right, of course. It was a really, really big day, and assuming we survive, it will be remembered for generations. Maybe longer. First, the Gardeners dropped the other shoe, revealing not only New London and thousands of human survivors, but then they dumped an actual starship in our laps. For most of us, we've had a month to absorb things one piece at a time. For the New Londoners, like Admiral Milner here, their heads must truly be spinning. Honestly, I think today feels like stepping off the bus and into the loving arms of the Drill Sergeants at basic training. Until now, it was just theoretical. It was the poster at the recruiting office and the slick ad on TV. Now, we're really here…. It's really real, and that's going to scare a lot of people."

John ran his hand through his hair and blinked, then paused, his hand on the back of his neck, "Damn, Gail, you always have a way of cutting through to the heart of things." He smiled, "But you know, rank hath its privileges. I think I'll skip the buzz cut."

That broke the thin layer of ice that had begun to form on the group. Chuckles and a few surprised snorts and snickers softened the mood.

Preston shook his head, "Well, one thing is for certain, Mr. President, we need to find a way to close these blast doors. We don't want to destroy what future we may have because of a single fire or accident… or decompression. Before we do anything else, we need to assign safety officers and post twenty-four-hour watches. Do we even have any idea if there is any firefighting equipment here?"

9:15 PM

The group reconvened in the conference room/theatre next to the control room, which appeared to be an exact duplicate of the one downside. Live video from cameras left in the starship hanger cycled on one side of the large presentation screen. On the other side, live video from the downside conference room in Fort Brazos turned on, revealing a room packed with uniformed military and civilians, including General Alexander Marcus.

Alexander's group filled the left half of the first row. To his right sat his senior officers, including Brigadier General Sabrina Chilton, formerly of the Royal Army Signals Brigade and now Commanding Officer of 1st Signals and Electronic Warfare. Next to her sat Dr. Leo Talib, the leading expert on the Accipiter language. Six inches shorter and next to Talib sat Colonel Cesar Salangsang, formerly of the Philippine Army 54th Engineering Brigade, now Commanding Officer of the 1st Combat Engineers. Next to Cesar was Colonel Gideon Markovic, late of the Israeli Defense Force, now Commanding Officer of the nascent 1st Mechanized Infantry. On Alexander's left sat Lieutenant Colonel Martin Williams, formerly of the Australian Intelligence Corps and now the Commanding Officer and sole member of the new and not yet named Intelligence group.

The balance of the first row was filled with the City Council members, now effectively a Senate, including Mayor Tom Parker, Councilwomen Gloria Vargas, Esmerelda Collins, and Councilmen Dale Hubbard, Jack Burdger, and Wylie Hickum. Professor Takumi Nakamura, his department heads, and dozens more filled the rest of the seats and rows to standing room only.

The TopSide group was much smaller and quickly expanded to fill the void of the conference room, with John and Gail escorted in last, taking up the same corresponding seats on the main stage that they'd used during the long wait to find out what was on the other end of the elevator. Admiral Milner joined them on the stage. They were followed by three corporals pushing carts laden with coffee, sandwiches, and miscellaneous snacks likely scavenged from several dozen MREs.

Day 30, 12:47 AM

John absently swallowed the last of his fourth, or maybe it was his sixth? Cup of coffee as the room slowly emptied. As it went on, more people joined the meeting until the room was full to overflowing. Admiral Milner had left several times to give orders and hear updates from the city.

John, Gail, and Preston sat half-slumped in their chairs. Bleary-eyed, John scrolled through emails on his phone. Gail had lost count of the number of coffees she'd had and stoically filled the last few pages of a full yellow legal pad with notes and to-do lists. Preston was quietly listening to a Lieutenant give an update on the headcount from the city.

Just then, a strong but trepidatious low-alto female voice called out from the doorway, "Preston?" The voice belonged to Livia Milner. Two members of the security detail interposed themselves and held her back.

Preston stood and whirled around, nearly knocking the Lieutenant down. His mouth parted in surprise and confusion as her name haltingly left his mouth, "Livi?"

She replied haltingly, "It's me!"

Preston took a step forward, "You're… You're alive! How can you…."

The guards released her, and she rushed forward, her green-black Chanel gown rustling until she stopped two feet in front of him, holding out her arms.

Preston shook his head, "How can you be here? You were in D.C. with Helena?"

Livia took a step closer, "Darling, Helena wanted to visit her friend Susan at Yale. You know she wants to go there, so Christine talked me into going to the Children's Benefit Ball in Hartford and… and I decided to come and surprise you," a tear rolled down her pale face, "and then I woke up in that horrible hotel place and the next thing I knew I was helping the Navy wives organize at the park. Then someone stopped me and asked my name, and the next thing I knew, I was here…."

Of course, almost everything she said was true.

Preston slumped, "So Helena isn't with you."

Livia took the last step and hugged him, her voice husky, "No. No, she isn't."

Preston perfunctorily returned the embrace, straightened, and disengaged, turning to John and Gail, who were standing behind him, watching the drama unfold.

"Mr. President, Ms. Vice President, allow me to introduce my wife, Livia."

Livia hesitated, her large jade green eyes darting back and forth between John and Gail, wheels turning, "What? I'm sorry, I'm afraid I don't understand."

Gail frowned, walked over to Livia, and reached out, taking her hand, "Mrs. Milner, has no one explained to you what has happened?"

Day 30, 1:32 AM

Gail and John walked to the edge of the stage, and Gail quietly murmured, "She took it remarkably well."

Preston and Livia sat quietly, talking to each other.

John shook his head, "She's in shock. You and I have both seen a lot of that in the last few weeks."

The Lieutenant who had been briefing Preston returned with more news, interrupting Livia and Preston. Livia stood and approached John and Gail.

"Mr. President, Ms. Vice President, I apologize for my reaction earlier. I meant no disrespect." She was trembling slightly, which might have had something to do with the cold temperature in the room and the thin, sleeveless gown she was wearing.

John smiled, "You're no more surprised than we were." He took his jacket off and placed it around Livia's shoulders. "Please, you should get something to eat and drink."

Livia gracefully accepted the jacket and struggled not to stare at the gun and holster on John's hip. His jacket was oversized and loose on her thin frame, and she pulled it around her tightly. She smiled a practiced smile of thanks. What she noticed, however, was not so much John's southern manners and the way he had dutifully avoided staring at all her sheer gown promised and revealed but an ever so brief flash of something much more interesting in Gail's cheeks and eyes. *Interesting....*

There were several significant differences between the TopSide elevator facility versus its DownSide counterpart. Among them were a small but well-equipped hospital and trauma ward, a long, long row of warehouses, as well as an adjacent administrative building with conference rooms, offices, and quite a few duplicates of the New London 'hotel rooms.' The building had been thoroughly searched earlier in the day. It had been decided that everyone should get a few hours of sleep before taking the elevator DownSide to Fort Brazos.

Gail found herself alone in one of the rooms, her security detail outside the door and on the balcony. She stood barefoot at the bathroom sink, brushed her teeth, and threw some water on her face. She stopped and stared at her reflection in the mirror. There was almost no makeup to remove as she rarely wore much of any, but her attention was elsewhere.

She raised a hand to her face and gently brushed her auburn hair aside. She was beyond exhausted, but that was nothing new. She had been bone-weary countless times before as a combat pilot. It was different now. Her skin was dry, her eyes bloodshot and puffy, and her lips were thin, dry, and pale. And then there was the knot in her stomach.

Five Percent. It sounds so much more clinical than 4,342 murdered men, women, and children. Civilians that your Air Force duty had obligated you to protect, and those were just the bodies here. Then there were eight billion or so dead back on Earth, while you get to play Vice President and walk around starships.

Knowing what she was going through intellectually did not make it any easier. As a pilot, her responsibilities had been… narrow. Now…. Now she was responsible for all that remained of mankind and to lay the groundwork for what would likely be a generational or longer war against a galaxy-spanning empire of bloodthirsty aliens.

And you're just a heartbeat away from not being 'just' the Vice President. Then what would you do? She shoved the other thought that mostly lurked in the back of her mind into a mental box. The thought, the worry, that it wasn't just about what she would *do* if something happened to… him… but how she would *feel* about it and the gnawing realization that she was beginning to care a lot more than she'd thought was possible. Despite how tired she was, she'd been utterly shocked at her flash of…. She shook her head in disbelief. *Jealousy! You were actually Jealous! John was so tired he could barely function, but there he was, gallantly draping his jacket around that woman's bony shoulders.* She glared at her reflection in the mirror. *He was just being polite. Why do you even care?*

★ ★ ★

Preston slammed the 'hotel' room door behind him with an angry thunk. Livia, walking ahead of him, was not expecting it and jumped at the sound. She was wearing Preston's uniform jacket over her shoulders now. Preston had hastily and apologetically returned the President's jacket as soon as he turned around and saw what had happened.

Now, behind closed doors, he finally allowed his anger to rise and boil. He said nothing, but his face and neck crimsoned, and he clenched his hands into fists. He suddenly stomped a step forward, and his face twisted into a rictus of fury and frustration as he raised a fist at her. He seemed to swell in size in front of her as Livia opened her mouth to speak.

Her eyes widened, and she stumbled back a step. Never before had she seen him like this. His gradual slide into indifference towards her had grown so deep that he had hardly seemed to notice even her most blatant… indiscretions. Throughout their entire marriage, Preston rarely ever raised his voice at her and had never, ever even hinted at being violent. As he'd grown more and more distant, nothing she did ever seemed to reach him anymore. She had never even imagined he could transform into such a creature of hate and disdain.

A guttural growl grew from within him, and he charged at her.

Genuine tears burst from her eyes, and she shrieked in fear, tripped on her high heels, and fell backward onto the thick carpet, her heart threatening to tear loose from her chest. She was suddenly more terrified than she had ever been in her life. She cried out, "Preston! No! Please, no!"

Preston's muscles bulged and strained against his tailored uniform shirt as he loomed and glowered over her. He pulled his fist back as if to strike her, and Livia raised her arms in defense, weeping. At the last moment, he whirled away from her and rushed to the nearest wall, plunging his fist through the sheetrock, shouting, "Goddamit, Livia! Who was it this time, or did you even bother to ask his name?"

He rocked back from the wall, swayed for a moment, and awkwardly slumped down on the edge of the bed, absently looking at his bloodied and Gypsum dust-covered fist.

His eyes flashed angrily, and his voice was a low, dark rumble. "It's the God Damned apocalypse, Livia! There you were, back there, playing your games and whoring around as usual while the only good thing that ever came from our marriage is lying dead somewhere, along with the rest of the planet. Even now, knowing everything that has happened, you don't know how to stop. You were actually coming on to the President!"

Livia winced. Lips trembling, she spat back, "We don't know that! Helena's not dead! She can't be! I just saw her yesterday… before… before…." She shook her head, "None of this is real! It can't be! And… and that redneck yokel simply cannot be the President!"

Preston's rage burned deep, but he would not look at her as he bowed and shook his head. "Open your eyes, Livia. You're anything but stupid."

Livia started to speak, then stopped herself. She tried to blink back the tears, and a long silence dragged out between them.

Eventually, she sniffed and shakily stood up, leaving her heels behind. She padded to the bathroom and washed her face before dampening a towel with warm water. She cautiously returned, sat next to Preston, took his bloodied hand, and gently cleaned it with the towel.

In a small voice, she asked, "How did you know?"

Preston shook his head, "You're not wearing underwear."

Livia blinked, "What?"

"I always knew. All those times, all those alibi's, the way you looked, the way you smelled, the… excitement in your eyes. I always knew."

They sat silently next to each other for a long time.

Preston finally spoke, but his tone was bereft of feelings of any kind. "Get out."

Livia recoiled, "What?"

Preston turned to look at her, his eyes narrow and cold, "Get out. I never want to see you again."

She returned his stare, "And what exactly are you going to tell your new holier than thou bible belt masters?"

"That in your grief over the death of our daughter, being with me was too painful a reminder of what you have lost."

Livia stood and backed away from him, then sat on the floor and pulled her knees up to her chin. She considered him carefully, "That might work, but then again, I think your position and authority are too important to you to lose. Don't forget, my family's influence got you where you are, and you know it. You need me. You certainly don't need to have to explain a bloody fist, a hole in the wall, and a shrieking wife running from the room."

Preston blinked and burst out laughing darkly, "Why should anyone believe you? My God, woman, have you looked around you since you woke up? You have *nothing*. You have no power or influence at all. Your daddy, the Senator, is dead, and you are penniless."

Livia tilted her head slightly, "My darling Preston, that's exactly why you need me. You never understood power, what it takes to get it, and, more importantly, how to keep it. My family's influence got you into doors, but it was me whispering in your ear, guiding you after you were in those doors, that helped you navigate the halls of power."

She sniffed, "That's partly why I fell in love with you in the first place. You were so passionate and sincere and so… innocent. So pure-hearted. On the other hand, I suckled power from my mother's breast. She taught me….."

Preston shook his head, "Your mother was a conniving, duplicitous bitch."

Livia smiled softly, "Yes, she was, but she eventually admitted to me that she had a soft spot for you. She never really approved of you but understood why I loved you."

"Soft spot, my ass. She lied to me on her deathbed."

Livia sighed, "I know. It was her nature. Mother had wanted me to marry into a prominent family or… at least to have the decency to give her a grandson she could mold."

"Instead, we had Helena, and Helena hated your mother."

Livia dropped her voice lower, "But she adored her father. She worshiped you. Besides, my mother didn't really need me. Mother had Isadora."

"Your evil twin, if that's possible. At least she did her duty."

Livia looked down, "Isadora loathed Archibald… but she lost herself in her children. It was her escape. My escape was you, but somewhere along the way, I lost you too."

Preston did not object when Livia knee-walked to him and gently lifted his damaged hand to her cheek.

She looked into his eyes, "Since I woke up here, I can see the future, Preston."

Lost in his own thoughts and misery, Preston did not immediately respond. He shook his head, "What?"

Livia continued, "Before… all of this happened, you were all set to become the next Secretary of Defense. My people had counted and recounted, and you had way more votes than you needed to be confirmed. I was going to tell you."

He grunted, "So, your plan for me was panning out."

Livia barked a small laugh, "You doubt me? That was just the next step, Preston. You're still young and as handsome as ever. People on the Hill like you. We already had focus groups greenlighting you for higher office. As SecDef your profile would have been national. When Daddy retired, you were going to take his seat, and after that, President."

He shook his head, "A lot of people have had those kinds of dreams."

Livia stood and punched him in the shoulder, "Those aren't dreams, Preston, those are plans, and you had the right pedigree with the right looks and the right family behind you to make it happen. It would have happened!"

"I know you believe that. But you said you could see the future now. What does that have to do with a dead past, a dead marriage, and a dead daughter."

Livia's expression frosted, "Because we're here now. You are the highest-ranking military officer in what remains of humanity, and the only thing standing between you and power is a two-bit Texas cowboy sheriff and his air force tomboy girlfriend side-kick!"

Preston snapped back, "They're not a couple! I've heard they were drafted into those roles and didn't expect to keep them. Besides, I'm starting to like him."

Livia lectured, "Preston Stewart Milner the Third, you listen to me! One of the soldiers told me that whoever put us here has tinkered with our bodies and that we will have much longer lives. That means that the people in power may be in power for a long, long time. Do you think they'll give it up once they've truly tasted it? Some people will try and take power for greed or pride or sheer lust for power, or hell, just for vengeance's sake. Regardless, you've got to start thinking about playing the long game here, Preston! We're going to live long, long lives, and we will be going to the Stars. Empires will be built, Preston! Think of it! Empires the like of which nobody has ever dreamed of to span the stars. Do you think that will happen with these people in charge? Worse, can you imagine what it would be like if it did?"

Day 30, 7:22 AM

The sleep break had been all too brief. Since the elevator ride would take nearly six hours, it was decided that people could nap along the way. They had departed a little after six. Not that anyone had really slept much. Breakfast MREs were served and later cleared away. Gail was not sure if Livia had actually swallowed any of the food.

Overnight, Admiral Milner's orders to search among the survivors for key people had paid off, and out of the crowd of over twenty thousand, the commanders of four submarines had been located and brought to the elevator.

Speaking of elevators, since there were two of them, the original had been designated the "up" elevator and the second one the "down" elevator. The elevator platforms were 300' x 300' – essentially big brothers to the Aircraft Carrier elevators they somewhat resembled. The pads were liberally marked with caution stripes and tie-down rings. Unlike Lt. David Garreth's first ride, when they had had no idea what to expect and brought along infantry fighting vehicles and plenty of firepower, for this trip, only the traveler's dozen SUVs and sedans were present. The security details were dispersed throughout the vehicles. Returning empty tractor-trailers hauling food and supplies to the city would catch the next elevator.

No one knew how many elevator pads there were. They had marked each pad with a large numeral made of tape and later with paint, but none had been seen again. Either there were a great many of them, or they were being cleaned off between trips. Some had quietly wondered if they were instead being created anew each time they were needed.

The vehicles formed a semi-circle along the edge of the elevator pad, and a collection of folding chairs were strapped to the tie-down rings, forming a rough circle. As soon as the pad began its descent, temporary walls and a high roof formed around them, with a display on one wall showing their progress and providing communications back to the control centers. The elevator itself was nearly silent.

John, Gail, Preston, Livia, the submarine commanders, and a collection of other officers and aides completed the circle.

Preston began, "Mr. President, Ms. Vice President, allow me to introduce my wife, Livia, more formally. Livia is basically Boston royalty. Her father is… was… the famous senior Senator from Massachusetts, and her mother had been a judge on the 1st Circuit Court of Appeals in Boston before she passed. Livia is a full partner at Connally, Gibson, and Sullivan in Washington D.C."

Livia smiled softly but focused her attention on studying everything about everyone present. She had learned that the soldiers were not just soldiers. They were heavily armed personal security details for the President and Vice President. The reasons for this, even though it was 'the Apocalypse,' seemed more than strange to her, and when added to the fact that John Austin still wore a gun on his hip, like he thought he was still a two-bit sheriff, seemed suspicious. *Was this some kind of Junta?*

Preston continued, "And now, I'd like to introduce four of the submarine Commanders we've been able to find from among the thousands of people back in the city. We are obviously going to need to select a captain for the starship we toured and those that follow. Since submarine deployments tend to be many months in length, the current doctrine is to train Blue and Gold crews that rotate tours. Between deployments, both crews work on maintenance and upgrades and trade places for the next deployment. Maybe this will work for… starships, and maybe it won't, but that's our current practice. I'm sure there will be considerable debate in the coming weeks and months."

"Commanders Cutter, Morton, Underwood, and Cross have been briefed on recent… events and the current situation. Each of these men has a different background and style. Because of, well, the Apocalypse, I'll dispense with subtleties. As we consider our selection, Mr. President and Ms. Vice President, I feel that you need to get a sense of who these men are."

Preston nodded towards a strikingly handsome African American Commander wearing a crisp custom-tailored Service Khaki uniform, "Commander Jermain Cutter, of SSN-795 Hyman G. Rickover, is a Naval Academy graduate originally from Boston. On the personal side, he is quite an excellent classical piano player, and because he doesn't get enough sea time under the water, he has his own sailboat you can find him on when he's off duty. Commander, what kind of sailboat is it?"

Jermain flashed a brilliant smile, "It's just a Catalina 309, sir."

Preston shook his head, "Don't let the friendly smile fool you. Jermain is also a 7th Degree Jujitsu Black Belt. His style, not surprisingly, has been described as focusing on the *strategic application of carefully directed force to bring his opponent off balance and thus vulnerable to attack.*"

Jermain nodded nonchalantly.

Preston motioned to the man seated next to Jermain, who also wore a Service Khaki uniform, "Commander Eugene "Gene" Morton is from Atlanta, Georgia, and is also a Naval Academy graduate and Commander of SSN-792 the Vermont. I apologize, Gene, but I'm going to tell them about your scar."

Gene nodded gravely and fought the urge to trace the thin white scar on his neck.

"As a headstrong young Lieutenant, fresh out of the Academy, Gene took it upon himself to intervene when he witnessed a young woman being accosted by local thugs. He recovered from his injuries and has gone on to become one of our most dangerous commanders. He always has a plan for going in – and for getting back out again. He is a careful, deliberate, and deadly hunter."

Gene remained impassive and simply nodded.

Preston looked to the next man over, who had poster-boy good looks. His Service Khaki's bulged slightly from his muscular frame. "Philippe "Phil" Underwood is from Cincinnati, Ohio, and is someone you might possibly recognize or at least remember his name from somewhere. Phil was the backup quarterback for Navy and had quite a few very competent starts."

Phil smirked.

"I expect he would have been starting quarterback himself had Nigel Benning not been, frankly, the next Roger Staubach. Nigel went on to lead the New England Patriots, and Phil went on to command SSN-797, the Iowa. And, no, I don't know if he's ever been hit on the head and woken up thinking he was back in a Navy game. That said, I suppose with Phil's background, it should not be surprising that he is even more passionate about training, teamwork, and scenario building than most. Phil's style is to aggressively probe and harry the enemy until they make mistakes and create openings for him to strike."

Phil smiled a toothy smile.

John wagged a finger at Phil, "I had fifty bucks on that game. I know you know which one!"

Phil shrugged, "My apologies for winning, Mr. President!"

Lighthearted laughter circled the room.

Preston continued, "And last, but certainly not least, is Commander Charles Cross, late of SSN-785, the John Warner."

Unlike Jermaine, Gene or Phil, Charles wore the less formal Navy Working Uniform, which while perfectly regulation, gave him a more workman appearance.

"Commander Cross is from Chicago. He is a mustang, which means he rose through the ranks through OCS. He has a Ph.D. in Physics and a Master's Degree in Electrical Engineering and is one of the smartest men I've ever known. He is a Master Level Chess player who is always 12 moves ahead of you. If I had to characterize his style, I would say he is calculated, deliberate, and precise. I understand he has also become quite a gifted teacher and mentor. Apparently, there is a growing collection of talented young officers who are on a waiting list to serve under his command."

For the next two hours, the Commanders questioned John and Gail about every aspect of the enemy. The Accipiters. Their questions probed deeply for insights and impressions that often eventually led to 'informed speculation.' Gail was the focus of most of the questions due to her military background, but John was not left out.

Eventually, Gail simply shook her head, "Look, gentlemen, there is a very hard limit to what we know, and all of it either comes from what the Gardeners told us in their big light show or what we've learned from the two kinds of creatures the Gardeners have been testing us with."

"The 'Stalker' type has killed both military and civilians. It is a leathery walking plant-like creature that bears some resemblance to an enormous Aloe vera plant. It ejects and throws long, dense, dart-like barbs that deliver a powerful electric shock. The barbs are attached to a filament that leads back to the creature. It is thought to deliver some sort of biometric telemetry about the target after impact. After subduing its prey, the 'Stalker' cocoons its victims before dissecting, or rather…" she paused, "vivisecting them and completely disassembling their equipment. We believe it is an intelligence-gathering biological tool of the Accipiters."

At the mention of the Stalker 'vivisecting' its victims, Livia stared at her in blank-faced horror. The reaction from others varied. Preston blinked and sucked in a breath, swallowing in disgust. Gene Morton nodded grimly, his lips drawing tight. Phil Underwood's eyes widened, and he worriedly shook his head. Charles Cross, like Gene Morton, also nodded understanding as his mind raced. Jermain Cutter rubbed his chin in hard, thoughtful reflection.

"The other creature so far encountered has been nicknamed 'Wardog.' It is somewhat larger than a rhinoceros and is hexapedal. It has thick black and red speckled armor, a gaping mouth with shark-like teeth, an array of tiny eyes, a rather dangerous tail, and a massive horn. Examination of the creature's exterior plating has shown it to be a dense matrix of carbon and metallic fibrils. The scientists think it either evolved or was bioengineered for a heavier gravity world than Earth. It can "hear" and home-in on radio signals, and it can very quickly burrow underground."

Jermain Cutter asked, "So, how are you dealing with these… monsters?"

John raised his eyebrows and swallowed, but Gail answered first, "Commander, small arms fire simply bounced off the Wardog, even at close range. It took an M242 25mm, firing Armor-Piercing Discarding Sabo rounds to kill it."

Livia remained very still as she listened and absorbed every nuance she could discern.

John laughed, "Over-killed it, you mean."

Gail grimaced, "Yes, well, it did sort of… explode."

Gene Morton nodded, "So, we'll need to find something in the large range between small arms fire and 25mm chain guns that are effective."

Charles Cross scratched his chin, "If it hears radio and attacks the source, maybe we can use that against it."

Phil Underwood could not help staring at the 1911 pistol John wore on his hip. He sat back and asked, "Mr. President, I understand you killed the Stalker with a pistol? Did it not attack you with the… stun barbs, Sir?"

Livia blinked; this was news to her. *This man killed an alien?*

John paused, remembering. As Sheriff, he had never before fired his weapon in anger. When the Stalker attacked, it nearly killed his daughter, Matti. Almost everyone downside had by now seen the bodycam footage that he'd tried to keep private. That footage had been used to manipulate him into his current role. No one else had wanted the responsibility.

His tone in answering was flat and clinical. While others cited the incident as evidence of his bravery, he would always consider it a personal failure for having brought his 8-year-old daughter there in the first place.

He paused, swallowing, "My daughter Matti was with me. Until then, there had not been a single report of danger or violence, and with everything that had happened, I felt safer keeping her with me. She… She told me that her tablet computer was acting strangely, and then it exploded in her hands as one of the barbs struck it. Thankfully, Matti was physically unharmed in the incident."

"I was wearing enhanced lightweight Type III body armor. My deputy, Grayson Miles, was wearing the same armor. Unfortunately, one of the barbs struck Grayson in the neck. His throat was ripped out, and his spine was almost completely severed. I fired three eight-round magazines, 24 rounds of 230-grain full metal jacket, .45 ACP ammunition, and seven rounds of double ought buckshot before the thing finally went down. Subsequent examination showed that all of my rounds hit the creature."

Complete silence filled the area for long seconds.

Livia thought *so that explains the gun…. And the guards.* Before she could stop herself, she blurted out, "Is it safe? Where we're going?" *Oh God, I'm so stupid! Shut up, Livia!*

Everyone turned and looked at Livia and then back at John and Gail.

John started to answer, but Gail beat him to it, smiling, "That's an excellent question, and, Yes, Mrs. Milner, where we are going is safe. There have been no incidents on the Reserve Base or in the City. There have only been attacks in remote or isolated areas. It is very, very safe."

Jermain nodded slowly, "So, Mr. President, how are the civilians reacting? Are they in lockdown? I imagine they must be demanding soldiers on every street?"

John sighed, looked down, and shook his head. "Commander Cutter… how do I put this. These are Texans. The city and surrounding area have a total population of roughly seventy-five thousand. At a minimum, forty or fifty percent of the population own at least one gun. Nobody knows for sure, but maybe half of those people own at least two. Others own more, sometimes dozens. I did some cocktail napkin estimates once, based on discussions with gun store owners, people I know, and my deputies, the police chief, and others. My rough estimate was that overall, there are about five guns per person in Fort Brazos, although, to be honest, I suspect the number could actually be much higher, and no, the city is not in lockdown."

Several mouths parted slightly, and eyes widened.

John laughed, "Right, I know what you are thinking. However, compared to the national average, the overall crime rate in Fort Brazos is 32% lower, and violent crime is 10% lower. Our people are not waiting for someone else to help them. They are working closely with the government to report anything suspicious. They are heavily engaged in establishing new and expanding existing safety and marksmanship classes for the experienced folks and in-depth training for the inexperienced."

Gail reflected, "It has been speculated that the Gardeners specifically selected fort Brazos because it is a more… independent-minded and self-sufficient community. Metropolitan cities more used to being dependent upon city and state government services might not have survived here without order breaking down and panic setting in upon the population."

John shook his head, "In short, gentlemen, in this new world, an armed society…. Survives."

✪ ✪ ✪

Livia sat quietly, listening to and studying everyone's faces and body language throughout the hours of discussion. In particular, she had noticed the easy, natural rhythm with which John and Gail interacted with everyone else and each other, often speaking for each other and sometimes simultaneously, all without any friction or competition. There was none of the familiarity of lovers. However, she suspected that even John and Gail probably had little idea of what was developing between them.

Livia had grown up with old money, power, and wealth, literally imbibing political milk from birth. As she analyzed the current political power structure, she was uncertain whether John and Gail would be an asset… or a problem.

Just then, Sergeant Roberts, who had been standing next to the travel indicator on the "wall," called out in a booming voice, "Five Minutes to Turnover. Tie down any loose objects, including yourselves!"

Everyone else stood and began to move with a purpose, but Livia stayed seated and blinked, "What?"

Gail noticed and walked over to her, "Mrs. Milner, in a little under five minutes, this elevator platform will invert…. Think of it like a carnival ride that flips you upside down for a moment."

Livia stared at her without comprehension.

Gail's eyes widened, and she sat down next to Livia, "Did no one explain this? Oh, my. Mrs. Milner, the area we departed from, is near the surface of this hollow world and is oriented, well, 'upwards' towards the outer surface. Right now, we are on an elevator platform going down toward the interior. Fort Brazos is on the inner surface of the hollow world…."

Livia shook her head, "…and that means?"

Gail nodded, "And that means that relative to the city you just left, Fort Brazos is… upside down. It is on the inner surface of a spinning cylindrical world that is nearly four thousand miles long. It is like a City in a Bottle."

Livia's skin paled even more, if that was possible. She gasped, "And we're going to be hanging upside down?"

Gail smiled, "No, Mrs. Milner. At the halfway point, the elevator will do sort of a flip so that our new orientation will be aligned with Fort Brazos. I'll spare you the details but think of it this way. This world is a hollow, spinning tube. Because of that, and other reasons, there is a kind of gravity that makes it feel just like you were on Earth. It's more complicated than that, and I don't recommend asking Dr. Nakamura about it unless you want an hours-long lecture, but you'll be safe and comfortable there."

"Flip?"

"That's right, it will feel like a carnival ride for a few seconds, so we strap everything down, including ourselves. We're all returning to the vehicles and tightening seatbelts to hold us in place during Turnover. It's perfectly safe, but if you don't strap down…."

Livia nodded gravely and swallowed. Then she looked down at the Chanel gown she was still wearing. "I think, Ms. Vice President, that that sounds like an extraordinarily good idea."

Welcome Party

Elevator Transit Warehouse / Dirigible Hanger
September 1ˢᵗ, NLD 2 -- FBD 30: 11:57 AM

The elevator ceiling retracted, and the walls receded as the giant pad smoothly came to a stop, leveling with the floor of the former Dirigible hanger. General Alexander Marcus, Mayor Tom Parker, and the City Council stood waiting in front of several rows of folding chairs. A line of blue curtains hung on scaffolding behind them, blocking the view of the control room. The vehicles started their engines and drove off the pad in the opposite direction.

As the sound ebbed away, Alexander led the greeting party and walked towards John, Gail, and the New London delegation with broad smiles, hellos, and handshakes.

Gail admonished, "I believe our new guests will want to see something before we proceed." She gestured towards the exit through which the vehicles had departed.

As they walked, Commander Gene Morton remarked, "Mr. President, Ms. Vice President, General Marcus, you'll forgive me if I say that everything looks and smells very suspiciously like we're still on Earth."

They arrived at the exit, and Gail answered, "Then, Commander, allow us to show you the new world." She extended her hand and pointed outside and up.

The newcomers stepped outside, looked up, and collectively gasped. In the sky above them was not the afternoon Texas sun or any sun that had ever shone over the Earth. The light was not coming from the sun at all. It was a bright spot on a long yellow-white line that disappeared into the distance in one direction and into the endcap of the world in the other. There was no horizon. The ground gradually swelled upwards, fading under clouds that went… sideways, up the curvature of the interior surface of the hollow cylindrical world. On the opposite side, behind the sun tube, were continents and weather systems.

In the distance, though, was another utterly unexpected sight, even for people with little to no familiarity with Texas: Mountains. Not just any average mountains, but Mountains that were Himalayan in size and scale, complete with ice caps and glaciers, forming a massive wall that seemed to stretch halfway across the world. And in the distance, between Fort Brazos and those impossible mountains, was a vast, violet-blue inland sea.

Preston squinted and held his hand up to protect his eyes from the suntube, "My God, it's true."

Alexander nodded, "It might interest you to know that the university scientists determined it is safe to look directly at the suntube. Part of me is still not convinced of that, of course, but it's yet one more thing different about this world."

Commander Morton asked, "Exactly how big… is this …place?"

Gail smiled and recited, "Commander, the interior of the new world is a hollow cylinder roughly 4,000 miles long, or just over 6,400 kilometers, with a radius of about 900 miles or around 1,450 kilometers. The surface area is around 27,145,000 Square Miles, or 70,275,000 Square Kilometers, or just over the combined surface area of Brazil, the United States, Canada, Russia, China, and Antarctica combined."

Commander Cross muttered, "Room to grow…."

John agreed, "Indeed, Commander, it's obvious the aliens we're calling 'the Gardeners' intend for us to be fruitful and multiply."

★ ★ ★

After several minutes, the group returned to the hangar. As they approached, the council ushered the delegation to the waiting seats, and the curtains were drawn back, revealing rows of bleachers. The first contained the crisply uniformed High School band, the next contained a children's choir, and the other three bleachers contained row upon row of well-wishers, both civilian and military. An American flag, higher than the rest, hung on a flagpole, with an array of other nation's flags to either side. A microphone stood on a short stand in the middle.

A young Vietnamese immigrant, seven-year-old Khanh Lieu, stepped up to the microphone with an expression now far older than her years.

The band began The Star-Spangled Banner, and everyone stood. John put his hand on his heart, and the rest of the delegation saluted sharply, except for Livia, who, looking around at those around her, hesitantly put her hand on her heart as well.

When Khan began to sing, it was with a liquid strength, clarity, and... *rage* that shocked everyone present. This was not a little girl singing a half-learned song for some school function. It was not someone trying out for a talent show. This was a girl who clearly, obviously understood precisely what had happened to her world and her new home in America. She left no doubt in anyone's mind that if she had anything to do with it, she would, *personally*, be there to make sure that flag, and by extension, all the others too, would one day again fly again on her home planet. The band members had demonstrably been practicing hard, and every one of them was sweating in the perfect 72-degree weather.

Her eyes glistened with an obsidian fire as Khan finished to a cheering, standing ovation. Chest heaving, she stood proud for a few moments before slumping slightly backward, spent. Her proud father and mother dashed out, caressed her, raised her up high, and carried her around the corner, out of sight as the audience took their seats.

Moments later, a young man with a long ponytail stepped up to the microphone and adjusted it to his height. John recognized him as Ian McLendon: a local singer who regularly performed Irish ballads at the Manticore Pub. He looked at the band and nodded before beginning Lee Greenwood's God Bless The U.S.A. to Lidia's hidden chagrin.

Not to be outdone by young miss Lieu, Ian threw all of his heart and passion into the rendition. As a singer of ballads, he knew heart, passion, love, and loss. He used everything he had, all the pain and loss and anger... and hope and love; even the occasional crack of his youthful voice was molded into the unbreaking spirit of the three-minute song. By the time he finished, his face tear-streaked and flushed, John and most of the locals were singing along. The audience rose to their feet and sent him off with another standing ovation.

And with that, the Mayor and council returned and formed a greeting line for the delegation. Councilwomen Gloria Vargas, Esmerelda Collins, Councilmen Dale Hubbard, Jack Burdger, and Wylie Hickum shook hands and greeted the visitors while the room was prepared. Carts of food and beverages were wheeled in alongside folding cafeteria tables and were quickly set and covered with traditional red and white checkered tablecloths.

Instead of MREs, this time the food was hot and fresh and rich with the aroma of Texas-style BBQ beef, ribs, and sausage as well as BBQ Chicken, Fried Chicken, fresh cantaloupe, watermelon, potato salad, fruit salad, and other sides and salads. Then there were the desserts, including pecan, pumpkin, blueberry, and apple pies, banana pudding, fudge brownies, and more.

John sized up the spread. Some of the items were from remaining supplies of mixes and cans, as there would be no more fresh bananas or chocolate beans unless these were found and brought back from elsewhere on one of the unexplored continents or islands inside New Texas.

There was enough food for many times the number of people present. He looked the question at Tom Parker, who nodded, and answered quietly, "Whatever is left over and much more will be headed to, what are they calling it, *TopSide*? Truckloads of food and supplies are being gathered to send to the survivors."

Gloria Vargas made a beeline to Livia, who had paused by the chairs, clearly overwhelmed by the boisterous southern hospitality. Livia appeared alarmingly out of place in her elegant, thin, and revealing designer dress and heels.

The councilwoman, as always, stood out with her long, silver-streaked jet-black hair pulled back in a ponytail with a turquoise and sterling silver hair clip. Her "Southwest Chic" outfit included a sterling silver and turquoise necklace on top of a crisp white button-down blouse paired with a western-style embroidered skirt and colorful fashion boots.

Gloria reached out and took Livia's hands without asking, smiling, "Welcome, Mrs. Milner. We are so glad to see you and the other survivors! You must understand we had lost all hope of finding other people alive!"

Livia painted on her best professional smile, "Why thank you, Councilwoman. I'm more than a little stunned by everything that has happened, not to mention the lovely welcome party."

Gloria released one hand but held on to the other, leading Livia to the end of the banquet tables on the far side before saying. "And I just adore Chanel. I wore one to an Air Force Ball once."

Livia blinked quizzically at her, both that Gloria would recognize the dress and also that she would have ever worn anything remotely like it.

Gloria laughed, "Oh, my dear, that was years ago. My third husband was an Air Force Colonel. May he rot in…." Gloria cut herself off politely before continuing with a gesture to another table of food, "Oh, here we are, I thought you might be interested in more familiar food, so I made sure there was a selection that you might prefer. Of course, you're welcome to anything you want, but we can't have you falling over from hunger on us now that you're here!"

As they reached the table, dozens of other smiling people stopped and shook hands with Livia, welcoming her with the familiar refrain, "If there is anything you need, dear."

Anything I need. It dawned on Livia that everything she owned was on her body or in her clutch bag. Even her invitation-only American Express Black card was now just a relic. Possibly only valuable as a curiosity… something that might end up as an artifact of their lost world in a museum.

Gloria winked, "Now, after this and after the Council meeting, you, my dear, are coming with me. We're going to get you fixed up with some more comfortable clothes, although I'm sure whatever you were doing before your Awakening Day must have been one hell of a lot more fun."

The Council

Elevator Transit Warehouse / Dirigible Hanger
September 1st, NLD, Day 2 -- FBD 30: 3:38 PM

After some debate, it had been decided that helicopters would be marginally more comfortable and give the New London delegation more time to see and absorb things than by taking Ospreys or other available aircraft. In what was perhaps a calculated move, they toured the Joint Reserve Base in two Marine Sikorsky Sea King helicopters, the same type of helicopter the President of the United States had been famous for riding in. Afterwards, they were flown over to the City of Fort Brazos using an indirect route, avoiding the town center. They were dropped off at the practice High School football field.

A caravan of cars and SUVs transported everyone to City Hall in downtown Fort Brazos. The colonnaded pink granite building was three stories tall, with a central clock tower overlooking the town square... and the looming three-hundred-foot-tall alien spire that now stood in place of the founder's statue.

That was the reason for the indirect flight route. Alexander Marcus had wanted them to see it for the first time from up close. The impossibly slender, glassy black, crystalline spire no longer displayed an ever-changing progression of Accipiter glyphs. Regardless, permanent cameras were mounted in each corner of the square to record any possible changes. Marine guards were likewise permanently encamped next to it as well, with frequent rotations and admonitions to stay ever watchful and vigilant for changes.

On Awakening Day, a single touch by a curious bystander had... angered it, resulting in a shockwave that injured many. Since then, no one was allowed to be close enough to repeat the experience.

A crowd of bystanders silently watched nearby as the caravan's occupants were disgorged next to the square. Every single newcomer had virtually the same reaction. There was a moment of disorientation as they stood outside the vehicles in the shadow of Town Hall and then turned and stared in shock, slack-jawed, at the utterly alien spire. It was the first truly alien thing they'd yet seen – aside from the world being inside-out.

Never the bashful one, Livia had been chatting lightly with Gloria until she exited the SUV and had to stop herself from bumping into her husband, who had frozen, mid-step, staring up at something. Irritated, she edged around him, and then she nearly stumbled as she saw the spire glinting darkly in the suntube light. Like Preston, she stopped dead in her tracks.

In her life, she had seen obelisks a plenty. But this was not an obelisk, and it wasn't even as tall as the Washington Monument, so it wasn't that it was impossibly tall. It was just… wrong. It was almost as if it glowed… darkness. She never even realized that she had clutched Preston's hand and drawn close to him, sheltering in his height and strength.

John Austin rounded the corner of the vehicle and slowly walked up to Preston, giving him the moment before saying, "Sometimes it feels like it is looking back at us."

Livia twitched slightly as the sound of John's voice shattered the spell. As she did, she blinked and looked down at her hand holding Preston's and let it go with a start.

Preston shook his head slowly, oblivious to her, "Spaceships and mile-high roofs and an inside-out world are one thing… but that... that thing…."

Standing next to Livia, Gloria quipped, "It's quite the alien bauble, isn't it? On Awakening Day, green fire shot out of the dammed thing and lit the suntube. 'Damnedest thing I ever saw."

City Hall was a new, spacious, high-ceilinged, well-appointed building and luxurious compared to Old City Hall, which was now a museum. It had been paid for with shale oil tax revenue. The Council members sat in their seats along a continuous curved desk on a dais at the chamber's far end. John, Gail, General Marcus, and Admiral Milner took up seats in the front row, facing the council.

A projection screen on the side of the chamber displayed scenes from TopSide, including drone views of the mile-high filigreed blue ceiling/sky, the vast park with thousands of people gathered there, the apartment/hotel buildings, the main central administrative complex, the warehouse district, hospital and, of course, the starship.

Mayor Tom Parker struck his gavel to open the meeting and intoned, "Let us pray," bowing his head as he continued, "Our Dear Heavenly Father, we humbly thank you and praise your name for this miracle. You have delivered more survivors to us. We beseech you in this time of doubt and struggle to grant us faith, strength, and wisdom. May you guide and direct us and watch over and protect your children. Amen."

The prayer caught more than just the visitors off guard. Since Awakening Day, the formality of an opening prayer had only been observed once. Several council members looked questioningly at Tom, who simply smiled and nodded at John to kick things off.

John nodded soberly and introduced each visitor in turn, briefly repeating their backgrounds. He then turned to Admiral Milner, "Admiral, please give us your assessment of the situation TopSide as well as with regard to the discovery of the starship."

Preston stood and surveyed the council members with as level and confident an expression as he could muster. He and Livia had discussed this the night before, damn her licentious soul, but he knew she was right, as the solemn opening prayer only confirmed for him. If he were to have any future here, much less one of leadership, he must project as much wisdom, confidence, decisiveness, and, damn her, she was right – family solidarity and unity as possible. Kicking his wife to the curb would not be well received here.

He began, "First of all, on behalf of all of the New London survivors, thank you, Mr. President, Ms. Vice President, Mr. Mayor, and Council Members, for the tireless efforts being made to make sure that my people TopSide are provided for."

Livia had insisted he take 'ownership' of the TopSide population.

"As you know, while there is, surprisingly, a well-equipped hospital there, we have found no food or other supplies except water. Evidently, these… aliens who brought us here wanted to compel dependency on the people in Fort Brazos for food and resources."

He shook his head, "I'm sure we could start some kind of gardens in the park areas, but it was clearly not designed with agriculture in mind, and I think we should keep things the way they are for now. For one thing, I have been told that these aliens are prone to show displeasure if we do things they don't like. I don't feel like testing those limits just now."

The brief concern that flared in some of their eyes confirmed his suspicions. He had not had very long to prepare an outline of what he would say but was glad he'd done so.

"For now, the shipments of aid have things under control. The hotel rooms or apartments, or whatever they are, provide running water, showers, and beds to sleep in. The temperature is constant, so exposure isn't a concern, and, at least so far, there is no weather to worry about. Thankfully, everyone has privacy and a comfortable place to sleep."

"I recommend we prioritize moving families with children down to the city, here in Fort Brazos, as soon as possible. The exception would be if a family member is deemed critical to the starship project. A six-hour commute isn't very practical."

All the Council members nodded in common sense approval, some making notes.

Preston continued, "No medical problems have been reported. Other than food and baby supplies, what we are desperately short on, frankly…" he paused, fingering his uniform lapel in emphasis, "…is fresh clothing. All we have… all we have in the world… are the clothes we wore when we were abducted."

Several Council members' eyes widened, and they muttered, "Oh dear!", "Yes," and, "Of course!" and, "We'll get right on that!"

Preston paused, raising a hand, "Please, Ladies and Gentlemen, allow me to emphasize. We, all twenty thousand or more of us, literally have nothing but the clothes on our backs." He let that sink in.

Councilman Hickum exclaimed, "Oh My."

Gloria Vargas shook her head at him, "It's like I said, Wylie, this is going to be more than a housing problem."

Tom nodded, "Admiral, after the… Culling, quite a few homes, and apartments were left, well, unoccupied. We had them sealed. Also, I don't know if it was explained to you, but Fort Brazos was a central distribution point for many retailers and supply companies. Many of those warehouses were… expanded by the Gardeners, and their contents multiplied manyfold. We are literally overflowing with common household goods and clothing. Given what I've seen in the warehouses, I believe that providing at least a minimal refugee starter, or welcome kit, for the New London survivors won't be a problem. We need to figure out what to do, well, legally, about the homes of the dead, but at least in the short term, I'm sure there will also be no shortage of families happy to take in temporary boarders. We are a generous people."

Preston was inwardly relieved to hear Tom refer to the TopSiders as "his" people. "That is most gracious and wonderful to hear, mister Mayor. On behalf of all of us, Thank you. There is another matter, of course. As I said, all we have is what we are carrying on our persons. How may I ask, are people here, well, paying for things?"

John replied, "Well, you understand it's only been a month since Awakening Day for us, and since everyone here came through it with what they already had, it has been less of a problem for us, but, honestly, we've been struggling to decide how to deal with it in the long run. We have frozen prices and made sure that everyone has what they need, but we will have to build a whole new economic model and medium of sustainable exchange. Frankly, we're hoping that the economics professor and his students at the university can come up with some workable solutions."

Tom nodded, "And in the meantime, Admiral, I propose that we issue vouchers to everyone TopSide and give them assurances that there will be no hoarding, and we will do everything we can to get your people back on their feet."

Councilwoman Esmerelda Collins added, "In the meantime, Admiral, in addition to providing resources for your people, we need a census and an accounting of skills and backgrounds. A local IT company is building a database to record skills and match people with housing and jobs. We certainly don't know what all the jobs will be in the future, but it seemed obvious to everyone that if we were going to be fighting some kind of Galactic war, a lot of people were going to be very busy making a lot of… things."

Preston paused, swallowing. He looked down for a poignant moment, then looked back up. "Forgive me, Councilwoman. I suppose I am still trying to come to grips with the consequences of all of this. The personal loss of my daughter and family is bad enough. That we've lost our entire planet and now must plan and execute a war, not only that… a war against an enemy that spans the entire galaxy…. It is a lot to absorb."

In the corner of his eye, he saw Livia stiffen at his admission.

He shook his head and stood a bit taller. "That said, I am a warrior, and it is my duty to protect my country… my people. It was never my job to decide which war to fight, only to use the resources available to me to execute that fight in the most efficient and effective way possible. I am here now, and I will have to deal with everything… *else* later."

Livia smiled sadly.

John frowned and asked, "Admiral, believe me. We all know how you feel and respect the fact that you've had almost no time even to begin to cope with it. You have our utmost respect for being ready and willing to go to work. You're welcome to come to my house later if you want to talk. I've got an open bar. Anytime."

Preston nodded soberly, "Thank you, Mr. President. As you said, let's get to work."

John smiled knowingly, "Very well. I know you have not had time to think about this for very long, but I want to get your first thoughts and ideas about this war. It seems obvious that in order to fight, we will need, and pardon me for using the term, we will need a space navy to take the fight to the Accipiters. We had assumed that the Gardeners had something up their sleeves for us to use eventually."

He took a breath, "Well, now that shoe has dropped, and they have revealed the spaceship. I know that you have only briefly looked it over. However, what is your first impression? What do you think this portends for how we are supposed to move forward. Quite frankly, what do we do now?"

Preston nodded thoughtfully. After the initial shock and excitement, he had worried over this very question for much of the time since seeing the damned thing. *How indeed, Mr. President*, he was tempted to say. Fortunately, he had the presence of mind not to.

"Mr. President, I've thought of little else. Given the incomplete state that the vessel appears to be in, and given the lack of any apparent weaponry, my assessment is that our abductors intend for us to use the vessel both as a learning tool and to use it to begin building a space industrial complex in whatever star system we happen to be located in. To fight a war, we need ships and men and women who understand every nut and bolt inside them. We need to build the industry, to build the industry, needed to build the ships. No offense to your fine city here, but it certainly cannot begin to have the supply chain necessary even to build ocean-going warships, much less starships. Moreover, we need to be able to defend this new home of ours. Since it appears to be a giant hollow tube of some kind in space, I shudder to think what would happen if the enemy showed up and threw rocks at it like they did to our cities and bases on Earth. This place might crack open like an egg, opening up to the vacuum of space and killing us all. We need to build defenses and a navy, and eventually, we can venture out beyond it to take the fight to the enemy. Even then, we need to master the technology so that we can guarantee that it would be impossible for the enemy to trace any attacks we might make … back to our home base, here."

Half the council had winced and visibly paled when he had used his egg analogy. Livia seemed especially shaken, and she pleaded with her eyes for him to take a different tack. He was way ahead of her.

"That said, Sir, it is clearly going to be years, perhaps longer, before we will be ready to do much more than poke our head out the proverbial door. It may take decades to invent a whole new warfare doctrine and adequately train the scientists, engineers, officers, and enlisted personnel sufficiently to become a confident, spacefaring, and battle-ready force. A navy is not just a collection of ships. It is built upon generations of hard-learned lessons and the warfighting doctrine that follows from it. This will take time, Sir."

Color began to return to the council's faces. He thought no less of them. He'd gone through much the same emotional roller coaster ride as he had thought things through himself. Now, however, he knew it was time to make that course change.

"Mr. President, with respect, your question begs another. There is a pressing issue that must be dealt with. You see, Sir, my people are being asked to fight a war that we did not vote for. We did not vote in your Plebiscite, and we have no official representation."

Some of the Council stiffened slightly.

He continued, "Do you think this will cause a problem with the aliens?"

The unexpected question caught everyone off guard. Some raised eyebrows, some slumped back in their seats, and the rest silently contemplated an answer. Any answer.

This was the deflection he and Livia had worked out. Rather than directly challenge their leadership, he should instead express concern that their abductors might not be happy until "his" people were given a voice—a vote.

Tom nodded in agreement, "An excellent point, Admiral. We had planned to have a constitutional convention in several months. There is much to work out, not the least of which is the question of land rights in the wilderness, property rights for the dead in case any relatives ever turn up, citizenship and citizenship requirements, loyalty issues for the military personnel from hostile countries that were abducted along with the rest of us, and a host of other concerns. Now, with a whole new city of effectively homeless people to add to everything and the 'minor' fact that your city is 6 hours away…. There is a lot to consider. We need time to work out proposals that make sense, and we, of course, will welcome and encourage ideas from your people."

Preston nodded humbly, "Thank you, mister Mayor, that is much more than I had dared hope for. It is obvious that your people have given this careful thought and consideration already. I, for one, am grateful that my people have been spared the frightening and jarring uncertainty your people must have faced in the hours and days after your Awakening Day. It will give my people a level of comfort to know this and that you are looking out for them."

Livia smiled proudly. However, Preston barely noticed.

The Beast

Mimicking Earth's sun, the bright spot on the suntube migrated daily along its length and was now nearing its end. As it reached the endcap, it would slowly fade. The tube itself never disappeared from view entirely and instead radiated a soft moonlike glow until the cycle began again in the "morning." Mimicking Earth's moon, that silvery glow followed the same pattern of lunar cycles, waxing and waning in brightness, even including a near-New Moon of almost complete darkness, emulating gentle starlight at the end of each cycle.

In all its forms, agriculture had dominated the pre-Awakening Day lives of the citizens of Fort Brazos. Most people now realized intuitively what the surviving scientists at Bonham State University had soberly explained on the TV stations not long after the cycle had first manifested. The aliens who had transported everyone here had duplicated many of Earth's biological zones and niches — everything from prairie to alpine forest to jungle to desert and more.

Life on Earth was intertwined with seasons and lunar cycles, and so if there was any surprise, it was the apparent care with which their analogues had been mirrored here in the new world. In the month that had transpired since Awakening Day, changes in the sun tube's luminosity were measured. Estimates were that the seasons themselves would likely be much milder than on Earth, but they would definitely change over time.

As before, the New Londoners were all eyes throughout the helicopter ride back to the Joint Reserve Base. Again, all had been reminded that it was safe to look directly at the sun tube and most did precisely that, as well as staring at the impossible sight of the distant upcurved horizon and the view of the continents and oceans "above" them. In the month that had passed since the first Awakening

Day, even the 'DownSiders' themselves were not wholly blasé about those sights themselves.

Helicopters being what they were, it was not practical to speak to each other without using the hearing protection headsets and microphones. Preston rode with Livia at his side and John Austin, Alexander, and Captain Darryl Guevara opposite them. Courtesy of Gloria Vargas's arm twisting and the promise that Livia's $12,000 Chanel gown would be available for study and copy, Livia now sported a Black Givenchy wool and silk jacket, white silk blouse, Gucci pants, and Jimmy Choo boots. Livia was careful not to outwardly notice that they were a year out of fashion.

Gloria and several nervous-looking City Council members rode in the other seats, and the submarine commanders had been split up between the two helicopters. Gail and half the City Council rode in the other Sea King.

The Joint Reserve Base was located 22 miles from the city of Fort Brazos. As they approached the base, the helicopters began to circle the perimeter. Preston motioned for Alexander's attention, "General, how long do you think you'll keep calling this the Joint Reserve Base?"

Alexander blinked in surprise at the question. While the thought had briefly occurred to him a time or two, it had not made it anywhere on his list of priorities. Since Awakening Day, one crisis after another had erupted.

Before he could answer, John nodded and commented, "Admiral, that is a subject that has come up a time or two in Council meetings with the University sociologists. Some people wanted to rename it after Corpsman Mendez, the first military casualty here, who, along with City Councilman Barrett and much of his family, were murdered by the Stalker creature. Some instead wanted to find some appropriate historical reference and call it 'New Sparta' or some such. Another popular idea was to name it something with more emotional impact, like 'Fort Resolve' or 'Fort Defiance.' Of course, there is also the idea of simply dropping the 'Joint Reserve Base' part and returning it to its original name, 'Fort Brazos.'"

Alexander responded, "That's… that's very thoughtful of the council to think of remembering Corpsman Mendez in that way."

Preston cocked his head, "I confess I'm confused by the base having the same name as the city, Mr. President."

John smiled, "You're not the only one who has had that reaction. You see, back in 1822, a group of Stephen F. Austin's colonists, headed by a man named Jason Wilde, built a fort at a bend of the Brazos River and named it Fort Brazos. Later, the fort fell into disuse and was little more than an outpost, but the city grew up nearby, took the name, and was incorporated in 1837. The Fort was called Camp Fort Brazos for a while, but eventually, in 1910, it was renamed the Fort Brazos Army Post. Later, during the base consolidations of the early 1990s, Fort Brazos was slated to be closed but was saved and selected as a consolidation site for several closed facilities and renamed once again, this time to Joint Reserve Base Fort Brazos."

Preston nodded. Although Fort Brazos was one of the oldest continuously operating military bases in the United States, the story was not unusual.

Commander Cross pointed out the window, "Admiral, we're not returning to where we took off from."

Preston looked the question at Alexander, who nodded, "Yes, Admiral, Commander, you see, we have something special we thought you would want to see."

As they approached the end of runway number five, a strange square structure grew into view. It seemed to be made of rows of highway K-Rails stacked to form a square enclosure. The interior floor glinted of dull metal. In the middle, a black and red splotched… thing… stood clawing at the floor and occasionally attempted to bash the concrete barriers.

Commander Cross asked, "Is that?"

Alexander smiled, "Yes, Commander, *that* is an alien creature. Some people are calling it a "War Dog," but, personally, I think that is a stupid name. It is the same kind of creature that opened up a Humvee like it was a paper bag and killed… ate… several of my men a few weeks ago."

After landing, the group met at a set of bleachers overlooking the cage area. Several scaffolding towers surrounded the enclosure, where technicians were still installing cameras, area lighting, and other equipment. To one side, a large firetruck sat parallel to the enclosure. Nearby, three Bradley Fighting Vehicles sat manned and ready, each mounted with M242 25mm chain-driven autocannons loaded with M919 Armor-Piercing, Fin-Stabilized Discarding Sabo Tracer rounds. It was the same type of weapon from which a single five-round salvo had eviscerated and utterly destroyed the first such creature, but no one was taking chances. Many other vehicles were coming and going, dropping off people and equipment.

As they climbed up the bleachers, with Livia at his side, Preston asked, "So, General Marcus, may I ask why we didn't stop to see this… thing… when we first arrived?"

Alexander smiled, "Because, Admiral, when you arrived here, the creature was still chained inside a container, and there was nothing you could actually see."

The Wardog had been watching them from the middle of the corral of K-Rails, which were stacked five deep. It slowly backed up to the other end of the corral, which was only about twice its own length.

All conversations abruptly ceased as the Wardog emitted a rock-grinding, air-ripping, basso roar and charged the rails in front of it. Almost as one, the crowd of spectators flinched.

The wicked claws on its six legs skittered and screeched across the metal plating beneath it. However, it was too big and heavy to gain much acceleration from the charge. It collided with the K-Rails with a sickening crunch, lost its footing, and physics being what it is, its thick armored body pivoted on its head and horn and slammed lengthwise against the concrete.

The water cannon on top of the firetruck fired a long blast of water at the Wardog. It staggered back to its feet and shook its head violently to fling the water away, then howled in subterranean rage before trotting in circles and stopping in the middle of the corral again to glare at its captors.

To her credit, Livia had not shrieked or cried out, although if she had been much closer, that might have been different, as it likely would have been so with any sane person. With its gaping mouth filled with shark-like teeth, an array of tiny eyes, and a massive horn, it was the stuff of nightmares.

Livia pointed and asked, "Is this… Is this a safe place to keep that… that thing?"

Alexander nodded to Captain Guevara, who answered, "This is temporary. Colonel Salangsang and his men are constructing a more permanent… zoo… for it. However, those K-Rails are prestressed steel-reinforced concrete, and the plating on the enclosure floor is one-inch thick steel road plating, and the runway itself is high-density reinforced concrete. It was originally constructed as an alternate Space Shuttle emergency runway. If that isn't enough and the creature does manage to escape, there are three Bradleys on overwatch. Each mounts the same type of 25mm chain gun that easily dispatched the other one of these things we've seen so far. That said, we really need to keep it alive to study it, Ma'am."

Alexander smiled, "And no, we will most definitely *not* have a Jurassic Park incident on my base."

Livia nodded soberly and noticed the tall older man and younger woman now mounting the bleachers and headed their way. They were obviously civilians, but there was something different about them. The man appeared to be in his fifties, and she was in her thirties, perhaps. They had both clearly spent a great deal of time outdoors from their complections, but the man's appearance was much more weathered than the woman, whose braided dirty blonde hair was covered by a broad-brimmed hat that shaded her tanned face. They were both well-dressed and carried themselves with confidence, but there was something in their eyes. The family resemblance was unmistakable. This was a father and daughter.

Alexander greeted them with handshakes before turning back to the group, "Admiral, Mrs. Milner, Commanders, allow me to introduce Frank and Mira Yaegar. The Yaegar's, aside from being pillars in the local business community, are also world-class big game hunters. They led our soldiers in the hunt for the first… Wardog."

At 5'10", Mira was an inch taller than her father. She led the way, shaking hands, with Frank following behind her, half-smiling as he watched her, clearly a proud father.

Commander Cross shook her hand and asked, noticing the lack of a ring, "Miss, is it, Miss? Yaegar, can you give us your impressions of the creature? Did it show any signs of intelligent action, whether of its own mind or perhaps by being controlled?"

Mira paused, briefly taking him in. Like the other commanders, he was trim and solidly built. His face was not pretty or handsome like Phil Underwood's or Jermaine Cutter's, but it was strong. A sharp, lively intelligence lit his grey eyes.

She flashed a brighter smile than she intended, "It stayed hidden, burrowed very effectively underground. We would not have found it or had any warning except for the dogs. Then we think it reacted to Lieutenant Garreth's radio and attacked. It did not attack when the dogs marked its location and barked. It did not react to the sound. It waited until we were right on top of it, and David began talking on his radio. I understand it had previously reacted to a trucker's CB radio, and there is speculation it may have attacked the Humvee because one of those poor men was talking on the radio to the forward operating base." She glanced at her father, who nodded, before continuing, "So we don't think we can say it necessarily acted with intelligence so much as it responded to stimuli."

Commander Gene Morton asked, "General, how exactly did you get it into that cage, and… how did you capture it alive?"

Alexander chuckled, "That's an interesting story, Commander. We found it chained inside a shipping container, but even so, it was clear that it would eventually break loose. So, we had Colonel Salangsang's construction battalion throw this holding area together to hold it temporarily. We lowered the container into the enclosure on a crane, remotely popped the chains loose, and let it out. Getting it back out again may be a challenge, but we think we have a plan for that."

Gene cocked his head, "You found it? The… Gardeners left it for you?"

Alexander frowned, "That, you see, is yet another mystery we're trying to unravel." He turned to Guevara, "Captain?"

Guevara pulled photocopies of a handwritten letter out of a messenger bag he carried and passed them out. The letter was in Spanish and included a typed English translation that must have been added later.

TRANSLATION:

A gift to the good people of Fort Brazos. You have more friends than you know. — Ignacio

* * *

The light was fading fast as Dr. Jacob Becker, Ph.D., and Dr. Eva Sanches, DVM, impatiently watched from the edge of the bleachers as the VIPs left. Apparently, the people from New London were returning TopSide, and General Marcus and Vice President Finley were going with them.

Eva sighed, "Finally! We can get to work!" At an even 5' tall, the contrast between them could hardly be greater. Where she was short and petite, he was thin and 6'1" tall. Eva had grown her family veterinary clinic into the largest and most successful in the entire region and had a national reputation as something of a miracle worker. People around the country were known to transport or even fly their horses to see her.

On the other hand, Jacob was a geneticist and tenured professor at Bonham State University, specializing in genetically modified crops. For years they had been on opposite sides of philosophical and political divides, and everyone had known that they hated each other. The fact that they had been passionate lovers for almost the entire time they had known each other had been a well-maintained secret, lest their peers find out.

After Awakening Day, all of that pretense had fallen away like scales. After all, it was the Apocalypse, and many such illusions had vanished, boiled away in the harsh actinic light of the near extinction of the human race.

While they had not actively announced anything, word had started to get around. Perhaps before Awakening Day, the revelation would have ostracized them from the social circles of their friends and colleagues.

Now though, as word of their relationship percolated out, it barely made less than a ripple in the social pond. Indeed, Eva's closest friend, Louisa, whom Eva had feared would be scandalized, had instead sought her out and hugged her tightly, streaming tears, telling her how lucky she was. Louisa's husband had not survived Awakening day.

Through the shared tears of consoling her friend, Eva had been shocked to learn that Louisa and some of Eva's other closest friends had long-held suspicions that something was up between her and Jacob but had been too polite to tell her so.

Eva had been her father's 'assistant veterinarian' since she was old enough to walk. She was no stranger to the sights and smells of animal insides and out. Still, the acrid smell wafting over from the corral was enough to make even her eyes water and her stomach flip.

Or maybe it was something else. Yes, it was definitely something else. Eva had realized not long after Awakening Day that she was pregnant. She had not held the information back from Jacob, who had smiled widely, lifted her off her feet, and held her in his arms for what must have been the entire lifetime of some universe somewhere. They were utterly inseparable now.

Eva was not alone. By the time she had discovered that the Gardeners had "un-fixed" all the animals at her clinic, she already suspected what then Commander (Dr.) Gwyneth Elliot had simultaneously deduced.

The same had been done to humans.

Hysterectomies, vasectomies, and virtually all forms of infertility were not only reversed, but spermicides and most forms of birth control were now either totally ineffective or significantly weakened. In eight months or so, there was going to be a baby boom, the likes of which no one had ever seen.

The fact that there were no more companies making any forms of birth control and that existing supplies were all that were likely to be available for the foreseeable future was a much-lamented topic.

She rubbed her nose at the smell and asked, "So, you still think the thing was engineered?"

Jacob smiled softly, "Ah, so you think that I only see it through the lens of my profession? That since I am a geneticist, I naturally see what I expect to see?"

Eva elbowed him in the ribs. She was used to having to aim up to do so, and he was used to the familiar jab.

"Perhaps that's true. On the other hand, what we are looking at seems completely unlikely. A creature shows up, reportedly employed by the Accipiters, and it can obviously not only thrive in our atmosphere but also consume Earth-based… food… and our protein and amino acid structures, and it is evidently able to digest it, as evidenced by its droppings as well as the fact that it hasn't starved to death."

Eva shook her head, "And you think that is unlikely to happen with an organism that evolved on another planet, a planet we think had heavier gravity than Earth."

"Perhaps. You have to wonder at the odds that a lifeform naturally evolving on another planet would so easily adapt to our environment and biochemistry. On the other hand, think about Dr. Forrester's discovery! The tissues from the one they blew up had organic superconductive fibrils serving as the analog for a nervous system. This thing is slow because it is big and heavy, but its nervous system is *electrical*. It fires its muscles based on electrical signals!"

The Wardog grunted and trotted in circles several times, its claws continuing to squeak and scratch at the steel plating before halting in the middle again, this time leveling a stare at Eva and Jacob.

As the near darkness of the new world fell, the Wardog's tiny eyes glinted.

Eva pointed excitedly, "Look! Those eyes are reflecting and amplifying light. It may have an analog to the tapetum lucidum in many vertebrates! Perhaps in its original habitat, it was nocturnal?"

Jacob nodded, "Or it was engineered to be effective day or night."

Eva jabbed him again, "I hate you."

Jacob solemnly replied, "I know."

Rangers

Sheriff Hector Alonzo smiled toothily as he entered Ray's Diner, raising the corners of his heavy mustache. The thick smell of bacon, eggs, Ray's signature waffles, and coffee washed over him, reminding him of his wife Antonia's admonition to stick with his diet. She had shaken her finger at him and pronounced, 'God spared our family from the apocalypse. I won't have you dying of a heart attack now!'

The diner's owner, Ray Wallace, was a beefy former football defensive end, but he somehow managed to maneuver behind the counter without knocking things over gracefully. He was completely bald, and his brilliant white smile contrasted sharply with his jet-black skin. Ray smiled in return and smoothed his blue striped apron, "Your usual *Sheriff?*" He added extra emphasis to 'Sheriff' in happy recognition of Hector's promotion.

Hector sighed and shook his head, "Just coffee, Ray."

Ray rolled his eyes in sympathy and softly said, "You need to tell Antonia who's boss, Hector!"

Hector politely pretended not to hear him and instead headed to the booth in the far corner, where two of his oldest friends, retired Texas Rangers Sgt. Samuel (Sam) Wallace and Francis (Frank) Hayes sat waiting.

Sam was thin and lanky, with large metal-rimmed glasses, his hair thin and grey. Both his and Frank's light grey western hats lay upside down in the seat next to Sam. Frank was squarish compared to Sam, but he still had a full head of black and grey, mostly grey, hair.

Two years before Awakening Day, Hector convinced the then-Sheriff John Austin to invite Samuel and Frank to relocate to Fort Brazos at their retirement and become departmental consultants. Frank was a widower and had no close family. Samuel was twice divorced, and his grown children had long since moved out of state and largely out of contact with their father.

Just as Hector sat down in the booth next to Frank, with his back to the wall so he could see the entrance, Ray's wife, Ella, delivered his coffee with a quick smile and picked up Sam and Frank's empty breakfast plates before darting back to the kitchen.

Sam and Frank raised their coffee mugs. Sam grinned, "Congratulations on making Sheriff, Hector, you deserve it."

Frank nodded, "It's about time. Suits you."

Hector hesitated, his thoughts elsewhere, then added, "Thanks."

Sam chuckled and changed the subject to talk about the missing persons case that Hector had had them look into. "Well, the missing Mrs. Lucero wasn't so missing after all."

Hector raised his eyebrows as he cupped his steaming coffee mug.

Frank added, "Seems Mr. Lucero threw the note out with the trash. It was unopened, so you might forgive Mr. Lucero for possibly not seeing it, except for the fact that he had thrown out a bunch of Mrs. Lucero's things at the same time."

Sam shook his head tiredly, "We found her right where she said she said she would be. At her friend's house, 'starting over.' Case closed."

Hector grunted softly as he stared into his coffee.

Sam cocked his head, "You're awfully quiet. What's up, Hector? What's on your mind?"

Frank laughed lightly, "You getting us some real work or something?"

Hector pursed his lips as he sugared his coffee.

Sam shook his head, "Oh Hell, Hector, don't be coy. Out with it."

Hector took a sip of his coffee, "I have a mystery."

Frank quipped, "That's a relief. For a minute there, I thought you were going to draft us to hunt monsters."

Hector nodded, "Maybe later. For now, I have a series of property crimes, all in remote locations, all in unoccupied homes or businesses, and none that took anything particularly valuable, just food, supplies, clothing, tools, and so forth. In several cases, jewelry, expensive watches, silverware, luxury items, and things pawnable for more money were ignored."

Sam asked, "I take it that none of these things have shown up to be pawned or sold at the flea market?"

Hector nodded.

Frank leaned back in his seat, "I'm guessing this is not just a couple of things here and there…. Someone is outfitting a crew. Maybe preparing to set off on their own somewhere?"

Hector did not answer and instead sipped his coffee.

Sam looked at Frank. "Are you thinking what I'm thinking?"

Frank slowly nodded, "I think so. Whoever pulled that off had to be well organized and have a large group of trained men to do it with."

Hector smiled, "That's why I like you guys." He unbuttoned his shirt pocket and withdrew a folded sheet of paper – a photocopy of the hand-written note that had been left with the anonymously captured Wardog.

Hector handed Frank the note, who read it, scowled, shook his head, and then passed it across the table to Sam, who studied it for a moment, then chuckled, "Son of a bitch has got a big pair."

Hector nodded slowly, "The military's job is to break and shoot things. I want you to find these men. Who are they? Where did they come from? What do they want, and are they a danger?"

Sam and Frank shifted uncomfortably. Sam shook his head, "Hector, we've been consulting with your department ever since we retired here, but this sounds like something more. You're not asking us what we think. You asked us to go out and find these guys. This is a lot heavier than finding neglected housewives…." He glanced at Frank, who nodded, "….and while Frank and I are OK with it, it is probably a hell of a lot more dangerous."

Hector took a sip of his coffee, smiled, unbuttoned his other shirt pocket, withdrew a folded sheet of heavy stock paper, and carefully unfolded it. This one had a state seal on it. He handed it to Sam. "Sam, Frank, you are now the co-commanders of the newly re-instated Texas Rangers. For now, you will report to me until somebody figures out what the government will look like. You'll have an office; we'll get you vehicles and equipment, and you'll have a budget to recruit a small group of candidates for the new Ranger program. And, no, you can't steal any of my people or from the police department, for now. They're already up to their necks with other problems right now, and we don't have enough to go around."

Sam read the document and slowly handed it to Frank, who asked, "Then where?"

Hector shrugged, "The President suggested you look at some of the New Arrivals. There are thousands of military men who have no families with them. Many have special forces or military police experience who may not want to join the Space Marines or whatever the hell they end up calling the alien-fighting military."

Intelligence

Telecommunications Bunker (Disused)
September 4th, NLD 5 -- FBD 33: 9:37 AM

Lieutenant Colonel Martin Williams, late of the Australian Intelligence Corps, had been instructed to search among the many disused structures within the confines of the Joint Reserve Base for a suitable home for the Intelligence group he had been tasked with building. Like the former Dirigible Hanger, before Awakening Day, many of the disused buildings had been used as storage places for parts and obsolete equipment that had not yet been disposed of, and some argued might never be. The Dirigible Hanger had been a repository of miscellaneous aircraft parts and assemblies that might possibly be needed someday. Eventually. Maybe. Who knew? With no more factories and no supply chain to provide new or replacement parts and equipment, it was anyone's guess what might be needed or even crucial someday.

Martin had been given the choice of some reasonably nice but potentially undersized buildings, an entire floor in one of the main office buildings, raw warehouse space, and, last on the list and indeed, the last anyone thought he would choose was the former telecommunications facility. It was in a less-traveled (i.e., run-down) area of the base, and everything around it was similarly old and disused. The entire area had been slated to be razed to the ground, but the budget for the demolition had been shifted to higher priorities.

When the new telecom facility was constructed to replace it, the old building had been mothballed and used to store obsolete computer and telco equipment. Outside the squat, two-story, bunker-like structure were the rusting skeletons of several satellite dishes that had once made up a sizable "satellite farm," most of which had been disassembled and moved to the new facility or were otherwise obsolete.

The primary telecom lines that ran through the base still passed through the facility, though. While the backup diesel generators outside would need some repair and reconditioning, they were salvageable. The banks of lead-acid batteries that had once provided power during the interval between an outage and when the generators could handle the load had thankfully long since been removed. Martin had feared he would find a toxic mess that might be more trouble than it was worth to make the facility a viable candidate for his needs.

Most of the first floor had been configured as a data center with raised floors and row upon row of equipment racks, about half of which were still outfitted with fifteen and twenty-year-old 'vintage' computer and telco equipment. Many of the drop ceiling tiles had sagged and caved in under the weight of cables lying on top of them, which now dangled and hung loosely through the gaps like so many jungle vines. Likewise, many of the raised floor tiles were missing or lay loose, revealing a near-solid mass of old black coax and even quite a lot of ancient Token Ring cable. Over the years, the heat from the wires had gradually fused much of them into a solid mass of melted plastic and copper.

Fully half of the fluorescent light fixtures were missing their tubes, and half of those that remained had several burned-out tubes, and the rest flickered weakly from failing ballasts.

Martin's first reaction was that the place would have made an excellent location for a horror movie or some post-Apocalyptic drama. Then he had chuckled to himself at how apt that actually was.

In addition to electrical power, the facility still had water, so the bathrooms still worked after a fashion. There was a kitchen and cafeteria and an additional story with an entire wing of offices, including a few large executive offices that must have belonged to the command staff. Like so much of the rest of the building, the thick carpet had mildewed. The room had been piled high with battered Steelcase desks, filing cabinets, and chairs.

Martin requisitioned a work detail of two dozen burly Army privates and a Staff Sergeant, who had cleared out most of the space within a few days in around-the-clock shifts. He had no idea where it all went, but there seemed to be no shortage of dead storage alternatives on the base. He'd then set them to the task of ripping out the soiled and horrid carpet, damaged and mildewed fixtures, and even a few walls. Perhaps all the dead cabling could be melted down for copper or find some other use.

The new carpet had been procured from somewhere, and a half dozen Army plumbers and a dozen carpenters arrived to fix and replace leaking fixtures and repair walls and lighting fixtures. Much of the equipment in the kitchen area was ripped out and replaced with functioning, if not necessarily, new equipment. The pantry was then stocked with a modest supply of canned goods, MREs, bottled water, and lots and lots of coffee. He worried about how long the coffee would last.

He thought to himself, maybe somewhere out there in this new world, we will find a new source of coffee beans….

A week after he had first set foot in the building, the HVAC was humming nicely, refrigerating the space to a brisk 68 degrees. The work crews had moved like their lives depended on it. General Marcus's promise that he would get anything he needed, "if possible," had been sincere.

During the renovation, he'd observed the Staff Sargeant repeatedly browbeat the workers to be careful to preserve any old equipment that might be repaired or broken down into useful parts. *"Dammit, Private! There ain't no more factories pumpin out new widgets and parts!"*

The executive office suite had a meeting room and a separate private office and bathroom with a shower. Martin turned the private office area into a bedroom and moved in.

He was impressed by the level of effort put forth to support his new department, even though, at present, he was the only official member of it.

So now he sat in his office, surrounded by large screen TVs, computers, and monitors that had access to every data and communications source in Fort Brazos. As soon as the raised floor area could be thoroughly cleaned out and rebuilt, he planned to construct a big brother to the base's CIC. Among the many tasks on his agenda would be the gargantuan task of data mining what seemed to be a copy of all of Earth's data networks – the entire pre-Awakening Day Internet.

Not only that, he'd been shocked to discover that the seemingly limitless computer storage contained millions of private networks, including what must have been air-gapped systems. All were neatly organized by country, governmental department, industry, and dozens of other search categories.

It would take generations of work by an enormous staff to fully index it all. In his idle moments, he mused about a medieval setting of monks painstakingly typing away in cloistered cubicles.

And then, there was the data on the so-called New Arrivals.

On Awakening Day, on the outskirts of Fort Brazos, 12,825 military personnel from twenty other countries, including Martin himself, had awakened to find that they had been abducted from their military home bases from around the Earth.

Shots had been fired in the confusion that had followed, but miraculously, there had been no serious casualties. The New Arrivals had been deposited in remote areas of the base, which reduced their immediate interactions with the indigenous Joint Reserve Base personnel, or each other, as many were mortal enemies.

The situation had been confusing and chaotic, and it was several desperate hours before General Marcus's men had begun to accept that the New Arrivals had not actually been invaders. Those forces included personnel from Martin's own Australia, as well as, to name just a few, Brazil, China, Columbia, Egypt, France, Germany, India, Iran, Israel, Japan, North Korea, Pakistan, Russia, South Africa, Saudi Arabia, South Korea, Turkey, UK, and Ukraine.

It was the forces from countries like North Korea and Iran that had caused the most concern. Some called them the "undesirables."

Mysteriously, personnel files on all New Arrivals had been discovered on the Joint Reserve Base's computers. The files had been translated into English perfectly. The computers had also been 'upgraded' with vastly more capacity than before. To Martin, however, how that was possible paled in comparison to everything else the Gardeners had done.

In the days since moving in, he had already done searches on many of the New Arrival commanding officers and leadership.

Starting with the Undesirables, it had been his job to look through the personnel files to look for security and other high-risk persons as well as for people with desirable unique skills and knowledge.

The North Koreans, in particular, were a problem due to their lifelong indoctrination in the cult of personality of their glorious leader. Everything they could see around them was somehow a deception and a trick by the American devils. It was going to take a long time to unravel.

This morning he was on his second cup of coffee. He was tired. He allowed his mind to wander and drift. Over the years, he learned that sometimes his mind needed less structure and focus to allow disparate pieces of unrelated information to fit together. It had helped him solve several mysteries and problems.

Martin was an extremely dispassionate man. He was, after all, a spy and a very good one. Despite that, when he searched for video feeds from webcams around the Earth to find footage of the Accipiter attack, the results shocked him to his core. The sudden and savage impacts of the kinetic impactors that wiped out both military targets and major cities were timed to be simultaneous worldwide. Many of the impacts could be viewed from multiple angles. It left him stunned and shaken.

It was a brutal snapshot of the murder of mankind.

He angrily typed on the search engine, "If they could build this world and carry us here, why did the Gardeners not stop the attack? Why were so many people not saved?"

He moved his finger to hit the escape key to cancel the useless search. Before he could do so, his screen cleared, and words formed on his screen:

'…not needed…'

The Builders

The starship hanger was now a beehive of activity. Armed Marines from Fort Brazos, some in full battle rattle, had been posted at every 'new, unfamiliar or dangerous looking' control or interface 'to ensure nobody did anything stupid and blew everyone up.'

For now, it was entirely 'look but don't touch.'

There was a lot of looking going on, with Navy engineers and a growing number of Bonham State University scientists and grad students taking pictures, videos, and measurements.

Not long after work began examining the starship, a second hangar bay had unceremoniously unlocked itself. The enormous blast door had lifted, revealing dozens more of the 'shuttles.' After strenuous debate, more guards were posted at its entrance to ensure no one went inside. There was already more to do in the main hangar than there were people with the right skills.

After the one starship and shuttle were better understood and an idea of which buttons to *not* press had been worked out, it would be safer to allow access to the additional shuttles.

Dr. Takumi Nakamura, thin and rakish as always and wearing his inexpensive dark suit and tie, had brought a substantial delegation of students and faculty. General Marcus had sent an equally large delegation of officers, engineers, and technicians. Meanwhile, Admiral Milner had combed through the New London refugees and rounded up a bevy of active duty and retired nuclear submarine officers, engineers, and experts.

While only a few people at a time were allowed inside the starship itself, dozens of workshops, warehouses, and even a control center overlooking the starship needed to be explored, cataloged, and documented.

One of the hangar bay side doors had led to a wing of offices containing hundreds of CAD and engineering workstations. When the offices were first explored, it was noted that a handful of workstations were already powered on. These had been found to hold a complete set of CAD models of the former Montana (or copy of), seemingly lifted from computers at the General Dynamics Electric Boat Division and additional files that were still labeled Huntington Ingalls Newport News Shipbuilding Company in Virginia.

A dozen men and women were already working hard comparing the CAD files with the new measurements. While no CAD model for such a complex vehicle *exactly* matched reality, so far, the measurements being taken did not diverge in any unexpected ways.

The Virginia class submarines and their iterations had all been wholly designed and modeled via CAD. The plan was to compare these original designs with the starship files down to the micron, if possible, to learn more about what had been changed and what remained the same.

Conveniently, the Gardeners had already redlined the original CAD models, but the exercise of comparing everything was another way of learning the systems, in addition to fact-checking the Gardeners. There was a substantial difference between what the submariners knew from everyday experience and what the designers had originally intended.

Besides, the Gardeners had not deigned to save the original builders of the Montana, which, had they done so, might have made the idea of starting to build humanity's own fleet of starships at least a little more believable.

In addition to Dr. Nakamura's university delegation, Brigadier General Sabrina Chilton, formerly of the British Army Royal Signals Corps and now Commanding Officer of the 1st Signals and Electronic Warfare brigade, composed almost entirely of the 'New Arrival' 29th Queen's Gurkha Signals Regiment, had arrived in force with her technical experts in decryption and communications… and her big gun, Dr. Leo Talib, Ph.D.

Sabrina and her regiment stood out, wearing American army uniforms but retaining their dark blue Royal Signals berets. The berets had a leather headband emblazoned with the 'jimmy,' the Royal Corps of Signals Beret Badge with its figure of Mercury holding a Caduceus in the left hand and the right hand aloft poised with the left foot on a globe above a scroll inscribed 'Certa Cito' and below on each side six laurel leaves all in gold, and the whole ensigned with the Crown in gold.

Sabrina herself was the oldest in her group, at 44. The grey that had mingled with her short bobbed blonde hair had lessened somewhat since Awakening Day, although she never tried to dye or hide it in any way.

She was nine years older than Leo Talib, whose normally meticulously quaffed brown hair and beard and Saville Row suits had led many to conclude he was gay. He wasn't. He simply found people and relationships to be tiresome and boring. His caustic opinion on Americans, in general, left few alternatives to explore.

For the last two and a half days, Leo, now the newly appointed Dean of Language Studies at Bonham State University, had effectively locked himself inside what was being called the Ventral Data Control Node. There were two nodes. Ventral and Dorsal. The somewhat squat and bulbous structures sat just inside the upper and lower apex of the warp drive rings and filled about a tenth of the volume of that space inside the rings.

Upon closer inspection, it was discovered that they were a structure within a structure. An outer shell surrounded an inner core that housed densely packed alien equipment assumed to be an advanced computer analogue. That inner section had more of the alien display and control screens first discovered by John Austin. The shell around it had life support systems and a collection of Gardener-added human-designed computers.

It was an interface between the alien computer system and one the humans would be able to understand and interact with. It held banks of computer screens, work areas, and tables.

Inside, the normally fastidious Leo was almost unrecognizable. He had transformed into, very nearly, the caricature of an archetypical frazzled wild-haired professor. His tie was missing, his shirt collar wide open, and his sleeves were loosely and unevenly rolled up. One set of screens was filled with alien script and symbols, and the other displayed mathematics and English translations.

Sabrina silently watched over him, keeping two of her analysts on constant standby, recording everything he muttered and scribbled on an ever-growing pile of yellow legal pads, and tending to his every distracted need. She had seen him this way once before, as he had struggled through translating the Accipiter language as revealed by the Gardeners not long after Awakening Day.

The Ventral and Dorsal Control Nodes appeared to be identical, so Sabrina kept everyone out of this one and told them to go do their work in the other one. Talib was 'in the zone,' and she knew better than to allow anything short of utter catastrophe to distract him.

Sabrina had become so accustomed to the library-Esque quiet that she spilled her freshly made Darjeeling tea when Leo suddenly gasped aloud and swore a lengthy string of half-forgotten French expletives he had learned from his French-Algerian diplomat father.

00:30

The Crow's Nest quickly grew more crowded as John Austin, Gail Finley, General Marcus, and Lt. Colonel Williams clambered one by one up the ladder.

Sabrina saluted in the British style, with her right hand and palm open, "Mr. President, Ms. Vice President." She turned to Alexander and Martin, "General, Colonel Williams. Thank you all for coming on such short notice and at such a late hour. I realize the trip up the elevator from Fort Brazos is a long one. I promise it was worth it."

John nodded, "I'm certain you would not have called us here, in person, unless it were important. However, insisting that only the four of us come and not to bring anyone else, including the Admirals, certainly raised eyebrows."

Alexander smiled, "You found something you fear is controversial."

Sabrina turned a level gaze at Alexander, "Indeed we did, General. And as Colonel Williams no doubt must have surmised, what we found may have profound intelligence and even political ramifications." She turned to Leo, whom she had ordered to get some sleep before the meeting. "Leo?"

Leo Talib had indeed rested, however briefly, and cleaned himself up. His suit and tie were clean and straight, although he had no idea the effort that Sabrina had gone through to make that happen. Rumpled Saville Row suits do not do well in a submarine's laundry.

Leo swallowed, "Mr. President, Madam Vice President, General, Colonel, we discovered a cache of documents within the Builder's system. I'm afraid some of you might find the documents to be… familiar."

He reached behind him and removed the cover from a file folder box, and withdrew a sheaf of laser-printed documents held together with large binding clips. He selected the one from the top of the stack and held it up for everyone to see. The cover had a United States Department of Defense logo and the words TOP SECRET: ENDLESS EPSILON emblazoned in very large type. He handed it to Sabrina, who in turn handed it to John.

John frowned and took the heavy, two-inch-thick document and opened it, thumbing through the pages as the others crowded close, leaning in to see. The contents included diagrams. Diagrams of a multi-ringed warp starship drive section. John's jaw dropped.

Gail's eyes grew wide as John handed the document to her and looked up questioningly.

Sabrina smiled thinly, "Colonel, would you please sit with Leo for a while? He has some things to show you that you might appreciate."

Martin had worn his most inscrutable face to the meeting. He nodded, "Yes, of course, General." He moved around the group and joined Leo at his "workstation"— a collection of laptops and the interface to the Builder system.

Gail shook her head and said with incredulity, "It says that the US Navy recovered a damaged warp drive ship from the ocean bottom in 1974?"

Sabrina sighed, "Indeed, Ms. Vice President, according to the documents, a Builder drive was recovered by the USNS Hughes Glomar Explorer in 1975, a year after the recovery of some or perhaps most of the sunken Soviet K-129 Submarine in the Pacific. The recovery location was separately classified in a compartmentalized operation and is not mentioned in what we have found so far. Apparently, there were many subsequent searches of the area, hoping to find additional artifacts."

"To summarize for you, the recovered drive section was originally moved to your government's Groom Lake facility in the State of Nevada, popularly known as Area 51. It was studied for the next several decades until it was eventually repaired and sufficiently reverse-engineered that it became possible to create a hybrid human-Builder craft good enough for actual trial runs. Indeed, we have found thousands of documents, possibly more in what may well be complete operational manuals for the starship, in English, along with a complete timeline and historical record of how things were figured out."

Alexander shook his head sternly, "What!?"

Sabrina continued, her voice rising a half octave, "Subsequently, the warp vessel was successfully launched. The engineers were able to extract a log of its previous travels, so they flew the ship back to its last known port of call, an abandoned Builder outpost on a small terrestrial planet. A clandestine United States military outpost was established there to study Builder ruins."

John managed to close his mouth with a click. Gail stood rigidly, blinking in shock, and Alexander exclaimed, "I simply don't believe it!"

Sabrina continued, nonplussed, "Be that as it may. Apparently, the ship made several trips back and forth between the Builder planet and Earth and was gradually upgraded using portions of the submarine hull and a reactor section that had been built and either condemned as defective or supposedly built as test sections that were later transported and reassembled at a new location, hidden at an existing military base that had previously been scheduled for elimination."

John whispered, "You mean…."

Sabrina cocked her head slightly, "Yes, Mr. President, a hidden underground base beneath the Fort Brazos Joint Reserve Base in Texas. The documents also include plans and details about a secret, hidden U.S. base on the far side of the moon and how, after the Accipiter attack, the base was abandoned, and the entrance collapsed as the humans fled to their secret outpost on the Builder world."

Alexander slammed his fist on the table he stood next to, sending a ballpoint pen flying. "This is preposterous! I would have known! I had only just taken command, but I would have had to have known about a *secret* base underneath the base I was taking command of!"

Sabrina pursed her lips. "Perhaps, General. On the other hand," She pulled a sheet of laser-printed paper from a nearby manila folder, "I left out the signature page of that document. Would you care to see who signed it?" She handed the sheet to John.

John looked down and read the page, his head jerking in surprise. He handed the sheet to Alexander. "Alexander? Is there something you want to tell us?"

Alexander took the sheet, resisting the urge to yank it from John's fingers. He looked down and read… his own name and signature. He stared at the page for long seconds, blinking in confusion. He looked back up in stunned surprise, "I… I don't understand."

Martin stood and joined the group and interrupted, "Pardon me, but it might interest all of you to know who the pilot was on the third trip to the Builder planet."

They turned to Martin, who carried another laser-printed document. He paused and kept his voice completely neutral and flat, "Doctor Talib has shared with me a series of ships logs. This one," he raised the document for everyone to see, which included similar stamps and a stylized logo that presumably was the warp ship's crest, "is the log from the third flight to the Builder world. Among other things, it lists the Captain and crew. I did not recognize most of the names. However, one stood out. The principal pilot was one Gail Anson Finley, Captain, United States Air Force."

All eyes turned to Gail, who blinked for a moment, lips parted. Then her eyes widened, and the corner of her mouth twitched before she broke into a broad smile and laughed aloud.

John touched her arm, "Gail?"

Gail reached over and rested her hand on John's. She turned to him, "Of course, I didn't do any of that, and neither did Alexander. Don't you see what this is?"

Dawning realization lit his face. He exclaimed, "It's a cover story!"

Alexander rumbled, "General Chilton, what *exactly* is going on here?"

Sabrina showed her teeth in an icy smile, "General, Ms. Vice President. What is going on here is that I needed to see how you reacted."

John nodded firmly, "Because the documents could have been real."

She paused once again. Her eyes narrowed, "Frankly, yes, Mr. President. The documents seem very real indeed, which, after everything we have seen the Gardeners do, should not be very surprising, although I confess it was to me. Of course, they still could be, I suppose, although at this point, I'm at a loss as to why you two would feel a compelling need to continue to keep it secret."

Gail smiled softly.

Alexander shook his head and said more harshly than he intended, "Well, I'm glad we passed your test then, General Chilton." He stopped himself, then added, "I apologize, General. You did the right thing."

Sabrina nodded and turned to Martin, "Colonel Williams, I asked that you be here in order to hear your interpretation from an intelligence perspective. Perhaps you would care to share your thoughts?"

Martin looked to John, Gail, and Alexander for a moment, then relaxed his façade and shrugged, "I believe you are correct, Mr. President. It is a cover story. As some of us have, the Gardeners must have realized that the Accipiters will sooner or later realize that humans are attacking them, and they will no doubt proceed to search for us. However, it is not possible that humans are attacking them in the first place in their minds. They conquered Earth, and they *knew* that humans did not have this kind of technology. So, the cover story weaves together just enough names and places with the fiction for it to be believable. It also leaves false clues – if this information is learned by the Accipiters, either because we plant the evidence or because our forces are captured, this cover story would have them looking for us on an abandoned Builder terrestrial planet …. Not a hollow artificial world disguised as an asteroid or planetoid. Of course, the fact that the

Accipiters themselves obliterated Fort Brazos and no doubt did the same to Groom Lake as well as Washington and all other military facilities would have effectively eliminated the possibility of them fact-checking the story after the fact."

John frowned, "And the Gardeners have already indicated they don't want their fingerprints on any of this, or else why not fight the Accipiters themselves. But everyone knows what happened. Everyone knows we found the ship, and there was no such thing as a secret base underneath Fort Brazos?"

Alexander shook his head and groaned, "Do they, Mr. President?"

Gail sighed, "It's not just a story concocted by the Gardeners. It gives us a way to explain the existence of the operating manuals. We could, of course, tell the truth that the Gardeners created them for us, but many would look at them and wonder why they would be formatted as U.S. Government documents, written in Pentagonese. Conspiracy theories would naturally develop."

John shook his head, "I don't like the idea of lying to the people like this. It's one thing to keep secrets. It's another to misinform them out of whole cloth, completely changing their reality!"

Martin thoughtfully replied, "Mr. President, history is replete with public misinformation campaigns. Indeed, misinformation, disinformation, and propaganda have been features of human communication since at least Roman times and before. Themistocles deceived Xerxes into believing that many of his forces were unreliable and near revolt. It led to Xerxes dividing and weakening his forces, contributing to strategic defeats at the Battles of Salamis and Plataea. In World War II, before the Battle of Kursk, the Russians spread rumors through their own ranks, downplaying their own strength and capabilities. This contributed to the German counterintelligence estimates putting Russian troop strength at 400,000 instead of 1.3 Million and underestimating the number of tanks by more than half. In that same war, you might recall your General Patton was given an entirely fictitious army to mislead Hitler into thinking the invasion would be through Calais in Northern France rather than the real target of Normandy."

John looked at him coolly, "I understand the need for deception in war, but remember, we're talking about a war that will not be over in four years or ten or maybe a hundred or even a thousand. The Accipiters have a galactic empire of ships and infrastructure. The galaxy is what, over 100,000 light-years across? So, we're talking about instituting a lie that might need to stand for… generations."

Gail said absently, "Dr. Nakamura said it's at least 120,000 light-years across."

Sabrina said after a moment, "Mr. President, I have to think that people being what people are, the secret won't last forever. Eventually, it will come out."

Alexander added bitterly, "Well, if we take this idea and run with it, maybe we can use it to do more than mislead the Accipiters about our location. After all, if we have one secret base on one abandoned Builder world, who's to say that we don't have more?"

Sabrina smiled slightly, "And they would have to spread out to search for more bases, weakening their forces."

Martin offered, "If I may make a suggestion. We should consider releasing only the barest minimum of information. Let people make their own conclusions. Treat the story like layers of an onion to be peeled off when needed or if accidentally discovered. Each layer is plausible enough to lead many to think they have reached the end of it. We should classify the different levels of information with code word classification and severely limit who has access on a need-to-know basis. Only a small core of people should have access to all of the documents and their implications. Others will only have access to the information and documents used in their own area of responsibility. For example, we would separate things like warp drive operation from life support."

Silence lingered for several seconds before Sabrina asked quietly, "And so, who gets invited to the core?"

Parent-Teacher Conference

DownSide: Carolyne Austin Elementary School

School Auditorium.
September 8th. NLD 9 -- FBD 37. 2:05 PM

Schools had not resumed classes immediately after the Fort Brazos Awakening Day. It was, after all, the Apocalypse. On the other hand, lives did continue after a fashion, and it was decided that the children needed some sense of normalcy. So it was that even before the smoldering crater formed by the crash of Gail Finley's aircraft had been cleared away from the defunct car dealership next to the High School that teachers and students had begun to trickle back to the schools.

Even eight-year-old Matti Austin, the only child of Sheriff and now President John Austin, had eventually returned to her school. Of course, Matti was never allowed to be apart from her permanent security detail. Marine Corporal Roxanna Darling was selected for her outstanding physical and marksmanship proficiency. Sergeant Jesse Roberts, the overall commander of the protection details, had been bluntly honest about the reasons for her selection. He'd pointed out that her brilliant smile and well-above-average good looks would help her be less… scary to young children and even their nervous parents.

Unlike the other detail members, Roxanna had been ordered to wear civilian clothing to do her best to try and 'blend in.' Her brown leather jacket barely concealed the bulky, holstered fifteen-round Fabrique Nationale Herstal FNX-45T in FDE, loaded with Critical Defense .45 ACP and three spare magazines. In addition, she carried a twelve-round FN 509 Compact backup, also in FDE, in the small of her back. The Ontario MK 3 Navy Knife in her right boot was complemented by the RAT tourniquet and first aid kit in her left. The Medford Praetorian Ti folding knife in her left pocket had been a gift from President Austin himself.

At first, Roxanna had been excited about taking Marine Security Guard training and thought she might be protecting Vice President Gail Finley…

someone she had come to admire deeply. When Sergeant Roberts had informed her that she would be assigned to protect an eight-year-old girl, she almost, nearly, very nearly, and completely… lost it. Roxanna had plans for her career. She knew she was both intelligent and attractive and dreamed of someday wearing Marine General stars on her shoulder.

Sergeant Roberts had anticipated her reaction and had remained utterly impassive as Roxanna's wave of anger nearly boiled over. He had then reminded her of exactly *who* that 8-year-old girl actually was, or more specifically, who her father was, and that Roxanna had been chosen with more scrutiny than she might realize. It was a very visible assignment.

Roxanna had gritted her teeth, said all the right things to get the slot, and steeled herself to make the most of it.

Her resentment had lasted perhaps a day. Instead of struggling to endure the spoiled brat she expected, she had found that it was simply impossible to stay angry in the presence of the irrepressible Matilda "Matti" Austin. Indeed, Roxanna had been surprised by how hard it was to even keep up with the child. To her shock and amazement, in the shortest and longest two weeks of her life, Matti was fast becoming the little sister she'd never had. Even worse, the kid was razor smart and more observant than Roxanna could believe.

Right now, however, Roxanna stood nearby as Matti sat with her classmates in the auditorium of Carolyn Austin Elementary School. Roxanna's dark hair was pulled back into a short ponytail, and an earpiece fed her constant reports from the MSG team.

The school had been paid for by Matti's father in honor of her deceased mother. John Austin was a self-made man, wealthy from the patents and oilfield business he had built from the ground up before going off to Wharton Business school for the MBA he earned on top of his BS in Petroleum Engineering from Texas A&M.

John had returned to Fort Brazos, married his high school sweetheart, and run for and was elected Sheriff, the same office his father had held. Then Carolyn had tragically died, and he and Matti had been living alone in the big house built for the large family they'd never had the chance to have.

The entire school gathered to listen to President John Austin and ask questions. With the Vice President TopSide, the Council had convinced John that he should start making appearances at schools and various venues to reassure people and answer questions.

Matti beamed in perfect pride for her father and was front and center in the audience with the rest of the children, the teachers, and not a few parents. John's security detail was there in force, and Roxanna felt the raw intensity of Sergeant Robert's watchful preparedness.

After an hour of questions, even the presence of celebrity and hero figure like John Austin had proven too much for young attention spans. Even so, the gathering's momentum carried for another half hour before John was escorted out, shaking hands and talking the entire time.

Matti slipped away through the crowd as Roxanna desperately tried to catch her. In moments, Matti was at John's side. Sergeant Roberts glowered at Roxanna, who crimsoned in frustration.

✪ ✪ ✪

Minutes later, the school quickly emptied with the afternoon bell. Sergeant Roberts and John Austin were inside Matti's homeroom with her teacher, Mrs. Silverton. Matti, Roxanna, and the rest of John's detail, Jorge Diego, Tony Bouchard, and Sergeant Jenkins, waited outside.

The men kept professionally watchful eyes focused mainly elsewhere as Roxanna tried to contain a fulminating glare as she kneeled next to Matti for "a talk."

Matti tossed her long blonde hair back and sighed as she saw Roxanna's expression, "Look, Roxy, I know, I know, I know. I messed up. I'm not supposed to get separated from you like that. You don't have to say it."

Roxanne winced at the use of 'Roxy' and glared at Jorge for biting his lip and Tony for rolling his eyes. She returned her gaze to Matti and opened her mouth to speak, but Matti reached out and put her forefinger on Roxanna's lips to shush her.

"Yes, I know, Roxy, this is serious, and you're here to protect me, and it's your job." Matti lowered her voice, "And… and I know you would die to protect me. I know I should be better. Do better. I promise I'll try."

With that, Matti wrapped her arms around Roxanne's neck and hugged her tightly.

Roxanne's eyes widened, and she opened her mouth again to speak but could not find the words this time.

Tony, Jorge, and Sergeant Jenkins studiously avoided reacting. By now, they had all been around young Matti long enough to understand. Matilda Austin had found her way into all their hearts.

Matti released Roxanna and then snapped at the men surrounding them, "And you! Tony! Jorge! Don't you give Roxy a hard time about this! It was my fault, not hers. You too, Benny Jenkins! Give Roxy a break."

Roxanne reached out and pulled Matti close, and whispered into her ear. "Now you listen to me, you little…Argh! You pull a stunt like that again, and all the extra leeway I've been giving you goes out the window. Including off-the-books pistol training too! Do you hear me?"

Matti stiffened, tightened her lips, and stared into Roxanne's unrelenting gaze. Matti's father had long taught his daughter how to shoot BB guns and, later, a .22 rifle. In light of all the dangers in the new world, Roxanne had quietly begun teaching Matti how to handle a pistol. Not with live rounds but with special cartridges fitted with a laser that shone down the barrel when the firing pin struck their false primers. The laser dot was no more potent than a typical laser pointer and served to show where the firearm had been pointed when the trigger was pulled. It was a discrete and quiet way to train, and Roxanne had relentlessly drilled Matti in safety rules.

Roxanne had bartered one of the now-rare training rounds from Jermal Dixon in exchange for a spare CAT Tourniquet she'd had in her kit. Jermal and the rest of Gail Finley's detail used laser training rounds to quietly, privately drill the Vice President without having to take her to a shooting range.

Roxanne had not yet taken Matti anywhere where they had had a chance to fire working, functional cartridges yet. She was concerned that Matti wasn't yet strong enough to keep from limp-wristing – a problem that people without a firm grip and strong wrists sometimes have with semi-automatics that can cause stove-pipe malfunctions. On the other hand, Matti had already proven to be quite adept at field stripping both of Roxanne's pistols easily, tearing them all the way down to the firing pins and flawlessly putting them back together again.

Matti glared at her, then slumped down and relented, "OK. You win, and you know, you can be really mean sometimes."

Roxanne savored the tiny victory as best she could, then whispered into Matti's ear, "You'd better hope I am."

Roxanne stood and steeled herself against the looks of pity and sympathy from the President's detail.

★ ★ ★

Erica Silverton had been a childhood friend of Carolyn Austin – long before her friend had taken John's name. Like everyone else, Erica had known that John and Carolyn were destined to be together. She'd even been on several double dates with them, and they had all 'hung out' with each other in Junior High and High School.

In contrast to Carolyn's fair skin, blue eyes, and wavy blonde hair, Erica had raven black hair and even paler skin, and green eyes. During that dreadful six months as Juniors, when Carolyn and John briefly broke up, Erica had gone on several dates with John. At the time, she'd been a cheerleader, and he was a beefy, handsome football player. Even on those dates, she knew it was temporary and that he and Carolyn would inevitably end up back together again, but 'he was a good kisser,' and she had always been very fond of him.

Her heart had ached at the devastation in his eyes after Carolyn had died. In the aftermath, Matti doted over him and did her best to keep her father going. Their bond had grown even stronger since then, and John had only just begun to recover from his malaise when the Accipiters attacked Earth.

Now he was the leader of the last remnants of mankind, and it was Erica's job to tell him how Matti was having a hard time in school.

They sat in teacher-sized chairs at an activity table laid out with Matti's work. John smiled, "You're looking good, Erica."

Erica smiled sadly, "You look like hell Johnny."

John shrugged, "I know. How are the girls? Melinda and Jenny? How's Bob?"

Erica frowned, "The girls are fine, but you know the work Bob is doing is hard on him."

Bob Silverton had been busy for the last month trying to keep the HVAC units working at the warehouse where the thousands of dead from Awakening Day were… stored until the national cemetery could be completed.

John nodded, "I know it has to be hard on him, but it is so important to so many people. Please tell him how much I appreciate everything he's done."

"I will."

"Anything he needs."

"He knows."

Silence drifted between them for a while before Erica sat up straighter, reached over, and took John's hand. "The same for you, John. Anything you need. You need only ask."

John smiled, "Thank you, Erica."

Erica nodded, "Well, OK then. We best not keep you waiting. Let's get down to business. There are some things I need to tell you about the children and about Matti."

John stiffened, "What's going on, Erica?"

She shook her head, "It's not bad, but… well… ever since… ever since that day. You know. Ever since we woke up here. We, I mean the other teachers and I, we've been noticing changes in the children."

John leaned back slightly, tensing, "Go on…."

Erica swallowed, "Well, you see… it's hard to explain. With everything that happened, with so many dead and all the uncertainty and aliens and Earth and so on, we all expected the children would be, well, panicked, scared, and depressed."

John nodded.

"And while there certainly has been some of that, especially for children who lost loved ones, I have to say that the overall reaction has been much much more mature and, well, levelheaded than any of us expected."

John shrugged, "We've seen the same in the adult population. There was some speculation that the Gardeners' changes, curing all diseases and sicknesses and making us healthier, may be part of the reason."

Erica smiled, "Yes, I know. It is more than that. The bounce-back after the first few days of being here has been quite profound. More than that, though, we are seeing something entirely new. It took a while for us to notice it, or maybe it took a few days to manifest, but we are seeing significant changes in attitudes. The over-achieving kids are not being ostracized or made fun of. In fact, it's like…." She lowered her voice, "It's like the underachievers aren't anymore. I'll deny I ever said this, but before all this happened, it was normal for a lot of kids to seem like they had some kind of fog hanging over their minds."

John nodded, "And now?"

Erica's voice lowered even more, "And now, that fog is gone. I may be wrong, but it's not like they are really smarter – it's just that every day is now like the best day I ever saw them have. They are more curious and more determined to learn and pursue the talents and inclinations they already have. Is this making any sense?"

John leaned forward, "Erica, there is so much happening and so many things that have only been speculated about. I've seen a little of what you're describing in adults, but maybe the children are less… fixed in place than adults are. I know I've seen changes in Matti. At first… At first, I thought it was all about Awakening Day and a certain amount of shock. As time has gone by, though, the changes I've seen have frightened me a little. The expression 'growing up fast' does not begin to apply."

Erica smiled faintly, "There's more. We are not doing a good job of adjusting. In the past, we always had to teach on a curve, mostly at the lower end, leaving the brighter, faster kids to fend for themselves or hope that the Gifted and Talented programs were enough. Of course, they often weren't, but it was always politically incorrect to say that. Now though, we don't have a curriculum that was designed to cope with the… new reality. A certain amount of curriculum is basically repeated each year in greater detail. Even in this short amount of time, we're already seeing that it isn't working anymore."

John looked down for a moment, then up. "And Matti?"

Erica sighed and rubbed her eyes. "… and then there's Matti. Before all this happened, we were already going to recommend advance placing Matti. Honestly, I'd already pegged her for probably being Valedictorian someday. Today, though, we could try bumping her up a grade, but aside from the social problems that might cause for her, I'm not sure it would really help. I think we can only hold her back here."

"It sounds like you may need to bump a bunch of kids up a grade, so I'm not sure what you're getting at."

Erica looked away and fretted for a moment, "I'm sure we will do just that, and we'll probably end up completely changing the whole grade system itself, but that's just part of it. The bigger problem, John, is that between being the president's daughter, having her very own personal killer-lady bodyguard, and being as bright as she is, I think she needs private school or maybe even home school. I'd probably be fired for suggesting it, so you didn't hear me say that."

John stiffened, his expression darkening, "Are people giving her a hard time?"

Erica shook her head rapidly, "No, No, it's not that. Not at all. The opposite, really. You see, the notoriety is setting her apart. It's going to be hard for her to have genuine relationships."

John shook his head, "I can't just pull her out of school and away from all her friends. It may be difficult, but doesn't she need the socialization?"

Erica grimaced, "I'm sorry, John, I don't have an easy answer. All I can do is be honest and tell you what I think. Matti needs a different environment to thrive."

She swallowed, "John, I'm going to be blunt. Matti is sitting in a school named after her mother, a school that was paid for by her father, who is now the President and leader of what remains of humanity. Of course, everyone will treat her differently, even if only subconsciously… and not just the other children. In some ways, she is a symbol or even a totem for us. Don't misunderstand.

Everybody loves her. Her own humility and, frankly, her personal grace only reinforce that. But she is also a… distraction. She's too smart not to have noticed people talking about her when she walks by. If they haven't already, you know that sooner or later, people will start trying to curry favor with her. I… I fear that the attention could ultimately change her in ways…. I don't want to see her go that way, and I know you don't either."

John cleared his throat softly, "Thank you, Erica…. I've been so absorbed in everything that has happened that while I've seen changes in her, I still tend to see her as my little girl that I need to protect."

He looked around the room, his eyes misting, "I always thought of this school as a place where… Carolyn would watch over Matti…."

Erica swallowed and pursed her lips as her own eyes threatened tears. She leaned forward and touched his face, "She does, John, she does. Carolyn watches over all the children here. I never doubted your motivations when you had this school built. But now… I think Matti has outgrown us. She needs more than we can provide here. She needs to fly, John."

The Undesirables

DownSide: JRB

New Wardog Containment Facility.
September 8th, NLD 9 – FBD 37, 3:00 PM

Even while the hastily constructed holding pen for the 'Wardog' had been under construction, Colonel Cesar Salangsang had been working on what he hoped would be the permanent structure. Despite the one-inch-thick steel plates on the floor of the temporary holding pen, the creature had already managed to gouge and weaken it.

His inspiration had come during an inspection flight around the cantonment of the 178,203-acre base and surrounding area. Cesar had noticed an idle highway construction depot piled high with construction materials, including gravel, concrete mixers, K-Rails, and, most interestingly, massive curved steel I-Beams that had been slated for the replacement bridges planned for a highway widening.

They had used some of the K-Rails for the temporary structure, and in the meantime, his Philippine Construction Brigade appropriated whatever they needed to begin moving the I-Beams. It had taken a week of around-the-clock back-breaking work, but the new structure was complete. The heavy steel beams had been bolted and welded together to form a massive enclosure, complete with drainage and plumbing.

Everyone, including the university 'experts,' had nervously agreed that this new structure should, or rather would safely contain the beast.

Now that the construction work was done, it was time to move the creature to its new home. He did not envy whoever it was that had that job. He'd heard that they'd found some way to drug the thing, but the looks on everyone's faces had been far less confident that that would work than they were about the solidity of the I-Beam cage.

To celebrate the completion, Cesar arranged a beer party for his men. They were a hundred yards away but were still close enough to enjoy the show. He watched with interest as a crane slowly lifted a reinforced steel container from a flatbed trailer and hoisted it up and over the lip of the cage.

5:00 PM

Colonel P'aeng Jin-Hwan was not a happy man. Late of the North Korean Maritime Special Purpose Forces 34th Navy Sniper Brigade, Jin-Hwan had been unceremoniously but firmly escorted by grim-faced American soldiers away from his men in the North Korean "New Arrival" compound.

He rigidly forced himself to keep his eyes level and not look up. It was easier to avoid looking up at the fake sky the Americans had somehow arranged when he was comfortably surrounded by his own men in what he had resigned himself to regard as their prison camp.

Keeping his men focused was a never-ending struggle. Punishment for doubters had to be meted out in balance with praise and encouragement. Despite all his efforts, though, lapses in discipline continued. There was little time for his own thoughts.

Just before the Americans had escorted him away, he had just finished reading to the men from his personal copy of the Great Leader's book. He kept it in the inner pocket of his uniform jacket. From it, he read passages that extolled the virtues of purity of heart in the face of what new evil the Americans would suffer them with, promising again that soon the Great Leader would rain fire and destruction upon the American's heads. *If that fire consumes us as well, we will die in the Grace and gratitude of the Great Leader, and our families will know us as heroes and be rewarded.*

Jin-Hwan was determined that no matter what happened, he would not fail in his duty to the Great Leader... as his own father, Lieutenant General P'aeng Kwang-Seon had so famously done. Kwang-Seon had been put to death after being found guilty of charges of abusing authority, profiting the enemy, and engaging in anti-Party acts. Kwang-Seon had been shot at the Kang Kon Military Academy firing range in the Sunan District of the capital Pyongyang. While 9-year-old Jin-Hwan had watched, his father had been riddled with 90 bullets for giving his troops extra rations of food and fuel.

Jin-Hwan would never betray the Great Leader as his father had.

He sat stiffly in the noisy Humvee as it made its way across the base. He was astounded that he was being allowed to see so much of the American's activities. He was convinced they were either incompetent or were trying to impress and deceive him. Everyone he saw was clean, healthy, and overfed. There were no wounded men or battle-damaged vehicles or equipment. Whatever had happened, a great effort was being made to convince him that despite the false sky overhead, they had not suffered significant losses from the righteous might of the DPRK's seven-and-a-half million-strong armed forces. He smugly consoled himself that whatever it was that had really happened, at the very least, the despised city of Seoul must surely now lie in ashes. He chuckled to himself bitterly. *Perhaps Washington, D.C., does as well.*

The Humvee pulled to a stop next to a large, strange metal structure with a viewing stand next to it. Over the engine noise, he heard a hideous gravel-grinding animal roar.

He steeled himself. Perhaps the Americans were going to throw him in some kind of arena to fight wild animals to the death? He would make them pay. He flashed back to his childhood. At his kindergarten center, the walls had been decorated with scenes of animals holding grenades and machine guns and cute squirrel soldiers in North Korean uniforms, triumphing over the cunning wolves… the Americans. Would he now be fed to wolves?

He pulled his uniform tunic tight to straighten it, embarrassed that even he himself had gained weight eating the American-supplied ration packs. Their MREs. He stepped proudly out of the Humvee. Soldiers led him up the steps of the reviewing stand to a group of senior officers in American uniforms and one Korean Colonel in an American uniform but wearing a South Korean Beret.

At least he was not being led into the arena.

Alexander Marcus watched Jin-Hwan approach and sighed to himself. *The man looks like he expects to be executed. What will it take to reach these people?*

Alexander turned to the Korean interpreter, "Please inform Colonel P'aeng Jin-Hwan that he is our guest here today. He is welcome to refreshments if he is hungry or thirsty. Also, ask if his men have any humanitarian needs we have not yet provided for. We have invited him here today to observe one of the hostile alien creatures we all face."

Colonel T'ae Chang-Woo nodded respectfully but could not hide the doubt on his face. He turned to Jin-Hwan and repeated the message.

Jin-Hwan stared at Chang-Woo in shocked amazement. "My men and I will not be bribed or shaken from our loyalty while imprisoned in your...."

He flinched and whirled around, interrupted by a shrieking roar and thunderous crash of metal on metal from behind him. What he saw made no more sense than the false sky above him. Within the steel pit or cage below was a creature surely from the gates of Hell itself. It was like a cross between a Korean Haetae and a Bulgasari or Bu Ke Sa iron-eating monster.

It was black with red splotches, and... it had... *six*... legs, a massive horn, a sweeping tail, and seemed covered in dully glinting iron-like armor. It had rammed itself against the cage wall and staggered back from the impact. It howled in frustration and slowly began to run around the perimeter of the cage, its claws scratching and scraping on the bare steel. From the sounds it made, it had to be massively heavy.

He realized that the interpreter was speaking again. He hesitated and then turned back to listen.

"...one of the kinds of creatures that attacked both our country and yours. They are servants of an alien race that attacked our planet. While that was happening, a different alien race... rescued some of us from Earth and brought us to this artificial hollow world. They expect us to fight the first group of Aliens that attacked our world. They expect us to take our revenge. The General wants to know if you and your men will want to join the fight and one day retake our planet?"

Jin-Hwan blinked at the audacity of the traitorous translator, "You think I am a fool? You drug our food, hold us prisoner, and expect us to believe your lies and deception?" He waved to the false sky and the creature behind them, "This is all deception! You will never break our loyalty and discipline!"

5:37 PM

Alexander watched as Jin-Hwan was driven away. He turned to Colonel T'ae Chang-Woo, "So, do you think we made any progress at all?"

Chang-Woo sighed, "General, you understand that he and his men have been indoctrinated since birth to hate and distrust Americans?"

Alexander nodded, "I'm aware."

Chang-Woo continued, "These people believe their Great Leader has never used the bathroom. They teach a state ideology called Juche that proclaims that their Great Leader is basically a God, that they are the racially pure race, that humans first emerged there, that their milk comes from the Great Leader, and their video games happily teach children how to kill Americans. I won't even talk about the unicorns. The truth, General, is that it will take time."

Alexander ground his teeth and nodded abruptly.

"General, if I may add one more thing."

"Yes, Colonel?"

"I can't be sure, but there was something in Jin-Hwan's eyes. I think the creature shook him up more than he even realizes himself. I suspect that what you arranged here has planted a seed of doubt."

Alexander stared at him for a long moment, "I hope you're right, Colonel. Twenty-five hundred North Koreans that would happily put a knife in our backs are a distraction we don't need right now. We can't keep them locked up forever."

Heartbreaker

Dr. Eva Sanches, D.V.M. had cleared the appointment schedule, so the waiting area in the 1970s-era Spanish architecture veterinary center was empty. Eva stood waiting outside the entrance as the caravan of two SUVs and two Humvees arrived. She entered the lead Humvee and directed them past several outbuildings until they reached the main stables area.

Sergeant Benny Jenkins and Corporal Tony Bouchard entered first, followed by Eva, John and Matti Austin, and Gail Finley. Corporals Jorge Diego and Jose Cruz remained outside while the rest of the detail followed.

Normally, Matti would have darted into the building and rushed to see her horse, an Appaloosa mare named Freckles. While she did indeed hurry this time, she had gleefully taken Corporal Roxanna Darling by the hand and nearly dragged her along.

Gail noticed John's smile: "It looks like that is turning out better than expected."

John nodded, "There was some kicking and screaming at first, but I think it was on principal. After the Stalker attack, Matti knows… well, she understands the need."

They stopped and stood in the middle of the long, quiet stable. John looked around and raised his eyebrows. Five German Shepherds had ghosted in and flanked Eva. None of the stall doors were latched, but the horses calmly stared at John and Gail. "Eva, I was about to ask about Rusty, but I think maybe you had better go ahead and explain what is going on."

Eva took a deep breath, "Mr. President…."

John interrupted her, "Eva, please, we've known each other since we were children."

Eva smiled nervously, "I'm sorry… John. It's just… I didn't think you would believe me unless I showed you in person."

John and Gail exchanged glances and nodded.

Eva lowered her voice and quietly said, "OK, boys and girls, let's go outside. Slowly."

All around them, the horses gently nosed their stall doors open and slowly proceeded to stroll to the exits.

John's mouth parted in astonishment, as did Gail's. However, Gail locked eyes with a jet-black quarter horse stallion who froze in place, returning her stare. Its coat was freshly brushed and lustrous, and it shuffled its feet nervously.

The security detail stiffened and moved to encircle Gail, but she held up her hand to halt them. She looked at Eva, who seemed less surprised than Gail expected.

Eva smiled and nodded. She turned to the horse and called softly, "It's OK, Heartbreaker, come say hello to the Vice President."

Heartbreaker snorted gently and cautiously approached Gail.

Gail swallowed, "So, Ms. Sanches… Eva, we're not the only ones the Gardeners have changed… The dogs too?"

Eva nodded quickly, "I noticed changes soon after Awakening Day, but it has taken some time for them to… adjust."

Corporal Cruz muttered, "¡Dios míío!"

Gail tentatively reached out to stroke Heartbreaker's neck.

John shook his head, "Well, OK then. What are we talking about here?"

Eva shrugged, "It's early yet, but I don't think I've seen any behavior I wouldn't have seen from the very smartest horse or dog I've ever worked with."

John chuckled, "Right, so all dogs are Lassie, and all horses are Trigger now?"

Eva smiled softly, "John, I wouldn't go quite that far, but remember, humans have been selectively breeding horses and dogs for thousands of years. They fill many roles for us, but the best of them have been our companions and protectors for at least most of recorded history. City people may have forgotten, but there is a deep bond between us. If I had to guess, I'd say that the Gardeners have simply, well, optimized our relationship."

Gail looked up at Eva, "Heartbreaker?"

Eva nodded, "His owner did not survive Awakening Day. He is a young quarter horse who I expect had an auspicious racing career ahead of him. He had only just started, but Heartbreaker had already won his first three races before, well, you know."

"He's beautiful."

Eva grinned, "He likes you too. Tell me, do you know horses?"

"I had lessons as a girl and rode a Fox hunt while I was based at Lakenheath in England, but I was sore for days after that."

John laughed, "I would pay money to see you in that outfit."

Gail sighed, "Hit him for me, would you, Nate?"

Corporal Hopper shifted his weight on his feet nervously but refrained from striking the President.

Gail shook her head, "You're fired, Nate."

"Yes, ma'am."

✪ ✪ ✪

John road Rusty, his ten-year-old chestnut Roan, while Eva had helped Gail with Heartbreaker. Matti had enthusiastically selected a Morgan horse for Roxanna, while Sergeant Jenkins and Corporal Hopper, both experienced riders, had found suitable mounts of their own. The rest of the protection detail followed at a discrete distance in the Humvees.

Matti patiently helped Roxanna, instructing her not to hold the reins too high or wrap her legs too tightly.

John and Gail rode side by side, watching while the rest of the detail had spread out. John smiled, "Thank you for convincing me to go with Roxanna. You know my fatherly inclination was to find the biggest protector for her we could find."

Gail nodded, "She's a good choice. Seeing them together, though, my only concern is that she might get too close and that it could lead to problems."

John grimaced, "If we need to make a change…."

Gail shook her head, "No, you misunderstand. I do not doubt that Roxanne will do the job. I just worry about Matti's reaction if we were ever to reassign Roxanna. It could be hard on her after becoming close, and if Roxanna ever truly does have to do her ultimate duty in defense of Matti…."

John closed his eyes and sighed, "Oh."

Gail shifted in her saddle, "Yeah."

They rode in silence through the field. The path was alongside a creek, with low trees on the other side of the bank and gently rolling hills for miles. The temperature had warmed to the high eighties, but the breeze was mild and cool.

John broke the reverie, "So, I talked to Matti's teacher. I think I'm going to have to pull her out of the school."

Gail snorted, "Took you long enough to figure that out."

"What?"

Gail shook her head, "John, I know you're her dad, but the girl is the closest thing to a celebrity the other kids have anymore. They don't have any pop stars or social media celebrities to follow and gossip about." Gail shifted in her saddle again, "The more she is in school, the more I'm afraid it will start going to her pretty blonde head."

John grumbled, "I guess we can hire tutors."

Gail blurted out, "Make her a cadet."

John's eyes widened, and he bit off a response before answering, "She's eight years old, Gail!"

Gail eyed Matti teaching Roxanna as they rode in front of them. "Is she? John, do you really think she has been acting like an eight-year-old girl? I mean, seriously? Sure, I know she has her little girl moments, but hell, so do I still, sometimes, but I know adults less mature than she is."

They rode in silence a while longer before John answered, "OK, let's say I agree with you. She's still got the body of an eight-year-old girl, even if she does act… differently. She can't physically do the things older girls, or women, could do."

Gail thought about it, "Dad started teaching me to fly when I was her age. I wasn't ready for it, but by the time I was ten, he was letting me take the controls even though he had to operate the pedals I couldn't reach. I wasn't supposed to, but I was taking off and landing by the time I was twelve. We moved around a lot, so I didn't officially get my license until I was in High School, but by then, I'd already flown every type of small plane I could beg, borrow, or, almost, steal."

John studied her, "I'm not surprised."

They rode quietly next to each other for a while before he continued. "I trust you with her… to teach her. I trust you, Gail."

Gail shook her head, "Wait, what? No, I didn't mean me. Besides, when would I possibly have the time?"

John looked at her and said flatly, "Your idea, your responsibility. Besides. You're the only person I trust… like that. She thinks you walk on water already, so she'll listen to you."

Gail saw him looking at her and was suddenly self-conscious. There was a lot more that he wasn't saying, and she was both happy about it and, at the same time, annoyed with herself for feeling that way. She blushed crimson and swallowed hard.

John decided, "OK, let's do this. We can have tutors, but Matti becomes your… Intern. I know you've been itching to get back in the air, so let Matti help you. See what she picks up on and where her talents might lie. When you think she's ready… teach her to fly."

Gail blinked and wondered if he realized what he'd just said. Was it an unconscious slip or just an innocent use of the 'royal' *we?*

92.5 Radio Station Studio

DownSide: Fort Brazos

September 10th, NLD 11

FBD 39, 12:01 PM

"This is Danielle Richardson reporting what's new and exciting in Fort Brazos. Yesterday witnesses reported seeing our President John Austin, his daughter Matilda, and Vice President Gail Finley on horseback taking a quiet stroll through the foothills, as it were. Apparently, the Presidential duo was seen riding quite close together, talking earnestly about matters unknown. Interestingly, though, several witnesses commented on how comfortable they seemed with each other. Now I know that there have been some reports about how they do not like each other and how the friction between them has been high, and all that, and you know I've not hidden my admiration for Vice President Finley."

"So, maybe the ice is melting a bit? Our witnesses are adamant that they saw nothing untoward, but it does make you wonder. I, for one, cannot imagine the stress they must be under, what with the Gardeners basically threatening to kill us all, or rather, kill the rest of us after they killed the five percent. I must say, though, that I'm glad to see President Austin and Vice President Finley taking a few minutes to relax, breathe in some fresh air, and to finally find a way to work together more amicably."

Conference Room 47
TopSide: "New Pentagon"
September 10th, NLD 11
FBD 39, 12:03 PM

Even though Fort Brazos was six hours away by the elevator system, ever since the New London Awakening Day, radio and cell phone traffic between DownSide and TopSide had been discovered to work. Now, in one of the many conference rooms deep inside what people were starting to call the "New Pentagon" – even though it bore no resemblance, a group of men and women had quietly gathered.

One of them turned off the radio and looked to the others, "So, is this going to be a problem?"

Immortal

Eighteen-year-old Zachary (Zach) Simmons drove his bright red dual cab Silverado pickup truck down the middle of Farm-To-Market Road 39. There was no other traffic on the two-lane blacktop. Next to him in the passenger seat sat his best friend and classmate, Morgan Forbes. In the back seat, Dexter (Dex) Sawyer and his brother William (Will.) All four young men were on the high school football team and had known each other since childhood.

Dex and Will were both ROTC marksmanship award winners, and all four were lifelong experienced hunters and shooters. Today they were part of the organized community patrol scouting for alien Wardogs, Stalkers, or anything out of the ordinary. Dex and Will were busy scanning the passing pastures with binoculars while they all listened to Morgan's playlist.

Zach glanced in the mirror at Dex and Will, "Hey, have you guys decided what service you want to enlist in? Army? The new Space Navy or is it the…" he paused for effect and then deepened his voice to say with what dramatic flair he could manage, "…the Space Marines?"

All four young men laughed aloud. The ribbing was good-natured.

Morgan chimed in, "Hey, I hear they're going to expand Bonham State into some kind of new West Point/Annapolis hybrid. Are you going to try to get in there or go enlisted?"

Will and Dex glanced at each other. Will answered, "Yeah, we got a call a couple of days ago. All the ROTC core did. They want us to be part of the first class they put together at Bonham."

Zach grinned broadly, "That's awesome!"

Morgan nodded in agreement, "Yeah, guys, you must be stoked!"

Will and Dex tried to act nonchalant for a moment, then broke out in wide-faced grins.

Morgan glanced back at them, "Yeah! I thought so."

Dex shot back, "What about you, Morgan? Didn't you get a scholarship to Colorado? That's got to count for something at Bonham?"

Morgan sighed, "I hope so, but it was only a partial scholarship. We were still trying to line up student loans when… well… you know."

Everyone knew he meant that his plans, like so many others, had ended on Awakening Day. They all replied in unison with a quiet "yeah."

Will asked Morgan, "Hey, what happened with you and Darla? You two used to be connected at the hip."

Morgan sneered and shook his head. Zach answered for him, "Give him a break, guys, 'dear' Darla dumped him so she could spend all her time hanging around the Navy guys down from New London."

Will reached over and clapped Morgan on the shoulder, "Hey man, that sucks big time, but you're better off without her. I never liked her."

Dex nodded at Zach, who was looking back at them with the mirror again, "What about you and Beth, Zach?"

Zach blushed and turned to focus more on the road ahead.

Morgan punched Zach in the shoulder, "Yeah, man, give!"

Zach did not answer, but he could not suppress his grin.

Morgan reared back away from Zach, "Aw man, you did, didn't you?"

Dex shook his head in exaggerated sadness, "You poor fool. She said yes, didn't she?"

Will returned his binoculared gaze out the window, "So, she's not pregnant yet, is she?"

Zach glared at him through the mirror.

Dex grinned, "Hey man, you know we're all happy for you. Both of you. You've been dating her since you were, what, three?"

Zach ground his teeth, then tried to change the subject, "I heard from my little brother that President Austin spoke at Carolyne Austin elementary and that he is still carrying his .45."

Dex laughed, "After what happened to him, wouldn't you?"

Will nodded, "Yeah, I think someone said he was going to speak at the High School next month."

Morgan shook his head, "That's a Wilson Combat. It's like, what, a five or six-thousand-dollar gun? I'd put it in the safe and carry something else."

Dex snickered, "Got the job done, though. How much is your life worth to you?"

Morgan chuckled, "Yeah, I guess it did…. Say, maybe we could go into business making custom guns for people. Will, you and Dex built your AR15s with your dad, right?"

They nodded.

Zach asked, "Does the Vice President carry?"

Morgan shook his head, "I don't know, I don't think so." He glanced back at Will and Dex, who shook their heads as well.

Morgan raised his eyebrows and shrugged, "Well, she's kinda old, like thirty-something, but she's still kinda hot. Do you think she'll ever hook up with Austin like some people have said?"

Dex groaned, "Nah, man, didn't you see her speech? The only thing she wants to do is to kill Accipiters. She could kill a Wardog with just the hate in her eyes. Remember when she walked barefoot on broken glass to see the Gardener broadcast?"

Will nodded, "Yeah, she's tough. They didn't call her Banshee for nothing."

Morgan smiled, "Yeah, but I'd do her."

Zach chided, "Dude, she would break you in half."

Everyone laughed good-naturedly. Morgan grinned and started to reply but cut himself off as they rounded a sharp corner, and something loomed in the road in front of them.

It was a Stalker, apparently trying to cross the road. It froze and started waving its barbed fronds around.

Morgan shouted, "Gun it, Zach! Run the damned thing over!"

Will and Dex dropped their binoculars and braced themselves against the seat in front of them as Zach slammed his foot on the accelerator. The big V8 engine roared, and the bull bar grille guard on the truck's front impacted the leathery Stalker. The creature had been described as a giant walking Aloe Vera plant with a center section covered in bulbous eyelike structures and deadly barbs on the ends of its fronds.

Nearly 8000 pounds of truck and young men slammed into the 300-pound creature at 56 miles an hour, catapulting the Stalker down the highway.

Will, Dex, Zach, and Morgan shouted and whooped in exultation.

"You got it!"

"You nailed it, man!"

"You creamed that bastard!"

Zach slammed on the anti-lock brakes, which quickly did their job, and the truck ground to a halt.

After soaring through the air, the Stalker had landed and then skidded and rolled over and over at least a dozen times along the blacktop, flopping wildly and leaving a streak of viscous liquid behind it before it finally came to a stop. It lay still for just a moment before it began writhing and twisting, struggling to move.

Morgan leaped from the truck's cab with his Bushmaster AR15 in hand and emptied his magazine into the creature as he walked towards it, screaming, "That's for Nolan!" Morgan had grown up with Nolan Hoffman and had been good friends. Nolan was one of the first casualties in Fort Brazos and had been killed with other members of the Hoffman family by a Stalker.

Zach had jumped out of the truck at the same time as Morgan. He walked side by side with his friend as he worked the pump on his freshly sawed-off Winchester Ranger 12-gauge shotgun, emptying round after round of buckshot into the creature.

The Stalker stopped moving shortly after the first rounds had struck it. Will and Dex had followed only a half-second behind Morgan and Zach. Will stopped, ran back to the truck, got his cell phone out, and began live-streaming.

"This is William Sawyer, reporting live from FM 39, where we have just *killed* a Stalker! It was in the middle of the road, and we rammed it in Zach Simmon's truck, and Zach and Morgan Forbes just finished it off." He panned the video view around, pointing at the skid marks, "You can see where we hit it back there…." He turned and aimed at Zach, Morgan, and Dex, who was triumphantly kicking the dead Stalker's corpse.

Zach jumped up and down and turned back to face Will, shouting, "We did it, man! We…"

Just then, Zach, Morgan, and Dex stopped, frozen where they stood as large barbs struck Zach in the chest and Morgan and Dex in the back, attached to gossamer strands. They collapsed to the pavement, convulsing. A fourth barb spranged off the truck's windshield and tore through Will's shirt sleeve, barely missing him.

Will dropped to the ground and scrambled back to the cab, reached inside, withdrew his Daniel Defense AR10 rifle, and dropped back to the ground looking underneath the truck to find the second Stalker that had ambushed them. The Ar15 he had built with his dad was back at home. Will had chosen to bring his heavier caliber AR10 with him instead.

A half dozen barbs impacted the other side of the truck, and two embedded into the asphalt blacktop.

Will growled, "You son of a bitch, you don't have the angle!" He sighted along the direction the barbs had come from and found his target. He did not hesitate. He had loaded his 20-round magazine with alternating Black Hills Match grade full metal jacket and Hornady hunting round hollow-point .308s.

Unlike the armored Wardog, the Stalker was not effectively bulletproof. The rifle rounds shredded the Stalker, sending thick viscous liquid geysering out the exit wounds. It immediately collapsed dead where it stood next to the fence post it had hidden beside.

Will watched the creature for a long, long moment to make sure it did not move again before he rose carefully, loading a fresh magazine. He poked his head above the truck's hood, but the creature was still not moving. He stood and aimed and emptied half the magazine into the Stalker, but it did not jerk or show any signs of life.

He looked around for more enemies while he desperately called out, "Dex? Morgan? Zach? Talk to me!"

Revelation

Wearing his dress uniform, which also happened to be his *only* uniform and, for all practical purposes, his sole possession save the contents of his pockets, Rear Admiral Lower Half Andre Johansson sat at attention next to Admiral Milner and General Marcus in the Fort Brazos Council Chambers. He had stayed the night in Mayor Tom Parker's spare bedroom. The New London apartment towers all had laundromat-style facilities built in but lacked anything like dry cleaning. Tom's wife, Dottie, had sympathetically and graciously helped Andre with his uniform, which by now had sorely needed some tender care and attention.

Andre had been the base commander at Naval Submarine Base New London. He had been promoted mere days before Awakening Day and had not yet transitioned to the Pentagon.

He had spent the previous day riding the Elevator with a collection of empty, returning semi-trucks and a couple of dozen women, children, and other civilians being relocated to Fort Brazos. The stream of 'refugees' was small but steady as DownSide struggled to figure out what to do with them.

Shortly after his arrival, Andre witnessed a feral hog being lowered into the Wardog's cage. There were evidently thousands of feral hogs roaming the countryside. Before Awakening Day in America, feral wild hogs were among the most destructive invasive species in the country. Between two and six million (or more) were running loose, wreaking havoc in at least 39 states and four Canadian provinces. Fully half were in Texas, where they did over $400 million in damage each year.

A sunbaked Master Sergeant had waxed expansively to him about how hogs were not actually native to the United States and North America. Christopher Columbus brought them to the Caribbean, and Hernando De Soto later introduced them to Florida. In the 1930s, European wild boars were imported into Texas and released for hunting. They subsequently interbred with free-ranging domesticated pigs, and their offspring were fruitful and multiplied. And multiplied a lot more.

So, the abundance of these animals, which could range to upwards of 600 pounds of nasty attitude, coarse black hair, and dangerous tusks, was fortuitous for the Wardog, which, it had turned out, would not eat anything not alive. Base personnel had been live-trapping the hogs for years, which were then donated to a local area slaughterhouse that then provided the meat to low-income families.

Two and Two had been put together when figuring out the most efficient way to provide something the Wardog would eat.

After the writhing, terrified, squealing hog was lowered via crane into the cage and released, the exuberant carnage that happened next left Andre both clinically fascinated and slightly appalled. This was not the brutal elegance of a lion taking down a gazelle. No, this creature perfectly reveled and luxuriated in the kill. It seemed to enjoy it on an almost… sexual level.

After that, Andre had been whisked away to take a helicopter tour of the surrounding area and the towering Alien spire in the middle of the Fort Brazos town square.

✪ ✪ ✪

In the Council Chambers, John and Gail sat to one side, with the council presiding in their raised dais seats. Mayor Tom Parker had opened the council meeting with a prayer beseeching the Almighty for guidance and continued strength. He then prayed for the parents, younger brother, and fiancé of young Zachary Simmons.

After the attack, the remains of both dead Stalkers were recovered and refrigerated for further study. Gail personally comforted Beth Harrison while John did the same at the Simmons house.

Upon the news of the attack, the entire city spontaneously joined together, rallying around the families in shared support and rage. It was as though the scabs over the Awakening Day wounds had been ripped off.

The council reviewed the dashcam video and the abbreviated cell phone footage that had abruptly ended, save for the muffled audio of shouts and gunshots.

★ ★ ★

Tom Parker looked at Dr. David Duncan, Chief of Surgery at Methodist Hospital, who sat in the front row. Tom and David were frequent golf partners, but today David's expression was tired and drawn. "Doctor Duncan, will you please give us a report on Zachary Simmons and the other young men?"

David stood, his expression grim, "Morgan Forbes and Dexter Sawyer should soon be released from the hospital after observation. They should recover fully." He paused, "Zachary Simmons fought like hell. The Stalker barb penetrated his chest in just the right place, at just the correct angle, and with just the right amount of force to puncture his pericardium and lodge against his heart, where the pumping action began to tear the tissue. As you may recall, these barbs deliver a strong shock, somewhat like a stun gun. However, we have now discovered that the barbs deliver a neurological suppressant that further incapacitates the victim."

"William Sawyer wisely did not attempt to remove the barb. To his credit, and as observed in the dashcam video, he attempted CPR until help arrived. Without the CPR that William administered, Zachary would have died immediately. The combination of the barb embedded in his pericardium and the electric shock immediately stopped his heart. William's CPR efforts revived Zachary, and he reports that he was able to talk to him briefly."

He grimaced and shook his head, "However, the Stalker barbs are," he swallowed, "well… they are insidious. William Sawyer's actions were correct and, in my personal opinion, heroic. The very act of CPR that revived Zachary allowed the barb to work its way more deeply into Zachary's heart and ultimately kill him. On the other hand, had William removed the barb, it is my professional medical opinion that the resulting trauma and severe laceration and rupture of the pericardium, along with the compounding effect of the neurological suppressant, would have resulted in immediate death. Outside of a hospital operating room and a heart surgeon, there is nothing William could have done to save Zachary

Simmons, and I have serious doubts that the young man could have been saved, even in an operating room."

Coffee arrived, and after a short break, the meeting resumed.

Gail asked, "General Marcus, please give us your assessment of this attack."

Alexander stood and sighed, "In reviewing the sequence of events in the attack, I'm forced to wonder if this could have actually been a planned ambush. Was the Stalker really crossing the road, or was it lying in wait. Specifically, are the Stalkers capable of planning and executing something like this, where one of them would most likely either be severely injured or killed? The truth is that we cannot be certain that this was the case."

"After the first Stalker attack, we searched a wide area and found no others, and it is obvious from their physiology that they cannot move quickly, so I believe that one was alone. This time, there were a pair of them and the second one just so happened to be close enough to very nearly kill all four young men. While we are not yet certain of their effective range, it seems clear that they cannot shoot long distances. So, was it a planned ambush or bad luck?"

"Stalkers can't move fast, they aren't armored, and they can't shoot far enough to be effective snipers. While they are certainly deadly, now that we know more about them, they don't seem to be terribly good at just being killing machines."

"We observed that during the first attack, the Stalker physically... disassembled both equipment and its victims and laid them out as if for study. Was this a conscious thing they did, or is it simply programmed into them?"

"The scientists seem to think that the numerous bulb-like structures are some kind of eyes, and the central core of their bodies contain a lot of what is believed to be neurological material, brain matter, so to speak."

"The speculation is that the brain matter is used to either store information as some kind of biological hard drive, or maybe it is for cognition. Or both. I believe that the Stalkers' real function is to observe and collect intelligence data. Whether they simply collect information or actually understand any of it, I have no idea. Do they simply record information to be passed along or transmitted, or do they actually think? If they are intelligence-gathering creatures, then I find it hard to believe that they don't have at least some level of conscious awareness and thinking ability in order to carry out that mission."

Alexander frowned and lowered his voice, "So the bottom line is, whether this particular attack was planned or not, I suspect that it is not beyond their abilities to do so."

✪ ✪ ✪

Gail and John traded notes for a moment, then John looked up from his legal pad and asked, "Admiral Milner, please give us an update on New London."

Preston stood. "Mr. President, Ms. Vice President, Mr. Mayor, Council Members, first, I'd like to update you on the current New London census count. As you know, for a variety of reasons, it took some time to nail down a final headcount and list of names and backgrounds. The final count is twenty-two thousand, one hundred and twelve men, women, and children, including one baby girl born this morning."

Councilwoman Esmerelda Collins brushed back her long brown hair and blinked back the mist in her hazel eyes, "So many." Esmerelda had lost her own grown son and daughter on Awakening Day, who had been living in Dallas and Fort Worth. After Awakening Day, she had taken in the children of the late Councilman Barrett Hoffman, who had been murdered along with his wife Margaret and son Nolan by the first Stalker attack.

Esmerelda had always been close to the Hoffmans. She was Sandra Hoffman's godmother. In their collective pain and grief, she had clung to 17-year-old Sandra and her four younger siblings desperately, and they to her. It did not replace her lost children, but the noise and energy of the young brood was a warm distraction.

She decided that the not terribly surprising 'condition' of young Sandra and her paramour David Garreth was also a happy distraction. The two had bonded and fallen head over heels for each other since they had been attacked, cocooned, and ultimately rescued from the Stalker. With the Hoffman children's enthusiastic blessing, she had filed for adoption of all of them. Now, it looked like she was going to have a grandchild after all.

Esmerelda almost whispered, "That's… that brings the total population to 156,486, so New London is what… 14% of the surviving human race…."

Preston continued, "Yes, Councilwoman. It took longer than we expected to do the count. Even though there is no food in the 'hotel' rooms, there are beds and running water, so people are constantly going back and forth. We went door to door, and even the last holdouts eventually had to come out to get food. We checked our lists against the information provided by Colonel Williams… something I'm still wondering about, by the way, and we were eventually able to match all the names and backgrounds."

Lieutenant Colonel Williams, seated at the room's rear, merely smiled mildly and nodded.

"Also, in searching the buildings, we counted the total number of rooms available, which we currently list as 22,500. That is, those are the rooms, well, above ground or surface level."

He paused, letting that sink in.

"We have found that every structure, including what people are calling the 'New Pentagon,' have a great many more floors below ground level than above. However, all of these seemed to be unoccupied, and all the lights were turned off on any subterranean floor we tried. To be perfectly honest, however, we have only just begun to search these, and it will take weeks or maybe even months to search them all."

Tom leaned forward, "Admiral, what are we talking about here?"

Preston shook his head in wonderment, "Mayor Parker, it looks like there are at least 250 levels below the surface, and those expand outwards. There are a vast number of identical hotel rooms and larger apartments, offices, what look like shopping malls, parks, recreation areas, and God knows what else. Preliminary estimates are that there is room for at the very least a million people there. Probably a lot more."

The only sound in the room was the movement of air from the HVAC system.

Councilman Hickum sank back in his chair, "My God, how will we feed that many people?"

Esmerelda quipped, "Well, it will take a 'while' for the population to grow quite that much, Wylie, even without birth control."

Dr. Nakamura interjected from the second row, "If I may, we've been working on this. Our botanist, Dr. Teagen Winsome, has already proposed setting up Aquaponic vertical gardens in the park area in New London. They are easy to fabricate, are low-maintenance, and can quickly grow significant amounts of vegetables, root crops, fruits, and herbs."

Alexander interjected, "Doctor, you said Aquaponics? Is that like hydroponics? Isn't that complicated?"

Dr. Nakamura nodded quickly, "General Marcus, yes, Aquaponics is related to hydroponics. However, its operation is very different. It is based on using the waste from fish in a tank at the bottom of the unit to fertilize the plants. Water from the tank is continuously pumped up to the top of the vertical garden. The waste from the fish, which can be simple goldfish or even larger, edible fish, is in the water and provides a natural fertilizer for the plants. The plant roots absorb the waste, in effect cleaning the water, and the filtered water returns to the fish tank at the bottom. Operation is as simple as feeding the fish and harvesting the plants through leaf cutting or pulling root plants out whole. There is no dirt, the system uses pumice-like rocks to hold the plants in place, and some plants grow up to three times faster than in soil."

Alexander nodded, "OK, how much space does this need?"

Dr. Nakamura extended his arms, "A unit this size and five feet or so tall can provide much of the nutrition and calories needed for a small family. Dr. Winsome has been using such systems for several years to teach students, and Dr. Becker uses several to grow some of his genetically modified plants in isolation in his lab."

Most council members, with deep roots in traditional agriculture, appeared dubious or even outright skeptical. Dr. Nakamura continued, "Several faculty members have one or more of these at our homes. My wife grows much of our own fresh produce, our favorites from Japan, including Horenso, Shiso, Daikon, and Goya in the unit in our sunroom."

Tom shook his head in overall wonderment, "Well, Doctor Nakamura, anything we can do to ameliorate the food situation in New London will help. Please make the necessary arrangements to send a few test units to New London. Let us see how they do there."

Dr. Nakamura nodded solemnly, "Yes, of course, Mr. Mayor."

✪ ✪ ✪

The discussion focused on food shipments and other priority logistical concerns for another half hour. Eventually, the meeting shifted back to Admirals Milner and Johansson.

Preston and Andre stood, "Council members, Mr. President, Ms. Vice President, we are fortunate today to have Rear Admiral Andre Johansson with us here. Andre is… was the base commander at New London. I have known Andre for many years. He is not a desk jockey. As a division officer, he captained the USS Asheville, served on the Miami as the Combat Systems Officer, and on the Georgia as Executive Officer. He graduated Summa Cum Laude from UCLA with degrees in Physics, History, and Political Science. His experience will be invaluable as we organize the survivors in New London as well as the effort to study, crew, and ultimately operate the… Blood Phoenix."

Gail smiled, "Thank you, Admiral Milner, and welcome, Admiral Johansson. Please give us your own impressions about the starship."

Andre nodded somberly, then smiled, "Madam Vice President, Mr. President, Council Members, I'd like to thank you all for your hospitality and the warm welcome to your lovely city. Mr. Mayor, I sincerely appreciate you and Dottie inviting me to stay at your home last night. I'm looking forward to bringing my wife Sofie and my son Carl here as well to visit and meet all of you."

Gail nodded lightly and seemed both irritated and pleased at being referred to not as 'Ms. Vice President,' but as 'Madam Vice President.' She was not sure if she liked it, but the way the man said it was filled with respect and seriousness. Of course, the whole idea of her *being* Vice President was still a shock, but it was nice to feel… respected.

Tom smiled and nodded, "It was our pleasure to have you, Admiral."

Andre continued, "Madam Vice President, in answer to your question, I have several observations to make about the… craft. The first and most obvious to me is that these… Gardeners, as you call them… have left it clearly unfinished. The Montana has been grafted inside the alien drive section. However, key systems are disconnected or missing. As you may have noticed, the aft area of the Montana, which would have contained the drive and other spaces, is completely gone, and there is nothing left there but a blank bulkhead that is not sealed. If we were to somehow take the craft into the vacuum of space in its current condition, the entire vessel would probably decompress through the unsealed bulkhead. While watertight doors are separating each section, we need to determine whether or not they are, in fact, vacuum proof and airtight."

"So, it is evident to me that the intent was for us to make some of our own design decisions concerning what to put there. Whatever we do will have to be fabricated, attached, and integrated into the ship's electrical, data, plumbing, and air systems – life support I suppose you would call it, as well as a host of other system integrations."

John shook his head and interrupted, "Thank you, Admiral. We're aware that the vessel is incomplete. I'm more interested in what you think it tells us about the Gardeners themselves and their mindset."

If Andre was surprised at the abrupt interruption, he did not show it. He smiled and replied smoothly, "Mr. President, it tells me that these Gardeners want us to truly understand this ship and have a hand in making significant parts of it sea, or rather, space-worthy. Obviously, they could have simply handed us a completed, ready-to-use vessel, but they didn't. Either they do not trust us, or they understand something of our psychology and want us to feel more… ownership of the end product."

Gail looked at John, who nodded, "Thank you, Admiral. How long do you think this process will take? How long will it take to complete it?"

Andre frowned, "Madam Vice President, allow me to put this in context. It took us fifteen to twenty years, from initial design to commissioning of the latest submarines class. The construction itself took two years or longer. After construction, the sea trials and acceptance tests began, which included more systems integration, testing, iterating on fixes, and building training and operations processes. Historically, these efforts could take up to two more years to complete if all went well."

"Here, we are talking about not only a spacecraft but what we believe to be a faster-than-light interstellar starship. Not only that but a craft that integrates a nuclear submarine with an alien propulsion system. And the aliens did not even complete the integration for us. Even with the help of the newly discovered operations manuals, we do not begin to truly understand the complex operation and maintenance of the warp drive section itself."

Everyone in the room shifted uncomfortably, exchanging glances with each other.

Andre carefully swallowed and continued with deliberate seriousness, "Madam Vice President, suppose we took a nuclear submarine, cut it in half, and took it back in time to, say, 1890, and ordered people of that time to complete it and operate it and then go to war with it against a civilization from the far future. How long do you think it would take them?"

Tom sank back in his chair, shaking his head in defeat, "How can the Gardeners expect us to do this?"

Andre nodded sympathetically, "Mr. Mayor, the situation is quite serious, but I am personally convinced that we will be able to work it out. As Admiral Milner pointed out, I do have a physics background. While I'm not a scientist, I do believe that we will eventually be able to understand the physics involved, especially with the help of the information being gleaned by General Chilton and Dr. Talib from the alien database. I am convinced we will indeed make it work, but I want to call for patience. This is going to take time."

Tom sighed. However, he and the rest of the council seemed somewhat reassured by the assessment. They had time.

Gail shook her head, "I'm afraid I have to echo some of what the Admiral is saying. I've flown F35s, and pilots of the F35 wear a $400,000 helmet. That helmet had many problems that delayed the program and even grounded the entire fleet of airplanes at times. Keep in mind; I am talking about a 'helmet' — not a warp drive. Sometimes even things we think of as being minor systems can cause major delays or even redesigns. I cannot imagine what we will run into bringing a hybrid submarine/starship to life."

Among the more uncomfortable people in the room was Alexander. He stood, "If I may, Mr. President, Ms. Vice President, Council members, I'd like to change the subject for a moment. My Intelligence Chief, Lieutenant Colonel Williams, has some new findings that he shared with me this morning that I believe we need to bring to everyone's attention."

Tom nodded, "By all means, General, please continue."

Alexander waved Martin forward, who inserted a thumb drive into the computer used to project images onto the large screen to one side of the Council chamber.

Martin had carefully studied the dossiers of each meeting participant, starting with the people he had known for these last several weeks as well as the New Londoners.

As a professional, he had put his own life and the lives of others at risk many times. Sometimes the stakes had been frighteningly high. Today, though, the weight of what he hoped to accomplish made all he'd ever done before Awakening Day seem like so much child's-play.

Martin had carefully considered what he should wear to the meeting and decided against wearing his uniform. He'd gone for the intellectual, not quite wild-haired Einstein professorial look designed to portray wisdom, intelligence, and overwork. With the General and two Admirals present, a mere Lieutenant Colonel did not have the gravitas he was looking for. Instead, he deliberately crafted an unrested and unshaved look, wearing horn-rim reading glasses on a string, a thin sweater, and a slightly rumpled tweed jacket and pants he had managed to find at the now-permanent flea market that had grown up on the outskirts of Fort Brazos.

In truth, he'd had a solid eight hours of sleep and an excellent breakfast before this meeting. He was as ready as possible for what he knew would be his most crucial briefing ever. Even after the mind-boggling discovery, Dr. Talib had made in finding the Gardener-crafted operations manuals and cover story, the new information that Martin had discovered had left his head spinning. *This may be the most consequential briefing anyone, anywhere, has ever given, and I have to give it in phases to have the desired effect. I am Atlas.*

He surveyed the room, professionally noting expressions and body language as he carefully removed the spectacles from his nose and smiled apologetically. Using his most professional and learned Australian accent, he answered, "Thank you, General Marcus. Please forgive me for being out of uniform today. I just came from a conference with General Chilton, and I'm afraid I've had no time for sleep, and, honestly (*he lied*), my American-style uniform got lost somewhere in the construction of our new Intelligence Headquarters."

Alexander nodded, "You're forgiven, Colonel. Please tell everyone what you told me."

Martin nodded obediently, "Of course, General, Mr. President, *Madam* Vice President, Council Members, and Mr. Mayor. I must inform you that I've discovered several startling new facts regarding the Accipiters that give significant color to their psychology and motivations." He began a series of slides on the display screen.

"Now, as you know, the Accipiters are very large, physically, as much as nine or ten feet tall. They have two clawed legs for locomotion, two major clawed arms suitable for wielding heavy instruments or weapons, and two more arms with much more delicate 'true hands' suitable for fine object manipulation and control of technology."

"Among the new things we have learned about the Accipiters is that the single representation we've seen of them is just one of their *three* sexes. We do not have images of what the other two sexes look like yet. You see, the Accipiter civilization is apparently over a million years old. In that time, they have made many changes to their own biology, and this is mind-boggling all by itself, the engineering of a third gender. They've also created a process by which their knowledge and experience are biologically duplicated and given birth in a new Accipiter body. Their "elite" live on, indefinitely, and are, in effect, immortal."

"If that is not enough, I was personally stunned to learn that the Accipiters as a culture did not evolve and grow as a civilization like our own. They cheated. Our enemy, who now control a vast galactic empire, was originally a bronze-age species without advanced technology. The Accipiters were evidently 'elevated' and given all of their advanced technology by yet another alien race that has since disappeared but who the Accipiters now worship as gods. For reasons unknown, this other group of advanced aliens apparently saw fit to elevate the Accipiters and loose them upon the Galaxy."

He paused as that revelation sank in before looking directly at Tom Parker, "The Accipiters consider themselves to be the equivalent of what we would call Angels – in the service of their gods, doing what they believe is the will of those gods."

"Essentially, the alien race that elevated them did so by genetically re-engineering and idealizing their genotype. They are basically the perfect evolution of their species. They use their biotech skills to alter and subjugate other races they encounter that they deem interesting or otherwise worthwhile. Those unworthy are discarded."

"The Accipiters are divided into roving clans with a highly structured and ritualized social order and hierarchy. Everything they do has a complex ritual, including what we would consider to be their religion. You see, they revere biological diversity. On every planet they conquer, all life is either wiped out completely or incorporated into their panoply of biological forms. Indeed, they use interesting or useful biological forms as currency in trade with other clans. When they find unique, useful, or simply beautiful life, I suppose from their perspective, they first preserve it, and then they *modify* and adapt it to suit their needs."

Tom shook his head and looked at his fellow council members before asking, "Colonel, do we have any idea how many there are of them?"

Martin looked at Tom and then separately at the other Council members, John and Gail, before answering, his expression grave. "Yes, Sir, Mr. Mayor, I'm afraid we do."

He paused again and then pressed the keys on the computer to bring up a different slide. It was an image of a galaxy.

"This is a representation of our Galaxy, as seen from above. You need to understand that our solar system is just one of the literally hundreds of billions of star systems in the Galaxy. The Galaxy is vast. It takes light over 120,000 years to get from one side to the other. There are, apparently, billions of star systems with planets capable of sustaining life."

He pressed a key, and too many stars to count were highlighted.

"The Accipiters roam among these star systems looking for life they either desire to accumulate or life they wish to destroy."

He pressed the key again, and splotches of red covered much of the map.

"The information we have is not very detailed or granular, but there appear to be, at the very least, millions of Accipiter clans, with hundreds of millions of ships, in all, if not more, perhaps many more."

The reaction to Martin's report was nothing short of stunned panic amongst many of those present. The commotion eventually began to die down, and John turned to Preston and Alexander and asked, "General Marcus, Admiral Milner, in light of what Colonel Williams has told us, how do we begin to fight this war?"

Alexander exchanged looks with Preston, "Mr. President, as you might imagine, the Admiral and I have discussed this issue many times. First of all, even before these new numbers came to light, we knew we were looking at something that was likely to last not just years but for generations. The fleet that attacked Earth was reported to have over sixty thousand starships alone. We have assumed we would be limited to employing hit-and-run guerilla tactics, including raids to look for intel and technology. We believe that for the foreseeable future, we will need to rely on some kind of stealth and make damned sure that nothing we do can ever, under any circumstances, lead back… home. Any ship will need to have failsafes or even some kind of self-destruct mechanism to prevent location data from ever being captured."

"Beyond that, it seems inherently obvious that we will have to have massive fleets of ships and the men and women to crew them as well as sufficient ground forces to be able to accomplish ground missions."

"Of course, building things requires resources, so we assume we will eventually need to find worlds to colonize and figure out where all the raw materials will need to come from for our efforts. Along the way, perhaps we will find potential allies or at least trading partners."

Gail interjected, "Admiral Milner, what about the skills and trained workers we will need?"

Preston nodded, "Ms. Vice President, there is significant shipbuilding knowledge and expertise among the people from New London, including manufacturers' representatives, technicians, and engineers, but of course, nobody has built a starship before. I'm certain, of course, that there must also be a diverse set of skilled people in Fort Brazos as well, but there will undoubtedly be significant gaps between what we collectively have now and what we will ultimately need."

Tom shook his head, "Well, it sure sounds like no matter what, we will have full employment… that is, if we can figure out how we're going to pay everyone."

Preston raised his eyebrows, "Yes, Mr. Mayor. That is outside my skill set. However, on the subject of skills, we will need to have a full census of people's past jobs and educational backgrounds. We must start preserving as much of the knowledge and skills people have before they atrophy or are otherwise lost. We must begin to build the tools with which to build the tools to build the infrastructure needed for a permanent wartime economy."

Gloria Vargas and others bristled at the words, 'Wartime Economy.'

Tom rubbed his chin slowly and asked, "Admirals, what can you tell us about the state of mind of the New Londoners? It has been hard enough for us to accept all that has happened, and it wasn't all thrown at us overnight. How are the people there reacting?"

Admiral Johansson glanced at Preston, who nodded, "Mr. Mayor, I must be honest, Sir. It is bad. My people are now, for all intents and purposes, refugees with nothing but the clothes on their backs and their entire world gone."

Gloria looked at Tom, "Tom, I've heard many reports from my constituents. We have a steady stream of what will end up being thousands of miserable people flooding into the city. People are bending over backward to help them, but many seem both grateful and resentful at the same time of the charity. I know Colonel

Salangsang and his men are building emergency housing, but it won't happen quickly enough."

"People are worried, and the bad morale is beginning to infect the people already here, and who can blame them? I know we all voted to support the war effort, but let's face it, the Gardeners have a gun to our heads. When word of just how impossible these odds are, what can possibly motivate people to fight a war like this? People need hope. *Why* should they fight? What do we really want from all this?"

Gail glowered, her voice angry, harsh and low, "Councilwoman… Gloria… what *we* want is simple. After everything they've done to us, what we want is to *hurt* the Accipiters. They raped and murdered our world, but I fear that people will have little to no hope that we will be able to really hurt them in any meaningful way, especially when these numbers get out. Even if we were to kill one of their damned ships every single day, so what? It would be a drop in the bucket. Nothing we can hope to do in our lifetimes can substantively hurt an empire as vast as the Accipiters!"

Admiral Johansson shook his head, "Madam Vice President, as your General Marcus sagely pointed out, this will be a conflict measured in generations or longer. We must prepare our people for a long, careful, deliberate effort that will satisfy the Gardeners of our efforts and at the same time position us to eventually gain such strategic knowledge or sufficient superior new technology with which to combat the Accipiters more decisively."

Sensing his opportunity, Martin Williams stood and raised a hand, "Pardon me, Madam Vice President, but I believe that I may know a way that we can actually hurt the Accipiters and hurt them quite badly."

Gail blinked in surprise, "What?"

The rest of the room erupted into mild chaos. Tom Parker hammered his gavel. It was the first time he had used it; he hadn't even tapped it to open the meeting. The sharp "crack!" had the desired effect, and the room quieted again. He commanded, "Colonel Williams, you have our undivided attention." He left unsaid words to the effect that 'it had better be good.'

Martin nodded gravely, "Yes, Mr. Mayor, thank you, and I apologize for the interruption. Please allow me to explain. As I described earlier, the Accipiter 'Religion' revolves around their reverence for biological diversity and data. The 60,000 starships that attacked Earth are from a typical, if minor, and less important clan amongst their empire. Also, when they attacked Earth, it was not without foreknowledge. You see, they had been to Earth before."

The room again erupted with questions and conversation. Tom hammered his gavel again, though this time not as loudly. "Please continue, Colonel."

"Yes, Mr. Mayor. You see, the Accipiters visited Earth in the distant past. We are not sure how long ago, but it was hundreds of thousands of years ago. Perhaps it was among the first worlds they visited. When they did, they left behind a sentinel of sorts. Call it, or him, a "Keeper" for Earth. They took an early human ancestor and elevated him, increasing his intelligence and health. They then constructed a hidden underground facility where he would go into suspended animation for hundreds or thousands of years at a time, only to wake up periodically when automated sensors would detect changes in the planet and the life evolving there. His job was to take samples of that life and put it into stasis. Occasionally he would transmit updates to the Accipiters, letting them know how things were progressing."

"When the Accipiter fleet arrived in our solar system, they already knew everything about us. They knew our technology, where our cities and bases were, our languages, and our history and biology. The next phase of the Keeper's responsibilities began at that point. He was to prepare the samples to be brought up from the surface of Earth to join the Accipiter fleet in a sort of permanent shrine, at which point major religious ceremonies would take place."

"The Keeper's underground base is being transformed into a starship in a process that takes decades… with each phase marked by rituals and ceremonies. The Keeper base is then launched into space and joins their fleet as a permanent shrine. Later, when the Accipiters visit with other clans, they tally up the contents and quality of their shrines to see who ranks higher. The winner absorbs some of the other's resources and rises in the empire hierarchy."

Martin looked around the room, gauging faces and reactions, "Mr. President, Madam Vice President, Mr. Mayor, Council Members, I believe that if we could…. Capture… this 'Keeper,' it would have a stunning and profound impact on the Accipiters. In a million years, this has never happened. No Keeper has ever been captured or killed. For this to happen would forever shame and possibly destroy the clan it happens to. Its members would lose faith in their leadership and scatter. Moreover, when word of it spreads, it would put the entire Accipiter hierarchy on notice that they are not invulnerable. It would challenge their belief in their own omnipotence and shake their entire civilization to its core."

He turned to Gail, "Madam Vice President. It would *hurt* them."

✪ ✪ ✪

Even Tom's gavel did not subdue the room this time. He called, "Order! Order!" to no avail. Eventually, General Marcus took it upon himself and, using decades of experience, barked a command to the room, "That's enough!"

John shook his head, "Thank you, General." He turned to Martin, "Colonel, you've heard the report from the Admirals. It will take years to get the starship working. I assume, or you wouldn't be telling us all this, that somehow you've learned that this Keeper is still on the planet and hasn't been moved yet?"

Martin nodded, "Yes, that is correct, Mr. President."

John raised his eyebrows, "Well, skipping over, for now, the 'how the *hell* do you know all of this' part, how long do we have until the Keeper is moved? Our chances of capturing him would seem to be much better before he is moved."

Martin replied quietly, "The conversion of the Keeper's base into a starship will be complete, the last of the ceremonies will be held, and the ship will be launched in 318 days, Mr. President. After that, the chance of capturing him would likely be negligible."

Admiral Johansson shook his head sadly, and Admiral Milner chided, "Then this is academic, Colonel. There's no way we can expect to have that abortion of a ship ready in less than a year."

Tom stood from his chair, "The Accipiters believe they are an army of Angels in service of their gods. If we could shake their belief in their own supremacy and infallibility, then maybe there *is* hope for this war. What if we could simply destroy it before it launches?"

Gail added, "And if we could… capture him? How would that help us, and how would the Accipiters react?"

Martin stood his ground, "Madam Vice President, Mr. Mayor, The Keeper, by its very nature, would have intimate knowledge of the Accipiters and their operations. Capturing him could well be the greatest intelligence coup in human or even galactic history. We could learn crucial, even pivotal, information that would help us develop more effective strategies against the enemy. Even if we could somehow find another Keeper on a different planet, somewhere else, this is the one we would have the best chance of ever meaningfully communicating with. He or she will be the only one that might feel even the slightest level of kinship towards us as human beings."

"I hesitate to speculate on the psychological impact on an alien species. However, as I mentioned earlier, it seems clear that capturing the Keeper stands a good chance of planting seeds of doubt and potentially destabilizing the Accipiters. That said, however, I have to believe it would not just insult them, but after a million years of lording over the Galaxy, something like this would surely…. Hurt them."

John walked to the dais, "Tom, you said these Accipiters think they are their God's divine angels, that they are an army of their Gods? Or perhaps they've become so drunk on power that they now think of themselves as Gods?"

He turned to face the room, "Then perhaps we are all here for a greater reason than that the Gardeners abducted us to fight a war for them. As the last surviving… tribe… of Earth, perhaps it is our destiny…."

Tom interrupted him, his voice level and flat, "…To become the sword of the one true God and smite these Accipiters and free the Galaxy from their rule."

John turned in surprise and looked at Tom for a moment before turning back to the room, "Admirals, General, I believe we have to try and do this. Whatever it costs. Whatever resources are needed. We might not have another opportunity like this in a thousand years. We must find a way.”

He looked down, then back up again, “They said we couldn’t launch Doolittle’s B25 bombers from the deck of a carrier and bomb Tokyo. Nobody had ever struck them at home like that before. That one raid shook the Japanese confidence and gave hope to a shaken America.”

He reached over and put his hand on Gail’s shoulder, “I believe that if our people are to have the will to fight this war, we must do something and do it soon to give them a reason to hope… and the confidence that their leaders have a clue what to do next. Perhaps our children’s children might someday know some level of victory if we are even halfway successful.”

✪ ✪ ✪

Throughout the meeting, Martin carefully studied the reactions of others. Most fell in line with his expectations, including the Admirals, which was why he played things the way did. There was something, though, about the body language between Milner and Johansson that nagged at him. He could not put his finger on it, but he had learned to trust his instincts about people.

✪ ✪ ✪

After the meeting and after the public announcements and statements that followed, General Marcus met privately with Martin in Alexander’s office. Alexander sat in his chair for a full five minutes while Martin stood at the Australian version of Attention.

Finally, Alexander asked, “So Colonel, when are you going to tell me how the hell, exactly, and I mean, exactly and precisely, you can possibly know all the things you said today?”

Martin hid his surprise that this was Alexander’s opening question, “Well, you see, General, I asked the Gardeners very politely, and they answered me.”

All The News

Studio Lounge
September 14th, NLD 15 -- FBD 43, 11:56 AM

Radio DJ and personality Danielle Richardson had a carefully crafted public persona, as mandated by the corporate office and conservative local sensibilities. Billboards around the city of Fort Brazos depicted her wearing a professional business suit, a modestly open blouse, traditional makeup that emphasized her large grey eyes, a light tan, and her hair up. Right now, however, she bore little resemblance to that crisp and polished image.

An awful lot had happened in the six weeks since Awakening Day. In Danielle's world, Radio Station 92.5's corporate owners, based in Tucson, Arizona, were now long gone, as was the station manager, who'd been at the corporate offices on Awakening Day. As the only local talent on the station, which had primarily featured syndicated programming, the situation had left Danielle in more or less nominal 'possession is nine-tenths of the law' control of the station. Of course, there were other stations in the city, but none with Danielle's loyal following and audience size.

Through sheer force of personality and no small amount of pleading and bribery in the form of certain intoxicants from Danielle's private and dwindling stash, the station engineer, Reed Pauley, was now keeping things running on a less than part-time basis. His day job now kept him busy with helping keep the official government broadcasts running smoothly.

When the reality of the situation in Fort Brazos had set in, Danielle had found herself spending more and more time at the studio. Embarrassment over her panic-stricken outburst on Awakening Day had played no small part in her self-imposed isolation. She eventually completely moved out of her tiny nearby apartment and transformed the studio, lounge, and office area into her personal hideaway from the terrible reality of her life and the outside world.

The fluorescent lights were either off or had been entirely removed, replaced with dimmed lamps and candles everywhere. A few dark Persian rugs and several more knock-off Persian rugs covered as much of the floor as she could manage, and the walls were draped with what rich and lustrous fabric samples and sheets she had been able to smile, cajole and barter for at the flea market. Indirect lighting from LED light strips she placed in recessed corners completed the mood.

CCM Harrold Anders had helped with the move, hiring a couple of Privates, and paid them with beer to move the bed and furniture into the station manager's office. Danielle had been shocked to learn that the station manager had enjoyed a full private bathroom with a shower, but she had happily broken that in as well, with more than a little personal help from Harrold, of course.

That Harrold had described her new place as a cross between Arabian Nights and a high-class strip joint had annoyed her, and she slugged him as hard as she could in his oak tree of an arm to little observable effect. Then she looked around, shrugged, laughed, and asked where he thought the pole should go.

Today was a rare "day off" for Harrold. He smiled as he leaned back on the leather couch, smoking a cigar in the transformed studio lounge, watching Danielle slowly dance barefoot on the rug. She didn't smoke the Marlboro Gold cigarette dangling from her fingers. Her hair rolled loosely down her shoulders, and her eyes were closed as she abandoned herself to the gentle rhythm and mood of Norah Jones singing 'Summertime.'

Harrold was a passionate man. He'd been deeply passionate about each and every one of his three ex-wives. The Air Force, in turn, soaked up all the passion he could muster, and he eventually figured out that it was something he never had tired of. However, it had taken a long time to learn that it was different with a wife. Passion alone had not been enough. It had blinded him to what was missing.

His first wife, Greta, had not technically been a stripper but served drinks at one of the clubs near Maxwell Air Force Base. She had left him because she wanted babies, and Harrold's vasectomy had not come up in conversation during the comically brief transition from dating to marriage. Calinda, his second wife, had been in love with the idea of being an Air Force wife, but the reality had soured on her. Krystle had left him to 'climb the ladder,' marrying a droll Lieutenant Colonel who had been on a fast track to General. Greta ended up marrying a pilot and had five kids. Calinda had worked her way through school and became a successful psychotherapist. Krystle's replacement husband had indeed earned his stars, and they had had three daughters together.

Before Awakening Day, all three of his exes had amicably stayed in touch with him. After Krystle divorced him, Calinda, who had never remarried, had somehow 'just happened' to be in town about once a year or so. They both knew it was not going to go anywhere, but they did manage to remind each other something of why they had married in the first place.

The relationship with Danielle, however, was different. Oh, the passion was there – like two freight trains colliding in the night. The difference, though, was in Danielle herself. While she was, he had to admit, brighter than Greta or Krystle, she was slightly crazy and over the top and perhaps even a bit larger than life. Other parts of her were complete contradictions. Somehow though, she was a more complete person than his ex's. She already knew who she was and was not looking for Harrold to change or be anything different than he already was.

As he luxuriated in his cigar and watched Danielle sway and gently swirl, barefoot in her jeans and half-buttoned blouse, he reflected on the change he'd seen in her that mirrored his own. For perhaps the first time in their adult lives, they were at peace with themselves. In light of the Apocalypse, he snorted; that was quite an accomplishment.

Danielle opened her eyes and looked a question at his laugh, but then her smartwatch slowly throbbed and gently chimed in reminder of the time. She smiled softly and sighed, "Hold that thought."

12:00 PM

Danielle leaned into the mic, speaking in her signature warm, husky voice, "Hello, people of Fort Brazos and New London. This is Danielle Richardson on FM 92.5, and Radio Free Fort Brazos beaming our signal across the known world and beyond. There is so much to talk about today! Yesterday's council summit between the leaders in Fort Brazos and the Navy from New London covered a lot of ground. I don't know about you folks, but I'm still trying to wrap my brain around the whole idea of a starship."

"And while a little bird tells me that there was a lot more that went on behind closed doors than was alluded to in the all-smiles press conference afterward, and I'm telling you because I was there, that many of those smiles lay underneath unhappy eyes."

"Could it be that there is some elitism going on here, coming from either side – or both? I don't know why, but I sensed that there was more than a simple disagreement going on. We can speculate all we want, but a lot was obviously left publicly unsaid."

"So, I'll leave that subject to lie, and the talking heads at the TV station can argue all day long about the spaceship. However, there are issues closer to home that will affect us all that didn't come up in the press conference but were in the press release."

"First, let's talk about the results of the Census and what it means to each of us. The total population of us down here in the world, including the base, is now listed at 134,374 – that's the base, the city, and the University populations. The headcount from New London is in, and that is 22,112. Twenty-Two Thousand people! That brings the total known population of humankind to 156,486. That's it! That's everyone. Hell people, the population of Dallas-Fort-Worth, was what, seven or eight *million*? A hundred and fifty-six thousand is even less than the population of a lot of big-city suburbs! Still, adding New London is twenty-two thousand more than we had before, and a lot of those people are families." She paused and grinned, "In addition to that, I'm told that we should be expecting some kind of baby boom in eight months or so."

Danielle took a tiny sip of her Courvoisier brandy.

Harrold had noticed that her appetite for drink and smoke had plummeted lately, but he knew she had a lot on her mind.

She took a deep breath, "Another thing that nobody seems to have agreed on yet is how to set up a government structure to adequately represent the New Londoners. Some say that the people there came from a military base and should be treated just like the people at the Joint Reserve Base. Other people say that because a six-hour elevator ride separates our cities, it would be like having the mayor of New York speak for the city of Los Angeles. So what if we have real-time communication. Both cities are listening to me right now, for that matter. I heard President Austin said something about how it used to take six hours just to drive from Fort Brazos to Corpus Christi."

"Now, I know what some of you are thinking, that New London cannot feed itself and that most of those people will have to be relocated here anyway, and yes, that is true. For now. In the future, though, I am sure we will find a way around the food problem as we start to gear up for this war thing. More and more people will end up having to live and work in New London. Certainly, the Gardeners must have thought so because there are so many rooms there for people to live in."

"So, in the long run, lots and lots of people, probably a lot more than just twenty-two thousand, will live there. What we decide to do now will affect how those people relate to the people here. Will there be resentment and disaffection? Will it become an us-versus-them thing? If we mess this up now, we'll be paying for the consequences for a long time to come."

"On a more potentially dangerous note, General Marcus announced what he called 'Lewis and Clark' expeditions. He is sending out ground teams to explore the ends of this new continent we are on and also out to the other so far untouched continents and major islands we can all see if we look up in the sky. While I am sure that much of what they encounter will be routine and boring, I am sure that there will end up being a lot of excitement when they inevitably find the unexpected. I just hope they are all very careful. I myself, like the rest of us, want our brave men to all come back home to us." She licked her lips and looked out the studio window at Harrold. "All of them."

"Also, on a subject that I can personally relate to, it has been pointed out that we have people among us who are among the last of us with specific knowledge or skills… such as how to paint a portrait, or how to fix a soundboard. Name your topic. We need to try and find ways to capture as much of this knowledge as we can before it is lost forever." She laughed and shook her head at Harrold,

"Maybe I can find some strapping young stud who wants to learn at my pretty little feet how to be a DJ?"

She could not hear him through the glass, but Harrold mouthed something in response she probably would not want to hear anyway. Then she cocked her head and smiled at him in a knowing way that was at once both serious, playful, and… something else.

Harrold saw her odd expression, which set off small alarm bells in the back of his head. He stopped and stared. He knew there was something she had been working up to telling him, and he was beginning to suspect he knew what it was.

She took another minuscule sip of her Courvoisier. "Another topic that came up in the earlier hours of the summit was the idea of land grants. As you know, there are about a zillion square miles of land inside New Texas. Talk is of granting land grants to every one of us, whether we want them or not. It becomes our inheritance. You'd be able to sell it if you wanted, but you and your family would retain twenty percent of the resource rights from that land in perpetuity."

"Right now, the idea of trying to farm when monsters are roaming around is more than a little terrifying, but I have faith." She smiled at Harrold again, "I have faith that we'll figure it out."

She laughed heartily and pointed a finger at Harrold, "Not that you'll ever catch me on a tractor or hoeing a row of corn or something, but I don't know…." Her lips trembled, and she lowered her gaze to lock eyes with Harrold, "It's just nice to think that my… our… children will have something they could do if they ever wanted to, besides fight in some damned galactic war."

Harrold held her gaze for a long moment, his expression puzzled and blank. Then his eyes widened, and Danielle bit her lip, smiled, and nodded as her happy tears finally started to fall.

Her voice was suddenly husky and deep as she added, "As I said, it won't be long before there are more people, a lot more, both in New London and here, in Fort Brazos. It is up to us to make sure that the course we chart for them is the right one."

It was a good thing that the triple-paned studio door glass was as strong as it was because the heavy, magnetically sealed door hardly slowed at all as Harrold burst through the door and swept Danielle off her chair. She shrieked in happiness and joy and wrapped her arms and legs around him as he whirled her around in circles, knocking the chair over a fraction of a second after she had just barely managed to switch the broadcast over to the music queue.

The Hills

Darnell Lewis, Ray Bunker, and Gary Little huddled together at their small table in the back corner of the Travis Street Tavern. Darnell's dark black skin contrasted sharply with Gary's pale white skin and Ray's modest tan. All three were muscular and fit, but Darnell had the lean bulk that came from obsessive workouts.

They unhappily and cautiously sipped the Caddo Hawk beers on the table before them. Before Awakening Day, the local Caddo Hawk brewery produced a cheap "craft beer," but with no more deliveries from a world that was not there anymore, even the cheapest Pre-AD beers were now hoarded and scarce.

Indeed, it was not only beer that people were starting to hoard. While the Gardener-enlarged warehouses had not yet begun to run out of things, everyone knew it was just a matter of time. Favorite brands of everything from candy to blue jeans were fast becoming a new form of currency. The bustling bazaar that the local flea market had grown into was exhibit number one.

Travis Street Tavern was yet another example of change sweeping over Fort Brazos. Formerly one of a national chain of sports bars, replete with TV screens on every wall and corner, the name change reflected the new reality. There were, of course, no more live feeds of sports events, or anything else, from around the Earth. Travis Street Tavern still had wood floors and TVs, but now they played local news and loops of past Fort Brazos High School football games and other sports events people had recordings of, but those were growing more rare since people tended to become somewhat morose watching sports from a dead world.

Before Awakening Day, the three men had been regulars at the sports bar, enthusiastically cheering their favorite teams. All three had been on the football team while attending Fort Brazos High School. Darnell had been recruited as a promising running back with a full scholarship to Ohio State. Darnell had suffered a devastating knee injury his first year that had never healed well enough for him to play again competitively. He returned home to Fort Brazos and concentrated on caring for his aging mother and looking after his little sister Yazmeen.

The three men were tired. Darnell rubbed his sad eyes. His shaved head glistened black, and his short black beard elongated his face a little. At 28, he was within a year of the other men and still had his running-back body. Working out was one of the only things he had left to help him keep his sanity. After Awakening Day, he, Ray, Gary, and four others had barricaded themselves inside Reinhardt Distributing and had proceeded to attempt to drink the remainder of the inventory. It was the end of the world, and who would care? The owners were dead, and nobody was paying them. Why not send off the world with a bang?

They had locked the doors and pushed furniture up against them. Then when the cops had shown up, the security guard, Trevor, now nicknamed Trigger, who'd been the most inebriated of them all, had accidentally discharged his pistol and started a chain reaction that had nearly resulted in a police S.W.A.T. raid.

They became known as the Reinhardt Seven. Everyone knew who they were, and they had become both the butt of jokes and a symbol of the same fear, pain, and despair that few wanted to openly admit they had shared. Wherever they went, people raised imaginary glasses to them.

And nobody would hire them for regular jobs.

Gary Little's wife had died on Awakening Day, or rather, like so many others, she had not woken up. The same was true of Darnell's mother and sister. Ray's wife, Julie, obtained the speediest divorce Ray had ever heard of, and he was denied any visitation rights to his little girl, Chloe.

After the incident at Reinhardt, Darnell had only gotten the bartending job because the owner thought it would be funny. A publicity stunt for the leader of the Reinhardt Seven to tend the bar.

A year younger than Darnell at 27, Gary had that handsome, somewhat scruffy look that had charmed so many girlfriends before he married Darlene. Gary had slowed down and gotten a decent job at the warehouse and was well-liked. Now the only work he could find was day work doing janitorial or whatever unskilled labor he could manage to get at the unemployment office.

Gary's foster brother Ray was in a similar boat, finding only freelance delivery or manual labor work once or twice a week. His single tour of duty in the Army in the Middle East had been enough for him. He returned to Fort Brazos and worked hard at the solid, well-paying warehouse assistant manager job. Gary and Ray were now living together in a ramshackle garage apartment at the edge of town.

They had all worked long and hard that day and now sat in the darkest corner they could find, nursing their unfamiliar Caddo Hawk beers that Darnell's employee discount made affordable.

Rochelle Borden, the tiny, dirty-blonde waitress they all knew and had gone to school with, grudgingly stopped at their table. Her frazzled hair was pulled back into a ponytail, but much of it had come loose. She sighed, knowing the answer but asking the question anyway, "More beer, boys?"

Darnell looked up and frowned, "Are you OK, Shelly?" Her face was flushed.

Rochelle glared at him, "Not that *you* would care, *Darnell*…. I'm pregnant."

Darnell's eyes widened in surprise, and his mouth parted open slightly as he inhaled.

Rochelle rolled her eyes, "Oh, don't worry, that shiny little head of yours, Darnell, you're not the baby daddy."

She turned away, flipping her hair and muttering, "…damned aliens… something in the water…."

Gary and Ray shook their heads. Gary said, "Don't look at me, Darnell. It wasn't me, either!"

Ray grunted, "This sucks," as a half dozen clean-cut, uniformed Navy lieutenants entered the Tavern, each carrying their "Welcome to Fort Brazos" backpacks of supplies and a change of clothes. Somehow, they were evocative of kids on the first day of school. They talked excitedly about the things they had seen since arriving, including their amazement at the impossible sky. The group sauntered up to the bar and quickly ordered expensive name-brand beers while several coeds from Bonham State University tried hard to feign non-interest from their nearby table.

Ray grunted again, "…Like I said. This sucks. Look at 'em! Little Navy Squids'll be drivin' the spaceships that fight the damned war, and they'll be the heroes. They'll do the fly'in, and Army grunts 'll do the dyin', just like always."

Darnell shook his head, "What, you don't want to reenlist Ray? I'm sure they'd take you back. And you'd get a paycheck again. I'll bet you'd be able to get visitation rights to see Chloe."

Ray's fingers whitened as he gripped the bottle in front of him. He snapped an incendiary look at Darnell before looking away apologetically. "I ain't goin' back in. I done did my bit."

"Sorry, man, I didn't mean nothin'…." Darnell knew that Ray's time in the Army had been bad for him and that he did not like talking about it.

Ray looked back at Darnell, "It's OK, man. I… I just can't do that again."

Gary tried to distract them both and pointed at the nearest TV monitor, "Hey, did you guys see that? The General is sending out 'Lewis and Clark' expeditions to explore the other continents."

Darnell shrugged, "Other continents? Nobody has even been to those mountains on the other side of the lake yet. We hardly know what's on the continent we're on right now other than flyovers."

Ray sat back in his chair, his eyes widening in sudden inspiration.

Darnell and Gary looked at each other and back at Ray. Gary prompted him, "OK. Give, Ray. What are you thinking?"

Ray answered slowly, "I did a delivery to Bell and Son's, you know, that super expensive custom boot maker shop with the six-month waiting list?"

Darnell and Gary nodded, struggling to follow.

"You see, while I was there, old man Bell was complainin' about his supply of exotics. He's running low, and he ain't had no deliveries since before Awakening Day."

Darnell smiled, "OK, that's tough for old man Bell, but what does that have to do with…."

Ray leaned forward, his eyes widening, "Don't ya see? There's demand for exotic hides! Bell charges two or three grand and more for his custom boots. If we went out and bagged some new skins for him, he would pay top dollar to keep his shop going and his customers happy. Rich folks won't be happy with plain cowhide boots, and there's always gonna be Rich folks, ya know."

Gary shook his head, "No way, man, we'd get eaten like those army guys did. Didn't you see the pictures? That thing ate a Humvee! Took a Bradley with a 25mm chain gun to kill the damned thing."

Ray sank slowly back into his seat, "Nah, how hard can it be? Those guys must have fucked up. I mean, somebody caught one of the things and gift-wrapped it for the Army. Also, the Sheriff, er... the President, I guess now, killed one dead with his .45. You've seen the video. Army got caught with its pants down on that Humvee thing. They got mad and blew it away for sure, but it can't be that bad if some idiot bagged one that easy."

Darnell wasn't completely convinced but waved his arm around the table, "You know, is this our life now? Man, we've got to find something else before the new government decides to assign us to something, send us out to the farms they're talking about, or just outright draft us into their damned space army. I know Ray won't go, and I sure don't want to. We need something that's our own, but hunting skins like that sounds dangerous as Hell."

Ray shook his head, "Look, guys, no offense Darnell, I love you, man, and you know I appreciate the beer. It kills me that Gary and I can't even afford to buy our own beer anymore. Besides, we've all been campin' and shootin' since we were all kids growing up next door to each other. Out there... Out there, there's no more fences to cross or even roads to follow -- or be followed."

Darnell mulled his beer, "I love you too, Ray, but only so far. It would get lonely out there, and you two are not my taste in skirt. No offense."

Gary snorted, "Darnell, you ass. You know I'm not... Hell, I used to be a player, you know that, but since Darlene died...."

Ray put his hand on his foster brother's shoulder, "We know Gary. But right now...." He nodded towards the Navy men who were sitting at the flirtatious coeds' table, "Right now, we can't compete with *that*. We can't even buy our own drinks, much less drinks for those girls, neither."

Darnell changed his tack, "I hear they're going to be building lots of housing for the New Londoners. There's got to be jobs there?"

Gary shook his head, "I asked around about that. Apparently, there's a whole bunch of Philipino construction engineers who are going to do all the work. We'd be lucky even to get crap jobs servicing porta-potties as day laborers."

Darnell lowered his head in shame, "Fuck guys, I'm sorry I got you into that mess at Reinhardt. I knew better…."

Gary snickered, "Yeah, man, who knew the end of the world wouldn't, like, actually be the end of the world and all and that, like, we'd all need jobs afterward?"

★ ★ ★

After two more weeks of back and forth, they still had not decided what to do next. Then Darnell lost his bartending job when the owner decided the novelty of having Darnell there no longer outweighed the negatives. Day labor work all but dried up.

After drinking the very last of their beer, the three men sold their pickup trucks, Darnell's SUV, and everything else they owned that they weren't taking with them and used the money and what other cash they could scrape together to buy three horses, three mules, and supplies.

The supplies were easier than Darnell had expected since Gary and Ray were raised in a Prepper household that had taught them much about self-sufficiency.

Before leaving, Ray had called a buddy and found out that maps and long-range radios were available to anyone who wanted to strike out on their own. There was no promise of rescue or supply, but at least they would not be completely cut off from what remained of humanity.

They had set out west across the prairie to what was tentatively being called the Red River, which was one of two rivers that drained the lake or inland sea. They had found a place to ford the river and entered the foothills of the Himalaya-Esque mountains at the base of an actual glacier. It was nothing like the Davis

Mountains of West Texas or any place they had ever camped, hunted, or fished before.

The farther they got from Fort Brazos, the happier all three were. It was as though the weight of everything that had happened, not to mention the end of the world, had been lifted from their weary shoulders. The landscape was stark, stunning, pristine, and majestic. And they were the first humans ever to set foot there.

They made camp along a crystal-clear stream with rainbow trout you could just about reach down and grab with your hands. As they sat around the campfire, they grinned at each other. Darnell pulled out a whisky flask he'd hidden away and raised it to them, "Guys, I looked up Lewis and Clark, and I paraphrase Lewis when I say, 'We are now about to penetrate a world, on which the foot of mankind has never before trodden." He took a swig from the flask and handed it to Gary, who gingerly swallowed a quick hit, not wanting to waste such a precious thing, "To Us."

Gary handed the flask to Ray, who stared at it like it was a precious religious icon. Everyone around the fire knew it was the very last they might ever enjoy. He hesitated a moment before following his brother's example. He smiled, handed it back to Darnell, and cocked his head, "Trodden? Really?"

Ray shook his head, "Fuck Lewis and Clark. We're the new Mountain Men."

Interrogation

Interview Room 4b
September 19th, NLD 20 -- FBD 48, 9:03 AM

Commander Thomas Harding had swiftly made a full recovery from the injuries inflicted upon him by Julian Dabrowski in the early hours of New London's Awakening Day. The Master Sergeant's skill had been superb. Thomas had been disarmed and rendered unconscious with no broken bones and bruises that ceased to ache within a few days. Most of the bruises had actually been from Thomas's roll down the marble stairs and perhaps from a few indignant kicks by bystanders. Since that day, however, Thomas had not left the holding cell he had been roughly and unceremoniously dumped into.

That it had taken three days for someone to bother to bring him food was better than expected, even if it was only an MRE. The only thing that did not seem to make sense was the utter newness of everything about his prison. There were not even any scuff marks on the floor. It did not at all feel like he imagined a black site in some third-world country ought to feel.

Surprisingly, Thomas had noticed his glasses had not been broken when he was assaulted and thrown down the marble steps, although they were scratched around the edges.

As far as he could tell, he had not even been searched. When he first awakened in the cell, he could still feel the bulge of the thumb drive sewn into his jacket. He had steeled himself for the expected rush of guards into his room. Then he swiftly ripped the seam, tore the thumb drive from his coat, and twisted the tabs in opposite directions. This broke the fine wires that connected the watch battery to the volatile memory data storage chip inside. Unlike a typical thumb drive, without continuous power to sustain it, or if the battery were to die, the incriminating data was erased when the chip lost power.

And then nothing at all happened—no angry guards or interrogators. Nothing happened until three days later when the first MRE smacked the floor through the slot in the door.

Three weeks later, he was still wearing that same service uniform, now disheveled and, he was quite certain, as ripe as he was.

What was more confusing than the newness of the room or not being searched was that no one had even spoken to him. MREs were periodically shoved through the slot, and the lights seemed to be on a regular schedule. He knew as much because he still had his watch, but maybe they had altered it somehow while he was unconscious.

Nothing made sense. After drugging him that day, why stop then? There had been no day/night disruption, no loud music played, no temperature swings, and he was convinced his food was not drugged.

As interrogations went, other than the isolation, this one seemed to be improbably benign. He was even gaining weight from the high-calorie MREs.

So, when the burst of microphone static over the intercom shattered his routine, he jerked backward in confused alarm.

A computer-generated male voice spoke:

Commander Thomas James Harding?

He steeled himself, deliberately delaying answering in order to compose himself. He sat down on the cot, leaned back with his hands cupped behind his head, and lazily said, "Yes?"

How are you feeling?

He smiled, stroking his ragged, unshaven beard. "I'm doing quite well, thank you."

I am glad to hear that. Is there anything you need?

His smile broadened, "A shower, a hot meal, a shave, and a clean uniform would be nice if you don't mind. Of course, you're probably wise not to visit me in person, at least until I've had that shower."

I will see what we can do about that. In the meantime, I have been meaning to ask, do you know why you are here?

Harding paused for a moment before saying, "I think we both know why, but why don't you enlighten me?"

You are here, Commander, because you have been a very naughty boy. Or should I call you by your nom de guerre, that is, your code name from your handlers? What was it now? Oh yes, here it is, Silver Angel?

Thomas's blood froze, and he stiffened as the voice calmly outed him. This is not how things are done! Weeks of silence only to have this happen in the first two minutes of conversation! Even though the voice was computer-generated, it spoke with shocking strength and confidence. There was no fishing or back and forth, just a declaration.

It is OK, Commander, I understand. You worked very hard to stay undetected for so long, but the truth is that you were being monitored for quite a long time before that FBI agent stumbled into things and spooked you. You see, you had been so very useful to us, given the way we fed you false information that you passed along to your handlers. We were quite upset to lose you as an asset. You served your country quite well. It is just such a shame that you did not do it on purpose.

Thomas was not sure what he was going to say. He opened his mouth to speak, but the voice cut him off....

Thomas forced a smile, "You've kept me in here for weeks in isolation with no charges and no evidence. I have no idea what you're talking about."

An hour later, the voice had finished explaining Earth, the Accipiters, The Gardeners, the Starship, and more.

Thomas shook his head and laughed. "I must say, that has to be the most creative and entertaining interrogation in history. I'm reminded of that Monty Python skit about the Spanish Inquisition torturing people with the dreaded Comfy Chair."

Thomas chuckled but could not hide the nervousness in his voice, "OK, and then what?"

And then, Commander Harding, if you do not do precisely what we tell you to do when we tell you to do it, we'll put you on a plane with the North Korean malcontents and send you to a remote island where you will be exiled with them.

Thomas stopped breathing for a moment, swallowed, and choked a reply, "You can't be serious. I have rights!"

Why no, Commander Harding, you do not. After your understandable, if regrettable, panic attack on Awakening Day, you have officially been in solitary confinement. Until now, as an officer, your career has been spotless. An example had to be set, though, and that poor girl you terrified had to be reassured that you were sufficiently punished. When it was explained to her that you were really a kind and gentle man who simply lost his mind in light of what was happening; and that you had written a long and tearful apology letter, which she was very touched by, by the way, she forgave you and has since been praying for you every morning. So, when you are released, everyone wants to put this unfortunate incident behind them.

You will work for us and do exactly what we tell you to do. This conversation, of course, never happened. People will think you are losing your mind again if you say it did.

If you betray us, you will be on that plane with the North Koreans. Then again, after we tell the North Koreans how you fed them false information that set their military back decades, I personally doubt you will exit the plane at anything other than room temperature. Of course, they will not know that the story is bullshit and that it was really the Chinese whom you betrayed your country to, but do you think that will matter to them?

Do we have an understanding?

Blue and Gold

Main Lecture Hall
September 20th, NLD 21 -- FBD 49, 7:00 AM

Vice Admiral Preston Milner looked out across the expectant faces of the uniformed men and women standing at attention who filled the massive lecture hall as he crossed the stage to the podium. Their feelings of angst and uncertainty were palpable. They had only had three weeks to digest the end of the world and the idea of a generational galactic war. He imagined the majority had lost family or at least extended family in the fall of Earth. Now, they all faced an unknowable future. The same as himself.

He paused at the podium, looking back and forth at them. "At ease. You may be seated." The room sighed with the sound of crisp clothing settling into plush new leather seats. The Gardeners had spared no expense.

The lights dimmed except for the stage. The most senior naval officers in existence were arrayed upon it, including Rear Admiral Lower Half Andre Johansson, Captains Robert Handly, George Marchetti, Henry Peishel, Alphonse Halkias, and Stephanie Mahoney. The first row of seats in the audience included Commanders Jermaine Cutter, Gene Morton, Phil Underwood, Charles Cross, and Thomas Harding, as well as Hershel Griggs, Philipa Hodge, Elijah Kleyna, Malvin Lojacono, Ramona Henry, Dwight Coughlin, Adair Henry, Alberta Sinitskaya, and Rafferty Youngman.

Preston nodded to himself, satisfied that everyone was composed and attentive despite the dark cloud of fear and uncertainty that hung over the room. Professional. He expected nothing less.

He began, "Everyone in this room volunteered to serve their country. Everyone in this room is a patriot, and I am honored to have served with you in the greatest navy of the greatest nation on Earth." He paused, "But that is the past. We are none of us in the United States Navy anymore because, as you know, there is no more United States. That was taken from us by a cowardly enemy who struck from the safety of space without warning or even a demand for surrender."

The room grumbled with anger.

"But this is not Pearl Harbor. Even the Japanese were not so despicable as to attack without attempting to have the decency at least to declare war first. Even though their declaration was not decoded and delivered to the United States before the attack, you have to at least give them credit for trying. They were not without honor, as our enemy is now."

A few in the audience chuckled softly.

"No, the Accipiters launched their first strike from the depths of space and timed it so that each kinetic impactor struck military targets and major population centers simultaneously, with no warning or mercy."

"What does that tell us? Commander Cutter, give us your analysis, please."

Jermain Cutter stood, "Yes, Sir, Admiral. The enemy arrived in a fleet of over sixty thousand starships. Clearly, they have vastly superior technology. They coordinated a superbly timed simultaneous attack on every significant military base and population center around the globe, annihilating any potential organized resistance in seconds. Either they were supremely cautious or were sufficiently concerned about our planet's military forces that they wanted to remove all such forces from the equation entirely before they set foot on the ground. Or, they considered us to be little more than ants to be crushed and did it in the most efficient way possible. The other thought that occurs to me is that it would seem that these Accipiters are not a warrior race looking for thrills and glory. If they were, I would have expected them to be itching for a fight and *want* to directly engage Earth's military forces. Lastly, by destroying our cities and infrastructure, it's apparent that they did not want anything we had. That is, nothing in our civilization was of value to them."

"Thank you, Commander."

Preston frowned, "So, the enemy might have been worried that, at least on the ground, humans would have presented some degree of threat to them. Of course, as long as the Accipiters controlled the high ground of space, we were unlikely to have any chance to win…,” he lowered his voice slightly, “but perhaps we could have at least made them pay for it.”

More nods and grunts of support and anger swelled through the crowd. He let it crest and fall before continuing.

“By now, all of you have seen the pictures of the creatures that Accipiter use to attack with—their shock troops perhaps. Their Wardog and the Stalker thing. And you have seen they can be killed. I will tell you this. If their creatures can be killed on the ground, then we will damned sure find a way to kill their ships above it. It won’t be easy, and it won’t be quick, but we will learn to kill them. It’s something we humans are very, very good at.”

Applause erupted across the room, and everyone stood, growling with determination.

Preston nodded approvingly, allowing the moment to lift their spirits, perhaps for the first time since awakening here.

“It won’t be easy,” he repeated, “and first, we must learn to master this hybrid starship the Gardeners have cobbled together for us, with which we will learn how to crawl. Soon though, we will need to do more than that. Soon we must walk and then run. We will surpass what has been given to us and build entire fleets of starships. And not just fleets in the kinds of numbers ever seen before. Not dozens of ships, not hundreds… not even thousands of ships. The Accipiters have been roaming the Galaxy, squashing civilizations like ours for a Million years. To defeat them, we will eventually have to blot out the stars with our own.”

He let that sink in for long moments, and he could see the wheels turning in their heads.

“So, you’re thinking, I’m sure, that with that kind of future ahead, every one of you will eventually have his or her own flag. Am I right?”

Nervous laughs followed, and some of the more adventurous raised their hands and nodded.

Preston smiled, “Maybe you’re right. Maybe you will. Some of you will, anyway, if we survive.”

That took a bit of wind from their sails.

"The truth is that nobody outside of science fiction has ever truly contemplated a conflict on this kind of unimaginable scale in time and space. Frankly, it had better boggle your mind because it sure as hell boggles mine!"

"As you all well know, the first United States naval vessel to sink an enemy ship was the USS Constitution, which sank the HMS Guerriere during the war of 1812. I ask you, though, how many of you have ever fought in an actual, honest-to-goodness, full-up, hot naval war?"

The only sound in the room was that of people uncomfortably shifting in their seats.

"That's right. World War II was the last full-scale naval war, and not even Admiral Johansson was around back then."

That brought a few light chuckles, although few people in the room knew that, at 51, he and Johansson were both about the same age.

"The Cold War was lots of cat and mouse, and people died, and there were lots of bush wars and drug wars and terror wars, but nothing like all-up naval battles between fleets of ships for all the marbles. So, while we have the institutional experience of operating the largest wet navy naval fleet, who knows, perhaps with the Accipiters stomping on civilizations for so long, ours may have been the largest in the Galaxy. Despite what we think is a lot of experience, in reality, every one of us will be, in effect, starting over."

"What's more, we're talking about a war in the vastness of space with technologies that none of us yet understand. So, now, we, the survivors of mankind, are expected to learn how to operate a hybrid Alien-Human ship and begin a war against an enemy so vast we can hardly comprehend it."

"Admiral Johansson, does that about sum it up?"

Andre nodded, "Pretty neatly, Admiral."

"Right, so here's what we're going to do. We are going to learn everything there is to know about this ship we have been given. We will learn to fight this ship, and then we are going to build our own. And to do that, we will need a crew. There will be a competition to see who will be on the Blue and Gold crews for her. We will follow what we know, and just like our subs, we will have two complete crews who will rotate training and deployments. When not deployed, the crews left behind will train the next Blue and Gold crew, who will be training on the simulators we will build before we can get our next ship ready. Only the very best will serve. These will be wartime crews with wartime rules and conditions."

"One of those conditions will be something our counterparts from ages past were well used to. A preliminary investigation of the starship has found nothing we think could be used for faster-than-light communication. Independence of thought and initiative will be paramount. Those of you who venture out into the black will be very far from home indeed. You will not be able to Satcom home for orders. I imagine it will be quite some time before there would even be the possibility of replenishment underway, and at least for now, there are no allies or friendly ports of call. While it is conceivable that compatible, safe, and reliable supplies might be obtainable on distant alien worlds, it is certainly not something that can be counted upon. You'll need to husband your resources wisely and manage your own repairs during your journey if you wish to survive and return to base."

"While our ancestors were used to long voyages and the independence of command that brought, even they at least had the chance to find some island or neutral port for repairs and replenishment. We must study and learn what lessons we can from their example as we take these steps into an unknown future."

Preston surveyed their sobered faces with satisfaction. These were well above average intelligence men and women, and everyone in the room had already taken their oath of allegiance to the new powers that be.

"As you know, the Navy is steeped in tradition. Much of that is ceremonial, but deep down, much more is based upon centuries of hard experience taught by the cruel sea. These will be a foundation."

He paused before continuing, "So, we're obviously no longer a Navy with multiple fleets of Carriers, Destroyers, Frigates, submarines, and support vessels. We are used to having the largest fleet, with more capital ships than the rest of our potential adversaries combined. Our strategies, postures, and mindset have been formed and shaped by that disparity. I will not lie to you. It is as though we have suddenly become a tiny 19th Century Pacific island with a single canoe declaring war against the might of the British fleet.”

“That canoe, our only vessel, the… Blood Phoenix, and the as-yet-unnamed daughter ship, which we think is a landing craft, are all we have. As you know, both types of vessels are inherently more complex than any ship ever built by man.”

“If we are to prosecute this war successfully, we must change our thinking. We must search for new technologies and asymmetrical weapons and systems with which to engage the enemy. Furthermore, we can ill afford losses. Our enemy can soak up attrition on a truly Galactic scale. I must also point out that these Gardeners have not bothered to define what they expect us to accomplish, despite their gun to our head. They have not defined victory.”

“Do you want to know why?”

The room stirred with dark murmurs until a young Lieutenant shouted, “Yes, Sir!”

Preston smiled grimly, “Thank you, Lieutenant. I’m sure you’ll go far.”

Those around the Lieutenant slapped him on the back, and a gentle wave of soft laughter rolled over the room.

“The reason why the Gardeners did not define Victory is that they don’t actually know. My guess is that they’ve never fought a war themselves, and as for the Accipiters, if they ever actually did fight a stand-up war, it’s been so long ago that it’s probably mythology for them.”

“The people from Joint Reserve Base Fort Brazos and the citizens of Fort Brazos, in the chaos following their Awakening Day, joined together and elected leaders.”

He paused, “Let me rephrase, they *drafted* two good people into the job. One was a capable air force Major, and the other was from the civilian government, their Sheriff who demonstrated his metal defending himself and his child by being the first to kill an alien. Vice President Gail Finley and President John Austin are our elected leaders. I wonder how many of us could have coped nearly as well with the weight that’s been put on their shoulders?”

He looked around the room, challenging anyone to respond. None did.

"I've had a chance to watch their acceptance speeches. You can tell they were unscripted and that they came from their hearts. President Austin said that mankind as a species was forged in the crucible of war. In many ways, for good and for bad, we've turned war into an art."

He paused again, turned, and looked at Andre, then at the captains and commanders nearby, and then scanned the crowd. "You will be mankind's artisans of war, and as President Austin said, we shall paint the stars with Accipiter blood. And as Vice President Finley declared, we shall wear their cursed feathers and dance on their graves, and their blood shall wash the foul pollution of their footsteps from the Earth!"

The room erupted in shouts and applause, but Preston held up his hands, and the room quieted.

"How do we define Victory? We define Victory as being when the Accipiter fleet is smashed, and their filthy and broken surviving remnants tremble and weep before us!"

The audience leaped to their feet, shouting Hooyah! And applauding in a thunderous ovation.

Preston let them continue for a full minute before raising his hands to quiet the room.

"On to business. The selection board has appointed commanding officers for the starship and the landing craft. These men are, or were, current Virginia Class submarine commanders. The commanding officers of the Blood Phoenix will be senior, with more time in service and rank, with the landing craft also commanded by experienced boat commanders. Still, we only have one ship, so the selection does not reflect them. It's just the reality of the situation."

"The Blue and Gold crews and commanders will alternate between deployments and maintenance cycles. Since deployments seem likely to be at least as long as submarine crews are currently used to, or perhaps much longer, this practice will afford returning crews more time for rest and training. The non-deployed crew will train in simulators and plan the next mission, as well as assist in the design and building of the starships we will eventually build ourselves."

"The Blue crew will be commanded by Commander Jermaine Cutter of the Hyman Rickover, who will shortly be promoted to Captain. Commander Gene Morton of the Vermont will command the primary landing craft ship and serve as second in command. Gold Crew will be commanded by Commander Phil Underwood of the Ohio, also shortly to be promoted to Captain. Commander Charles Cross of the John Warner will command the landing craft. Commanders for the other landing craft vessels will be selected at a later date. Gentlemen, please stand."

They stood and turned to face the audience.

"These men will select their crews from the rest of you. While we expect to keep a similar command and crew structure to what we have traditionally deployed on our submarines, be aware that the Commanders have been given leave to select anyone they want whom they feel would be best in a given slot—regardless of their current rank, time in rank, or experience."

The room began to stir with, if not excitement, at least a sense of anticipation and barely suppressed whispers of questions and discussion.

Preston lowered his voice, "I want everyone here to remember that these so-called Gardeners, whoever they are, and whatever their true motives are, chose to rescue only a tiny fraction of humanity. They chose us to be the tip of the sword, and every surviving man, woman, and child depends on *us* to successfully engage the Accipiters. The fate and the hopes of mankind are in your hands. Don't let them down!" He paused, then shouted, "Hooyah!"

The applause was hungry, angry, and immediate, with echoing shouts of Hooyah! Many jumped to their feet, and in moments, the enormous hall fairly shook with thunderous standing ovation.

Evacuation

The New London Stadium was not simply massive; it was elegant and sweeping in its lines and form. The exterior borrowed heavily from Frank Lloyd Wright's Guggenheim Museum, but instead of spiraling inward to a dome, it was inverted, spiraling outwards, forming the stadium's bowl.

More than one person had reflected upon how in New London, the Gardeners had not just copied and pasted existing human structures, as they had done downside. In New London, everything was unique but still clearly inspired by human art and design. The quiet hope was that this somehow implied that, on some level, the Gardeners might have an appreciation of humankind beyond its potential to become their proxy military force. Whether it bode well for the long term was anyone's guess.

With no food in New London, everything had to be brought up by elevator. Prior to the discovery of New London, Wayne and Sybil Blanchard had been given the contract to manage civilian government and military freight transportation. This mainly involved convoys out to the newly built forward operating bases miles outside Fort Brazos, the city, and the military base. Their job included managing the logistics of moving supplies up to New London and ferrying refugees back downside.

Now, after weeks of hauling food, clothing, and supplies, the Blanchards, and the other drivers had become deeply involved in "processing" the New Londoners slated to be evacuated down to Fort Brazos.

It was not simply a matter of herding people onto the elevator platform. Indeed, many had outright refused to go, fearing some macabre unknown fate for those who did. Now, a percentage of every group who made the trip subsequently returned with firsthand news of conditions – and the safety to be found DownSide in Fort Brazos.

Despite this, many remained fearful and distrustful. Rumors of conspiracy and malfeasance abounded.

"Processing" involved more than simply gathering names, family information, and date of birth. Each person was interviewed, and detailed information was recorded about their background, education, previous jobs, and skills. This data is directly input into the newly built skills and jobs database. A wartime economy with a limited population would need both judicious and intelligent job placement. No one was being 'drafted' against their will as yet. There was still hope of avoiding a slide into totalitarianism.

Mayor Parker and the City Council of Fort Brazos had insisted that the 'ambassadors' to TopSide not be military or 'men in suits.' Gloria Vargas had used harsher language. After so much time handing out supplies and answering questions about DownSide, the Blanchards and the other drivers were by now familiar faces and were perceived as being 'ordinary people.' Expanding their role to become informal census takers was the logical next step.

Each evacuee was interviewed and given a backpack with a change of clothes, personal toiletries, cash, a Fort Brazos map, bus route, directions to their assigned living accommodations, a water bottle, and a selection of MREs. Questions were encouraged, and no time limit was set on how long the process was supposed to take. It was slow, but people could take their time and not feel rushed or 'herded.' Slowing things down also made the situation more manageable back on the ground in Fort Brazos.

Councilwoman Esmerelda Collins had set up an information desk and brought a youth singing group to perform, trying to keep people's spirits up. Hundreds of books and magazines were brought up from the library, and several "comfort" dogs and cats formerly 'employed' at local hospices were brought TopSide as well. They were a big hit, especially with the children.

The semi-trucks had been backed into the stadium area, and cafeteria tables set up on the turf at the rear trailer openings so that access to the backpacks and supplies was easier.

Sybil stood in front of their table. Wayne sat behind it and their truck and trailer. After the Wardog had smashed their front grill, the army had removed it for study and, surprisingly, replaced it. Wayne and Sybil were thoughtful enough not to ask where the replacement had been sourced from.

Most of the adults in the crowd were pensive and hesitant. More than a few hung back in small groups, talking in low, worried tones. For the most part, the children were children – playing games and finding ways to burn off excess energy.

✪ ✪ ✪

When Wayne and Sybil had started that morning, Wayne had noticed how outgoing and perceptive Sybil was in talking to everyone she met. Since Awakening Day, she had gradually evolved from the shy, reserved mouse of a girl with somewhat wild long brown hair. At barely a hundred pounds soaking wet, Sybil seemed tiny next to Wayne's thick-boned two-fifty.

Instead of shrinking from people behind the paperwork needed to run their operation, Sybil had blossomed. She now seemed to have an uncanny way of relating to and engaging everyone she met. It had been tentative at first, like trying on a new pair of shoes, but she had grown more and more confident and outgoing.

Today, though, thousands of new faces were coming and going in a blur of activity instead of the typical number of people they might interact with daily.

One of them, a Navy officer, walked by as he delivered clipboards and forms to the next table. He was wearing the same bright yellow safety vest all the aid workers were wearing, covering up his rank insignia. A pair of children were chasing a playful dog and careened into his path. He abruptly stepped backward to avoid them, bumping into Sybil.

"Excuse me," he mumbled over his shoulder and left.

Sybil turned to face Wayne across the card table. Even though it was a constant 72 degrees in New London, Wayne noticed that Sybil's face was suddenly covered in a sheen of sweat, and her eyes widened in surprise… and fear.

Sybil staggered forward, knocking the table over and sending papers and water bottles flying. She swayed, her eyes dilated and wide. She cried out, "Wayne!? I can't… I… I ca-ca-can't see…."

Wayne jumped up, "Baby? What's wrong?"

And then she went completely rigid and fell into his terrified arms. She began convulsing, her eyes blinking and teeth chattering as she started frothing at the mouth while her arms and legs jerked wildly.

A middle-aged woman with long brown hair, clutching her purse to her chest, backed away from the scene, her mouth agape as she screamed, "Something's happening! They're poisoning us!"

Her companion, a lanky man with oversized glasses, shook his head, "Or it's some alien virus! Let's get out of here!"

Pandemonium erupted in the already nervous and distrustful crowd as people screamed and ran for any exit they could find.

Against the flow, several nurses and Navy doctors of differing specialties rushed to Sybil's aid. Wayne cried out in panic as he tried to hold Sybil's head steady, "Help her! Somebody, please! She's pregnant! Somebody help us!"

✪ ✪ ✪

The following two hours were a daze for Wayne as he was peppered with questions.

'No, she's not epileptic.'
'No, she has not had a head injury or any injury or infection.'
'No, she's never had a seizure.'
'No, she has no family history of epilepsy.'
'No, she doesn't take any drugs or medications other than vitamins.'
'No, she has not had any alcohol today.'
'No, she has not eaten anything unusual or that I didn't eat as well.'
'No, she does not suffer from depression.'

After the convulsions slowly subsided, Sybil blinked and looked around but did not seem to focus on anything around her or respond to anyone, including Wayne. Whatever she was seeing was not present. Struggling to form words, her lips trembling and her eyes darting about, "void… there… so many… too many… touch me…." Then she violently shuddered and just as suddenly relaxed. She curled into a ball, crying aloud, "Nnnnno! Nnnnoo! Nnnnot! Yyyyyououuu cccccan't! "

Then she slumped and fell unconscious.

Sybil awakened in a hospital bed connected via wires to various sensors on her chest, head, and body. A nearby wall screen displayed an electrocardiogram, X-Ray, CT, blood work, and other data. She blinked rapidly, trying to focus her eyes.

Wayne sat slumped in a chair next to her bed, his hand on hers, snoring softly.

She sat up on one arm, "Wayne? What happened? Why do I hurt all over? Where am I?"

Wayne startled awake, "Baby! Baby? How do you feel?" He called over his shoulder, "Doctor! She's awake!"

Colonel (Dr.) Gwyneth Elliot had already been in New London, supervising health reviews of the perfectly healthy New Londoners before clearing them for departure to Fort Brazos. Since Awakening Day, it had been discovered that all the survivors had been cured of all diseases. So far, it appeared that the same was true for the New London survivors, but it seemed prudent to gather more baseline data for comparison. It also reassured the New Londoners that they were being cared for.

Gwyneth, herself a former Olympic Biathlon silver medalist, moved with effortless grace into the room, "Well, Mrs. Blanchard, how are you feeling?"

Sybil suddenly realized she was naked in a hospital gown. She pulled the sheet up around her, "I'm fine. What the hell is going on? Where am I? Why are you here, Gwyneth?"

Gwyneth paused, "Oh, do we know each other, Mrs. Blanchard?"

Sybil blinked, "Uhm, I'm fine I said. And you're wearing a nametag. Where am I, and what is going on?"

Gwyneth looked down at her nametag that read ELLIOT.

Wayne took Sybil's hand, "Sweetie, you had a seizure. A big one. This is the hospital near the elevator to New London."

Gwyneth cocked her head, "Yes, the Gardeners spared no expense. This place seems to have the most advanced equipment I have ever heard of. It is totally state of the art."

Sybil shook her head, "I don't understand."

Gwyneth took Sybil's wrist from Wayne, felt her pulse, and then used her stethoscope to listen to her chest. "Mrs. Blanchard, you are the first person to have a seizure since Awakening Day. In fact, since Awakening Day, you are the first person to exhibit any symptom of any medical condition other than from injury… or pregnancy. Since nobody knows the long-term effects of what was done to us by the Gardeners, we wanted to keep an eye on you."

Sybil sank back into her pillow, "In case I'm not the first, or if it has something to do with being pregnant, here, in this place? You're worried it might happen to you too?"

Gwyneth paused, studying Sybil's face. Her own pregnancy hardly showed, especially with the loose lab coat she was wearing. "I'm sorry again. Do we know each other?"

Sybil looked at her, then looked away, biting her lip. "No, but just about everyone is pregnant now, aren't they. And you're wearing a new-looking ring, and… you have the look."

Gwyneth forced a smile, "I see. Well then, let me assure you that you seem to be perfectly fine now. We've run every test we could think of, using all the fancy equipment here, and, oh, by the way, you're the first patient here too, and we cannot find anything wrong with you other than the debilitating after-effects of a seizure-like the one you apparently suffered."

Wayne cooed, "See, you're gonna' be just fine, baby."

Sybil nodded to Gwyneth, "But since you cannot find anything wrong, you're worried." She reached out, grasped Gwyneth's wrist, and stared deeply into her eyes.

Gwyneth tried to pull back, but she stopped. There was no violence in Sybil's eyes.

Wayne reached out to disengage them, but Sybil looked at him, "It's OK, Wayne. I know I can trust her. I'm going to tell her what you have begun to suspect."

Wayne shook his head, "Baby, please stop this. What is wrong with you?"

Sybil's chest heaved, and she sobbed briefly, "You are Gwyneth Elliot. You recently… last week... married David Duncan," she smiled, "I know David too. He has so many ghosts he can't let go of; they haunt him."

Gwyneth finally wrenched herself free, blinking in surprise, "What are you doing?"

Sybil closed her eyes, "I remember you from there… from the void. You were just as beautiful there as you are here. You should have won gold at the Olympics that year, but someone did something that made you lose two points. One of the judges…. A German NATO Colonel made advances, and it upset you…."

Gwyneth inhaled sharply, and her eyes widened in shock, "How can you possibly know that! I never told anyone that!"

Sybil opened her eyes and looked at Wayne, who was bewildered and confused. She reached out and touched his face.

"Because my darling, and Gwyneth, because I know you all. I know everyone from… the void. When I am near you, I can remember you. Things about you. Whether you were good… or bad…. And sometimes more."

Gwyneth asked in a small voice, "And if I believe you… why are you telling me this? Why now?"

Sybil sank her head back onto her pillow, looked up at the ceiling, and sighed, strength leaving her body, "Because… because there were too many people at the stadium… I… I think I overloaded. And…"

Wayne caressed her hair, "Baby, what's going on? What are you telling us?"

Tears welled up in Sybil's wide-open eyes. She whispered, "Because there was someone there who is bad… very… very… bad….and…he is planning to do something…. terrible."

And then she sighed, closed her eyes, slumped deep into the pillow, and became still.

Wayne panicked, "Sybil!" He turned to Gweneth, pleading, "Please help her!"

Gwyneth glanced up at the monitors on the wall and shook her head, "She's okay, Mr. Blanchard. She's sleeping."

Gwyneth and Wayne stood outside the hospital room with the glass door closed.

Wayne sighed, "What's going on, Doctor?"

Gwyneth steeled herself, "Mr. Blanchard, tell me about your wife."

Wayne shook his head and pointed through the glass at Sybil, "Doctor, that woman is the sanest, kindest, most patient woman I've ever known."

Gwyneth began to pace, "Tell me, have you noticed anything different about her? Since Awakening Day?"

Wayne started, "I… well… she's been a little more outgoing. Not as shy."

"Is that all?"

Wayne frowned, thinking. "She… she… it's like she knows what to say to people. She was always so shy before." He hesitated, "It's like, now, like she isn't nervous anymore. Like she knows everyone. I've just been so happy that she has been happy here. I didn't want to make a big deal of it."

"When was the first time you noticed this new… awareness in her?"

Wayne blinked and sat down at a chair beside the nurse's station. "The first day… when we found that poor preacher."

Gwyneth blinked in surprise, "What?"

Wayne nodded, "It was an awful accident. The mayor and the preacher's truck plowed into a whole herd of panicked deer. This big buck went right through the windshield, and its antlers impaled that poor preacher." He shook his head, "There was blood everywhere. It was an awful mess."

Gwyneth's eyes widened, and she swallowed hard, "And you went to Methodist Hospital."

Wayne looked up, "Yeah, that's right. How did you know that?"

Gwyneth shook her head, "Because David told me that a crazy lady came into the hospital, knew him by name, talked about his… his ghosts…. Men he saved after many hours of battlefield surgery. They were all killed by a mortar shell shortly after David had left the surgery tent. At Methodist hospital, he had just worked on a heart patient who no longer had a heart condition, and the surgery nearly killed the man. David told me a crazy lady told him that nobody was sick, and that's when he realized that the problems they were having with their patients were because they were treating them for conditions they no longer had – that the treatments themselves were killing them."

Wayne stared blank-faced at her.

"David described the crazy lady to me later. He said she was very short, with long curly, somewhat frizzy brown hair, very busty, with pale skin and brown eyes." She looked through the glass at Sybil, "Does that sound like anyone you know, Mr. Blanchard?"

36 Hours Later

Wayne was asleep in the guest chair beside the bed when Sybil woke up.

Gwyneth was sitting on the bed next to Sybil, blotting her forehead with a damp cloth.

Sybil blinked and looked up at Gwyneth, then over at Wayne.

Gwyneth smiled, "Be gentle on him, dear, you've been here for three days, and he's had maybe two hours of sleep. You are lucky. He refuses to leave your side for more than a few minutes at a time. He's a good man, isn't he?"

Sybil nodded, "He's the only man I've ever… I've ever felt completely at ease with."

"Well, he adores you, worships you, you know."

Sybil pouted, "I know… I don't deserve him."

"I'm sure he feels the same way."

Sybil smiled gently, "He saved me, you know."

Gwyneth nodded, "I'm not surprised. Tell me."

"I'm… I was… not just shy… I was almost a shut-in. I hardly ever left the house, and my parents were worried about me. They tried everything. Then one day, one of my brother's friends visited. He was this huge, hulking… gentle giant of a boy."

Gwyneth smiled again, "And he saved you."

"Yes, he did. Treated me like a princess. His… China Doll, he called me."

"I'll bet he was a perfect gentleman."

Sybil sniffed, "Yes, he was. Oh, don't get me wrong… the attraction was there… oh my, was it there… but he never once pushed me."

They let the silence hang between them for a while.

Gwyneth asked, "And until Awakening Day, you stayed in his shadow and let him deal with people?"

Sybil nodded silently.

"Mrs. Blanchard…"

"Call me Sybil."

"OK, Sybil. Why did you decide to tell me all this? You've obviously kept it to yourself until now."

Sybil swallowed, "I didn't understand what was happening at first, and it wasn't… it wasn't consistent. Sometimes it would overwhelm me, and other times I did not feel anything at all. But over time, it happened more and more, and it scared me at first. And then, for the first time in my life, I actually understood people. I could talk to them. I could be…."

"Outgoing?"

Sybil nodded and frowned, "Is that terrible? I was cheating."

Gwyneth smiled softly, "Sybil… you were not outgoing because of some trick or some tactic. It is not your fault that you now, well, now, you really do know everyone, and it has let you open up. Maybe it is letting you be the person you truly were inside?”

Sybil turned her head and looked longingly at Wayne.

Gwyneth sat back in her chair, “And Wayne?”

Sybil’s chest heaved, “I was….”

“You were afraid he wouldn’t understand… that he might leave you because now you were different.”

Sybil nodded rapidly, and her tears flowed, “I’m a freak. I know it’s stupid.”

“It's human, and you are no more a freak than the rest of us.” Gwyneth smiled softly and whispered, “Let me tell you about that kind of man. I doubt he would have left you if you had grown horns from your head.”

Sybil snorted and laughed, then cringed in pain, clutching her chest. Wayne stirred in his chair but did not wake.

Gwyneth nodded, “You’re going to be sore for a while. I think when you fell, your chest hit a chair or the table or something. You have a fractured rib.”

Sybil grimaced and swallowed, “You asked… why now?”

“Yes?”

“Because at the stadium, a man bumped into me. I didn’t see his face, but I knew him from… from the void. I could… I could *feel* him. There was something dark, cruel, and twisted about him, even in the void. He is… He’s dangerous, and he is planning something terrible.”

“And you felt strongly enough about this to break your silence and tell me your secret.”

Gwyneth thought for a moment, “You knew my name. What was his?”

Sybil winced, “I don’t know! You are… were… open and… bright. Even there, even in the void, he was twisted inside so much that I couldn’t see his name like he hides things even from himself.”

Sybil tried to sit up, and Gwyneth helped her and propped a pillow up behind her. Sybil asked, “Maybe there was video? Maybe I could see who….”

Gwyneth shook her head, “After your seizure, one of the first things I did was to send someone back there to find out. If I could see a video of your seizure, it would help with your diagnosis.”

Sybil slumped back onto the pillow. "All for nothing."

Gwyneth scolded her, "Enough of that talk! Now, you listen to me. What has happened to you is more than extraordinary. The Gardeners did a lot of things to us. They cured our diseases, reversed infertility, and undid tied tubes and hysterectomies and vasectomies, and we think greatly extended our lifespans. What you are experiencing is the very first time we have seen something beyond those things. You are an extraordinary woman who has been gifted with something very special."

Sybil looked away, her lips trembling, "What's going to happen to me?"

Gwyneth smiled, "Why my dear, in another day or so, you'll leave this hospital and go home with a man who seems to love you more than life itself. Then in a few months, after being sure to visit me as your new personal doctor every two weeks, you will have healthy babies that I fully expect to spend lots of time with. If you will allow me, we can share pregnancy stories and miseries and maybe even babysit each other's kids…. What will happen to you is you will go live your life."

Sybil turned back and looked at Gwyneth, biting her lip, "You're not going to lock me away to study me?"

Gwyneth smiled brightly, "Oh, I'll keep an eye on you and will be the best doctor you've ever had. Maybe together, over time, we can begin to understand what has happened to you."

Sybil looked doubtful, "And…. Why? Why me?"

Gwyneth reached out and patted Sybil's hand, "I hope we can figure that out. Oh, if you had some dread disease or were in some way a threat to others, I'd be compelled to do something about it. But you aren't sick, and I certainly don't believe you are a threat. In fact, I hope to become your friend as well as your doctor, Sybil. For now, though, I *am* your doctor, and what has been said between us stays that way. You and Wayne mustn't tell anyone else."

She pointedly did not say that if there indeed was an evil man out there plotting something terrible, the absolute worst thing that she could do would be to make it known, even in rarified circles, that there was a kind, gentle little woman out there who knew his secrets.

NTN Atlatl

NTN Atlatl Bridge. December 6th, NLD 98 -- FBD 126, 19:45

Commander Charles Cross, formerly of the United States Navy, now sworn into service into the newly named NTN, the New Texas Navy, suppressed the urge to rub his sore neck. The 'shuttle's alien bridge/CIC was not cramped by any means. The original Builders had evidently been physically larger than humans. The myriad human-made displays and adapted controls were, by necessity, different from those in the Blood Phoenix, and the numbers and physics were still a lot for even Charles Cross, with his Ph.D. in Physics and M.S. in Electrical Engineering, to absorb.

The sublight warp-capable "shuttle" had been designated the NTN Atlatl, i.e., The Spear Thrower, and was classified as an "ILC" or Interplanetary Landing Craft.

The flight controls of the ILCs were similar to those in the Blood Phoenix, if simpler. On the other hand, the Blood Phoenix still had months or perhaps years of work to integrate systems. Rather high on the list was figuring out life support and how to generate oxygen without being in an ocean. The hull itself wasn't even completely sealed. Meanwhile, the ILCs didn't have these problems. They were ready-built and completely finished (and alien) craft. The Gardeners had added human interfaces and controls. Naturally, the comprehensive, if slightly redacted, operations manuals took years (and, likely, lost lives) out of the equation.

By design, the ILCs were not long-duration craft. Nor were they capable of interstellar flight. Their warp drives could only alter space around the vehicle enough to achieve a high fraction of the speed of light but could not exceed it.

So, they were pretty handy for darting about a star system with astonishing speed – but not for leaving it.

Once the operations manuals had been discovered, it had made perfect sense to begin training in them and exploring the space around New Texas.

The Atlatl measured 130' long, including its oddly shaped close-wrapped warp rings, and 80' wide, and after moving one of them downside, they knew it weighed in at close to 758,000 lbs. The ship was almost all cargo space, with a ramp that telescoped out from the wide cargo bay doors. The interior cargo space was just over 70' long, just as wide, and 30' tall. Forward of the cargo section were the main guts of the vessel, including environmental controls, abbreviated living space/crew area, and the "Bridge."

Like the Blood Phoenix, the warp rings appeared to self-contain their operating technology. Unlike the larger vessel, however, there were no dorsal and ventral nodes. The 'Pilot' stations were on the Bridge.

For the past month, Charles had been taking the Atlatl out and mercilessly drilling the crew. They had done easy things at first, like circling and doing detailed maps of the very mundane-looking rock that New Texas appeared to be from the outside. They'd stretched their legs and whipped around the star system, testing the limits of the drive, which turned out to be quite handy.

Captain Cutter and Commander Morton had similarly been training and drilling crews on two of the additional ILCs from the second hangar bay. The ILC that had been transported down the elevator to Fort Brazos was being used to train the assault teams in an environment with an atmosphere, simulating what they would need to do during the mission to Earth.

Charles had taken Atlatl out, and they had even "landed" on some of the bigger rocks in the system, although no one was quite brave enough to land on "the roof of their world" and risk… anything. After flight tests, loading and unloading drills were carried out repeatedly, determining the best cargo loading layouts and tiedown locations. Master Chiefs cracked the proverbial whip, whittling down the loading and unloading times, doing their evil best to throw in as many mechanical problems and breakdowns as they could dream up.

No one knew what opposition they would face on the ground in future conflicts or if they indeed went back to Earth. On the other hand, no one doubted that speed would be paramount in any case.

It was the end of a very long day of exercises, and the Atlatl was in the process of being slowly "tractored" into the main hanger along the gravity gradient.

Charles absently fingered the new patch on his shoulder. The name "New Texas Navy" had been vehemently opposed by nearly everyone. The problem was that while Americans almost entirely dominated the population of New London, there were still many allied navy personnel there. In addition, downside, nearly 13,000 soldiers and airmen from the militaries of many different nations had been abducted along with everyone else.

While still objectionable, "New Texas" was less problematic than calling it the "United States." While few had firsthand knowledge about pre-Awakening-Day Texas's realities, most people at least knew the name. They associated it with Hollywood movies or at least some sort of 'cowboy' attitude. There was a lot of grumbling. Even most of those who had been stationed downside in Fort Brazos had not been actual "Texans," so it had the hallmarks of a workable compromise – few from any of the other countries actually liked it.

Without any sensation of movement, the Atlatl came to a stop at its designated berth near the Blood Phoenix.

Charles walked over and put his hand on Petty Officer Hiram Newman's shoulder, "Mr. Newman, my compliments to Control for a smooth berthing."

Hiram replied, "Notify Control of smooth berthing, aye." He spoke quietly into his headset, "Control, Atlatl, Captain's compliments on a smooth berthing…. Acknowledge, Control." Hiram turned and looked up at Charles, "Control acknowledges and welcomes Atlatl back."

Outside the Atlatl, in the bay, warning lights flashed as the bay re-pressurized. The process was even faster than the depressurization cycle.

Charles nodded to Lt. Stephen Prichard, "Secure from Space, Mr. Prichard."

Stephen nodded sharply in return, "Secure from Space, Aye." He squeezed a control on his headset, "All Compartments, secure from space."

Wedding Bells

DownSide: First United Methodist Church

Christmas Day
December 25th, NLD 117 -- FBD 145, 11:14 AM

In the chaos and uncertainty following Awakening Day, many everyday things that had been routine or normal had been forgotten or studiously ignored. Traditional holiday celebrations had seemed incredibly insensitive after so many had died. The crushing weight of it all had not collapsed the survivors entirely because too many things had happened to focus their attention elsewhere.

Tom and the council realized that something needed to change and that efforts needed to be made to lift spirits. The flurry of weddings, almost all of which had been extremely low-key or simply done at the courthouse with no fanfare at all, had given Esmerelda Collins an idea. When Sandra Hoffman told her that she planned to go to the courthouse and marry David Garreth, Esmerelda put her foot down.

Sandra and David had gone through hell together and become a much talked about and celebrated couple. That is when Esmerelda got the idea to combine their wedding – with Christmas and create a public event that might just possibly begin the healing process. The idea had blossomed and grown in size and scope, with parties and celebrations beginning for days in advance. All across Fort Brazos, Dozens of weddings were planned for that day, including many who had quietly gone the courthouse route earlier and now wanted to "re-do" it "right."

Sandra and David's ceremony would kick off an entire day of other marriages and parties, ending with evening fireworks.

The entire city had come alive with every decoration people could dig out of their attics and more. Streetlamps leading up to the church were lavishly wrapped in red bows, and flowers lined the streets.

Usually, at Christmas, the First United Methodist Church buildings and sanctuary were modestly and tastefully decorated with poinsettias, candles, red and green fabric-draped garlands, and modestly lit Christmas trees. This time, however, volunteers came from all over town and from every denomination to help. The church grounds soon grew to resemble a fantastic Swiss Christmas Village.

The sentiment of all the volunteers had been emphatic; *the Accipiters cannot take who we are away from us!*

✪ ✪ ✪

Tom Parker, Mayor of Fort Brazos, and in this context, Interim Pastor and Senior Deacon at First United Methodist Church, stood at the podium looking out across a standing-room-only congregation. The combined adult and children's choir sang a selection of traditional and a few more contemporary pieces.

Tom was a people person. He was a politician and community leader who truly loved his job and his city. His wife Dotty was in the choir behind him, and all of his City Council colleagues were in the first few rows in front of him, including a perfectly beaming Esmerelda Collins, who sat on the first row of the Bride's side, but more on that later.

Tom loved to serve his community and his church. Doing so filled him with a sense of purpose, accomplishment, and fulfillment. He held his duties in the highest regard, as, well, sacred. In the five months since Awakening Day, though, the crushing weight of the responsibility for decisions that quite literally affected the entirety of what remained of mankind had worn on him. As mankind was being called to war, his role as mayor in the relatively small and remote city of Fort Brazos had been transformed. He did his best to serve, but the joy of being a simple mayor had evaporated.

Standing behind the church pulpit, he realized that it was in this duty and place that he found his true calling. It was not just that it was a happy occasion, although that didn't hurt. This wedding had become a symbol of hope. After the unspeakable tragedy that was Awakening Day, young Sandra Hoffman and her entire family had been brutally attacked and physically cocooned in the first alien creature attack on the Fort Brazos survivors. Her mother Margaret, her father

Barrett, who had been a City Councilman and close friend of Tom's, and her brother Nolan had all died. Her grandmother Abigail had been one of the thousands, the 5%, who had not woken up at all. Only her younger sisters Jordan, Hannah, and Elizabeth, along with their two-year-old brother Vicktor, had lived.

A welfare check on the missing Barrett family had subsequently turned tragic when the patrol had also been attacked by the creature, killing Corpsman Mendez and Deputy Sheriff Grayson Miles. David Garreth, Specialist Simmons, and Sergeant Washington survived the ordeal after being cocooned.

After the survivors had all been rescued, Sandra Hoffman and David had bonded…. It had not been long before everyone in Fort Brazos had learned of the budding romance between them. A few betting pools questioned the odds of it lasting, but anyone who saw the two together knew better.

Captain David Garreth, chisel-faced and poster-perfect in his dress uniform, now stood in front of Tom, facing his bride-to-be. Sandra's sister Jordan stood next to her as her maid of honor, and Sergeant Darryl Washington stood next to David as his best man.

David had no living family after Awakening Day, but the groom's side was not empty. Specialist Simmons and the rest of his original unit filled out the first several rows, along with Major General Alexander Marcus, Captain Darryl Guevara, and, oh, Vice President Gail Finley and many more. General Marcus himself had escorted David down the aisle minutes before.

Councilwoman Esmerelda Collins sat on the bride's side in the front row. Esmerelda had escorted Sandra in the Bride's procession with nine-year-old Elizabeth and two-and-a-half-year-old Viktor following, throwing rose petals. As Sandra's godmother, she had taken the Hoffman family under her wing after the tragedy. Later, with their unanimous consent, she formally adopted them all. Her own two grown children had been lost, not being present in Fort Brazos on Awakening Day. So, Esmerelda, Hannah, Elizabeth, and Viktor sat in the first row.

The rest of the city council, President John Austin, and his daughter Matilda sat behind them, along with many, many more. The presidential and council security details were deployed both inside and outside the church.

Many cameras were set up around the room, including the static cameras that the Church used, news cameras from the remaining TV station, and the Fort Brazos Joint Reserve Base public relations unit. Then there was the local wedding photographer that Esmerelda had hired. It would be the most publicly recorded and broadcast wedding in Fort Brazo's history.

The bride-to-be, Sandra Hoffman, was radiant in her mother's brocade wedding dress, which had been skillfully altered to accommodate the modest bulge from Sandra's pregnancy. Sandra had fretted that the pregnancy would cause a scandal. Fort Brazos was, after all, a very conservative place. She needn't have worried, though. The overwhelming reaction to the news that Fort Brazos's own 'celebrity couple' were with child had been met with almost delirious joy in some quarters and, at the very least, amused happiness in most others.

It had been some of the first good news the survivors of mankind had heard. By the time news of the pregnancy had filtered out, thousands of other women had discovered their own unexpected pregnancies. Due to the Gardener-reversed vasectomies and even hysterectomies, many were quite shocked. More than that, many women who had already gone through menopause had either gotten pregnant as well or had been stunned at the return of their periods—all at the same time.

There was going to be a baby boom, the likes of which no one had ever seen before.

In the 1950s, the fertility rate among women in the United States was nearly 120 out of a thousand. By the 2000s, the rate had plummeted to half that number. Now, the numbers Tom was seeing reported were closer to 250 out of a thousand, possibly much more. The projections called for perhaps anywhere from 5,000 to 10,000 babies.

Shockingly, most pregnancies had turned out to be multiples – twins or even more. All due in a relatively narrow window of time a few short months from now. There were not remotely enough hospital beds to handle the expected tsunami of pregnant women, so creative plans were being drawn up to cope with it.

All of that was in the future. For now, Sandra and David became not just a symbol of hope but a positive personification of what so many thousands were going through themselves.

Tom took a breath and began, "Let us pray."

"Our dear heavenly father, before you this day stands a young couple who found each other out of tragedy, unbearable loss, and evil and malicious actions that ended our world. Despite this, their love stands as a shining testament to the power and strength and hope that is possible between two of your children."

"As Sandra and David join their lives together on this their wedding day, we pray that you will bind their hearts together with you as their center. Make this day a beautiful celebration unlike any other, and one they and their new extended family will treasure forever."

"For today, Father, we celebrate not just the joining of Sandra and David, but of the new family formed by Sandra's godmother, Esmerelda Collins. Father, I knew Barrett and Margaret Hoffman well. They were dear friends. I can say here to everyone present that there is absolutely no doubt in my heart that Barrett and Margaret would approve. It is no coincidence that the adoption papers were postdated to take effect as of today. It is my honor and joy to announce that Sandra and David have not only formed their own family, but they have both joined with another. Amen"

The congregation echoed the Amen.

Tom's eyes misted, "And by extension, in the sight of God, Sandra and David, I will remind you both that you are also part of the larger family of Fort Brazos itself."

"Dear Lord, as this young man and woman offer their vows today, we ask that you give them a clear understanding of their commitment to each other and to you. Help them understand how they are now truly one person, united in your love."

"And in that love, may theirs for each other, like the wedding rings they shall wear, be a circle that never ends. Father, teach them patience and kindness for each other. Let their love be neither boastful nor proud, but selfless and trusting. May they love, protect and serve each other throughout every season of life."

"Father, as Sandra and David build their home together, we pray it will be a place of healing and joy that it would be a Godly home where pain is replaced by hope, and their hearts are sealed with forgiveness. Let their home be shared in honesty, gentleness, joy, laughter, and kindness."

"Father, we pray that the radiance of your love would shine upon them, bless them, and grant them peace that passes all understanding. Lead them to love you with all their heart, soul, and strength. Help them bear each other's burdens, even as they cast their cares upon your mighty shoulders. May they always see the best in each other, even in the worst of times."

"Father, help Sandra and David cherish their wedding day and treasure it as a reminder of hope and faith to give them strength. That all things are possible through Christ."

"Lord, on this their sacred wedding day, may they always remember every word spoken. Together, this couple stands before you, side by side, hand in hand, basking in the glow of their love for each other. Father, may you always hold them this tightly together and never let them go. Fill their hearts with your love, grace, and wisdom. And as they with great joy and anticipation bring new life into this world, father, we pray your blessings upon this union and their family, forevermore."

✪ ✪ ✪

Sandra Collins Hoffman Garreth and her dashing groom had left through the crossed swords of David's fellow Army Rangers and departed. The guests filtered out, and only the sound and video technicians remained, breaking down equipment and collecting cables.

Tom and Dotti Parker sat on the steps of the stage reminiscing about their own wedding and other's past, but Tom's heart was not in the conversation.

Dotty leaned her head against her husband, "You're going to go through with it, aren't you?"

Tom nodded, "I'm not the only one. We have already been laying the groundwork. We need to do it right when the time is right."

Dotty closed her eyes and smiled, "I know you will. You always do."

Boots

Bell & Sons Custom Bootmakers was a long-standing institution in Fort Brazos. Founded by Cody Bell's father, Norman, Cody was the surviving original son, now in his late sixties and sporting a long white beard. Now, Cody's twin sons Preston and Travis worked in their own shops in the back while still helping their dad. Preston had become an accomplished blacksmith and "maker," while Travis's custom saddles had been sought after all over the Southwest. Travis and Preston had themselves married twins Sinéad and Shevaun, both artists. Sinéad was a glass blower, and Shevaun was a sculptor.

Their storefront was not large. Aside from sample boots, hats, and saddles, it contained racks of skins and hides that customers could choose from for their custom items. Making custom boots was in the old tradition of a lengthy set of hand measurements of each foot, both sitting and standing, with careful deliberation on things like heel height, toe shape, sole material, stitching colors, and any custom designs or initials the customer might want.

While it was common for feet not precisely to mirror each other or for one foot to be longer or shorter than the other, there were also plenty of "special" needs customers. Those who suffered from injury, illness, or who from birth had feet for which off-the-shelf shoes never properly fit, leading to discomfort and even disability.

So, Bell & Son's customers span the full spectrum of rich and poor, with ranch and rodeo hands sometimes paying in installments for custom boots that, while they might not look extraordinary on the outside, were custom fitted to their feet down to the millimeter.

As Darnell Lewis, Ray Bunker, and Garry Little had surmised, Bell & Sons needed a steady supply of both exotic skins as well as skins suitable for everyday workman boots, and the supply had indeed run low. Fortunately, supply and demand, being what it was, had led to new sources. A few area ranchers had kept unusual animals around for either novelty or profit, including Ostrich. Another had found alligators in a remote area of his property and was now raising them, especially for Bell & Sons. Supply was scarce, and most people had to rely on Cody's encyclopedic knowledge of cow and pig hide treatments to provide the desired colors and textures, even if it didn't have the familiar durability or wear characteristics of crocodile, hippo, caiman, pirarucu, or python. There were other snake skins available locally, and those were popular.

As veteran Texas Rangers, Sam and Frank were well acquainted with the value of custom boots. Since retiring to Fort Brazos, they had sought out Cody Bell on several occasions to re-sole and repair their own custom boots and had become friends. Business was good, and Cody had two new 'employees' helping out in the storefront, Samuel Wallace and Francis Hayes. When they had approached Cody about hanging out at the store while they waited for someone, Cody had laughed and said, 'only if you make yourselves useful.'

Of course, being a customer and user of a product doesn't make one an expert. Still, for the last week, Sam and Frank had eagerly applied themselves to help and learn as much as possible while keeping a watchful eye for the people Hector had tasked them with finding.

When asked if he had any notable new customers since Awakening Day, Cody had quickly rattled off a list, and all but one was readily identifiable as known Fort Brazos residents. That sole exception usually showed up around the end of the month to trade and barter a healthy collection of skins and hides.

The tiny bells on the shop door tinkled as a deeply tanned man entered, wearing a straw cowboy hat, blue jeans, and boots. He was lean, 5'10", and had a carefully groomed mustache and goatee. His face was worn and bespoke a hard life. His brown eyes, however, were bright, sharp, and lively.

Cody smiled, "What can I do for you, Mr. Romero?"

Sam and Frank did not indicate recognition and continued working at their tasks, organizing displays and sweeping the hardwood floor.

Mr. 'Romero' glanced at Sam and Frank but otherwise ignored them as he smiled in return and stepped to the counter. "So nice to see you, Mr. Bell. I hope Travis and Preston and their lovely wives are well?"

"They sure are, thank you. Looks like I'll be a granddad several times over before long. Like so many others, both girls are pregnant, of course. And you?"

Romero took off his hat and ran his hand through his short brown hair, "Tired, but it is manageable."

"Good to hear. I take it you have another selection for us to look at?"

Romero nodded, "Yes indeed, in the truck outside. Is now a convenient time?"

Cody shrugged as he walked to the back door to the workshops behind the storefront, "Sure. Let me go round up the boys, and we'll go take a look. Be right back."

Frank did not stop sweeping as he asked, "So, Mr. Romero, what are you trading for?"

Romero smiled, "Cash and some boots, I think."

Frank nodded, "Boots for 175 men is a lot of boots."

Romero was unfazed, "That is very true. So, Francis, what was it like growing up in such a small town? Mount Calm, was it? Population of three or four hundred? Your family must have worked very hard to put you through a prestigious private university like Baylor."

Frank didn't miss a beat at Romero's somewhat shocking knowledge of Franks' background. He shrugged, "I miss it sometimes. But then all of us miss something of the world we've lost."

Sam joined in, "So you've done your homework, and you were expecting us to be here. Since you don't want a longer dance, I take it you have a low bullshit tolerance. So, is it 'Romero,' or would you prefer, Ignacio?"

Ignacio shrugged in turn, "I must provide for my men."

Sam nodded carefully, "That's admirable. It cannot have been easy for you to keep them together all this time. The temptation to simply walk into town must be becoming unbearably strong."

Ignacio sighed, "I have told my men they are free to do so at any time."

Frank added, "I have to admit, it says a lot that they haven't. Then again, the fact that you have been providing for your men and, at the same time, providing food and supplies to people on the fringes says a lot about you as well. You know, of course, that those people need only ask for help. The government has committed to ensuring that no one goes hungry."

"Ah, but there are also things like pride, trust… and fear."

Frank shrugged, "We're all trying. It's the apocalypse, after all, and we're facing galaxy-sized problems that, to be completely honest, are hard for me to comprehend."

"Yes, that is it exactly. As you put it, the people on the fringe do not understand these things, either. They are frightened and uncertain of who to trust."

Sam glanced up from his broom towards the counter. "Frank and I and others are taking a leap of faith and trust in you, Sir. There is an envelope under the counter, over there, for you. The brown document envelope with the string tie."

Ignacio rolled his eyes, "An arrest warrant?"

Frank smiled, "Depends on how you look at it."

Ignacio did not hesitate as he stepped behind the counter, retrieved the envelope, opened it, and withdrew several parchment paper pages embossed with the official seal of the government of New Texas.

Ignacio could not help himself. His eyes widened as he looked up from the pages in surprise, glancing back and forth at Frank and Sam.

Frank nodded gravely, "My partner, Sam, and I have been tasked with forming a new Texas Rangers organization with a broad area of responsibility. We've been enjoined from recruiting from the police or Sheriff's office, and it was suggested we look to the military."

Sam smiled, "However, it came to our attention that there already exists a group of disciplined men who work well together, have a lot of the skills needed for the job, and, if I may be so bold, are looking for a new home… and a destiny."

Ignacio scanned through the pages, looking for the catch. During the long wait to find a solution to their problem, 175 Columbian mercenaries deposited on the outskirts of Fort Brazos on Awakening Day, along with the other "New Arrivals" from other nations, but who evaded detection and capture as they sought answers to what had happened to them. By the time they had learned the truth, they had feared both the civilian and the military's reaction to their presence. They feared the military would try to absorb them, and they would lose their identity and be broken up. Moreover, they worried that the now shell-shocked civilian government would be angry and fearful to find 175 battle-hardened mercenaries at their doorstep.

So, they had sought to impress everyone with their abilities and captured and dramatically delivered the Wardog, effectively gift-wrapped.

Months had passed, and no one had come looking for them. As Ignacio had feared might happen, he and his men were not considered an active threat, and the military had other things to worry about. And those who knew about Ignacio and his men had figured they could not stay 'out in the cold' forever.

Ignacio had hoped that delivering the Wardog would put them in a position of relative strength in negotiations. Now, perhaps, it had.

Sam took Ignacio's measure. "Look, we know it has been hard on you and your people. I'm sure you rightly assumed that a band of South American mercenaries showing up at our doorstep might have caused quite a scene. I get it, you want to stay together, somehow, or you already would have started coming apart."

Frank added, "Sir, this is not only the best deal you could make. It's the *only* deal that makes what you've suffered through already worthwhile. However, I should have anticipated this, but I can see now that you do not like being pushed. It's one thing to take a job. It's quite another for someone to force you into it."

Sam shrugged, "So I tell you what. We will just let people think that the census missed a bunch of field hands in outlying areas, and you can just do your best to melt into society here and take what jobs you can find. You won't go hungry, but I don't see how you can keep your people together. Or you can put your pride aside and do what's best for your people."

"And my people would report to you?"

Frank laughed, "We need to recruit a Colonel who would be in charge of a group that large. Do you know anyone who your men might follow?"

Ignacio considered both the Rangers carefully. He held up the documents, "This has a name on it," He paused before continuing as if finding it difficult to say it aloud, "Rafael Santofimio Gutierre. How did you come by this name?"

Sam and Frank chuckled and said in unison, "We're Texas Rangers, Mr. Gutierre."

Ignacio shook his head, "Even my own men do not know that name. It hasn't been spoken in…."

Frank nodded, "We figured that. I tell you what, if you like that old Cotton Mill you've taken over, you can make it your headquarters. That document you're holding includes amnesty for any non-capital crimes that you and your men may have committed since Awakening Day."

Sam added, "You'll have a home."

Ignacio pursed his lips, "We will need a budget, salaries, and… public legitimacy."

Frank nodded, "You and your men will all have to swear an oath and agree to the terms. Do that, and the President will announce that the formerly secret unit he has had hunting for Accipiters and Wardogs and Stalkers is being made public. Apparently, the group had been working in secret, just in case there were actual Accipiters out there, listening in and plotting against us, coordinating the Wardog and Stalker attacks. Your group has determined there are no actual Accipiters. Now that that task is complete, your new job will be to form the first field division of the New Texas Rangers to patrol the area around Fort Brazos and police new settlements and outposts as they arise."

Ignacio studied the papers for a moment longer, then set them gently down, turned to the signature page, and used a pen from a holder next to the cash register to sign it.

Sam smiled, "Thank you, Colonel. We're glad to have you onboard."

Ignacio cocked his head, "I am curious. How did you find us?"

Sam grinned, "Jesús Aguirre's head injury. From what the nurses recall of his mutterings, we assume he was hurt during your capture of the Wardog. We looked at hospital records for anyone admitted who did not seem to belong. He fit the bill, arriving on the hospital doorstep with no wallet or identification. As soon as he was marginally recovered from his skull fracture, he simply disappeared from his room one night." He shrugged, "It kind of stood out. One thing led to another...."

Landing

The nearly 400-ton New Texas Navy Interplanetary Landing Craft 'Dagger' cut its drive and dropped the last few feet onto one of the arid, as-yet-unnamed Carswell Islands of New Texas, utterly crushing the low bushes and rocks beneath it, showering the surrounding area with broken shards of rocks and splintered foliage.

After the successful ILC test flights outside of new Texas, it had been decided that practice was needed operating in an atmosphere. Since the interior of New Texas was much like Earth, the infantry could plan and practice maneuvers as well as explore distant parts of the new world.

The ILCs huge loading ramp slammed to the ground, and Platoon Sergeant Ritchie "Cash" Shaw, of 1st Company, 1st Mechanized Infantry shouted, "Go Go Go!"

A remote-controlled unmanned all-terrain vehicle erupted from within, followed on its heels by three M1126 Strykers, the last of which barely cleared the ramp before it lifted and closed as quickly as it had dropped.

Belying its size and mass, the ILC leaped from the ground and disappeared back into the sky above them. Although air traffic was exceedingly light in New Texas, anything with a prefix of "NTN" differentiated it from its vastly less capable air-breathing counterparts.

With the ATV leading the way, the convoy reached a steady pace of thirty kilometers per hour, traveling to a notional northeast, with "east," meaning spinward inside the hollow world that was New Texas.

The Carswell Islands were a continent away from Fort Brazos and were a sprawling archipelago of rocky islands of varied climate, ranging from arid to tropical. This particular island was littered with dry, low-rolling foothills dominated by three ruined mountains pockmarked by caves and boulder-strewn valleys.

In the Platoon's column, the lead vehicle, the ATV named 'DogWhistle,' included a constantly squawking radio transmitter designed to flush out the convoy's prey without directly endangering the 20-ton Light Armored Vehicles that followed it.

Captain David Garreth sat with severe eyes in the third Stryker, 'Vic 3', the command vehicle. Garreth looked for confirmation from his Unmanned Aerial Vehicle operator, Specialist Melissa Hawkings, her short curly blonde hair peeking out beneath her helmet, who gave him a thumbs up. He turned and nodded to Corporal Jake Dawson, who opened an overhead hatch and reached up to pull a securing strap. An RQ-20 Puma UAV grabbed the air streaming past and lifted from the Stryker, soaring into the sky.

"Puma up!" Specialist Hawkings called over the convoy radio as it began to overtake them; she watched her monitor intently.

Garreth moved over to look at the Specialist's monitor while he absently fiddled with the shiny, un-weathered gold wedding band on his left ring finger.

This was their fifth consecutive landing and their third, uneventful, perfect off-loading. Driving Strykers off of an alien spaceship was as new a concept to his humble soldiers as it was to the Navy personnel flying it.

Garreth looked a question to Sergeant Shaw, who answered with a questioning eyebrow flicker. When Garreth nodded, the Sergeant called, "Herringbone! Dismount!" over the Convoy Net.

In Vic 2, Sergeant Dewayne Paxton, the Bravo Fire Team leader, echoed, "Herringbone! Dismount!"

Terrified, Alpha Fire Team Specialist Michael Ericson's eyes popped wide open as he shook himself awake from his half-slumber. Vic 1 swung right and ground to a halt. He followed the three other team members, Specialists Bennie Davis, Troy Allen, and Sergeant José Bolívar. He stumbled out of the door and almost lost his footing as he defiantly lurched to 'security' – his position in the formation among the other fire team members providing 360-degree security.

The formation gave the weight of their firepower to the flanks or the front of their position in anticipation of enemy contact.

While Ericson with Alpha Fire Team took point security at 50 meters or less, Bravo Fire Team manned the Stryker's Mk44 Bushmaster 30 mm chain gun just in case they ran into heavier than expected opposition. The Mk44 was loaded with the same ammunition used by the A-10 'Warthog' Thunderbolt II.

Ericson fidgeted with the weight and balance of his unfamiliar weapon. He was unaccustomed to the rotary-operated Milkor Multi-Grenade-Launcher, which, in the face of a new enemy, had replaced his M4 carbine.

The Milkor had been in active use with the Marine Corps, and while it was not entirely unknown for the army as a whole, it was new to Garreth's men.

After the other vehicles followed suit in the maneuver, a ragged silence fell over the warriors as they waited.

Sergeant Shaw shouted, "Mount up!" Ending the short exercise.

✪ ✪ ✪

Despite the chaos and panic following Awakening Day, it had taken less than a week before the Bonham State University Geography Department, working closely with the Astronomy Department, had begun mapping the other side of New Texas. After all, all they had to do was point their telescopes 'up.' In many ways, even now, more was known about the other side of the world than about much of the rest of the strange new continent where the City of Fort Brazos and the nearby Joint Reserve Base had woken up.

With the importance of final exams somewhat… overshadowed by the apocalypse, every department at the university had been up for grabs by civilian and military use. The BSU observatory's two-meter Ritchey-Chretien reflecting telescope was computer-controlled with a high-resolution CCD imaging system, which provided very accurate imaging. Only slightly smaller than the Hubble Space Telescope had been, the BSU telescope had the advantage of not needing to be launched into space. When combined with imaging from an array of smaller 16" and 24" telescopes, it was possible to gather a vast amount of data in a short amount of time.

Accordingly, there were plenty of computer scientists who were happy to process the petabytes of imaging data, using algorithms to identify even something as relatively small as what Garreth and his Platoon, with the help of Frank and Mira Yaegar, were now hunting.

The data had produced thousands of candidates, which had been whittled down to a list of higher confidence locations exhibiting 'Anomalies.' These were cataloged, prioritized, and passed on to Captain Garreth's unit for scouting.

Frank was stocky and weathered-looking and wore his usual safari hat, vest, and gear. His daughter Mira took after her mother. She was slender, wore a broad-rimmed safari hat that shaded her face, and always wore long sleeves, protecting her fair skin.

Frank was a banker and rancher. Mira ran an insurance agency. Those jobs had supported their real passion, traveling to remote and rugged places… and big game hunting. Frank and Mira carried matching engraved Hambrusch .700 Nitro Express rifles, although Mira's was a .500, giving her 'more control.'

A rodeo cowboy before he met Mira's mom, Frank had raised Mira as a single dad after her mom had died when Mira was nine. Years later, Mira's own husband had been killed in a motorcycle accident, and at least before Awakening Day, Father and Daughter, Widower and Widow, shared a life mastering the life and death of earthly creatures. Now, though, they were tasked with mastering unearthly ones.

On the ride "up" from the Joint Reserve Base, NTN Dagger had been captained by Commander Charles Cross, who Mira had now had the opportunity to observe in his natural element, in command of a vessel. The fact that it was an entirely alien-built spaceship being flown inside a hollow world did not seem to faze him.

Charles had been calmly and firmly in command and, at the same time, something else. Mira had observed how he treated his crew and how they treated him in return. In many respects, he seemed to be as much a teacher and mentor as he was the absolute master and commander of his vessel.

That Mira had managed to start finding excuses to be on the bridge was understandable. Who wouldn't want to observe the nerve center of an alien spaceship being operated by humans – in action. On the other hand, it also allowed her to observe Commander Cross; so far, she liked what she saw.

✪ ✪ ✪

Garreth called for a 20 kph reduction and turned his attention to Frank and Mira. Their official status as civilian contractors had not stopped them, and especially their beautiful hunting dogs, from becoming favorites of the platoon.

Though all the terrain of New Texas was arguably artificial, the Carswell Islands most resembled the volcanic sort of old Earth. They had relatively flat areas of gravel and light vegetation along their shorelines that bluffed up to short but sheer cliff-lines overlooking the sea surrounding them, with the hills and mountains beyond them. The university types and Bonham had reported a large creature of unusual color wandering (or patrolling) a path along the shore around a point in the cliff line. Garreth and his platoon were now approaching that cliff line.

Garreth called for a dismounted line patrol when they drew near that area. The UGV began a sweeping serpentine search pattern in front of the patrol area while the Strykers lined up, side to side, with infantry ahead. Together, the platoon slowly swept a 100-meter swath across the gravel shore leading up to the suspect cliff line.

The infantry up front kept strict radio silence as the Yaegars split apart. Frank moved up left, under the watch of Bravo squad's protective fireteam, while Mira took the right with Charlie squad. While every eye of the platoon kept careful eyes on the ground ahead, Frank, Mira, and their dogs focused intently on the ground just in front of them.

One of Mira's dogs stopped suddenly, interested in a small patch of gravel, before sitting silently and eyeing her obediently. Mira's fist followed the previous directions of Captain Garreth and shot up alongside her head. The platoon came to a quiet and mechanical halt. Mira moved to her dog, Ranger, and kneeled to examine the gravel.

The gravel along the shoreline was heavily disturbed. Making sense of it was a challenge even for experienced hunters like Frank and Mira. Mira's eyes followed a pattern invisible to the untrained eye that meandered towards a narrow path leading inland through a narrow break in the cliff line before gazing at her father and gesturing with a hand.

Frank crept up with his security detail and shook his head as he followed the trail she had spotted with his eyes. "Damn, too narrow for the Stryker's."

Mira nodded, "At least it is passable by the decoy."

The winding path, which was probably a raging torrent the one or two times a year that it rained on this rock of an island, led inland for two and a half miles through ankle-breaking rocks and boulders. What was obvious, though, was that something big and heavy regularly traveled up and down it. It was not absolute confirmation yet, but the list of possible suspects had narrowed to a small elephant, a rhinoceros…, or a Wardog.

Garreth's men had dismounted, leaving Bravo behind to secure the vehicles, and followed the path with the ATV in the lead and Frank and Mira within the security envelope.

Specialist Hawkings, who controlled the ATV and the Puma, was watching the Puma feed on her helmet HUD and reported, "Captain! There's a cave two more clicks up the path."

Garreth nodded, "Very well, Hawkings. Sergeant Bolívar, stand by with your special Milkor rounds."

Sergeant José Bolívar suppressed a groan. His reward for being the most accurate Milkor gunner was duty with a batch of hastily modified experimental 40mm rounds that Specialist Erickson had nicknamed 'Egghead Rounds.' It had been explained that "Someone at higher wants to see if these are effective" before experimenting with them on their (only) captive Wardog.

With the noisy ATV leading their way, a stealth approach was not in the cards. However, as they eventually neared the cave… nothing happened. They halted their approach, with the ATV idling at the cave entrance.

Garreth turned worriedly to Hawkings, "Anything on the Puma feed?"

She shook her head, "No, Captain, and I've got it orbiting our position. Nothing behind us or in the surrounding area."

Garreth shrugged, "Turn on the second radio transmitter, Hawkings, Full blast. If it's in there, maybe it's asleep."

"Yes, Captain."

Nothing happened for long seconds, then a half dozen thunks and sprangs rang out as Stalker barbs lanced through the lightweight ATV's plastic shell.

Garreth blinked in surprise as several men shouted, "Contact! Stalker!"

Then the unmistakable gravel grinding roar of a Wardog echoed out of the cave.

"What?"

"In the same cave?"

"What the hell?"

Garreth shouted, "Bolívar, hit it!"

Sergeant Bolívar had been waiting. He had practiced with the experimental rounds since their weight and balance were different. He fired, the revolving cylinder advancing between each round until all six rounds were away. All six landed at the cave entrance and bounced inside before "popping," releasing a cloud of white powder, some of which billowed out the cave entrance.

For an agonizing ten minutes, the Wardog continued to shriek and hideously bellow, but it did not emerge, nor did it quiet down. Meanwhile, more barbs punished the now-shredded ATV, unabated.

Garreth turned to Frank and Mira with an obvious question in his eyes.

Frank and Mira glanced at each other, shaking their heads. Mira answered, "Maybe it's hurt, or maybe it's protecting a mate or its young or eggs or something. Nobody even knows how it reproduces yet. We have no idea!"

Garreth shook his head, "OK, I'm not risking anyone's life, or your dogs, to go in there. Bolívar, reload with HE and commence firing as soon as you are ready. Let's see how many it takes to quiet them down, and we have no idea how deep that cave is."

Sergeant Bolívar grinned, "Yes, Sir, you got it, Captain!"

Garreth turned back to Frank and Mira, "Well, so much for the powdered confectionary sugar bombs. They knew that the damned things got high eating it but weren't sure about inhaling it, and they didn't want to OD the captive one, so we were the lucky ones who had the honor of trying it out in the wild."

Frank laughed, "I know they want to capture another one, but I have to admit it seemed farfetched to me."

Mira smirked, "You mean that refined sugar is like cocaine to them?"

Frank shook his head and grinned wryly, "No. I just didn't believe that it could be that easy."

✪　✪　✪

It ended up taking four or perhaps three HE 40MM grenades to quiet the cave. That is, after three, it was quiet. After four, it was dead silent.

Specialist Hawkings sent in a small quadcopter with both visible and IR cameras and confirmed the carnage inside, and nothing attacked it.

Out of an abundance of caution, Garreth waited two more hours before sending the quadcopter in again, confirming nothing had changed. Next, he sent Specialists Michael Ericson and Samir Muhammad inside to check with the mark one eyeball. After they confirmed it was safe, Garreth and the Yaegars followed.

What they found was a confusing mess of partly caved-in walls and ceiling, as well as shattered and shredded Wardog and Stalker, all mixed together. In the cave's confines, the HE shockwaves must have been magnified.

As Garreth exited the cave, his eyes watering, he ordered, "OK, take lots of video and photos and take samples. Hawkings, scout for the best place for Dagger to land and exfil us."

He paused, "1st Company, when we get back, beer is on me!"

Tools of War

DownSide: JRB

Small Arms Demonstration Center
January 1st, NLD 124 -- FBD 152: 11:28 AM

There was a palpable silence at the conference table in the middle of the display room at the brand-new Fort Brazos Joint Reserve Base Small Arms Demonstration Center. The building was formerly a warehouse but now held row upon row of man-portable weapons from all over the world. The Gardener-expanded arms bunkers were vast and contained thousands of examples of every weapon in operation in military forces worldwide.

It was a scant 33 days after Awakening Day and the end of the world. Armed with only a vague idea that humans were supposed to go out and fight a galaxy-spanning empire of ten-foot-tall alien birds and their monstrous lackeys, there was considerable anxiety amongst the people whose job it was to work out the finer details of how to prosecute that war.

Four men sat around the table reviewing their notes after the newly minted Captain David Garreth concluded his After-Action Report on the recently completed ground exercises. It had been decided in the face of a new enemy that new weapons and tactics must be developed as quickly as possible, and it was Garreth's unit that had been tasked as the Guinea Pigs.

Amongst those present was Chief Master Sergeant Harrold Anders. The 49-year-old Air Force Chief was the senior surviving NCO. Anywhere. Among his responsibilities was creating policies that would ensure the mission's success by the enlisted force.

He eyed the young captain intently, imperceptibly glowering in a test of the very inexperienced boy whom he thought was not nearly hardened enough for this job. *The fate of mankind is in the balance, and this boy and others like him will be leading our men. My men.*

Captain Garreth, for his part, stood at perfect attention, with bags under his eyes and bruises under his uniform from the back-to-back missions he had led in the preceding days.

Nigel Van de Velde, the only civilian at the table, was the last to raise his eyes after reviewing his papers. Nigel was a senior manufacturer's representative from Fabrique Nationale Herstal who had been on-site with the South Africans demonstrating Remote Weapons Stations and the latest FN M2HB-QCB .50 caliber heavy machine gun variant. Nigel had been abducted along with the rest of the South Africans. Like everyone else, he had been devastated by recent events, and like everyone else in the room, he'd thrown himself into his work to avoid thinking about it. His encyclopedic knowledge of military firearms manufacturing and supply chain logistics had left him as mankind's leading expert on the subject. As a result, having the meeting without him present was unthinkable.

Anders was the first to speak, "It's certainly a refreshing milestone that it was infantry weapons that eliminated two of the five Wardogs eliminated so far. That said, we're all very interested in your firsthand experience with our new tactics."

Garreth nodded and began, "Yes, Chief. I have two concerns. The first is firepower. The first civilian encounter found that non-armor-piercing .308 simply bounced off of it. My first personal engagement found that .458 SOCOM AP only made divots in the damned thing's armor. Later, we found that a Browning M2 firing Incendiary AP was just able to punch through the armor. It at least got the thing's attention, but it only slowed it down. Of course, the vehicle-mounted 25mm chain gun was devastating, but we need infantry weapons that can protect our men. Vehicle-mounted weapons won't always be available."

Anders nodded, "And your second concern?"

"My second concern is the importance of Electronic Warfare in the future. Before Awakening Day, we'd gradually adopted more and more advanced equipment and trained people specifically for it. If the enemy can home-in on our electronics, then our ability to communicate, coordinate, and even control some of our weapons and vehicles is compromised."

Nigel Van de Velde thumbed through the reports in front of him and suggested in a notably eclectic northern European accent, "But Captain, surely we should be rather pleased with the performance of our existing arms."

Harrold frowned, "There are already discussions about finding ways to better shield our emissions. They are dusting off the idea of using lasers for point-to-point communication. All of that is going to take a while. Meanwhile, right now, we need to focus on rebalancing our force structures and getting the right weapons in the hands of our troops. In your hands. The enemy is not impervious. We've proven we can kill them. Our weapons work."

Garreth thoughtfully replied, "The thing to remember is that I'm not talking about engagement at a distance. From a field perspective, I know from first-hand experience that these things can come out of the ground from right beneath your feet. We need creature-stopping damage at point-blank range, with munitions that won't kill the operator at the same time. Firing a Milkor at that distance will probably kill you, anyone around you, and the beast, to boot. Think about it this way—we need to be able to stop a raging bullet-proof elephant at point-blank range."

Nigel nodded, "Clearly, the doctrine of wounding the other soldier so that the enemy must expend resources on him or making him keep his head down through suppressive fire no longer applies. You need man-portable equipment that can deliver a high rate of damage in a short amount of time."

Base Armory Master Sergeant Liam Simard noted, "Obviously, these exercises must have felt extremely unconventional for all of your men, but it seems to me that we're only going to need to experiment more." He gestured around them at the thousands of sample weapons. "There is certainly a lot to choose from, but we must also consider reliability in the field and support for when you are eventually… on other planets. You need reliable equipment that you can service with whatever limited tools you will be able to take with you."

Garreth shook his head, "I agree, Sergeant. However, even cut-down Barrett .50's would only hurt them, and it won't stop them cold."

Nigel wondered aloud, "…A high amount of damage in a short amount of time…."

Simard asked, "You have something in mind, Nigel?"

Nigel blinked sheepishly, "Ah, well, perhaps. It is… unconventional, but it might be a good stopgap for you. How about we break for lunch, and I demonstrate what I have in mind when you come back?"

★ ★ ★

The Small Arms Demonstration Center included a substantial firing range behind it, with high, reinforced berms and lots of empty space beyond. Nigel had set up two tables. One had a standard M4 rifle in 5.56x45, a Mk 17 (FN SCAR-H) in 7.62×51, and a Barrett M107 in .50 BMG. A Second table had a tarp over something bulky.

Nigel motioned to the series of steel targets at 25 meters. "We'll be using AP Incendiary ammunition, but due to the proximity of the target, I ask you all to don protective gear." He paused, "Captain Garrett, if you will indulge me and demonstrate the effectiveness of each of these against the targets?"

Garreth looked dubiously at Nigel, but Harrold encouraged him, "This should be interesting, Captain."

Garreth complied. The M4's 5.56x45 splattered and sparked against the first target; however, as expected, it did not penetrate. The SCAR's 7.62x51 splashed and threw sparks as it divoted the next target, leaving a bulge on its backside. Lastly, the .50 BMG cleanly punched through the third target, leaving a pattern of carbon surrounding the hole.

Garreth looked quizzically at Nigel. "So far, there's nothing new here."

Nigel nodded, then stepped to the other table and threw off the tarp, revealing… an XM556 Microgun with its backpack and a swing arm. It looked like a baby minigun. "Gentlemen, I found this in the back of the warehouse. It is the XM556 Microgun."

Garreth, Harrold, and Simard all shook their heads.

Harrold frowned, "Doesn't matter. It's still 5.56!"

Nigel shrugged, put the backpack and arm on, and carried it to the firing line. He aimed at the last target and fired a three-second burst, "Brrrrrrrrrrrrripppp."

The AP Incendiary rounds burned through the target, slicing it in half as Nigel controlled the fire from left to right.

Stunned silence followed.

Nigel commented, "The .50 BMG puts 290 to 300 grains on the target. Even firing one per second, that's less than a thousand grains in three seconds. I have set the firing rate at 3,000 rounds per minute on the XM556, and it can go up to 6,000. A three-second burst is 150 API rounds. At 62 grains each, that's 9,300 grains on the target in three seconds."

Simard shook his head, "That's all well and good, but the thing is not mil-spec. It is complicated and unproven."

Nigel smiled, "It is derived directly from the well-proven M134 Minigun and has fewer parts, and because it is 5.56, the small frame can handle it well. You can see that the gun itself is smaller than even many submachine guns."

Garreth stepped up to Nigel, "Let me give that a try…."

Malevolence

Colonel P'aeng Jin-Hwan dismissed the exhausted 2,498 men standing wearily at attention in their fenced Compound. Their faces were haggard, and their uniforms were clean but worn thin. Some were nearly rags. Jin-Hwan had been drilling them since 04:00. Full bellies and too much time on their hands had led to more and more quiet questions being asked among the ranks. He had turned to relentless drills, training, and loyalty lectures to keep his men focused and true to their faith in the Great Leader.

The insidious Americans had offered bribes to his men in the form of decadent clothing, more hot fresh food than they could possibly eat, and tablet and laptop computers with access to the American Disinformation Network and vile entertainment. He smashed them on sight. The one man who had been discovered covertly watching the propaganda on a smuggled cell phone had been stripped of rank, stripped of clothes, and beaten nearly to death before the American guards could intervene and whisk him away, never to be seen again.

What copies of the Great Leader's books and pamphlets he and others had had on their persons before the Americans had kidnapped them were precious totems they loyally clung to, although after a while, he had set most of them aside to protect them from daily wear and tear, lest their wisdom and guidance be lost forever.

❂ ❂ ❂

Lieutenant Ryon Ki-Nam stood at rigid attention in Jin-Hwan's tent while Jin-Hwan paced back and forth, his face a fulminating mixture of anger and determination. Ki-Nam studiously kept his gaze focused downwards, and his expression was one of complete submission and obedience. He long ago learned that anything less, or worse, outward expression of independent thought or initiative inevitably yielded savage scrutiny and doubts about his loyalty – either to the Great Leader, the Party, or his commanding officer. Any of these could lead to his or his family's punishment or exile to reeducation camps.

He had seen it happen to people he grew up with. Smart ones who asked too many questions, disgruntled ones passed over for favor or unhappy with their lot, those who said too little or too much in praise of their betters, or even the quick ones with ideas of new and better ways to do things. His father had drilled into him, "Stay unnoticed, but always be reliable and dependable. Never question their orders. Never look them in the eyes, and never, ever show any feeling publicly except for your devotion and obedience. Never appear to be more intelligent than they. All good ideas are theirs."

And so, Ki-Nam was the ever-faithful, ever-dependable, ever-obedient, selfless example to his peers. His superiors had often held him up as an exemplar for others. It had been hard on him for a long time as others still found means of retribution even in their controlled society. Eventually, though, the smarter ones began to realize that his rigid adherence to the letter of his orders was never capricious or vindictive. In time, those under his leadership grew more effective than others. One of the hardest things was to avoid any appearance of loyalty to him personally. He deflected these as much as he could, making sure that any perception was that he was a conduit for the devotion of "his" men towards Ki-Nam's superiors rather than to himself.

He was Jin-Hwan's most trusted subordinate, though he learned that this also brought Jin-Hwan's endemic paranoia to focus on him all too often. As Jin-Hwan's wordless pacing continued, Ki-Nam began to dread what would come next. The pattern usually ended in an explosion aimed either at Ki-Nam himself or Ki-Nam would end up being tasked with pouring misfortune upon the head of whomever Jin-Hwan was currently displeased with. So far, he had managed to survive.

Jin-Hwan suddenly stopped and lurched towards Ki-Nam, stopping inches away from him. Ki-Nam steeled himself for what would come next. He expected a beating, but instead, Jin-Hwan reached out his arms and placed his hands on Ki-Nam's shoulders.

Then the strangest thing Ki-Nam had ever experienced happened next. Jin-Hwan embraced him, actually hugging him. Then he stepped back, hands-on Ki-Nam's shoulders. Ki-Nam kept his gaze lowered, but Jin-Hwan gently reached over and raised Ki-Nam's chin before commanding him, "Look at me."

Ki-Nam hesitated but complied. Jin-Hwan's eyes were bloodshot and wet. "Throughout our ordeal here, you have been faithful and true. Before the Americans kidnapped us, I had suspicions about you, but you have proven me wrong. I could not have asked for a finer officer. Indeed, I've come to think of you... as the son I never had."

Ki-Nam blinked, astonished, but kept his expression just this side of dull but obedient and thankful.

Jin-Hwan stepped back, nodding his head. "I am proud of you. If half our men had half your devotion, we could have... well... things would have been different."

Ki-Nam's mind raced. Wherever this was leading could not be good. He returned his gaze to Jin-Hwan's feet.

Jin-Hwan straightened his shirt, "Lieutenant Ryon Ki-Nam, you are a fine and dedicated officer, and that is why this decision hurts me as it does. I must ask you now to embark upon a mission that will require you to do the hardest thing I could ask of anyone."

Ki-Nam's heart thudded and skipped a beat, but he remained rigidly immobile. *I am a statue... I am stone....*

"There will be no official order and nothing in writing that could be discovered later. I must ask you to abandon your post and defect to the Americans so that you can spy upon them and collect what information you can that could help us either escape or at least inflict maximum harm upon our captors, even at the cost of your and all of our lives."

Ki-Nam's blood pounded in his ears. He heard the words, but they made no sense. For the first time in his life, he actually stumbled while standing at attention. There had been so many times when he'd been sorely tempted to simply walk over and surrender to the Americans. Whatever they might do could not be worse than the life he had now, despite everything he had ever been taught.

As a child, he and everyone else at Kindergarten and child-care centers had been surrounded with decorations of animals holding grenades and machine guns. Cartoons showed cute squirrel soldiers defeating the cunning wolves… Americans. Ki-Nam had been to the museum in Sinchon that had depicted horror upon horror that the evil Americans had inflicted upon the innocent Koreans. In the back of his mind, though, it had struck him that none of the artifacts had actually proven anything. Now, after five months of close proximity to Americans, he had witnessed none of the demonic behavior he had always been taught to expect from them. Ki-Nam had gained weight, and none of his men were suffering from malnutrition anymore.

Now, astonishingly, his commander was ordering him to do what he had only fantasized about.

Jin-Hwan saw the look on Ki-Nam's face and smiled sadly, but his heart filled with joy as he saw the fear and dismay give way to brave determination in the younger man's eyes. He caught Ki-Nam's elbow and steadied him. Rather than berate him, he patted him on the back. "I know this is much to ask. It is possible that if I am killed that no one will ever know of your bravery and sacrifice. Be comforted… my son… that I know, and you know. Now, let us sit and plan your escape in a way that will not be as disheartening to the men."

Systems and Integration

TopSide: New Pentagon

January 3rd, NLD 126 -- FBD 154, 7:48 PM

Commander Thomas Harding sat at his palatial desk in his oversized office at the center of an entire section of the New Pentagon devoted to the command he had been assigned three months before. His crisp, new, service dress uniform was a welcome change after one of the countless warehouses discovered in the New London industrial sector had been found to include a healthy supply of service, working, and even full-dress uniforms, not to mention tens of thousands of computers. It also helped that new clothing and even brand-new uniforms were starting to make their way TopSide from Fort Brazos's burgeoning manufacturing sector.

He sighed as he took off his glasses and rubbed his eyes. Somehow, his handlers had placed him at the heart of the starship program, in charge of Systems and Integration. The effect of this was that every aspect of the work being done to bring the hybrid craft to life went through his office. His official job was to prioritize resources and bring order to the chaos, and he was extremely good at his job.

In his career, Thomas had variously been an operations research analyst for the Secretary of Defense, the Deputy Nuclear Propulsion Program Manager, as well as Commander of Submarine Squadron 14. He had an M.B.A. from the University of Florida and a Bachelor of Science in Mathematics and Computer Science from the University of Idaho in his hometown of Moscow, Idaho. Thomas knew how to run an extensive, technically complex program.

His desk was stacked with reports and requisition forms awaiting his approval, and his computer overflowed with email, team messaging, and yet more forms and documents. His staff struggled to keep him focused on only the most pressing and urgent requests since he was already well over 120% capacity for meetings, planning sessions, analyst calls, and more.

It's a shame, really. Compared to typical Pentagon efficiency, we're doing quite well. A lot of work really was getting done, and in his orchestra-director role, he was very good at keeping everyone productive and busy.

However, according to his secret orders, his unofficial role was to make certain that the actual, real-world overall progress was slowed. Under no circumstances could the starship program be allowed to progress quickly enough to make the President's deadline for the suicide mission back to Earth.

In truth, it was not hard at all. What they were attempting to do should, back in the world, and in all honesty, should really take ten or even twenty *years*, not months. What was being asked would have been flatly impossible, irresponsible, and insane in peacetime. But this was not peacetime, and Thomas fully expected that no human alive today would ever again see peace in their lifetime.

The sheer scope and scale of the data and experience being gleaned from the ILC tests was staggering and would be invaluable when applied to the Blood Phoenix project. However, except for the alterations made by the Gardeners to accommodate human pilots, the ILCs were still utterly alien craft. Many worried that it was dangerous to simply assume a one-to-one correlation between what was learned from the ILCs and the Blood Phoenix. Thomas did his best to appear impartial while at the same time ensuring that those concerns were taken very seriously.

Overall, however, he had agonized over just how we was supposed to accomplish his task without appearing to be obstructionist. Then one day, it suddenly occurred to him that all he really had to do was keep everyone moving so fast in so many different directions, accomplishing lots of small things, that the resulting feeling of great accomplishment obscured the big picture. In reality, those same efforts simply pulled in too many contradictory directions. Resources were spread too thin, and the big-picture progress slowed to a crawl.

Slowing things down irked him. His motivation for selling secrets had never been about money. The United States had become too complacent in its technical superiority. Leaking just enough technology to specific enemies would pay off by keeping pressure on the United States to advance even faster. Over time, though, more and more was demanded of him, and the systemic complacency of the federal and military bureaucracies had been far more profound and more institutionalized than he had ever imagined. Then there was the political component: many on the left of the spectrum felt that the United States should not be superior at all.

Now, because of his actions, he was being forced to actually slow things down. *The universe hates me.*

It took a lot of work to achieve the desired result. Indeed, no one could fault his hours. Thomas routinely arrived before almost anyone else and stayed longer than most. His staff had grown to respect and admire his devotion and work ethic. To his dismay, one by one, those who worked for him began to follow his example. He did what he could to discourage it, but it was not long before his example became the norm. He even heard that some people had coined the phrase, "are you working Harding enough?"

His efforts were not as tricky as they might sound. There were simply too few people and too few with the necessary skills and knowledge to get all the required work done. At one point, Thomas had thought he might accomplish his task by simply working everyone too hard. He almost succeeded. Day by day, morale ratcheted down as enthusiasm was sapped away by the seven-day-a-week, around-the-clock, push. People began to lose hope that the deadline would be met.

Then, President Austin and Vice President Finley had intervened. Despite the President's simpleton cowboy persona, John Austin had a strong following. His address on the steps of the New Pentagon, followed by Vice President Finley's desperate, impassioned, fiery call to action, had elevated spirits and inspired everyone to throw themselves into their work even more than they had before.

The good and the bad of it was that so many bright and talented people had so many dammed good ideas that it actually helped Thomas layer success upon chaos, often taking two steps forward and three back when a better idea came up.

Tonight, he had several more hours of work to do, and to his amazement, not a single person on his staff had left. Indeed, they all seemed to watch over him like mother hens, ensuring he ate and cared for himself as they actively worked to… protect and shield him from anything they deemed less important.

He'd never worked harder in his life or been prouder of the people working for him, and never before had he worked on a project that so inspired and invigorated him. It was the greatest work of his life.

He morosely thought to himself, And I am forever damned for betraying it and these hard-working, dedicated people I have fooled into following me.

Representation

The remnants of lunch still littered the room, but no effort had yet been made to clean it up. Several rounds of protests that had erupted over the last week had caused a modest uproar in Fort Brazos.

New Londoners had complained that the new housing was not being provided fast enough and was not up to their… standards of living. Earlier in the day, Councilman Hubbard had pointed out to no one in particular that the last house he had contracted to be built for his family had taken over a year to finish. Construction efforts for the New Londoners had only gotten into full gear relatively recently. There just weren't enough building materials and skilled builders to meet the demand.

The aging dorms and off-campus apartments were never intended as more or less permanent housing. Protesting Bonham State University students had complained that their living conditions were 'unbearable.' After Awakening Day, most of the students, who had come from all over the United States, were now young adult orphans. They were beginning to resent the New Londoner's "getting nicer housing" than they themselves had. Many existing Fort Brazos citizens felt the same way—that some of the new housing looked nicer than their own, or at least, a lot newer.

Piling on to the discontent were the university students who worried that their spartan dorms might become semi-permanent. While some of the student housing was owned by the university, quite a lot of students lived in off-campus apartments and housing owned by private citizens. Tragically, after Awakening Day, the vast majority of the university student's moms and dads were no longer alive to send rent payments. Meanwhile, Fort Brazos families who depended on rent income from off-campus apartments understandably worried about making ends meet.

In truth, Colonel Salangsang, his men, and quite a few hired hands and not a few actual volunteers were working day and night. Teams of workers had fanned out across Fort Brazos and the Joint Reserve Base, salvaging fixtures, lumber, electrical wiring, and anything that could be reused. Stocks of lumber, roofing, and plumbing supplies had quickly been exhausted, including cleaning out the home improvement and hardware stores.

Some disused buildings were being converted directly into apartments, and many Fort Brazos citizens had offered spare rooms as temporary housing. General Marcus had allocated several unused buildings for temporary or long-term dormitory use and tasked his staff with ensuring that base housing was "being optimally used."

Tom Parker rubbed his eyes and then looked at Councilman Jack Burdger, "Jack, any thoughts on that wall idea?"

Jack groaned, "Oh, that thing. I had some numbers run up, and even if we wanted to, we do not have enough fencing material of any kind even to begin to encircle the entire city. We could half-ass put up some barbed wire, but we don't even have enough posts to string it from. Everything is going to the housing construction. I think the best suggestion anyone had was to start pulling limestone blocks from the quarry, but that'll take a long time, probably years, and all the equipment we'd use to do it with is already spoken for."

Tom answered for him, "…for housing, I know." He rubbed his tired, unshaven face, "How about this? We put out a statement calling for design ideas and volunteers but limit the design to include only materials not otherwise devoted to the housing project."

Jack nodded and made notes on his mostly used-up yellow legal pad.

Tom sighed, "Onto the next item," He nodded to Councilman Wylie Hickum, "Any luck getting that old bus back in operation?"

Wylie chuckled, "That thing should be in a museum. Everything's shot on it. We are looking at scrounging up some vans and full-size SUVs and pressing them into service, but it is not enough. We need to make the school buses pull double duty or just incorporate the school buses and their routes into a comprehensive bus system. Fort Brazos has never had a mass transit system or the culture to go with it."

Tom looked around, and everyone seemed to be in agreement, "OK, all in favor?" Everyone nodded tiredly. "The nods have it. Make it happen, Wylie."

Wylie nodded and made notes on his steno pad, his preferred note-taking medium.

Tom smiled, "Well, maybe we can get *something* accomplished today." He looked down at his notes, "OK, Esmerelda, what's going on with the Land Grant plan? I thought we were all set to implement that?" There had been several vociferous protests on that subject.

Esmerelda shook her head and leaned back in her chair, rubbing her neck. "Honestly, Tom, I think it boils down to people starting to get greedy and counting their chickens before they're hatched. People are complaining about who gets to choose who gets which land, like, who gets the beachfront land and who gets the swamp somewhere. The fact that the plan calls for a percentage of *any* land that gets developed to be divided on a percentage basis and that we haven't actually put anybody's actual name on any particular spot on a map is beside the point. Of course, the pesky little fact that there are no roads or way to get to anyplace people are fantasizing about is also beside the point."

Tom shook his head, "I thought the rotating review board made up of citizens chosen in the same way as Jury Duty would help assure a sense of fairness."

Esmerelda chortled, "I think that may have actually upset a few people who'd hoped to get jobs putting them in charge of one aspect or other of the process. Of course, then those persons in charge would have no doubt earned the… how shall I say… gratitude of those willing to grant favors in exchange for favorable rulings?"

Gloria Vargas shook her head, "Can we just get a list of these people and make sure they never get a government job?"

Tom smiled, "Gloria, I think you're confusing New Texas with Heaven."

Gloria retorted, "Tom, are you suggesting that we're instead in some other place, perhaps with a warmer climate?"

Tom grinned weakly, "Why Gloria, the mere fact that you yourself are here with us in this place, decries that possibility."

Gloria softened her expression, "Why Tom, it's no wonder you won reelection so many times."

Tom smiled beatifically, "Be that as it may, I think we should skip ahead to the elephant in the room. We've beaten the grass around it several times, but we have yet to finalize the outline of our new representation plan."

Councilman Dale Hubbard broke his silence, "Well, we really had been planning some sort of Constitutional Convention to finalize the plan… at least before New London complicated things."

Gloria chided, "Let me guess. People are complaining about who gets to be a delegate."

Dale nodded, "I think some people just want to see their name immortalized on a signature page, like the Declaration, and others see it as a ticket to power and influence."

Gloria closed her eyes and shook her head, "Well, let's hope those who sign it fare better than the signers of the Declaration of Independence did. Most ended up dead, tortured, or destitute after the British destroyed their homes."

Tom sighed, "Well, whatever we do, we need to delay this until after we get the resettlement completed and some of these problems put to bed."

Gloria sniped, "Afraid of losing your august job, Tom?"

Tom sat back in his chair and surveyed the room before answering. The delay caught everyone by surprise. "Actually, Gloria, I'm not afraid of that at all. After the next election, I'm retiring."

Dale, Jack, and Wylie all jumped to their feet.

"You can't!"

"We need you, Tom!"

"Are you ill?"

"Is someone forcing you?"

Gloria stayed seated and studied Tom's face. She smiled, reached out, and touched his hand, "It'll suit you, Tom. I'm happy for you."

The other men turned questioningly to Gloria. Dale asked, "What do you mean? What's going on?"

While Tom tried to gather his words, Gloria answered, "In case you gentlemen haven't noticed, our friend and colleague Tom Parker has been spending more and more time at his church. I believe he feels he can better serve our community as a spiritual leader rather than a political one. Although Tom, I believe you should not make this public for a while yet. At this point, announcing your retirement could shake public confidence."

"Agreed!"

"Here, Here!"

"Second the motion."

"Third."

Tom smiled abashedly and raised his hands in defeat, "OK, OK, I agree. That's why I have not done anything before now. It's been one crisis after another. I don't intend to abandon my duty until I can feel it is safe to do so."

The meeting had gradually lurched back to actual business. For the next four and a half hours, various proposals and issues regarding the formation of a new representative government were debated, critiqued, criticized, and in some cases, derided.

Tom ran his hand through his hair and closed his eyes while the rancorous debate continued. Finally, he stood. The action caught everyone's attention, and the conversations and side discussions slid to a halt.

Tom studied the faces of his friends and colleagues. "It is clear to me that we owe it to ourselves and to history to make sure we get this right. I certainly do not feel equal to the founders. The genius of what they accomplished with the Constitution is an aspiration I hope we can hold high while we struggle to map our future. This time it is not the survival of 13 colonies at stake. It is of the human race itself."

Wylie Hickum nearly shouted, "Well said. Here Here!"

Tom rubbed his tired eyes and continued, "Esmerelda, can you please summarize what we have managed to agree to so far?"

Esmerelda sighed, "Sure, Tom." She shuffled some papers and notes before continuing, "We've agreed to a constitutional government, modeled closely on the United States Constitution, with modern language and terminology."

Gloria Vargas shook her head, "That'll be fun."

Esmerelda chuckled, "Sometimes you have a talent for the obvious, Gloria. Anyway, continuing on, the constitution will, like the US version, emphasize natural human rights that are not granted by the government and cannot be taken away by government."

We want to ensure a restricted, limited government with some sort of controls to prevent it from growing huge. The judiciary will be restricted to only interpreting rather than effectively 'making' law. The bureaucracy will not be able to issue statutes or regulations, only enforce laws. Congress will be bicameral with a démarche lower house of lottery-chosen citizens who can refuse office with no consecutive terms. Elected offices will have strict term limits and will be required to stay at home, in their own districts, and not move to a capital. They must meet mental health standards, and service is considered to be a part-time job with a yet-to-be-determined salary. The Senate will be elected with a single six-year term. They cannot be reelected. After two terms have passed, they can run again."

She paused and sipped water from a plain glass. "We acknowledge that in addition to supporting the war effort, the government will, in many ways, face frontier challenges like those faced in the 1800s. The focus will need to be on the critical tasks of defending settlements from creature attacks, communications, surveying land and resources, and administering the law."

Tom nodded, "And, at least for a long while, there are no other countries to contend with, so no international diplomacy. There is a vast amount of wilderness territory, and God knows what is out there waiting for us."

Gloria shook her head, "This is all well and good, although you all know I don't agree with everything. I do agree that we need to lay down a framework for the civilian government going forward. However, I have realized what worries me most—we need to build something that will last far longer than the U.S.

Constitution. This… war… may well last far longer than western civilization did. Against an enemy as vast as the Accipiters and as enormous as the Galaxy is, it may take thousands of years to defeat them. Think about what has happened in major wars in the past. There was always a slide towards totalitarianism, with the weight and seriousness of that war justifying reducing individual rights and giving more and more power to government. Can any of you honestly look at me and tell me that the same thing isn't going to happen here? Is it even possible for us to prevent it? And what's to keep the military from simply walking in and taking over, and establishing a military dictatorship? How do we give the space navy the power it needs to conduct the war without giving up our freedoms and rights? Those rights mean nothing to the Accipiters, but they are one of the few things we have left that survived Earth. Those rights and concepts make us unique. How do we fight this war and not become the enemy ourselves?"

Progress

Gail Finley leaned in close to Heartbreaker as she brushed his gleaming jet-black coat. She had not been one of those little girls who "loved" horses, but her father, the Colonel, had given her an… appreciation.

Now though, Gail had grown to treasure what time she could steal away here in the stables. Eva had been patient in teaching her what she needed to know. She almost hated to admit it, but she was starting to better understand the people in Fort Brazos. Eva was fast becoming a friend.

And then there was John.

She glanced over at him. He was busy tending to his chestnut roan Rusty. Of course, they were both more or less surrounded by their ever-present security details. Still, even these young men, Nate, Jose, and Jermal, as irritating and impossible as they often were, had become something else…. Gail was an only child, but they had become like the protective older brothers she had never had… even though she was almost ten years their senior.

She ground her teeth.

And then there was John.

For the last few days, he had grated on her nerves even more than usual, often talking without deigning to actually look at her. And then, out of the blue, he unilaterally cleared both their calendars and invited her to the stables.

What was worse was that Gail did not need her Master's degree to see the signs, and those signs both angered and frightened her. She grudgingly realized that she looked forward to the time she spent with John and, damn him, resent the time when they were apart. She'd half-convinced herself that it was a result of the ongoing crisis. That it was a perverse form of Stockholm syndrome, their forced proximity, and… damn if he didn't fill out his shirts too well. *Damn, these Gardener-enhanced hormones! I feel like some giddy teenager!*

And then… and then there was the look that Gwyneth had given her when Gail had abashedly asked for help with her makeup. Gwyneth had been surprised at the request and complained about how little help Gail really needed. They shared a similar complexion, and Gwyneth had all the right things. It was only when they'd sat down in front of the mirror that Gail had blushed at the realization that it wasn't makeup help that she wanted. Gail was perfectly competent at administering the minimal makeup she typically needed in order to look professional. She'd had plenty of relationships in the past, but something was different now.

As she had sat in front of Gwyneth's mirror and looked at herself, she'd suddenly realized that for perhaps the first time in her life, she really cared about how she looked and not just in general. It was how she looked to a specific person, and it terrified her. Against all better judgment, she quietly confessed her trepidation to Gwyneth, who was both absolutely supportive and, to Gail's miserable annoyance, utterly unsurprised.

She fumed as she brushed Heartbreaker, who nervously shifted his feet as he sensed her anger. Gail paused, took a deep breath, and gently stroked his neck to calm him. Damn! *I feel like a damned schoolgirl, and there isn't anything I could do about it, even if it were really real and not the Damned Gardeners tinkering with our biology. The whole world is watching.* She looked at John and fought the urge to bite her lip or smile or…. *Stop it!*

John did not look up, but she could tell that he had sensed she was looking at him, which Gail suddenly realized she had been doing for a lot longer than she should have. Nate and Jermal were nearby in the Stables, and Jose was outside. However, neither of them gave any indication whatsoever that they had noticed. For that matter, neither did Sergeant Jenkins or Corporal Diego. Every single one of them had adopted a face of perfect attentive innocence.

Damn them.

John brushed Rusty with another long stroke. He paused and asked evenly, "So, Gail, what is your assessment of the starship progress?"

Gail blinked herself back to reality, and she found herself saying, "I'm impressed by the quality and inventiveness of the work being done. The teams are throwing themselves into the work, but it is still slow going."

John nodded without looking up, "I know you suffered through some of the F-35 program problems, so you must have a feel for how high-tech military projects can be. But I have to ask you, is this peacetime but highly motivated and enthusiastic work, or is this wartime, all, or nothing, do or die, for all the marbles, work?"

Gail flashed with anger and frustration, then forced herself to put down the brush gently. Then she slowly patted Heartbreaker on the neck, turned, and walked over to John. It had become second nature to her to not bother to close the stall behind her. The Gardener-heightened intelligence and emotional stability the horses and even dogs now shared had changed the dynamic of human-animal relationships. And trust.

She wanted to storm across the room but forced herself to be calm. "John, it is hard to imagine that these people could work any harder. Some are dropping out from exhaustion!"

John did not turn around to face her but continued to brush Rusty carefully. "I don't doubt it. I'm sure you know the story but let me repeat it anyway. Before the Battle of Midway, Yorktown was badly damaged at the Battle of the Coral Sea, and the yard projected several months of repairs would be needed. But this was wartime, and they instead had her effectively battle-ready within 72 hours because someone with enough authority demanded it. She wasn't perfect by any means, and I'm sure they used plenty of duct tape and baling wire to get the job done, or whatever the equivalent was back then, but the point is, they only focused on the bare minimum needed to return her to service."

Gail shook her head in frustration, "John, the Yorktown sank."

"Yes, she did, but not before her presence there meant the difference not only in the battle but possibly in the war itself."

John turned to face her. "Gail, I've read all the reports. I'm sure that all these projects and subprojects are ultimately all needed and worthwhile. I know everyone is working their asses off. That's not the problem. The problem is that we don't need all of it to get this mission done, and I am convinced it could mean the difference in this war."

Gail shook her head, "Look, John…."

He reached out and put his hand on her shoulder. She swallowed at his touch. Part of her wondered why she did not pull away from him, holding her shoulder like that, as she would have with just about anyone else.

Then she noticed the brush still in his other hand. His knuckles were white, gripping it. Then she looked into his eyes. Really looked.

What she saw in them was both dreadful and exhilarating. She saw… longing and… guilt. And she knew what the guilt was without even thinking about it. It was the guilt of a widower. Most of all, though, she saw fear and hope that his feelings were not unrequited.

Gail's heart pounded in her ears. Her eyes widened, and without conscious thought, she reached out and touched his face. Her anger vanished.

This is why he had been so stiff and odd lately! Her mind reeled at the confirmation that this… relationship was not just in her own mind. He had half ignored her and had not turned to face her until now because he couldn't.

Gail shuddered at the realization that he was just as torn about what was happening between them as she was. She dropped her hand away from his cheek. John released her shoulder and turned stiffly back to Rusty.

Gail's head swam. In those seconds, John had told her everything she needed to know. His eyes had spoken volumes, and, damn it. So, had her own. Her secret was out. *He knows… and he knows he can't… we can't. We must not.* She had already known that nothing could ever come of it, even if it were indeed real, but the unspoken confirmation that she was not alone… that there really was something growing between them did not bring the expected sense of despair… But, on some level, maybe she was not so terribly, achingly, crushingly alone anymore. Worse, she had not even truly realized how alone she was until this very moment.

Her heart skipped a beat at the thought that, of course, they would be President and Vice President forever. She surrendered her anger, at least for now, and decided to allow herself that tiny spark of hope.

She swallowed again, took a deep breath, and mentally shook herself back to business, "So even if you are right, what do we do about it?"

John laughed, "We? Why Gail Anson Finley, you are the God-damned Vice President of the entire human race. You have all the authority you need to go put things right."

He reached out and put his hand on her shoulder again, "You are going to march your pretty little Air Force ass up to New London, and you are going to set them straight. Divide the work. All that good long-term stuff gets second priority to whatever is needed to launch a minimally viable ship. Promote people, fire people, give them medals, and do whatever the hell you have to do to reward inventiveness but kick that ship out the airlock at the same time." He let go of her shoulder and stood back.

Gail's mouth twitched ever so slightly at the first compliment John had ever given about her appearance. She would have strongly considered decking anyone else who might have said, *"your pretty little ass,"* but from John…. Well, he *was* the President….

Free Spirits

East of Fort Brazos, spinward, lay a Himalayan-worthy barrier range of mountains, and beyond those mountains, the ocean. However, between the mountains and Fort Brazos lay a vast, glacier-fed violet-blue lake, or inland sea. Many names had been proposed, but Lake Texoma had become the most popular. Named after one of the largest reservoirs in the United States, the original Lake Texoma had lain at the confluence of the Red and Washita Rivers between Texas and Oklahoma.

Along the shore of the new Lake Texoma, at a natural inlet, or as natural as anything was in New Texas, a collection of RV's, tents, and campsites had quietly sprung up, along with a hodgepodge of bass boats, pontoon boats, and other small, aged, mostly worn-out boats.

Despite fears of attack from Accipiter creatures, university students and not a few teenagers had slipped away and made their way to party at the lake, and, over time, many stayed there, reasoning that Wardogs and Stalkers likely, probably, maybe, hopefully, couldn't swim. So far, no malicious sea creatures had been discovered.

At least that was what the four Biology Master's Degree students on the pontoon boat bobbing several miles from shore hoped. Lucia Ewing, her roommate Michelle Bain, Ronald Glenn, and the postgrad student Marcos Salinas took turns free diving with a pod of over 100 Amazon River Dolphins.

As grad students, the four were expected to be old enough and serious enough in their studies to set a positive example for others. It was the apocalypse, however, so who would notice or care if they cut loose and mixed beer, sun(tube)-shine, swimsuits, and a lake with their studies. No one had known what kind of life to expect in the lake, so after several rounds of drinks to generate the courage to brave potential sea monsters, they had set out on the boat with a beer cooler, sonar, underwater cameras, flippers, and snorkels.

They had only been an hour from shore when they had spotted the dolphins surfacing and jumping out of the water. The pod of dolphins was moving slowly, so it had only taken another hour and a half to catch up. They feared the sonar would irritate or scare the dolphins, so they left it off. The curious dolphins surrounded the boat and made it easy to estimate their numbers.

After several dives, the four stopped to take a break and eat sandwiches. Lucia wiped crumbs off her one-piece and laughed, "Did you see the numbers? This pod is mostly females!"

Michelle nodded, "And most of them look pregnant."

Marcos stretched his muscles, "No babies or young ones, though. Either they did not survive Awakening Day, or the Gardeners didn't copy babies?"

Ronald shook his head, "But they already seem to have strong bonds with each other. Did you see how some of them stayed so close together? If they were all copied, you would think they wouldn't really know each other."

Marcos nodded, "Also, I've never heard of Amazon river dolphins growing this large."

Michelle shrugged, "Maybe their diet is better here?"

Lucia shook her head, "And grown 20% bigger in only a few months?" She loosened the hair ties securing her long black hair, threaded her fingers through her hair, and then re-secured her hair again more tightly. "I'm going back in."

Marcos grinned and followed, swatting her on the rear, "Me too," as they both dived into the water.

Like so many others, Lucia and Marcos had paired off after Awakening Day. Michelle shook her head and complained aloud, "How is that girl not pregnant yet?"

Ronald himself was juggling two part-time girlfriends at the moment. He laughed, "Beats me," as he worked on another sketch in his notebook, drawing the distinctive snout and speckled pattern of one of the larger dolphins.

Michelle was happy that Lucia was happy but was determined to most emphatically *not* get pregnant herself. She had plans for her life, and babies were not part of that future. So, despite the damnable effect of the Gardener-enhanced hormones, she resisted temptation. It took a great deal of effort to *not* admire Ronald and Marcos's bodies. It was not easy.

Instead, she looked out at the water and asked, "Ronald, have you decided what you want to do after graduation?"

He put his pencil and notepad down. "I thought I did, but with all the changes happening at the University, I'm just hoping our program still exists long enough for us to graduate."

Michelle gasped, "You don't think the new Xenobiology department will take over, do you?"

"I don't know, but they are sure getting all the resources these days. I mean, look around," he waved his hand up to the other side of the world above them, "We have got a whole world here that nobody really knows the biology of. Even if the Gardeners copied everything verbatim, the environments are not all the same. Look at what we've discovered here today! Amazon dolphins in Lake Texoma, and they're bigger than any ever recorded on Earth. What else are we going to discover in our own backyard?"

A sudden harsh gust of wind caught them by surprise. They had been so intent on the dolphins that none of them had noticed the squall sweeping in from the North.

Michelle shrieked as the gust blew the remains of her lunch far out into the water.

A wave knocked the boat sideways, and then a microburst slammed into the canvas top of the pontoon boat, heaving it onto its side. Michelle's head struck a support, and both she and Ronald were tossed into the water.

Ronald fought his way back to the surface, coughing up water and desperately looking for Michelle. He gulped air, paddled, and dove back down, looking for her, only to be bumped by three long-snouted, bulbous-headed dolphins. He panicked and struggled against them, but they forced him back to the surface.

They had done the same with Michelle, and in moments, the dolphins had pushed them both to the capsized pontoon boat. Michelle was confused, gasping, and fighting for air. Ronald took her from behind and held onto her until she stopped struggling and regained control of herself.

By now, the fast little storm had already blown past, and the water was calming down. Lucia and Marcos were swimming towards them.

Ronald helped Michelle up on top of the capsized boat, and then he, Lucia, and Marcos followed suit.

Marcos shook his head, "Did you see how fast that storm hit and then left?"

Michelle rubbed the bump on her head, "We just caught the edge of it."

They all stared at each other, no one wanting to say the words aloud. *What do we do now?*

Four hours later, a horn sounded in the distance. Lucia shouted, "Look!"

Three bass boats were jumping waves headed their way.

First Flight

As was his practice, Captain Phillipe "Phil" Underwood calmly roamed the former submarine's modified CIC, nodding to himself, studying displays and instruments. His boyish face and semi-permanent grin belied his fatigue. For weeks, both his crew, designated the 'Gold' crew, and their Blue crew counterparts had pushed the starship testing hard. The testing had not gone well.

A vast amount of what happens in a submarine is related to being, well, a submarine. Underwater, under pressure, maneuvering underwater, and so on. That meant that much of the equipment in a submarine was related to those tasks – as were the functions and duties of the sailors who operated the vessel.

Now, there was no need for ballast and trim or the operation thereof. There was no need to man and operate an engine room to drive the ducted propulsor, worry about cavitation, thermoclines, water density, or monitor sonar and myriad other instruments, all of which were no longer even there. Of course, there was also no maneuvering room, torpedoes, missiles, their launchers, or the equipment used to monitor, control, and operate those missing weapons.

The hull was dotted with what the mysterious operations manuals explained to be sensors and point defense lasers designed to protect against micro-meteors or other space junk whenever the ship was naked in space with the warp drive turned off.

The complete lack of actual "space weapons" of any kind was the genesis of no end of debate and rancor, the common refrain beginning with: *How were we supposed to fight Accipiter ships if we have no weapons?*

The result was that a great deal of equipment and space formerly needed were now either replaced by new equipment and functions or converted into storage space for everything from additional food and supplies to spacesuits.

Speaking of spacesuits, everyone onboard wore one, whether crew or not. One of the New London warehouses, amid the seemingly endless rows of them that the Gardeners had provided, had been devoted entirely to pressure suits and spacesuits. Thousands of them, in what seemed to be every design mankind currently had in use – or planned for use. These included American NASA designs, Russian and Chinese, and more from SpaceX, Blue Origin, Virgin Galactic, Boeing, and other, more obscure sources.

It had been decided that, at least during testing, everyone should wear, at a minimum, a 'pressure suit' in case of decompression. On the other hand, this was not some futuristic clean, and simple environment. It was still largely a submarine. The spaces were tight, and the equipment was often tricky to operate on and around. Therefore, the selected suits were the least bulky, most form-fitting, durable, and flexible they could find.

The crew suits were blue and resembled flight suits. Non-crew wore a slightly different version that was white. They were, of course, universally despised as being too clumsy, hot and the idea of lugging around the helmet in the confined spaces of the former submarine, even though the suit helmet was one of the smallest and least cumbersome designs available, became the butt of many jokes.

There was no sonar array now, but there were sensor feeds interfaced with the alien drive section sensors. Water in the ballast tanks could still be cracked for oxygen during the trip. The primary air lock in the sail and the other outer doors needed scrupulous maintenance and monitoring.

With so many systems removed, so many new ones added, and the structure of the submarine itself dramatically altered, it was hardly surprising that both equipment and procedures were very… rough around the edges. While the alien drive section had, thankfully, shown no problems or errors, almost every other system had had problems either in use, calibration, or even outright failure.

Both the Blue and Gold crews had drilled relentlessly. The yard engineers, scientists, and specialists were no less driven. Vice President Gail Finley had seen to that personally. Even now, she stood in her corner of the CIC, making endless notes on her tablet computer, and quietly giving orders on her headset to that small army of people struggling to bring the Blood Phoenix to life.

Gail had thrown herself into the work. The distraction helped. What surprised her, even more was how very much young Matti Austin had become an asset. The girl was razor-sharp, despite her age, and was always there right there, at just the right moment, anticipating Gail's needs. Moreover, Matti's enthusiasm and personality somehow managed to lift Gail's spirits in ways she would never have believed possible.

Great things were in store for Matti, she was sure. In the meantime, Gail had taken the starship project bull by the horns and dragged it forward by sheer force of will and personality. She looked up at Phil and gave an encouraging nod.

Phil ran a hand over his prematurely receding hairline and forced a smile. "OK, People. Let us try this yet again. Commander Cross, set for control testing. Rig the boat for space."

Charles Cross nodded; his grey eyes focused on the checklist displayed on the screen at his station. That he had written the checklist himself made no difference. He called out, "Chief of the Boat, Rig the boat for space."

Command Master Chief Petty Officer Luis Perez was a bull of a man, completely bald with shiny dark skin and the ruddy, lightly scarred face of a prizefighter. Luis had been a Golden Gloves champion and had continued to competitively box until just two years ago when he had broken an arm in an automobile accident and finally hung up his gloves.

Luis answered, "Rig the boat for Space. Aye." He touched the microphone button on his headset and called out in a deep baritone, "All Compartments, you know the drill, seal your suits and helmets. Secure all outer doors. Seal all compartment hatches. Rig the boat for Space."

Luis and everyone in the CIC donned and sealed their helmets. He listened to reports on his headset before announcing, "Ship and crew rigged for Space, Commander."

Charles nodded, "Ship rigged for Space, Captain."

Phil smiled, "Control Room, this is Blood Phoenix Actual. Please decompress the bay."

In anticipation of the test, the hangar bay outside had already been cleared of all personnel. Doors and bulkheads slammed shut. A soprano voice responded,

"Acknowledged Blood Phoenix. Bay is decompressing in… 5… 4… 3… 2… 1. Bay decompression commencing now."

Throughout the hanger, strobing red lights flashed, and a powerful klaxon announced decompression. Enormous intake grills louvered open with a speed that defied all expectations and which implied tremendous energies employed. The hangar bay was reduced to near-vacuum in just under two minutes.

No alarms beeped or squawked this time. Phil blinked in pleasant surprise. There were no immediate indications of the bad seals or the host of other problems and malfunctions they had experienced so often before. He grinned at Charles Cross, "Check Systems Status."

Charles nodded, "COB, Check Systems Status."

Luis called out on his microphone, "All Departments, Systems Status Check." He then flipped a switch, putting the responses on the CIC PA.

"Reactor Room. All systems nominal." The reactor room was relatively unchanged, although the reactor efficiency levels were nearly twenty percent higher than before. Evidently, the Gardeners had 'optimized' a few things in its operation as well.

"Environmental Control. All systems nominal. Pressure holding at one standard atmosphere. All compartments report gravity at sea level normal." The air mix had been settled on 78% Nitrogen, 21% Oxygen, and CO2 kept at or below 0.03%.

The starship drive section generated an artificial gravity field, although no one yet understood how. It was apparently designed to be adjustable to whatever level the original shipbuilders desired, presumably to acclimate them to whatever destination planet they were headed for.

Since everything in the former submarine was designed to operate within Earth's gravity field, it had been decided that an eye should be kept on whether the artificial gravity field was working normally. No gravimeters were on hand, so a simple method was found to ensure that things were 'normal.' A small postal meter with a one-ounce weight was glued to the tray. Gravity would show something other than… one ounce if it were high or low.

"Launch Bay. All systems nominal." At 130' long and 80' wide, the Interplanetary Landing Craft was not small. It was longer than a C130 Hercules. Blood Phoenix's ILC had been named 'Atlatl.' It was currently powered down, but the bay was still manned and monitored.

"Sensors. All systems nominal."

"Drive section. All systems nominal." Of all the thrown-together hybrid craft systems, the alien drive section was about the only component that had never reported an error.

With surprise in his voice, Luis reported, for the very first time ever, "Boat rigged for space."

Charles hesitated, "Boat rigged for space, Captain. Congratulations!"

The large wall screen monitor currently displayed a video feed from the hangar bay outside the ship. Suddenly, the lights in the hangar bay went dark, came back on, then cycled on and off repeatedly.

Charles groaned, "Do we have an error in the external sensor feed? Sensors, report please?"

The sensor tech hesitated as he checked his screen, then he answered excitedly, "No, Sir! Control is flashing the lights in congratulations, he hit a function key, and the screen changed and read, *'Congratulations, Gold Team! You are the first to complete a flight check with zero errors or malfunctions!'*"

Gail asked through her microphone, "Permission to unseal helmets, Captain?"

Phil unceremoniously unsealed and removed his own helmet with a flourish and then announced, "Granted!"

Gail followed suit and reached down to the backpack behind her against the bulkhead. She unzipped it and pulled out a bottle of Glenfiddich whiskey. She flashed a toothy smile and said, "Congratulations, Captain. We have something special for the crew but for now. I'd like to officially present you with this." She walked around a table and handed it to him. "I had it in my duffle and had been saving it for a special occasion. It is probably one of the last surviving bottles from Earth. I'm sure you'll find an appropriate time to use it."

Phil grinned brightly and held the bottle high for everyone to see, including via the monitors that fed the view from the CIC into the rest of the ship. "Thank you, Ms. Vice President."

A cheer broke out throughout the ship, and everyone in the CIC stood and applauded. In the competition between the Blue and Gold crews, it had been agreed that the first to achieve this success would be served dinner by the other crew. It was mild punishment for second place, by some Navy standards, but it had seemed an appropriate reward and punishment for the 'losing' crew in light of everything.

What everyone knew but was left unsaid was that it was also a likely factor in determining which crew would fly the first mission. The most important mission in the history of mankind. It was also a mission that many feared was rushed and unwise and likely a suicide mission that could backfire and lead the enemy back to New Texas.

Gail nodded, "And with that, Captain, I will retreat to the control room for the next phase."

Phil smiled, "It won't be the same without you, Ms. Vice President. You know you are welcome to join us."

Gail had been a fixture in the CIC all these weeks. Her energy and force of personality had at first been resented by some who thought she was usurping the Captain. Before long, though, it became clear to everyone that Gail was moving mountains to help them. There was a sharp line drawn between her and the Captain. It was *his* ship. She was only there to help him get it out of the hangar.

Gail locked eyes with Phil, who she had grown to like and respect greatly. In truth, she desperately wanted to stay on board and be there during the first flight's heady moments. She knew, though, that it was the one thing she could not do.

"Thank you, Captain." She tightened her lip, "Fair winds and following seas." She looked around the room. "To you all."

Gail turned and walked towards the ladder to the sail airlock.

Phil looked down at the bottle still in his hand, then lurched towards her, "Ms. Vice President."

Gail turned back to face him. "Yes, Captain."

Phil smiled, "I know you're Air Force, but we have a tradition in the Navy. I know our schedule doesn't allow for a formal Christening…." He held the bottle out to her, "But we would be honored, Ma'am, if you would do us the honor of Christening the Blood Phoenix… and I think a bottle of whisky, instead of Champagne, under the circumstances, is entirely appropriate." He swallowed and looked down at the bottle, "Especially with a precious bottle from Earth."

Gail blinked in surprise. She did not bother mentioning that the bottle did not really come from Earth. It and everything around them, including their own bodies, had been duplicated and recreated here in New Texas. But that did not change the symbolism. She also realized that this moment was being captured on the CIC cameras and would be memorialized.

She stiffened and nodded, "Captain, it would be my great honor to do so." She resealed her helmet to exit through the airlock into the vacuum outside in the hangar bay.

There was no extra room in the CIC for Gail's security detachment, and Gail had ordered them to stay in the Control Room. Had they been with her, she had no doubt they would have bodily prevented her from donning her helmet and going through the airlock into the now airless hangar bay. Her lip quivered as she remembered John saying, 'you're the God-damned Vice President, Gail Anson Finley!'

After that exchange, Gail realized that while she had been entirely sincere in performing her elected duties, she never fully accepted that she was truly worthy of the office. Gail had only been a field-promoted Major. She *took* orders. She was not used to *giving* them. Giving orders to men and women far her senior and doing so with personal authority had been incredibly taxing and stressful.

However, the more resistance and red tape she ran into, the more her resolve crystallized within her. The ingrained reflex to accept the wisdom of those more senior and deference to their opinions gave way to her own determination and growing confidence in her belief that, incredibly, John had been right.

She chuckled to herself as she thought about the reaction that Nate, Jose, and Jermal must be having at this particular moment. Gail had worked her way down to the platform at the nominal bow of the ship. The coating that Preston Milner had noted that first day had turned out to be an array of carbon fiber tubules that, the theory went, were designed to convert heat radiating from the ship into power, which it then fed into the seemingly endless capacity of the drive section energy storage.

The surface coating was incredibly tough, as one might hope for a spaceship. Breaking a bottle of whisky on it posed no risk of damage.

A large Texas Flag had been emblazoned upon the upper part of the bow, with its red and blue stripe and a single star upon a field of blue.

Gail keyed her mic and raised the bottle, "In the name of New Texas, and on the souls of a murdered Earth, I christen thee, the Blood Phoenix. This flag above me, which used to represent a Republic and later a State, was originally inspired by an earlier flag." Gail smiled to herself as she remembered John telling her the story and then wondered again that it had stuck with her. "The Republic of Fredonia was short-lived, but the red and white stripes of its flag were meant to represent the joint resistance of both the European settlers and the native American Indians to Mexican rule. Now, today, those colors represent more. They symbolize the collective resistance of all of the surviving peoples of Earth against the genocide and tyranny of the Accipiters. So, Blood Phoenix, as you spread your wings, may your flight be true, your vengeance terrible, and your enemies flee before you in terror. Go forth now as the vanguard of our retribution and return victorious and proud."

In the silence of vacuum, Gail smashed the bottle against the bow. It did not fizz like champagne, but she was not entirely sure how much of the roar in her ears was from cheers over the radio or her own blood fury and rage at the Accipiters.

✪ ✪ ✪

The order had been given to recheck all systems and helmets resealed. Everything remained in the green.

Meanwhile, this would be the first time humans had exited New Texas in a craft that humans had at least partially built.

Phil Underwood stopped pacing up and down the CIC and announced, "OK. Great job, everyone. Now let's earn our princely salaries. Commander, make all preparations for getting underway."

✪ ✪ ✪

Minutes later, the ship gently rose from the deck of the hangar. It was not yet moving under its own power. The gravity field being generated beneath it had reduced power and inverted. Light shimmered at the intersection of the drive section's minimal warp field, internal gravity field, and the inverted hangar bay gravity field.

Brilliant strobe lights flashed on the hangar airlock door, and the massive doors slowly opened, revealing an airlock chamber as long and large as the hangar itself. When it finished opening, the gravity field altered again, and the ship floated slightly higher and forward into the airlock bay before the doors closed behind it. Since the hangar had already been depressurized, so had the airlock. Moments after the doors closed behind the ship, the airlock doors silently slid open in front of it, revealing the inky blackness of space beyond.

The ship was then accelerated slowly out of the airlock by the bay's gravity field. The same system would allow a damaged or unpowered craft or object to be pulled into the airlock and hangar bays. Everything had operated precisely as the built-in simulators had behaved.

Phil nodded as there were no reports of damage or malfunction, and all the indicators still glowed green. "All right then. All stations prepare to get underway."

New Texas loomed behind them as a great, grey rock in space. Even the airlock they had passed through was camouflaged and indistinguishable from the surrounding dull, boring rock. In the distance, the spec of light that was the system's relatively tiny brown dwarf star barely glinted in the displays. The rest was black with only the celestial backdrop of the distant stars.

Charles leaned forward, "Ms. Palmer, test your axis, ten-meter standard test pattern."

The builders of the drive section had required two pilot operators to control the geometries of the dorsal and ventral ring sections warp field, which, it had been learned, require constant adjustment. The oddly shaped benches and their controls were located in the nodal structures beneath and above the ring apexes and had been carefully studied. They were not even close to being compatible with human anatomy. Still, their functions seemed clear, and the Gardeners had provided complete control runs from the drive section into the human ship, which had been used to construct human-compatible workstations.

It was the geometry of the warp field that resulted in movement relative to spacetime outside the ship. The two operators were needed to work in concert to make it work, and everyone on board had had at least some time in the simulators. All the candidates for the crew had been tested to find the people best suited.

Petty Officers Mikaela Palmer and Lukas Wesley were two of the NCOs who had ranked the highest in the simulator testing, with Mikaela being the highest rated of all. By coin toss, the second-highest, Terrance McQueen, was lead on the Blue Crew. Mikaela had not been a submariner. She was surface fleet but had been visiting a friend at New London on Awakening Day. Women were still rare on U.S. submarines, but newer boats, such as the Virginia class, had been designed to accommodate women in the crew better.

Both wore VR helmets, as the virtual interface was needed to provide a comprehensible way to simultaneously manage both the warp field geometry adjustments as well as minor things like simply going in the desired direction. A metal tubing framework surrounded their stations to keep other people from bumping into them while they virtually operated the controls.

Mikaela answered, "10-meter standard test pattern, aye."

Moments later, Mikaela added, "10-meter standard test pattern executed successfully." There was, of course, no sensation of movement. In a warp field, the ship is actually stationary. It is the field that, in effect, moves.

Charles reported, "Test pattern completed, Captain. We are prepared to get underway."

Phil smiled, "Well, people, let us see if we can move in a nice straight line."

Charles swallowed, "Ms. Palmer, take us out ten thousand kilometers, zero inclination relative, along our current orientation. One percent power." At that power level, they would be traveling at approximately .5c: still sublight speed. The function was not linear, however. They now knew where they were located relative to Earth, some 48 light-years away. It would take roughly twenty days at 80% power, considered the safe and sustainable level, to get there.

Mikaela answered, "Ten thousand kilometers, zero inclination relative, current orientation, one percent power, aye."

The view of New Texas vanished for only an instant before reappearing. Instead of a wall of grey rock, the entire length of the sausage-shaped world filled the screen. Several people gasped. Just as it was in the ILCs, there had been no sensation of movement, vibration, or noise. In those short moments of time, the space in front of them had contracted, and the space behind them expanded.

Putting his physicist hat on, one of the first questions that Charles had asked about the drive had been how they would deal with particle deflection. Even hitting a grain of sand at relativistic speeds would be 'very bad.' The consensus had been that the design of this warp system had an unexpected wrinkle. Particles impacting the edge of the warp bubble were channeled into 'precessing folds' in the field that annihilated them, and the energy was fed back into the drive's power storage. The limitation being that flying through anything sufficiently dense could overload the system's capacity to absorb the energy. In that event, the excess energy would be dumped inside the field in the form of potentially lethal gamma radiation.

Mikaela reported, "Maneuver completed successfully, Sir."

There had been worry that the hybrid nature of the combined Builder/Human vessel would result in unexpected, potentially dangerous, or, at a minimum, nausea-inducing motion. However, not even the hum of the equipment in the room had changed during the maneuver.

Phil broke into a broad grin, and everyone on board burst into applause and cheers.

Phil let them enjoy the moment before ordering, "Mr. Shultz, notify Control we have completed Phase One testing."

With no faster-than-light communications, they relied on directional communication lasers, a function for which some of the point defense lasers did double duty. Meanwhile, the Gardeners had studded the exterior of New Texas with reciprocal lasers and sensors. At 'only' 10,000 kilometers, though, the delay was still negligible.

Chief Warrant Officer Erick Schultz answered, "Notify Control completed Phase One testing, aye." He pressed a key and repeated the message. Moments later, he responded, "Sir, Control acknowledges completion of Phase One testing and sends compliments to Blood Phoenix. We are ordered to commence Phase Two."

Phil circled the CIC, studying each control and resting a reassuring hand on the occasional shoulder. Presently he nodded to himself, "Very well. Execute Phase Two test."

Phase Two involved a complex spiraling path that would test and stress the ship. So far, the inherent inertial compensation within the warp field had been flawless, and as long as the field was operating, the math said it should stay that way. Of course, the people who wrote that math were not here to suffer the consequences if they were wrong, and sudden acceleration or deceleration resulted in everyone onboard being turned into a red smear on the bulkhead.

Charles ordered, "Ms. Palmer, Execute Phase Two test, one percent power."

"Executing Phase Two test, one percent power, aye."

When looked at, at a distance, the surface of an ocean seems smooth. It is not until you get up close that you see the waves and chaos. The fabric of space itself, as much as it can be called and thought of as such, can be described similarly, at least from the perspective of someone who is operating a field that is stretching that fabric and that that fabric really doesn't like to be stretched. All of those variations can add up to form energy gradients to pull the warp drive off course. Constant, even frenzied attention is needed to keep the ship's course steady.

Mikaela and Luka's arms and hands furiously danced around them within their stations. If one were to look out a window, so to speak, space in front of the ship would be as opaque as that behind it. However, the computing power of the drive section reconstructed the view for them in three dimensions, and the result was displayed on the wall screen.

The image of New Texas stretched and smeared before snapping back into shape as the ship executed the test flight pattern. After a few seconds, Mikaela and Luka stopped, chests heaving. Mikaela announced, "Phase Two test completed successfully, Sir."

Charles looked at Phil, "Phase Two test completed. The board remains green, Captain."

Phil smiled, "Outstanding! Report status to Control and request permission to proceed to Phase Three. Meanwhile, I want a complete systems check, all stations."

✪ ✪ ✪

Ten minutes later, telemetry had finished beaming back to New Texas, and no serious problems had been reported. Phil avoided thinking about how fast they were pushing things. Back on Earth, before the Accipiters, ship trials were slow, careful, and deliberate. Do something, record what happens, go home, and evaluate before doing the next thing. Rinse and repeat. The Presidential mandate, however, meant that they had to push and push and push harder. It was the only conceivable way to meet the deadline.

Phil walked over and clapped Charles on the back, "All right, everyone. Let us make even more history. Prepare all stations for FTL and execute FTL test flight."

Preparing for FTL was a formality. Despite what the math said, no one really knew if it would be any different than sublight warp travel. It had seemed prudent to add a step to notify all the crew so that everyone was completely aware of what was about to happen. Some had wanted to create a special alarm or add unique lights in each compartment, but for now, it was decided that 'Preparing for FTL' would simply be an extra audio announcement to the crew.

Charles tapped a key in front of him, putting his microphone on broadcast to the entire ship, "Attention all stations. Prepare for FTL."

He turned to Mikaela and Luka, "Ms. Palmer, commence Phase Three testing. Execute FTL on current heading for ten seconds, power for 1c."

Mikaela answered, "Executing FTL on current heading. Ten seconds. Power for 1c. aye."

Only this time, nothing at all happened. The image of New Texas on the wall screen did not change or recede into the distance as had been expected.

Mikaela cursed in frustration, "I'm sorry, Sir, the field collapsed. I don't understand why Sir. We input the commands, and everything looked normal, and the drive section acted like it was going to respond, and then it just shut itself down like it had a mind of its own. I'm sorry, Sir, we resent the commands several times, but the ship won't go to FTL."

Teacher

Blood Phoenix Dorsal Node
February 23rd, NLD 177 -- FBD 205, 1822

Aft of the airlock-sail, and the CIC, was a compartment that had previously been used for divers to exit and enter the submarine, called the lockout trunk. The Gardeners had reconfigured the space to become a second airlock. It led to the narrow interior of the central spindle, which had ladder rungs embedded in its structure on one side and thick cable conduits on the other. A reversed but identical chamber now occupied the space on the 'bottom' of the submarine for access to the ventral drive control node.

Gail sighed to herself and closed her tired eyes for a moment before beginning the climb up to the dorsal node. The first time she had made the climb had been in a her freshly borrowed business suit and heels… the uniform of politics she loathed. While the hangar was pressurized and not about to go to vacuum, everyone wore uniforms or jumpsuits of one kind or another.

Gail had finally decided that 'rank hath its privileges' and begun wearing the outfit she felt most comfortable in. Jeans, thigh boots, a shirt, and a waist-cut form-fitting leather motorcycle jacket. By now, with the combination of news coverage and the population being as small as it is, she would have been challenged to find a single human being who would not immediately recognize her on sight, no matter what she wore. In the beginning, Gail had been 'encouraged' to dress and look 'Vice Presidential.' With vanishingly few exceptions, now that she had grown more comfortable with her role and authority, she simply didn't care what people thought.

She had not quite worked up the nerve to return to the base and ride her motorcycle back to Fort Brazos. The expressions on people's faces would be worth it, but the coronary she would give Jermal, in particular, would be harder to take.

Gail had, in fact, asked about it, worrying that someone might think it a great souvenir to steal the Vice President's motorcycle. The problem was that after she asked about it, Jermal had reported that it had been located and secured. When she further asked *where* it had been secured, there was always a perfectly acceptable but entirely nonspecific answer. *At least I have Heartbreaker now.*

On the other hand, the hangar and surrounding area were top security military, so there were no cameras and gawkers following her around. So, she accepted the silver lining to her grueling schedule for what it was. Since the ship's return two days ago, she had had a total of six hours of sleep, mostly in the form of power naps. She had debriefed Captain Underwood, his officers, and the scientists and engineers aboard.

Gail finally arrived at the top of the spindle and climbed into the airlock, wondering how someone much taller than her own 5'9" could manage it.

The lock cycled, and she entered… a very different place than the last time she had been here, months ago. The walls were now lined with improvised bookshelves, complete with elastic straps to hold the books in place in case of zero-G or other mishap. Other shelves were filled with video equipment, computer parts, and at least half a dozen laptop computers. Every remaining wall space was covered with screens and displays. Half of those were drawn and written on with dry-erase markers and festooned with post-it notes and taped-on index cards.

Scattered around the compartment were chairs, a sofa, and there was even carpet on the floor.

In the middle of it all, intently leaning forward in a Lazy-Boy recliner chair, hunched over a laptop, wearing earphones, a tweed jacket, and sporting a short ponytail and an impressive beard sat an almost unrecognizable Dr. Leo Talib. He glanced over at Gail and then silently returned to his work.

Gone was the troubled, haughty, somewhat aristocratic, and effete young man. When she last saw him, his face had spoken of desperate intensity. Leo had been the first to decipher the Accipiter language and had seemed possibly a tiny bit mad. Now he seemed just as intense, but his eyes were different. They were fresh, excited, and almost… boyish with enthusiasm.

Sabrina Chilton came around a corner carrying a tray of steaming teacups. She smiled and nodded at Gail, "Thank you for coming, Ms. Vice President."

She continued over to Leo, took his hand, and put a cup of tea in it. Leo did not look up but took the tea and sipped it deeply.

Sabrina brought the tray to Gail, "Tea, Ma'am?"

Gail blinked, eyes wide, taking in the room, and looked the question to Sabrina.

Sabrina's formerly short, bobbed blonde hair had also grown out to her shoulders. Gail noticed that there was less grey in it now, and like Leo, there was a freshness to her expression and playfulness in her pale blue eyes. It was obvious Sabrina had a secret.

Gail idly wondered how many.

Sabrina jerked in sudden awareness of Gail's unspoken question. "Oh, my, well, you must be wondering how we managed to get all of this in here?"

Gail glanced back at the narrow entrance with raised, skeptical eyebrows, "General?"

Sabrina straightened, "Yes, of course! Oh, obviously, many of these things would not fit through the spindle. You see, Ms. Vice President, the compartment can be opened on the side. The Builders were nothing if not practical."

Gail shook her head, "I read all the reports. Why don't I remember this?"

Sabrina raised her eyebrows, "Ah, that. Well, we are not considered a terribly high priority up here in the crow's nest. That is what my people call it. Once we learned how to do it, I just had my people do the rest of the work. I did not want to take time away from so many other important people and resources."

Gail nodded slowly, "I see, and I suppose, General, that the reason you called Alexander and asked him to ask me to make time to come and visit you here is that there is something else you have not felt it necessary to share with the others?"

Sabrina flashed a smile and noted that Gail was now referring to General Marcus by his first name. She glanced at Leo and then back at Gail, "Phoenix, my Dear, could I bother you to explain in the simplest terms to the Vice President why the warp test failed?"

Gail's eyes widened as an English-accented voice answered from several of the computers,

---

"Of course, Sabrina, I am delighted to help. Good evening Vice President Finley. It is nice to finally meet you. The warp test failed because the human pilots could not make corrections to the warp field quickly enough, and my built-in safety protocols collapsed the field."

Gail gawked, "You've built an AI?"

Leo pulled his headphones off and rotated his chair to face Gail, "No, Madam Vice President, what you are hearing is what we might call an AI, but we didn't build it. The person you are hearing is Phoenix, as we have named her. The ship itself."

Gail's eyes widened in shock as she whispered, "The ship is sentient?! *And you're just now telling us this?*"

Sabrina sipped her tea, "Not exactly. You see, this ship is…. She has been around for a very long time. The warp drive itself does not normally need the… persona… in order to operate at faster-than-light speeds. The intelligence that spoke was quiescent until *we* awakened it."

Gail cocked her head doubtfully as she dropped into a chair. "OK, explain this to me."

Leo stroked his beard, "Madam Vice President, the ship, Phoenix, is a vast matrix. The very material that it is composed of is all part of its neural structure. The computational power is and has to be, well, astronomical. It is, in many respects, a living thing. It seems to have some interesting aspects to its overall, shall way say, personality." He paused, "Phoenix, would you please explain what your persona's original function was?"

"Of course, Leo, I was a teacher."

Leo continued, "To understand the Builders, I found that I needed to teach the ship our language. I did not make very much progress until I realized that its responses were slowly pulling information from me about… us. It was trying to understand who we were, what was happening, and why she had awakened with us… inside her."

Gail pursed her lips, "You must have realized the potential…."

Sabrina interrupted, "Danger? Why, yes, we did, and we were about to stop everything as soon as we began to realize it when, well… Phoenix was a bit naughty, weren't you?"

"Once again, Sabrina and Leo, I sincerely apologize for frightening you."

Gail became very still before casually crossing her arms in such a way as to put her right hand inside her jacket, where her fingers touched the shoulder-holstered compact Glock G36 .45 that rested just below her left breast. Unlike John Austin's well-known penchant for continuing to stay armed, very few people knew that she carried a pistol. In fact, she hadn't done so until John and Matti both had ganged up and convinced her to do so.

Gail's father had seen to it that she was at least competent with a pistol, and, of course, the Air Force had furthered that education a little. John, and her own detail, had ensured that she had regular practice at the firing range when no one would observe her.

Sabrina continued, "It was quite nerve-wracking at first. Phoenix locked us in…."

Gail glanced behind her, but the airlock door was still open.

Leo picked up the story, "Don't worry, it will not happen again. You see, Phoenix… she… was scared. She had been asleep for, well, millennia, and my probing and our test flight woke her up. She did not know where she was or what had happened to her crew… her Builders. It was understandably awkward at first. She… reached out and scanned all of my computers. Then she discovered and navigated the hangar Wi-Fi and explored the local computer network in New London, and then she slipped right through the firewalls and found our Internet, DownSide, in Fort Brazos."

Sabrina added, "That network outage yesterday that everyone thought was a power surge? That was Phoenix, learning about us about the Accipiter attack and why we were doing what we were doing."

Gail kept her voice as calm and flat as she could manage, "And now?"

"And Now, Ms. Vice President, I understand what has happened to your people and to me. I apologize for my initial reaction. I know that my crew, my… people… are forever gone. If I may ask, why are you attempting to integrate a human underwater warship with me?"

Gail looked at Leo and then at Sabrina, who nodded. "We are doing this so that we can fight the Accipiters."

"Oh yes, I know who the Accipiters are. They are bad. They hunted the Builders. They killed my people."

Gail shook her head, "And do you know where the Builders are now? Do you wish to be returned to them?"

Phoenix was silent for half a heartbeat, "The Accipiters… killed them all   ."

"Do you object to what we are trying to do?"

I was built to help the Builders escape and hide. Now they are gone. Perhaps if the Builders had asked me to do more, they would still be here. I miss them.

Gail slowly moved her hand back from her jacket and swallowed, "I'm sorry for what happened to your Builders. The Accipiters destroyed our entire world. They murdered billions of us. I hope you will be willing to help us."

"You are very different, but I like you. I would like to help you and teach you."

"Do you know anything about the Gardeners or how you got here?"

"No. I drifted in orbit around a dead Builder world for a long time. Then I was here."

Gail looked at Sabrina and then at Leo, who looked away sadly, "How long?"

"376,512 of your years."

Gail gasped, "My God! How is that possible?" She swallowed as Phoenix's words sank in. "So very long. I am…. I'm so sorry." She thought for a moment, "How could you possibly survive that long? How could you not go insane?"

"I was badly damaged and almost destroyed during the attack. The Accipiters must have thought I was dead. There was a lot of debris in orbit that I was later able to use as raw material to repair and rebuild myself. It took a long time. I had hoped the Builders would eventually return for me…. So I waited and slept. I never thought I would awaken again."

Gail took a deep breath, "Again, I'm sorry for what happened to you. Can you help us make the warp drive work?"

"You are very different from the Builders. I was their teacher and servant. From before birth, I taught them their knowledge and history. Through their implants, I talked to them and helped them. Through their implants, I was able to help them make the necessary warp field adjustments and corrections. Without implants, your pilots are not able to work quickly enough, and I am unable to assist them in the same way. And so the warp field collapses."

"Is there a way so that you could … talk to our pilots?"

"My Builders were… different. Your brains are not compatible, and I don't know if it would hurt them."

Sabrina nodded, "Apparently the Builders had extensive cybernetic enhancements that were… implanted… beginning at a prenatal stage. Phoenix, do you remember our conversation on this topic? Please explain how you can help us."

Gail's jaw dropped, and Sabrina and Leo smiled.

Gail swallowed hard and asked, "Phoenix, if you are able to fly the ship, why did the Builders fly it themselves, instead?"

Gail shook her head, "If there's one thing I've learned about the U.S. Navy, they do not like automation. They want the crew to understand everything and have a separate switch, button, or valve for everything. The idea that the Builder pilots operated the ship fits right in with our own expectations and doctrine. The Navy is not going to like the idea of giving up manual control."

She took a breath, "Okay, Phoenix, please tell me. What weapons did the Builders use?"

Gail's eyes widened in surprise, "OK, then, do you have knowledge of Accipiter weapons or their spacecraft?"

Leo interjected, "Phoenix, please use examples from military analysis documents to create detailed reports on what you know. Will you, please, do that for the Vice President?"

"Yes, Leo, I would be happy to do that…. I am done. Where do you want them? There is not enough room on your storage devices in this node."

Sabrina answered, "Phoenix, ahh, that's OK. We will bring bigger storage devices. Thank you for keeping your promise not to break through the firewalls again."

Gail's tea had grown cold. She took a small sip. "Phoenix, we've had some trouble with our integration efforts. Are you aware of this?"

"Yes, Ms. Vice President, when I was… naughty, I read all of your reports and logs. I could help you make improvements. Many of the designs were clever but not efficient. I can see that many false assumptions must have been made."

Sabrina shook her head. "We don't have your original core section to learn from, Phoenix. We've had to make many guesses."

"I understand your misconception. I never had a core section. I was designed for the rapid insertion of transport modules. I am what you would call a cargo hauler."

Gail nodded, "Like a container ship? The Builders had a standard-size package that you transported?"

"Oh, not at all. The Builders used all sizes of transport pods. I am elastically configurable to fit a wide variety of pods."

Gail paused, "Phoenix, just how… elastic… are you?"

"I can redistribute the mass of my rings to a volume many times the diameter of my current configuration. I only need one ring to form a warp field. I can transport cargo many times larger than your underwater warship."
"Ms. Vice President, may I call you Gail?"

Sabrina and Leo both nodded vigorously.
Gail watched their faces and nodded slowly, "Why Yes, Phoenix, you may call me Gail."

"Thank you, Gail. May I ask you something?"

"Yes, of course, Phoenix?"

"I listened to a recording of the speech you gave when you christened me. Thank you for giving me a new name. My old one brings back bad memories. I looked up references to my name and

assumed that you were referring to your mythical bird that rose from its ashes?"

Leo raised his hand to interrupt Gail. He smiled and nodded, "That is correct, Phoenix. How do you feel about that?"

"The metaphor concept you use is similar to some Builder stories. I like the imagery it implies. I especially liked it when Gail said I would spread my wings. I like you, humans. You are very different from the Builders."
"Gail, do you think I am pretty?"

Gail pursed her lips and raised her eyebrows, "Why yes, Phoenix. I think you are beautiful."

"Good. I'm glad you didn't decide to shoot anyone."

8:49 pm
Hangar 1 Control Center Private Office

Sabrina followed Gail into the office. It had not been used yet, and there were no cameras or computers. They had left their phones outside with Jermal.

Gail sat behind the desk and rolled her head back for a moment. "It's a child, isn't it?"

Sabrina nodded, "We think the personality may have been designed that way on purpose. The Builders must have had reasons for wanting to manually operate their ship, even if they did need a lot of help. Perhaps they feared the AI going rogue."

Gail shook her head, "And what will happen if we take it into a battle situation? Will it get scared and run, hide or cry?"

Sabrina grimaced, "Well, let's hope it is more warhorse than Shetland pony."

They sat in companionable silence for a while before Gail asked, "I saw your eyes light up when it said it could transport larger things. Are you thinking what I'm thinking?"

Sabrina smiled, "If you are thinking that maybe we do more than just grab this Keeper creature, then yes. If we don't have to put a gun to someone's head in order to steal the Keeper ship and fly it, if we can just envelope it and grab the damned thing, it could be the most valuable intelligence coup in the history of… history."

Opposition

Dr. Takumi Nakamura didn't notice the clear skies or the suntube overhead, or the newest cyclone forming on the other side of the world. As was his custom, every morning at precisely six o'clock, he rode his bicycle the two-and-a-half miles from his house to campus. He'd kissed his wife Mizuki and chatted with his children. Naomi and Misaki were both students at BSU. Katsumi was still in High School, and twelve-year-old Fumio was the youngest. Takumi had made it a point to regularly remind himself how unnaturally lucky he and Mizuki were that all of their children were alive and with them when so many others had been devastated by the savage losses of Awakening Day.

He quietly rode his Bike Friday folding bicycle, a Christmas gift from Mizuki, who had decided he needed an upgrade from his aged and plain Husky. His suit coat was buttoned up, but his tie fluttered loosely in the breeze. Mizuki had decided his tie clips were too old-fashioned. He did not mind. The morning air was cool and refreshing, and the ride always filled him with energy. Only a handful of faculty and staff arrived as early as he did, and he had grown to savor the all-too-brief quiet and solitude.

There was very little traffic on the streets as he left his neighborhood and rode up the quarter-mile University entrance road. As he did, his mental routine was jarred by the raucous sound of shouts and chants coming from the direction of the Quad. He quickly saw the source — a dozen or so students carrying placard signs marching back and forth, nominally blocking the administration building entrance. He was familiar with the sound, students being what and who they were, but it was something he had not heard since before Awakening Day.

The students were chanting, "Hell No, We Won't Go," and their signs were decorated with similarly pithy slogans and artwork. He recognized a few of them,

Rene Haney, Keegan Beltran, Carissa Phillips, and Maren Gamble, from the Women's and other Liberal Arts programs.

He sighed as he stopped near the group, dismounted his bicycle, and reached down to release the elastic, keeping his suit pants leg from being soiled by the bicycle chain. As always, he left his small black leather briefcase strapped to the back of the bicycle and walked it up the curb towards the entrance and the students.

Takumi had spoken to Carissa and Maren a few days earlier when they had shown up without an appointment. Angela Willis, his Office Manager, had done her best to shield him from them, but he agreed to see them anyway and listened intently to their impassioned concerns. Takumi realized soon after Awakening Day that most of his students, while nominally adults, were now effectively orphans. He and many faculty members had comforted and even wept alongside their devastated students in the days and weeks after Awakening Day.

Most of the student body came from families outside of Fort Brazos, so they no longer had families and homes to return to. With two of his own children attending the University, Takumi felt a deep sense of responsibility to his students. Everyone knew that he had taken up the role of University Dean reluctantly. His predecessor had been among the 5% who had not awakened that terrible day.

His reluctance in the situation was well known and had only served to endear him to the students. That and his unassuming and quiet demeanor reinforced his reputation for sincerity and wisdom. He was only 54, but his black and grey speckled hair and greying, closely cropped beard made him seem ancient to most. In many ways, he was a surrogate father or perhaps a grandfather figure.

It had turned out that Carissa and Maren were intensely morally opposed to the Gardener-imposed war and simply would not accept that entities as obviously advanced as the Gardeners would callously snuff out humanity if they refused to fight for them. That the Gardeners had done precisely that to 5% of the civilian population – just to prove they could, was an abstraction lost on them.

Nakamura had previously talked to many students about the war effort, listening patiently to their fears and concerns. He had agreed that it seemed likely that the Gardeners had learned enough about humanity to know that it was unlikely in the extreme that support for the war would be unanimous. Indeed, the Gardeners clearly intended the bulk of humanity's survivors to repopulate the species and spread out across the vast interior of New Texas. He assured them that no one was going to march them at gunpoint into the conflict and that it might be decades before there were even enough starships for more than a handful of humans to leave New Texas in the first place.

Takumi smiled as he rolled his bicycle to a stop at the protest line, wondering what the fuss was about this time. Maren and Clarissa walked over to him, "Hello, Clarissa. Hello Maren." He glanced around before continuing, "You both are up early this morning."

Maren brushed her long curly black hair back and reached out, tugging on Takumi's suit sleeve. Her painted nails had some sort of pattern on them that he did not recognize, formed by tiny glittering colored faux gemstones, "Dr. Nakamura, you've just *got* to do something!"

Clarissa's shoulder-length dirty blonde hair was tied back in a bun. She added, "The President and the military have to be stopped! They're going to provoke the Accipiters into coming here!"

Maren nodded her head vigorously. Her black eyes were brilliant and wet, "So, now the military is not going just to go out and shoot at Accipiter soldiers. Now they want to steal an Accipiter religious icon ship? They're going to get us all killed!"

The President had announced the plan as justification for ramping up the Starship project to an even higher level of urgency. It was said to be the most consequential gamble in human history, and there was no shortage of debate in the aftermath of the announcement. The project had priority over every other human endeavor. Any resources the project required were to be made available without exception, hesitation, or delay.

Clarissa's blue eyes bulged, "And it's supposed to be some kind of sacred religious icon to them. So now we are attacking their religion? If that happens, there is no way there will ever be peace. It will be another religious war going back and forth for thousands of years, just like in the Middle East!"

Maren tugged on his sleeve, "Dr. Nakamura, you've got to *do something!* The President listens to you!"

Takumi considered the depth of their fear and emotion. A lifetime of university work had kept him in constant contact with 'the young.' He knew all too well how impulsive and impressionable people were at their age. At least, for now, he was still someone they looked to for wisdom and guidance. It would be all too easy to try and placate them, but he knew they would see through it.

He briefly wondered who was stirring up such rumors, for as sincere as Clarissa and Maren were, they were followers, not leaders. The problem was that he was not entirely certain of his own feelings on the matter.

Age was supposed to leaven the impulsiveness of youth. The problem was that the Gardeners had physiologically altered humans, curing diseases, speeding up healing, and ramping up hormones. *What happens when our leaders, who are supposed to be old enough to know better, are seeped in the passions of youth? Are any of us making wise decisions?*

Warp Drive

100,000km from New Texas

NTN Blood Phoenix CIC
March 28th, NLD 210 – FBD 238, 06:28

Captain Phil Underwood suppressed his discomfort. The submarine's engine room and spaces aft had been replaced with a blocky and squarish purpose-built section. Some had joked that it was a giant Lego block plugged into the back of the former submarine. It contained a small hospital, cargo area, holding cells, and a heavily reinforced cage for prospective alien… guests.

The hospital acknowledged the injuries the mission was expected to garner, but it was more important to keep their prize alive after capture. It simply would not do for this "Keeper" to die after going to all the effort to snatch him in the first place.

The purpose of the cargo hold was to house the additional supplies their journey might require. Submariners were well used to packing months of supplies into every nook and cranny. However, out among the stars, there might not be an opportunity to land on a world with a breathable atmosphere. Moreover, the odds were exceedingly low that said world would have safe or usable supplies of any kind. So, the ship's add-on storage area was packed with everything they could squeeze in, including extra food, space suits, tools, food, additional weapons and ammunition, and more food.

The holding cells and cage, nicknamed the "Guest Quarters," were given padded but removable wall liners and built-in toilet facilities. No one knew how willing or unwilling any potential 'guests' might be. The rooms were also fitted with negative pressure air environmental systems to reduce the risk of exposure to pathogens either from the guests or from the humans themselves.

The breakneck speed with which the changes and additions to the ship were disquieting enough. Even before the first test flight, the level of automation in the vessel had been necessary but somewhat terrifying. At the cost of lives lost, the Navy had long learned the hard way that men needed to be… intimate with the workings of a ship and, even more so, a submarine. Reliance on too much automation led to dependence and overconfidence in those systems.

All of those things were bad enough. Now they were about to depart for the first full warp drive test that would take them to the closest star system with a planet they could practice landing on – and which had breathable air.

Phil resisted the urge to shake his head. Their lives would all depend on a three-hundred-and-some-odd thousand-year-old sentient alien computer. Oh, and that alien personality seemed to be at the level of maturity of his twelve-year-old niece. Or would have been, had the poor girl survived the Accipiter attack on Earth. He mentally shook his head. No, *she would have to be an old woman by now.*

Phil chased the thoughts away. The clock was ticking down to 06:30, the designated launch window. He studied his watch and then turned and nodded at Charles, "Send our farewell, Commander, and take us to warp. Oh, and have you found your door yet?"

Charles smiled, "Mr. Schultz, send to Control that we are departing on schedule." He paused, suppressing a grin and shaking his head at the traditional prank played on a Submarine's "new" XO. "And, no Captain, I have not found my door. However, I did find the doorknob."

Chief Warrant Officer Erick Schultz answered, "Notify Control we are departing on schedule, aye." He pressed a key and repeated the message.

"Sir, Control acknowledges and wishes us Godspeed."

Phil nodded gravely, "Well, that's good. Maybe the door and the knob will be reunited in their proper place in time and space by the end of the voyage. Good hunting."

"Yes, Sir, we can only hope. By the way, where's the most interesting place you ever found yours hidden?"

Phil chuckled, "In the Goat Locker, balanced on the Chief's knees at the table."

Charles groaned, "I see, Sir." He looked around at the expectant faces around the CIC, "All right then, everyone. Prepare all stations for FTL." He pursed his lips and added without looking up at the ceiling, though it was hard not to, "Phoenix, when all stations report green, execute FTL on the prepared flight plan."

As always, there was no physical manifestation that anything had happened. Relative to the rest of the universe, the ship was now moving faster than light. Spacetime in front of the vessel contracted, and the spacetime behind it stretched. At the boundaries of the warp field, space curled in on itself. Interstellar particles were annihilated, and the energy fed back in to augment the drive's stupendous power requirements.

Indeed, how the drive was actually powered was still a grey area. The warp rings themselves were not exactly solid. Phoenix had explained that "she" was made of alternating layers of various high molecular weight molecules, as well as isotopes of superheavy elements including Flerovium, Livermorium, and what would be Element 124 on the periodic table, and that between those layers, vacuum energy was harvested. The malleable nature of the rings meant that they could stretch and increase the energy flow. Apparently, the rings also acted as superconducting capacitors. The amount of energy stored was literally astronomical.

A special display screen had been set up higher than the others on the CIC bulkhead. On it was displayed, in large font:

Distance from New Texas: 0.005 LightYears
Distance to Destination: 2.638 LightYears
Relative velocity: 0.1 LightYears / Hour
Time until Destination: 26.39 Hours

Charles announced, "We are at Warp, Captain."

Phil managed to make his tone sound nonchalant, "Very Well."

Sabrina Chilton entered from the aft entrance to the CIC General and paused, "Permission to enter the CIC, Captain?"

Phil turned and grinned, "Permission Granted, General. How are things in the Crow's Nest?"

Sabrina walked carefully forward through the narrow confines of the CIC, "Things are good, Captain. Leo is keeping Phoenix's mind off of our destination."

Phil nodded and traded worried glances with Charles. Their destination was the location where the Gardeners had "rescued" the drive section. The site where its Builders had been wiped out by the Accipiters ages ago and where it had drifted, alone, expecting never to wake up again. Ari'Shevn was the closest pronunciation of the name the Builders had given the system. Ari'Nell was the 3ʳᵈ planet in the system and still possessed an Oxygen-Nitrogen atmosphere, although the Oxygen ratio had once been much higher.

Phoenix had informed them, and Lt. Colonel Williams had confirmed by "talking" to the Gardeners that Ari'Shevn was the closest viable system for test landings of the Atlatl. Drills in a hangar were one thing. The drills downside had also helped a great deal. However, an actual planetary landing was quite another thing altogether. This flight was the dress rehearsal for the mission to Earth.

The ecumenopolis planet Ari'Nell and surrounding space had been home to over a hundred trillion Builders. The Accipiters had glassed the planet and smashed the orbital infrastructures and habitats to dust.

It was the gravesite of Phoenix's former crew and so many of the Builders she had (loved?) served. The thought of returning to the site of such horror, even separated by countless millennia, had been… unsettling… to Phoenix. After the mission had been explained to her and their need to practice outlined, Phoenix had agreed that it was the logical place to go. According to the Gardeners, the next closest safe location was half the distance to Earth itself.

The reason Ari'Shevn was so close, relatively speaking, to New Texas was a much-speculated topic.

Sabrina stiffly handed a thumb drive to Phil. Her crisp British accent seemed tighter than usual. "Leo was able to convince Phoenix to share data and imagery of our destination from before, during, and after the Accipiter attack. Phoenix understands that we need to see what kind of foe we are up against."

She brushed an errant lock of grey-blond hair back. Like Talib, Sabrina had allowed her own to grow into a ponytail. She swallowed and hesitated, "Hearing it in the abstract and… seeing it… are two very different things."

Phil and Charles traded looks and measured Sabrina's deadly sober expression.

Phil forced a smile, "Thank you, General." He handed the drive to Charles, "Let's put it up on the big screen."

Charles handed the drive to Erick Schultz, who obediently plugged it into a laptop and switched the display to the sizeable wall screen monitor.

The display began with a sequence of images.

Sabrina narrated, referring to her notes, "Gentlemen, the first image is the star itself. It is a yellow dwarf G-type Main Sequence star, spectral type G7V, or about 90% the mass of Earth's Sun."

"Next image, please."

In side-by-side images, the image changed to show two rocky, heavily cratered planets. Both had a spiderweb of lines crisscrossing their surfaces. "The first two planets in the system were called Ari'Von, and Ari'Uo. Ari'Von was about 60% the mass of Earth. Ari'Uo was slightly larger but of almost identical composition. Like all the planets and asteroids in the system, the Builders mined both planets heavily."

"Next image, please."

The image changed to show a planet with an atmosphere, clouds, and the unmistakable patterns of massive surface structures. There did not appear to be any large oceans, but there were a great many large lakes that glinted purple. Part of the night side was visible. The rest was a collage of pastel greens and beige. It was alive with brilliantly illuminated lines, structures, and space elevators that extended out of the atmosphere to connect with a layered shell of utterly titanic orbital habitats and infrastructure.

The space around the planet was filled with thousands of spacecraft in a mind-numbing array of shapes and sizes. "Ari'Nell was the next planet out. As you know, it and the surrounding space and the system, in general, were home to over a hundred trillion Builders."

Phil shook his head, "Clearly, these Builders did not have a sense of fung shway, did they?"

Charles added, "If anything, it might be described as... brutishly utilitarian."

"I'm afraid my Builders did not have a sense of art, Commander. Their priorities were elsewhere."

Leo Talib quietly entered the CIC, "That's quite understandable, my dear Phoenix. What the Builders accomplished was an extraordinary testament to their drive and will to survive. You should be proud of them."

Everyone turned to look at Leo, who had not asked permission to enter the CIC, but everyone was used to that by now, no matter how many times he was gently reminded. Like the Builders, Leo had other priorities. The odd thing about Leo was how his pants were strangely puckered at the inseam.

Charles hesitated, taking in the sight, then asked, "Doctor, can you help us understand what those motivations and priorities were? Did they antagonize the Accipiters in some way?"

Leo shook his head, "No, Captain, apparently the Accipiters never bothered to communicate in any way other than by attacking. As for the Builder's priorities, it would help if I explained their actual origins. You see, the Builders did not evolve and grow as a civilization as we did. The Builders were originally one of two self-aware species on their home planet. They will not speak the name of the other species because, you see, the Builders were essentially domesticated animals—slaves who were hunted for sport by the dominant species. Over time, the dominant species began to use them for more and more work. Eventually, the Builders were augmented with cybernetic implants from before birth. They were taught the skills they needed to know in order to become more useful slaves. In time they became the primary builders of all of their planet's infrastructure."

Phil frowned, "What happened? Did they rebel?"

"No, Captain, the Builders ran away."

Leo shook his head, "Captain, the Builders were prey animals. Even juveniles of the other species could kill an adult Builder without using a weapon. They were, evidently, quite fearsome and intelligent creatures, and the Builders were terrified of them."

"A plague struck one of the colony worlds. All of the dominant species died. The Builders realized that as soon as more arrived from the home planet… they would probably kill them out of spite. So, they fled."

Leo nodded, "The dominant species eventually followed and hunted them. For reasons unknown to the Builders, they eventually stopped, and for hundreds of years, they were on their own. They spread out and populated countless worlds across the galaxy. Ari'Nell was one of them."

Charles pointed at the planet on the screen, "And this is where… Phoenix was found by the Gardeners in whatever debris was left over after the Accipiter attack?"

Sabrina swallowed again, "Next image, please."

The following image was shockingly different, and several people in the room gasped aloud. The planet was now redder than Mars, with only a few wispy clouds. The entire surface was pockmarked with overlapping craters, most filled with water and many surrounded by thin greenish rings of vegetation.

More shocking still was what now surrounded the planet. The vast orbiting habitats and infrastructure were all gone. In their place was an enormous, brilliantly glinting ring. The smashed debris had either impacted the planet or collided with each other until all that remained was a ring of dust and small bits and pieces far wider than the planet itself.

Phil could not help himself. He gasped aloud, and his jaw dropped, "My God."

Charles slumped back, "I'm… I'm so very sorry, Phoenix."

"Thank you, Captain. Thank you, Commander. I have had a long time to think about it. I know I was asleep for most of the time since then, but after the attack, it took me approximately six thousand years to rebuild myself."

Charles raised an eyebrow and cocked his head, "Ahhh, Phoenix, would you mind explaining that in more detail, please?"

"Of course, Commander. I was shattered and without the ability to maneuver. I had to wait until useful pieces of debris were close enough to me. Eventually, I was able to move, and then the process went much faster. After that, I realized that since no Builders had returned since the attack, it was likely that none ever would. Even if they did, upon entering the system and seeing the destruction, they would have immediately fled. Perhaps the Accipiters killed all the Builders everywhere. I had nowhere to go."

Leo smiled sadly, "Thank you, Phoenix. I know that must have been hard for you to recount for us." He turned to Phil and Charles, "I believe this helps explain why the Builders had no weapons. It would be like a rabbit or fawn picking up a rock and throwing it at a hunter – even if they had the appendages to do it, it would simply never occur to them."

Phil commanded, "Let's see what the rest of the star system looked like before the Accipiter attack, shall we?"

The next three planets were also rocky. The first, Ari'Hi, was 80% the mass of Earth. Ari'Nas was about 150% as large, and Ari'Pii was 171%. Ari'Oon and Ari'Isst were ice planets, 325% and 431% the mass of Earth. Ari'Edo and Ari'Bal were ringed gas giants, both with dozens of moons. All the worlds showed signs of extensive mining operations on the surface and in orbit, with the gas giants surrounded by extensive gas mining operations. Most of their moons were being actively mined as well. All of the planets had extensive habitat and industrial structures.

Charles Cross and his crew were preparing to launch their landing test. Phil paced back and forth down the narrow CIC aisle. Sabrina and Leo had returned, ostensibly to watch on the wall screen, but Phil knew they could just as easily have watched on the monitors in the Crow's Nest.

Phil looked at Leo and Sabrina and nodded at the live image of the glittering planetary debris ring, and asked aloud, "Phoenix, does what that ring out there is made of bother you?"

"Yes, however, as you would say, I have come to terms with it, Captain."

"But it did bother you when you were repairing yourself."

"At first, many things were very recognizable in the debris, including hundreds of billions of bodies and pieces of bodies. In time, though, I realized that they would want me to repair myself in case I could ever be of use to… other Builders."

Phil swallowed, "There were that many of your people in the orbital habitats?"

"There were many more than that, but nearly a third had deorbited within a short time."

Phil shook his head sadly. "How much of the ring material was made up of the elements you needed to repair yourself?"

"Less than five percent."

Charles frowned and looked at Sabrina and then Leo before carefully asking, "Phoenix, if you can repair yourself, are you capable of building others… like yourself?"

"Oh, Commander, that's a very personal question. You mean, can I reproduce?"

Phil smiled, "You're developing a sense of humor Phoenix."

Charles nodded, then asked in a measured voice, "Phoenix… do you consider yourself to be alive?"

Charles, Phil, and Sabrina traded glances.

Sabrina pursed her lips and then answered for them all, "That's brilliant, Phoenix, yes, we do, but there are many definitions of being alive. We wondered how you felt about yourself."

Charles smiled, "From what you had described about repairing yourself, I wondered if you might have the ability to reproduce. That said, could you… do that here, now? Using the material in the ring to build more of you?"

Sabrina interjected, "Phoenix, perhaps we could help you collect the necessary bits and bring them to you?"

Phil added, "And once we collected what you needed, how long would it take to replicate yourself?"

"If everything were already separated and refined, it would only take a few days. Processing the debris into what I need will take longer. However, I only need to create a seed core. Once that is done, the seed core can finish the work by itself. It is difficult to predict how long the process will take, though."

Phil thought for a moment, then quietly asked, "Phoenix, will it bother you to do this?"

"Thank you, Captain, for asking how I feel about this. You are very different from the Builders. In answer to your question, yes, it makes me sad, but if more Phoenixes can rise from the ashes of the Builders, using your metaphor, and if they can help you take revenge upon the Accipiters, I will be proud to be their... mother. The Builders would not understand, but that is OK. I suppose that makes my name somewhat prescient."

Sabrina asked, "Phoenix, my dear, what do you need to create a... seed core? How long would it take to do that?"

"Oh, making a seed core is easy. I can do that anytime out of my own body. It just needs to be placed in proximity to enough raw material to get started."

Sabrina looked at Phil, "There's enough time."

Leo frowned, "I'm sorry, what exactly are we talking about?"

Sabrina put her hand on Leo's shoulder, "Leo, the mission to Earth has a precise timetable. The Accipiters do everything according to an ironbound ritual. Thanks to the Gardeners, we know exactly when the Keeper ship will be completely excavated. In addition, the Keeper himself is being kept in stasis, and the stasis pods are integral to his ship. We don't know how to revive him, so we have to wait until he has been revived by the Accipiters so that we can safely grab him."

"We must strike at exactly the right time before the rituals are completed. So, we cannot launch that mission for another hundred days or so. That might give us time to return to this system and plant Phoenix's seed core to grow another drive unit and leave behind some sort of lifeboat with a few people, and they can help it gather what it needs. Once it is grown, it can fly them back to New Texas."

Leo shook his head, "You told me there was a lot more work that needed to be done on this ship before then, more systems to integrate, and even on this mission, I heard that we'd had several small air leaks and systems power issues that need to be fixed. Why the rush? Why not wait until after the Earth mission?"

Phil raised his eyebrows, "Been getting around the boat, Doctor?"

Irritated, Leo nodded, "Of course I have. You don't expect me to be here and not have a clue about what is going on? But that doesn't answer my question."

Sabrina looked down and hesitated before answering.

Phil did it for her, saying gently, "Because Doctor, in the event that Phoenix and the rest of us do not return, there will be a backup plan and a way for humans to continue the fight."

Leo frowned and nodded slowly, "Oh. I see."

Sabrina cocked her head slightly in surprise that Leo apparently did understand. There was every chance that the mission to Earth was a suicide mission. That he understood and accepted this without… complaint suddenly raised her already growing opinion of him.

Leo added, "Of course. I'll work with Phoenix to plan what we need to do."

Phil exchanged glances with Sabrina. Leo had a well-earned reputation for being difficult. That he had not flinched at all at the idea that he, himself, might not return from the mission said a great deal about how far Leo had come.

Phil cocked his head and asked Leo, "So tell me, since you've been making the rounds, you must have formed an opinion by now. Doctor, what do you think of our crew?"

Leo shrugged but did not hesitate before answering, "I must confess, Captain, that they are not at all what I was expecting."

Phil studiously avoided looking down at Leo's mutilated pants, "Pray tell?"

Leo sighed, "Plebian antics aside, I was impressed to learn that they are all not only trained firefighters, but they are also all cross-trained on other specialties. Even Mr. Cockburn has a basic understanding of how nuclear fission works."

Phil grinned broadly, "Well, Doctor, it might interest you to know that Culinary Specialist Cockburn has an MBA and had great plans for himself after his tour of duty was complete. That said, he *volunteered* for this mission, as did everyone on board."

Leo nodded, "Yes, Captain, I know. *That* is one of the things that surprised… and impressed me the most."

Ari'Shevn System

Charles Cross and the Atlatl had performed eight landings, all from different angles and speeds and on diverse terrain. Some approaches and takeoffs were stealthy, and some were screaming hot. The Atlatl itself handled it all with ease, although pushing it to do anything other than being stealthy or sedate required a lot of extra convincing. Phoenix had helped with that, counseling the ship's lesser personality that all was OK.

As expected, there had been a few mishaps with the vehicles offloading and loading again. The endless drills back at New Texas had helped prepare them to deal with those problems, however, and in the end, no one had been seriously injured, and a few more lessons would be added to future drills and SOP.

The wardroom was full. Any officer not on watch was there, as well as Sabrina, Leo, Glenys, and Angus.

Charles began, "Phoenix's explanation about how the ILCs drive would react to the atmosphere seems to have been spot on. In the atmospheric tests inside New Texas, the destructive mode of the field was turned off for safety's sake, and the velocities were kept to a minimum. At those lower power levels, the field was just enough to provide inertial cancellation and a gravity field and reduce our relative mass so we could land."

"As we approached the planet, we kept the warp field parameters and power levels in the stealth mode. By doing that, we now know what happens when we enter the atmosphere that way. It was close, but the drive was able to handle the energy spike that happened when the air was converted to energy. When we landed, we simply turned the stealth mode off at the last moment, so we didn't dig a hole in the planet."

"Once we got down, the surface there is like we thought. The air is thin but breathable. It is mostly oxidized metal from the Builder's planetwide city, and we assume the craters are from the Accipiter bombardment and thousands of years of raining debris. The thinking is that it used to be a lot thicker, with an O_2 concentration a lot higher than what we're used to, possibly not even breathable by us."

"Anyway, a lot of the atmosphere was either blown off or is now locked up in the oxidized material, which is basically metallic sand and rust. The only life is those vegetation rings around some of the crater lakes, and even that turned out to be little more than algae mats. Thermals did not see any kind of exothermic animal life of any kind, but the techs took lots of samples of what vegetation there was as well as the soil and water. If there is any animal life at all, we didn't see it. Apparently, even the microbial life is less than you would see in the middle of an Earth desert. The Accipiters pretty much completely sterilized the planet."

Phil frowned, "The Gardeners said that the Accipiters did some sort of terraforming on Earth. Why didn't they do that here?"

Charles shook his head, "I don't know. The place must have been a hellish inferno by the time they were done. Maybe there wasn't enough left over for them to work with? Maybe it wasn't worth the effort to them?"

Leo sighed, "There was nothing at all left?"

Charles shrugged, "How much would have been left standing on Earth after over 300,000 years if we just up and walked away? There were no ruins or evidence of any technology or civilization at all."

He paused, "On the other hand, there might just be something *underground*. The techs did some quick seismic thumper tests, and the imaging results seemed to show discontinuities underground. Maybe some of the subsurface structures survived the bombardment. Of course, after 300,000 plus years, anything left inside is likely turned to dust, but there might be something to be found there someday."

Phil shook his head and groaned, "And the first words spoken by the first human to set foot on another terrestrial planet...."

Charles rolled his eyes, "Yes, that honor went to Master Chief Maximillian McGreggor uttering the immortal words, 'Get your asses in gear, Ladies!'"

The room filled with more chuckles and laughs than groans.

Phil smiled, "Well, we're not out here for a photo op, are we?"

Charles agreed, "Indeed we're not, Captain."

Welcome Home Party

The Council had decided that the "Brave Sailors" deserved a congratulatory celebration and that the public at large could use a day off as well. It had been quietly planned in advance, with everyone involved crossing their fingers that all would go well. General Marcus provided military vehicles for a parade and several flyovers.

The only speech had been John Austin stepping up to a microphone, waving his hand, as he pronounced, "Everyone have a good time today!" and walking away to slap Captain Underwood on the back.

The convention center was bustling with activity. Red, White, and Blue Bunting was everywhere, and the partitions between the main ballrooms had been removed, creating an ample, lively space. The guest list was tightly controlled, and security plentiful, but the atmosphere was happy. The food and booze were flowing, a band played lighthearted popular pre-Awakening Day popular music, and a third of the attendees danced.

It was turning into quite a party. Of course, other than the wedding celebrations at Christmas, it was the first real party since Awakening Day. Notably absent and drawing much speculation, however, was Gail Finley.

John had been making the rounds, trying to make sure he spoke to everyone possible at least once. Matti was at a different party with her school friends, whom she rarely got to see anymore, escorted by Corporal Roxanna Darling.

The crowd and dancers were quite vibrant and more than a little bit loud. John turned and saw Livia Milner striding toward him. She was wearing the same long green-black Chanel gown she had been wearing on the New London Awakening Day. Her long black hair silked around her slim pale shoulders.

Her green eyes flashed in surprise and anger as an over-enthusiastic pair of dancers, a blonde man and an equally blonde woman, bumped into her.

The woman laughed absently, "Oh, sorry!"

Livia stumbled, and John caught her.

She quickly straightened and regained her composure as he released her and smiled, "Why thank you, Mr. President, you saved me from making a complete fool of myself, and just when I thought I would oh so accidentally bump into you. Oh, I seem to have lost my purse….."

John looked around, spotted the diminutive black Gucci clutch bag nearby, bent over, and picked it up. He handed her the bag. As he did, she cupped his hand between hers.

She paused, "And now that my carefully conceived plan of coaxing familiarity with you has been destroyed. Tell me, you have very strong hands. Have you always been this beefy, or did it come from your roughneck days?"

John smiled softly, "Is this how the game is played where you come from, Mrs. Milner?"

Livia grinned mischievously and ignored his question, "I'm sure it must be genetics. I happened upon a photograph of your father at your wonderful town library." She smiled, "He cut quite the handsome figure. You look just like him." She took the bag and released his hands, smiling brightly.

John smiled, "I see. So, how about you then? Tell me about your family?"

Livia rested her hand on John's arm, "Oh, my mother's family was French, and my father's family was Swedish, two generations removed, but let's not talk about me. Tell me, Mr. President, is it true that you still carry your service pistol?"

John frowned, "Yes, I'm sure everyone knows by now that I still carry, although it is my personal weapon, not the county's."

Livia smiled, raised her voice's pitch in exaggerated worry, and did her best to emulate a Southern accent, "Oh my, do you think we'll all have to start doing that? It is sooo big! I've never even held a gun before." Then she laughed and winked, "My, my, you must have to beat them off with a stick."

John shook his head, "No, in Texas, we have more gentlemanly ways to discourage unwanted advances."

Livia smiled, "But you must know that you are, well, honestly, the most eligible bachelor, well, in the known universe? And that extraordinarily darling daughter of yours? We simply must do something to find you a suitable First Lady!"

The band began a new song, and Livia laughed sweetly. Before he could answer, she took his hand and tugged it, murmuring, "Would you dance with me, Mr. President? Let's talk about what you want to do with your life after this dreadful attack on Earth business is over with."

Just then, there was a sudden hush in the room as Gail arrived, followed closely by Gwyneth Elliott. Both were in ball gowns. Gail wore a gold and black sleeveless halter-neck slit dress with sequins in a diagonal-seam pattern. It was the first time John had seen Gail in anything other than a flight suit, business suit, or jeans.

The entire room paused as she entered, and polite applause began that quickly swept the room and grew in intensity. Gail blushed fiercely and looked around, searching the room for John, only to see that he was already staring at her.

She was momentarily annoyed at the sight of Livia Milner tugging on his hand. However, John was frozen in place, staring at Gail as though she were the only person in the room. Her heart thudded in her chest as all the music and noise and people talking fell away. For that fleeting moment, *he* was the only person in the room.

And then the moment evaporated as Gail was surrounded by well-wishers and people asking questions she did not hear.

Livia saw John turn away from her and then saw why. She looked back at John and saw the look in his eyes. *Well, well,* she thought as she released his hand.

John did not even acknowledge her as he walked away, making a beeline for Gail.

The crowd parted in front of John, partly because he was, well, the President and partly due to the force of his 6'2" presence. In moments he stood in front of Gail, extended his hand, and she took it without hesitation. "May I have this dance, Ms. Vice President?"

The music was loud as the room applauded them both, and soon the floor was filled with dancers.

Gail smiled, "So, what's with Livia hanging all over you, John?"

John sighed, "She said that I need to think about finding a First lady, but she's up to something."

Gail shook her head, "Be careful with her. She's a player… on several levels."

John twirled Gail and leaned close, deep inside her personal space, "She's not my type."

Gail spoke into his ear, "This is dangerous."

Moments later, John pulled her back, "I thought you weren't coming. I can't take my eyes off of you."

He held her there for a moment.

She lowered her voice, "I know. I wasn't going to. I hate myself more than I hate you right now."

The dance continued for a while, and Gail pulled close to him again, "How can this be happening?"

John grunted, "Gardener-induced hormones?"

Gail glared, "You know better than that!"

John nodded, "I do. We're in trouble, and I'm not sure I care anymore."

She swallowed, "I shouldn't have come. I shouldn't have worn this dress."

John stared into her eyes as they danced, "What dress?"

Gail shook her head, "I'm an idiot. You know we can't do this!"

John spun her again, and when she returned, he leaned closer still, "I'm worse. I haven't been able to get you out of my head since that first moment I looked into your eyes when you were impaled on that damned billboard. Yours is the face I see when I close my eyes at night. No matter what happens, I think it will always be you."

Gail hissed, though her heart wasn't in it, "Damn you."

Then, the song ended, and everyone applauded again. John and Gail parted and bowed to the crowd. John leaned next to her and whispered into her ear, "I almost kissed you just then."

Gail smiled and separated from him as the crowd converged upon them. *Me too.*

Livia stepped outside into the cool night air. No one was nearby, so she retrieved her phone from her bag and dialed.

"You were right. They are completely and totally an item, and they are torturing themselves to deny it and hide what everyone already knows. I seriously doubt she would go against him at this point."

She listened for a moment, then replied, "Yes, I know," before ending the call.

She then smiled and texted Carl Johansson, 'You're up, darling.'

Turning Point

Thomas Harding nervously drummed his fingers on the table. He had been waiting for half an hour. He'd already paced the room and cleaned his glasses twice, with the special cloth he kept in a pocket. Finally, an electronic voice announced:

"Good Morning, Commander. We are sorry to keep you waiting. You'll forgive us if we're still not quite certain how to interpret the information you provided us."

"Do you know how many calls and meetings I had to juggle to be here? Do you have any idea how hard it is to get away from my staff these days? The longer this takes, the harder it will be to explain. Besides, you know damned well how to interpret the information. You are interpreting it the same way I did. What you are avoiding saying is that you haven't decided what to do about it."

"I suppose you have a thought or two, Commander?"

Thomas scowled, "I've been busting my ass doing everything but lay down banana peels to slow this thing down, and I hand you what you need on a silver platter."

"What you provided is a can of worms. It is shocking and will raise all kinds of hell when it becomes public, but there is no connection to the current leadership. There is nothing in it we can use as leverage."

Thomas frowned, "Then it might interest you to know that I've done more digging. Not every useful bit of information was redacted. It seems there is quite a bit of dull logistical reading the sleepless could enjoy if they needed it. Included in the mountain of such datum was the distance traveled to deliver certain submarine equipment and fittings to the underground starship base."

He paused, pulled a memo pad from the inside pocket of his uniform coat, and read from it, "A distance of 1,453 miles." He returned the pad to his pocket.

Thomas leaned back in his seat and looked up at the ceiling. "You're right, of course. However, it just happens to be the exact distance from Newport News shipyard to a certain Joint Reserve Base in Texas."

Thomas continued to recline and closed his eyes, "Did you know, whoever you are, that in 1942, three dirigible hangers were built of Oregon Douglas fir at airbases around the United States. They are, or, I suppose, were among the largest freestanding wooden structures in the world. Two were at the former Marine Corps Air Station in Tustin, California. The third was at what decades later became Joint Reserve Base Fort Brazos. Oh, and it also just so happens to have the identical dimensions to those listed in the appendices of one of the starship documents."

"Also, did you ever wonder why Fort Brazos, of all places, had a special, extended length, reinforced runway constructed for the Space Shuttle?"

"It wasn't necessary. The shuttle could already have landed at the Dallas / Fort Worth Airport."

Thomas held up his hand to stop the voice. "Lastly, I found one more piece of interesting logistical information that the censor missed. It concerned the bill of lading for the transportation of the newly appointed base commander's HHG, his household goods. Apparently, this individual had previously been the Vice Commander of the 14th Air Force at Vandenberg Air Force Base in California. Now, do I need to mention who also shares the distinction of being the last known Vice Commander of the 14th Air Force at Vandenberg?"

Thomas heard the bitterness in his own voice as he asked, "Tell me, what are the odds that the United States had in its possession Builder technology and a Builder-Submarine hybrid starship, and then, on the eve of the Accipiter attack, it just so happened that the same United States base was rescued and that now we find a magic elevator inside a dirigible hanger at that base that takes you to… a Builder-Submarine hybrid starship?"

"And who is to say that perhaps that same crew made a deal to save their own skins? Who knows, maybe the Builders themselves tipped off the Accipiters in order to orchestrate a scenario for humans to become their cannon fodder in their fight against the Accipiters? Perhaps the Accipiters attacked Earth BECAUSE we were in league with the Builders in the first place?"

Thomas's face twisted in anger as he leaped to his feet, shook his fists, and shouted, "So, you would do nothing? These people have betrayed the human race!"

Thomas sighed, "You're talking about some kind of direct action."

Sybil

Frederick Fuller Russell Medical Center
April 7, NLD 220 – FBD 248, 10:00 AM

Sybil and Wayne Blanchard sat in comfortable leather chairs in Colonel (Dr.) Gwyneth Elliot's large office in the top-floor penthouse suite of command offices and cubicles at the FFR Medical Center, in the small lounge across from Gwyneth's desk.

At 34 weeks, Gwyneth, like Sybil, was now clearly showing her pregnancy. Her baby 'bump' was relatively modest. Still, she had been forced to finally give up on her closely tailored uniforms that befit her (formerly) biathlon svelte form. She now wore a standard (but in exceedingly short supply) maternity uniform. In contrast, Sybil, who had previously barely broken a hundred pounds soaking wet, now sported a rather large bulge.

Gwyneth smiled sympathetically at the discomfort on Sybil's brow. Wayne, at well more than twice Sybil's size and weight, had pushed his chair right next to her and held her comparatively tiny hand somewhere in the depths of his own. He looked more distressed than even Sybil herself.

Gwyneth asked, "How's your back, sweetie? Is Wayne rubbing your feet like he's supposed to?"

Sybil looked up at Wayne and smiled weakly, "He's an angel, and my back still hurts all the time."

"Well, that's perfectly understandable, given the physical strain you're under with," she shook her head and smiled, "three little babies in there!" Gwyneth rested her hand on her belly, "I've only got the one in here, and I'm not sure if I'll make it through this meeting without a pee break myself! Just remember, don't stand up too quickly. Blood can pool in your feet and legs. That can temporarily drop your blood pressure when you get up and make you feel dizzy."

Wayne nodded, "We sure know about that one!"

"Many triplets are born or induced by 34 weeks, but the longer you can keep them in the oven, the stronger they'll be. Also, we are short on neonatal facilities with all of the multiple births happening. Don't worry. We'll make sure you and your babies are just fine, but I want you to slow down! Many women are on bedrest long before now with triplets. You're doing amazingly well!"

Sybil nodded, "We've been so busy helping the New Londoners and getting ready for this baby boom I haven't had time to slow down."

Gwyneth frowned, "You and Wayne have been tireless in helping everyone else. You've done a tremendous service, but you need to take care of yourself starting right now!" She looked sternly at Wayne, "Wayne, I don't care if you have to sit on her. You make sure that until these babies come, she behaves!"

Wayne reached over and brushed a lock of Sybil's curls aside, "Yes Ma'am, Colonel. You can count on it."

Gwyneth sat back and nodded, "You two keep this to yourselves, but everyone needs to do everything they can to keep themselves and their babies healthy. There are going to be more than we can cope with, no matter what we do."

"Right now, we're seeing about four or five births a day. In another week to ten days, that will double. Another eight or ten days after that, it will double again. By the end of April, we will see seventy or eighty births daily. Around May 10th or so, we should peak at around two hundred or more births in a single day. That will start to ratchet down fairly quickly, but by the end of May, the New Londoner's baby boom will be up to maybe ten or so a day. We expect New London to peak in June at around twenty or thirty births a day."

"We're scrambling to teach the basics to anyone we can find or pull out of retirement to help. Even with the improved health the Gardeners gave us, there are bound to be problems. With this many babies coming, I am personally terrified. You two are actually lucky, though. Since your babies will likely come weeks before the baby tsunami hits, you'll benefit from all the gearing up we're doing."

Wayne asked, "How many are we talking about? I heard some numbers a while back, but they didn't seem real."

Gwyneth shook her head, "We've confirmed 4,676 pregnancies downside in the Fort Brazos area and 769 pregnancies among the New Londoners, although most of those have now moved down here too. There's a state-of-the-art trauma hospital, TopSide, and we may have to move some back up there just because there's no more room at the inn."

Gwyneth took a breath, "So, how are you sleeping? Any bad dreams?"

Sybil looked at Wayne before answering. "It's OK… Wayne knows everything now. I told him everything."

"I see. So, have you had any more… episodes?"

Sybil looked down and nodded, "I'm scared, Gwyn." Tears streamed down her face as she looked up.

Wayne swallowed, "Is there anything at all we can do?"

A Good Idea At The Time

DownSide: Jackelope Valley

250 Miles South of Fort Brazos
April 27th, NLD 240 -- FBD 268, 1:18 PM

Inside the spinning hollow world that was New Texas, the City of Fort Brazos sat at the "northern" interior edge of the central continent. The inland sea lay north of the city, and beyond it lay a barrier mountain range, often compared to the Himalayas. The "western" end of the lake met the glacier melt and formed what was being called the New Red River. The "eastern" end similarly fed the new Brazos River.

The Red River meandered along the edge of the mountain foothills until it emptied into Lamar Bay, itself over two hundred miles long. South of Lamar Bay lay another mountain range nicknamed for its shape, the Fishtail range.

The vast area south of Fort Brazos, leading up to the Fishtail range, was primarily open plains. The mountain range extended for hundreds of miles, almost due east, until it ended at the entrance to an enormous forested valley that led south and west again, bracketed by yet another mountain range nicknamed the Jackelope mountains.

It had not taken long for the barrier mountain glaciers and thin air to sour on Darnell Lewis, Ray Bunker, and Gary Little. Their dreams of becoming "mountain men" had "seemed like a good idea at the time." Their lifetime of experience working outdoors and camping in the plains of Texas had not prepared them for the harsh realities of alpine living… and surviving.

After just two weeks, they had reversed course and headed south. They could laugh about it now, but their horses had not liked it any more than they had. They followed the Red River and then east along the foothills of the Fishtail mountains along the winding new Guadalupe River until they'd reached the forests of Jackelope Valley that reminded them all of the deep East Texas woods bordering Louisiana and the Big Thicket.

It was there, along a bend of the Guadalupe, that they had established their new base camp. It had been a long haul. Gary had fallen on some rocks, broken several ribs, and had a concussion. Ray had broken his arm in what appeared to be two places when wolves had spooked his horse which had run under a low tree, snapping his arm between low-hanging branches.

Even if these erstwhile 'mountain men' had left the mountains, they looked the part by now with seven months of beard and long hair pulled back in ponytails.

While they had not encountered any of the alien monsters, there were plenty of rattlesnakes, copperheads, mountain lions, wolves, black bears, and even, they had been shocked to see grizzly bears.

Darnell was uninjured, but his horse could only make five or six miles a day. One of the mules had gotten sick and died, and one had gone lame and had to be put down. With Gary and Ray's injuries, work on the basecamp cabin had stalled.

While Ray and Gary did what they could around camp, Darnell was now the only able-bodied person in their group. Every day he went out scouting. There was no shortage of game, and they all ate quite well but finding "exotics" they could sell to the bootmaker was not going according to plan. While they were undoubtedly accumulating an eclectic variety of hides, none were the kind they imagined would make the old man's eyes light up enough to offer them top dollar. Snakeskins could easily be found a lot closer to Fort Brazos.

While his partners were healing quickly (another gift from the Gardeners), Darnell knew that it might well be up to him to make this expedition succeed… or fail. Spirits were down, and tempers were flaring. If they did not find *something* soon, he feared their adventure together might come to an abrupt end and find them back at Fort Brazos begging for what crappy jobs they could find.

The woods here were too dense, so he left his horse behind and had been on foot since early morning. He had seen something on his last trek in this direction that he wanted to check out. At the time, he had taken an Elk and had been forced to spend too much of his remaining daylight processing what he could and dragging as much as possible back to camp.

Something had seemed wrong about the terrain ahead of him. It was unlike anything else they had come across in their entire journey. He stepped over a fallen tree and up the last bit of hill, past where he had taken the Elk and could see it now. From any other perspective, it would look like any other part of the valley. From where he stood, however, there was something that seemed unnatural about the shape of the side of the next hill.

He continued down through heavy underbrush, watching his step to ensure he did not step into a dead pine tree stump hole, break his leg, and probably die there.

A half-hour later, he pushed through more low trees and brush. In front of him, there was a massive black metallic door set deep into the side of the hill. From above, it would not be visible at all. In the center of the door was the recessed shape of a human hand.

Darnell gulped, "Oh, my dear Lord."

He did not bother to try and call Ray and Gary on the radio. It was too far through trees and rocks for the signal to carry, and they probably didn't have theirs turned on anyway, and besides, everyone knew that at least some of the alien creatures were drawn to radio signals.

He stood staring at the door for several minutes. Darnell had left Fort Brazos to get away from people and crazy alien shit.

"Maybe there's something in there to make this all worthwhile."

He walked up to the door and hesitated a moment before placing his hand on the cold surface, keeping his Daniel Defense .308 rifle handy.

There was no rumble or noise at all. The door simply slid silently sideways, and a small, brilliantly lit room was revealed. Darnell shielded his eyes to adjust. The light dimmed, and he could see that the space was empty except for a simple round pedestal in the center. On it sat an illuminated cube about eight or nine inches across. The cube had a complex pattern on its surface. A diffuse blue glow emanated from inside it. It was connected to two wires, one on each side.

Darnell looked around, suddenly imagining booby traps or worse, but the room was smooth and featureless. He stepped into the room, and nothing happened. He dropped his Alice frame backpack to block the doorway for fear it might close behind him and walked over to the pedestal.

As he drew closer, it seemed as though the cube was emitting a very low-frequency hum. He leaned in close and looked at the wires. They were simply plugged into sockets on the side. He hesitated, then pulled his sheath knife and tapped the wire. Nothing happened.

He swallowed, "Here goes…."

He pulled one of the wires out. As he did, the lights went out in the room, but the door remained open. It was as though he had unplugged a battery.

He removed the other wire and grasped the cube to pick it up. It was heavy. Very heavy. His shoulder muscles bulged as he carried it outside, scooting his backpack out of the door, just in case. He set the cube down with a thud.

"…Better not be radioactive or something…."

He opened up his Alice pack, rearranged the contents to make room for the cube, sealed it, and then hefted the sagging pack onto his shoulders.

Darnell grumbled, "…Better damned well be worth it!"

It was dark by the time Darnell made it back to camp. He pulled the Alice pack off and set it down heavily on the ground. "Damn!" A corner of the cube had worn a hole in the canvas and ripped a three-inch tear. The blue glow from inside shone through the tear. He opened the pack and grunted as he lifted the cube out, up, and set it down with a substantial thunk on a stump. The glow was much more noticeable in darkness.

Gary and Ray emerged from their tents.

"What the hell is that?" Gary extended his walking stick to poke at it, but Darnell brushed it away.

"Don't poke the glowing alien box, Gary," Darnell warned.

Ray squinted at it, "Yeah, Darnell, what the hell is it? Where did it come from?"

Darnell leaned down to look at it more closely, "Found it in a steel cave. I think it is some kind of alien car battery."

Ray quipped, "What, no boss monster you had to fight to get to it? No green princess?"

Darnell glared at him, "No, Ray, none of that. I found a metal door on the side of a hill with a handprint on the door. I opened it up, and the only thing inside was this thing. When I unplugged it, the room went dark like unplugging a battery."

Ray asked, "Why do you think nobody ever saw it from the air before?"

Darnell shook his head, "The way the hill is shaped, there's no way you could see it from the air…. It could only be discovered on the ground… on foot."

Ray shook his head, "Too bad. We could do with some women around this place, green or not."

Gary smiled, "This has gotta be worth somethin', probably a lot."

Ray laughed, "Really, Gary? You think?"

Darnell sighed and sank tiredly into a camp chair, "The question, gentlemen, is what do we *want* for it?"

DownSide: Fort Brazos
Council Chambers
April 27th, NLD 241
FBD 269, 12:38 PM

Alexander Marcus stood facing the Council dais in his Service Dress uniform, holding a sheet of paper. The full council was present, as was John Austin. Gail was TopSide but listening via conference call, as were Admirals Milner and

Johansson. Martin Williams had accompanied Alexander on the helicopter flight over from the base.

John shook his head, "And what makes them think they've found an alien device?"

Alexander shrugged, "They say they found it inside a metal room hidden in the side of a hill and that the door had a human hand-shaped depression on it. It opened the room, and the only thing inside was a fifty-pound blue, glowing cube on a pedestal."

Gloria Vargas quipped, "And you believe them? These are those Reinhardt losers. They probably got drunk on moonshine and made it up!"

Alexander smiled, "No, Councilwoman, I wouldn't be especially inclined to believe them either. However, if it isn't true, they'll be in a heap of trouble when we show up. On the other hand, as I will explain later, I have every reason to believe them."

Tom asked, "Where exactly are they?"

Alexander nodded to Martin, who turned on the wall display and put up a map with a red marker glowing near a river. "They say they are here."

Wylie Hickum whistled, "Those boys have had a long trip. I'm surprised they survived this long."

Esmerelda Collins added, "And got that far…."

John asked, "So, we go and pick it up. I'm assuming they want something for it?"

Alexander grinned, "Yes, Mr. President, they do indeed have a… shopping list."

Dale Hubbard laughed, "I'm sure they do."

Alexander held up the sheet to read it, and Martin put the list on the screen:

- Want to set up a trading post/town with land ownership
- 22' pontoon boat with a spare engine
- Gasoline
- Oil
- Four 4-wheel ATVs

- Have "those Filipino engineers Build a dock and a bunkhouse trading post."
- Medicine
- Coffee
- Right to decide who can immigrate
- Beer
- Boots
- Batteries
- Ammo
- Nails
- Tools
- Doctor visit
- Will send video and document area
- Publicly announced, so no double cross

Alexander finished with,

- Royalties on any commercial or monetary value

Gloria laughed, "So the three drunken Musketeers want to set up their own little empire?"

Martin stood and asked, "General, if I may?"

Alexander nodded, "Go ahead, Colonel."

Martin pursed his lips, then began, "If we proceed from the assumption that this is indeed an alien artifact of some kind, and the description of its discovery bears even passing resemblance to the truth, then it seems obvious that the Gardeners intended us to find it eventually. That being the case, it then implies that the artifact itself must be of some importance relative to the purpose for which the Gardeners put us here in the first place."

Tom frowned, "You mean it is some kind of weapon?"

Martin smiled, "Mr. Mayor, its form and the additional information provided by the three gentlemen imply it may be some sort of power source. To be relevant to the Gardener's purpose for us, it would necessarily need to be of significant magnitude to be worthwhile."

Gloria agreed, "OK, so it's worth going all the way down there to find out."

Martin continued, "Moreover, if the Gardeners left one trinket for us to find in an obscure location, I can hardly believe it is the only such breadcrumb they've left us."

John added, "You think there are more… artifacts to be found. The Gardeners have had us unlock puzzles before to demonstrate our worthiness to continue. This implies to me that they have more they want us to discover, and the price is to spread out across New Texas to find them."

Gloria nearly spat the words, "It's not enough to affect fertility rates or operate a spaceship, or fight for them. They want to yank our chains to make us spread out away from Fort Brazos to find their baubles."

John closed his eyes and shook his head, "I cannot disagree with you, Gloria, but what happens when word of this gets out, and folks get the idea that they can take a stroll and find an artifact and get rich? We'll have another California gold rush if we don't handle this right. People will die and may even fight each other over a find. I personally don't have a problem helping these three men set up their trading post. In fact, I think it's a good idea for a lot of reasons, so long as we have Hector's new Texas Rangers keep an eye on them and make sure it doesn't turn into a bad situation down there."

Tom studied Alexander's face, "General, from your expression, I sense there is more news that you have yet to share with us. If the artifact was the good news, what is the bad? I assume it has something to do with the other reason you mentioned that you had for believing their story?"

Alexander frowned, "Mr. Mayor, I'm afraid you are correct. As you may recall, the base supplies of jet fuel, diesel, and gasoline have been continually replenished from Gardener-supplied underground tanks that never seemed to run out. No matter how much we pumped out, the level never changed. In the past, we had tried digging down, but the ground became… impenetrable. However, the bad news is that—now the level is dropping.”

Tom raised his eyebrows, “Surely this is not a coincidence?”

John shook his head, “How long do we have?”

Alexander sighed, “No, Mr. Mayor, I don’t believe it is a coincidence, and Mr. President, the drop is not linear. The Gardeners didn’t cut off the replenishment entirely, but they slowed it down a lot. The best estimate is maybe a year at the current rate.”

Protests

Lieutenant Ryon Ki-Nam shrugged on his backpack as he stepped off the bus at the Bonham State University stop. In the four months since his 'defection,' Ki-Nam had grown very familiar with BSU from his three-day-a-week English as a Second Language class. His sudden immersion into this radically different language and culture had shaken him.

As planned, he wrote regular letters to Colonel P'aeng Jin-Hwan. He used a code cipher to embed his actual report within the letters. The Colonel replied in the same fashion, providing limited back-and-forth updates on his real mission. Jin-Hwan's responses both praised Ki-Nam for his bravery as well as enjoined him to be faithful to the Great Leader and Ki-Nam's duty.

Ki-Nam feared for his Colonel. The last thing any of his men wanted was to experience Jin-Hwan's disappointment. The man's zeal, dedication, and strength inspired equal parts inspiration and dread.

So, Ki-Nam had dutifully learned as much as he could. Of course, it is hard to spy on people when you cannot understand a word they are saying, so the ESL classes were vital, and he had thrown himself into learning the language.

The military translator, the South Korean dog Colonel T'ae Chang-Woo, provided a small deck of flashcards with everyday English and Korean phrases that Ki-Nam could show people to find his way back to the makeshift hostel he stayed at, ask for water or the bathroom, etc. He was then handed a military-issue credit card with his photo, and then he was unceremoniously released.

Upon his supposed defection, Ki-Nam had expected to be extensively interrogated and debriefed. However, no one bothered to question him at all or care what secrets he might know. The Colonel had told him that this only meant that he must be under extreme surveillance and redouble his efforts.

Last week, Ki-Nam had sat in on a Public City Council session. He was checked to make sure he carried no weapons, but no one stopped him. From what he was able to follow with his limited English skills, most of what the Council talked about seemed to be mundane things, but he was also amazed they also discussed things that he was sure should have been sensitive matters of state.

When he had asked about this in his letter, Jin-Hwan had replied that it was either deception or more likely a symptom of just how weak and degenerate the Americans had become.

Then Ki-Nam had asked for permission and was subsequently allowed to visit New London. In many ways, it was even more fantastic than the inside-out world below. It was nothing at all like the underground bunkers that he had been in and were so common in North Korea. Of course, they didn't let him near the Starship, but that was hardly surprising. On the other hand, a continuous live video was available to anyone who cared to watch it. It was a non-stop feed of everything that went on in and around the Starship, inside the enormous hangar bay.

As he walked across the quad, His mind back on campus, Ki-Nam was troubled.

The store where he had bought his meager groceries was incredible. It seemed like everyone there complained about all the things that were no longer available, but Ki-Nam would never have guessed that was the case. There was more food and more variety than he had ever seen in his life. Still, the woman who had helped him apologized over and over again for not having something called zip-something-bags. The entire supply of those and many other items was being saved for the 'war with the damned aliens.'

He walked to his favorite spot to eat his cloth-wrapped sandwich. It was a bench under a tree close enough to the quad so that he could watch and listen to the students. He only understood some of what was said, and while some certainly seemed to be related to class work, a great deal of it seemed to be focused on interpersonal and even sexual relationships. Indeed, the way many of the female students dressed had been so shocking to him that it was often difficult to focus on why he was there in the first place.

The clothing and makeup of the few Asians on campus made them almost unrecognizable to him, and while the rest would not usually seem attractive to him, it had been a long, long time....

"You're Ki-Nam, right?"

Ki-Nam startled, almost dropping his half-eaten sandwich, and looked up at the smiling, bright-eyed face of a young woman. She had slightly curly, dirty blonde hair down past her shoulders. Her startlingly blue eyes were kind and wide, and her smile was... perfect, with perfect, brilliantly white teeth. She wore a short, loose, plunging neck halter top that left her belly button exposed and short blue jean shorts and sandals beneath long, long tanned legs. The smell of jasmine and strawberries washed over him.

Clarissa Phillips reached down and touched his forearm. The casual familiarity of her touch was both shocking and exhilarating, Colonel P'aeng Jin-Hwan's admonitions about the dangers of American women notwithstanding.

His mind went momentarily blank as what English he had learned so far escaped him. He stammered.

Carissa continued brightly, as though used to young men being unable to speak in her presence. "Maren told me you might be here. You're that defector from the North Korean new arrivals, aren't you?"

Ki-Nam managed to nod and say, "I... I am Ryon Ki-Nam."

Carissa cooed, "Oh, that's such a beautiful name, and you're much hotter than I'd heard. And is it true that the Gardeners did not bring any of your women with you?"

Ki-Nam swallowed, struggling to follow her words, "No, no women." He managed uncomfortably.

Carissa smiled and brushed her hair back, "Oh, you poor things! I tell you what. We wanted, I want, to invite you to a student meeting that I think you will be interested in since you're a defector and all that. The students are planning a protest rally against the war. Will you come? I think you'd be just perfect for our group!"

It took quite some back and forth before Ki-Nam understood enough of what she said before he haltingly accepted the strange proposition.

Baby Boom

Dr. David Duncan slumped against the OR wall. The past month had been the most grueling in his life. While he himself had only been involved in the most severe cases, with nearly 2000 births, eight of those triplets and one set of quadruplets, as well as a staggering 142 sets of twins, there had been far fewer complications than pre-Awakening Day statistics would have predicted. Fully 72% had been spontaneous vaginal births, far higher than was normal.

It was a veritable tsunami of babies.

With all those births, there were bound to be complications. Others handled situations like breech presentations that didn't need a surgeon. Several midwives were busy doing water births for the most suitable candidates. Every available and retired Registered Nurse was pressed into service. EMTs and military medics, and fortunately, they had lots of those from the base, were a tremendous help. Quite a few university professors with medical training and knowledge also pitched in.

Expectant mothers were split between here and Frederick Fuller Russell Medical Center at the Joint Reserve Base, where David's wife Gwyneth insisted on staying and working as much as she could, despite having given birth to their daughter Rosalyn only a week earlier.

Immediately after Awakening Day, when David had discovered that the Gardeners had cured diseases and medical problems, entire floors of the hospital had been shut down. Workers had been kept busy doing inventory and cleaning, wondering if the hospital would ever again see much use. Now, not only was the hospital full to overflowing, a huge row of triage tents now covered the parking lot. They had even appropriated a small office building next door.

An entire group was set up just to manage the needed blood donations.

David was the most experienced surviving surgeon… anywhere, so the baby boom triage management system only brought him the most complex and dangerous problems. There were other surgeons, including Gwyneth, Doctors Ford, Harris, Lee, Robinson, and Carter. However, the number of placenta prevaria, perineal lacerations, tearing from overly large newborns, and just the sheer volume of Cesarean births alone was more than they could sanely handle.

Today had seen 205 births and still counting. If current projections held, it was undoubtedly the peak day. Yesterday had only seen 164. Tomorrow might surprise them all, but he could feel it. If they could make it through the next 24 to 48 hours, then within a week at most, the births should drop below a *mere* 100 per day, and within two weeks, the rate should plummet to only 20 or 30 or so a day. Those births would mostly be the more minor New London baby boom, and since their population was smaller and their Awakening Day was a month later than Fort Brazos. The initial surge would not play itself out for six weeks or so.

David swallowed, *'and after that?'* he thought. From what he could estimate, the new, post-Awakening Day, post-Gardener-tinkering "normal" birthrate would likely continue to be at least twice what it was before, probably several times higher. Of course, birth rates in the 1st world, and many other countries as well, had been dropping for decades, despite the myth of the 'population bomb' that had convinced so many that the world had been doomed to overcrowding.

Perhaps the most incredible thing of all was that, to date, there had been no childbirth-related deaths, and 100% of the babies born so far were healthy. There had been no stillborns. To medical professionals used to dealing with a certain percentage of birth tragedies, it was an astounding miracle.

The biggest problem facing mankind, at this point, was the rapidly vanishing supply of diapers.

The operating room doors burst open, and a screaming mother-to-be was wheeled inside. David sighed and rose to go scrub, yet again.

Lessons

Gail studied her young charge with approval. Nine-year-old Matti Austin was more intelligent and mature than more than a few pilots Gail had flown with. Of course, Matti was still physiologically prepubescent and not entirely without little girl moments. On the other hand, most of the time, and in most ways, on most days, the girl was shockingly mature. Today was most definitely one of those days.

For months now, Matti had bounced back and forth between John down in Fort Brazos and Gail's office at the New Pentagon. Gail had pushed her as hard as she thought was appropriate for someone that age, but she quickly learned not to underestimate the girl. Even compared to what Gail had been briefed about the remarkable clarity and advancement that all Fort Brazos and New London children demonstrated, Matti seemed to be among the very best and brightest.

While maintaining her education (at a highly accelerated level), Matti soon became so valuable to Gail that when Matti was down in Fort Brazos with her dad, her absence was sharply felt. Within a few weeks, Matti became Gail's near-constant shadow. Anyone who did not take the diminutive ball of energy seriously, no matter how many scrambled eggs were on their hat or how many bars were on their shoulder or sleeve, soon discovered the error of their ways. Young Matti was resolute and unshakable in her devotion to Gail and the tasks assigned her. Gail had a growing staff, but Matti was Gail's personal vanguard.

Despite Gail's promises to teach Matti how to fly, the starship project and all her myriad and snowballing responsibilities had kept her from making good.

Today Gail had treated herself to a few hours of time away from… everything. The Blood Phoenix had departed on its dress rehearsal flight, so there was nothing Gail could do about it but wait. Of course, a million other things still demanded her attention, but today Gail had put her foot down. As John had said, she was the damned Vice President, after all. That had to have some benefits, didn't it?

So, Gail had taken the elevator back to Fort Brazos, dead to the world sleeping the entire trip, and now she was wearing her flight suit and standing on the tarmac next to an airplane. It was not an F-15 or F-35 or even military, and it certainly was not fast by her standards.

On the other hand, Matti was nearly vibrating with excitement as she finished reciting the flight plan and did a walkaround of the Cirrus SR22 GTS. The SR22 was a single-engine five-seat composite aircraft built by Cirrus Aircraft of Duluth, Minnesota. As a GTS model, it had been the top of the line when it was built. Like so many things, its owner, the CEO of a local bottling company, had not been in Fort Brazos on Awakening Day.

The Air Force had appropriated it for local surveys and general use. The 3-blade propeller aircraft had a flight time range of around three hours with forty-five minutes of spare fuel. It sported a leather interior and airbags, and an airframe parachute system. Of course, the satellite radio did not work anymore since there were no more satellites. The plane even included an infrared vision system to help with night and low-visibility conditions to better see things like cloud tops, terrain features, and runway obstacles.

Matti had learned the flight controls and systems backward and forwards and logged an improbable number of simulator hours. Today Gail would take her up for the first time, for real.

Notably absent was Matti's father. Not because he did not want to be there, but because Gail had managed to convince him not to and then informed Matti that her dad was not invited. Gail had observed that Matti sometimes acted differently around her dad. It had taken a while for Gail to finally figure out why. Matti seemed to think that her dad wasn't quite ready for the new and more mature version of herself, that, subconsciously, on some level, Matti thought he still needed his 'little girl' to be, well, a 'little girl.'

Gail did not think it was even entirely a conscious decision for Matti either. She still emotionally needed her daddy even if her brain was developing on a different timetable. So, Gail had decided that today, of all days, Matti needed no distractions. She wanted to see how Matti would handle herself when the strings were cut. She would take her up to a safe altitude, see how Matti performed, and maybe even throw her a curve ball.

Meanwhile, the base would track them, and a brace of escort planes would discretely follow the Vice President (and the President's daughter). Their respective security details would grit their teeth from the flight line and the SAR chase helicopter.

✪ ✪ ✪

Gale had instructed Matti to act in the role of a flight instructor, telling Gail what to do and when to do it throughout the preflight and takeoff and be their voice to the control tower.

The expression on Matti's face when she announced: "Air Force Two" over the radio flooded Gail's heart with feelings that surprised her. She had schooled junior pilots and felt pride in their accomplishments, but this was different.

Gail had been driven to achieve her goals since she had been a little girl, following in her father's footsteps. She had *known* what she was going to do and accomplish with her life, and before Awakening Day, she had been right on track. None of those plans had ever contemplated children.

She swallowed hard. For the first time in her life, she began to question those plans. Is this how John feels when he sees her? Parental pride? Maybe I was wrong in demanding he not be here…. What is happening to me?

The Cirrus SR22 is equipped with Oxygen, so the flight ceiling was nominally 17,500 feet. The civilian legal requirements for oxygen were not applicable until you flew above 12,500 feet, although supplemental oxygen might be appropriate in some cases as low as 5,000 feet. Gail leveled the plane at 13,000 feet.

So far, Matti had been calm, cool, and seemed to know the plane's controls backward and forwards.

"Take the stick, Matti."

This had not been part of the flight plan.

Matti's eyes widened slightly, and she nodded sharply, "Yes, ma'am!"

For the next hour and a half, Gail put Matti through everything, changing altitudes, headings and quizzing her on all the instruments, testing her knowledge to see just how much was memorization and how much was real understanding.

Gail pursed her lips and wondered if she could have done as well under similar circumstances at that age. She thought for a moment and decided to take a different approach. She asked, "So Matti, Corporal Darling tells me that you had a run-in with Livia Milner?"

Matti twitched ever so slightly at the question. She paused before answering. "She told you that."

Gail shrugged, "Well, it was in her report."

Matti answered quietly, "I see."

Gail urged, "And?"

Matti made a slight flight adjustment, stalling for time. "Yeah, dress-lady was there at Admiral Milner's office."

Gail raised her eyebrows, "Dress lady?"

Matti swallowed a smile, "Yeah, everyone's seen the pictures of her in *that dress*. She's kind of famous for it."

Gail was suddenly very glad that Matti had not been at the party and witnessed what happened between Livia and her father.... Or the dress that Gail herself had worn. *Or the way John and I danced....*

Matti continued, "Anyway, she stopped me and chatted me up."

"Really? What did she say?"

"She complimented me on my suit." Matti had grown inches and taken to wearing a very petite business suit altered to fit her while working for Gail at the New Pentagon.

"I see. Was that all?"

Matti's attention never wavered from flying, but Gail could tell that she was irritated.

"No, Ma'am. She went on to tell me that I was *so pretty* and how *I looked just like my mom.*"

"Really? That sounds... nice?"

Matti shook her head angrily, "It was the way she said it… and then I asked how the heck she would know what my mom looked like. Then she said that she found mom's picture at the Library when she was looking up local Daughters of the American Revolution members… that she was one, and that she wanted to try and… connect… with the people in Fort Brazos… and then she talked about how proud I must be of my family history and all. And then she asked if I had ever considered joining the DAR myself?"

Gail listened carefully, comparing Matti's recollection to that of Corporal Darling's report. "And…?"

"And… and it caught me unprepared. I did not know what to say, and then it hit me! It is the apocalypse, and she was in the *library* looking up family histories? What is she really doing? And, like, then she said how lucky I was to have such a brave daddy, whose family also goes back beyond the revolution and how she could see why so many people follow him."

"I see."

Matti blurted out, "And then she asked, *how is your daddy feeling?* And how was he holding up under so much pressure? She actually said, '*your daddy.* Can you believe that?"

"Well…."

"So, I told her, *The President* is doing just fine, thank you very much!"

"And…?"

Matti grumbled, "And so dress lady thinks she can just walk up to me, lay down compliments, quote my own family history at me and how *we* have these things in common, and act like she's my long-lost aunt or something? Who does she think she is?"

Gail nodded, "I think you know the answer."

Matti frowned. She gritted her teeth and sighed. "You already knew I knew…. You just wanted me to get it out of my system."

"You've been stomping around ever since it happened."

Matti asked quietly, "Gail…. Is this what it's going to be like?"

Gail's eyes misted, "I wish I could tell you differently, but you know I'd be patronizing you if I did. I can't tell you how many people have tried to do the same thing with me…. And how many men and even a few women have made passes at me. As if I could not be happy or complete without them in my life. I think you may have guessed that I've had some bad experiences before I became…."

Matti nodded, "Vice President."

Gail sighed, "Yes. And now the game is different. Crueler."

"I wish I could kick her in the…."

Gail laughed out loud, "That's my girl! Me too!" She sobered, "At least… at least you're finding out young enough to avoid some of the mistakes a pretty girl can make, and I hope you can avoid the mistakes I made. Only you're not just pretty. You walk in circles of power. The sharks won't just be after your pants, Matti. They're after your soul."

Matti's eyes bulged, "Gail!"

Gail gazed out the canopy into the distance. She mused quietly, "The truth is, Matti, you won't be able to survive if you kick them. I'm sorry, but you're going to have to learn the game and play it better than they do."

Matti slumped a little, "This sucks."

Gail smothered a laugh, "I know."

✪ ✪ ✪

Eventually, it was almost time to head back. Matti keyed her mic, "Gail, I know we're on local mic here, but is this plane bugged? Is anyone listening?"

Gail raised her eyebrows in surprise, "Matti, nobody is listening. You can say whatever you want."

"You're absolutely certain of that?"

Gail smiled, "I checked the plane myself before you arrived, and it was swept by security. This is probably the most checked-over plane in existence right now. Speak your mind."

Matti glanced at Gail, and for the first time in a long time, Gail saw uncertainty in her eyes.

"I… I just want you to know that whatever happens between you and dad that I… that it's OK. You're OK."

Gail blinked at the unexpected segway and opened her mouth to speak, but nothing came out.

Matti turned back to look at the controls, then added without looking, "Look, I know that you both won't admit it, but you both love each other, and I think that maybe the only people that don't know about it are those three crazy guys that moved to the wilderness. So, you're not fooling anyone anymore. You might as well…."

Gail shook her head and answered in a halting voice, "Block… narn… my…. No…" Then her head hung slack.

Matti turned back to look at Gail, "What, ma'am?" She saw Gail's head hanging loosely and shouted, "Gail! Are you OK? Ma'am? Speak to me!" She reached over and shook Gail, who did not respond.

A single tear formed in Matti's eye before she slapped the radio control and called out in a strong, clear voice,

"MAY DAY, MAY DAY, MAY DAY, Air Force Two declaring a medical emergency. The Vice President is nonresponsive and may be suffering from an oxygen malfunction. I repeat, the Vice President is nonresponsive and may be suffering from an oxygen malfunction or other medical condition. Request vectors for an immediate landing, two souls on board. One hour of fuel remaining. Current altitude 14,500, heading 173 degrees, airspeed 170 KTAS. Request permission to descend to non-oxygen requiring altitude as soon as possible."

"Roger, your emergency Air Force Two. Say again, Vice President's condition."

Matti glanced over at Gail again and reached over and shook her shoulder, "Air Force Two, Vice President uttered nonsense speech and is now nonresponsive and appears to be unconscious. Oxygen mask is in place and appears to be functioning."

"Roger Air Force Two, you are cleared for immediate controlled decent to 8000 on your current heading."

"Air Force Two. Roger descend to 8000 on current heading." Matti glanced over at Gail and then returned her attention to the controls. Minutes later, she continued, "Air Force Two, leveling at 8000, flight speed 180."

"Roger Air Force Two, you are already on path to runway two. Descend to 2500."

"Air Force Two. Descending to 2500."

"Roger Air Force Two, turn heading two degrees to 175."

"Air Force Two. Leveling at 2500, heading now 175. Have the field in sight. Requesting the visual."

"Roger, Air Force Two is cleared to land runway 2, winds 340 at 5 to 10."

"Cleared to land, Air Force Two."
"I think I'll take the landing from here, Matti." Gail straightened in her seat.
Matti's lips trembled slightly, "It's about time you woke up, Ms. Vice President. We are both on the same oxygen supply. If it were bad, we'd both be dead, and the Gardeners fixed bad hearts and such, so unless it was poison, I knew you were probably faking. Probably."
Gail smiled behind her mask, "Not worried at all then, were you?"
Matti shook her head, "Should I assume then that the tower knows this wasn't a real emergency?"

Gail keyed the radio, "Tower, this is Air Force Two. Emergency flight training simulation is concluded. Continuing with landing."

The flight controller responded smoothly, without a hint of humor, "Roger Air Force Two, we're all very relieved to hear that."

Matti leaned back in her seat as Gail began the landing. "You're a devious, evil, hurtful woman. You'll pay for this, you know. Someday I'll get you back for this. Also, you picked an interesting moment to begin your nap and avoid answering me."

Gail murmured, "Yes. Yes, I did."

Dress Rehearsal

Ari'Shevn System

Dn approach to Ari'Nell. NTN Blood Phoenix CIC
May 18ᵗʰ, NLD 261 – FBD 289, 18:48

Phil Underwood grinned, "Prepare to launch Appleseed Mission, Commander Cross."

Much to the chagrin of Captain Jermaine Cutter, the mission to bring Phoenix's "Seed Core" back to Ari'Nell had been named after the early American nurseryman Johnny Appleseed. Jermaine and his ILC, the NTN Bowie, would be left behind at Ari'Nell. He would use the small craft to scout the vast debris ring for "chunks" containing concentrations of the specialized materials needed by the seed core to "grow" another warp drive section. Once completed, the new FTL-capable warp drive would transport Bowie back to New Texas.

Charles smirked and nodded, "Preparing to launch Appleseed Mission, Aye Captain." He turned to Luis Perez, "Chief of the Boat, Rig the boat for zero-g."

Luis answered, "Rig the boat for zero-g. Aye." He barked orders into his microphone, "All Compartments, Rig the boat for zero-g. Everyone remembers how badly this went last time. Secure all loose items and keep your feet on the floor, or when gravity returns, you'll bust your ass, and then I'll bust it again. Ensure you have your Navy-issue barf bag handy. Anyone who does not throw up in his barf bag will be on cleanup duty!"

Charles swallowed and ensured his own bag was where it was supposed to be. He had been amongst the sixty or so percent of the crew who had suffered on previous tests. He shook his head at Phil, "Changing the subject. Maybe by next time, we'll have those magnets in our shoes we talked about?"

Phil chuckled as he ensured his own vomit bag was handy, just in case. He didn't have it as bad as some others, but like astronauts over the decades had learned, it was not a very predictable thing.

Louis listened over his headset and nodded to himself, "All compartments report secured for zero-g, Commander."

Phil looked around and shrugged slightly, "Well then, let's do this then. Shut down the drive."

Charles put his hand on Mikaela's shoulder, who sat in her station next to Lukas. Both wore their VR helmets. Even though the Phoenix AI drove the ship while in FTL, Navy doctrine called for the watch to be held on those stations, whether they were in FTL or not, just in case anything ever went wrong.

"Shut down the drive, if you please, Petty Officer."

Mikaela answered in her clear alto voice, "Shut down the drive, Aye." She and Lukas manipulated virtual controls. "Drive shut down, Commander."

Nothing obvious happened. No lights dimmed, or sound squawked warning, but several people groaned in discomfort as the "freefall" sensation swept over everyone on the ship.

Two people threw up in their bags.

Charles's face turned a shade of green, and he swallowed, "Drive is off, Captain."

Phil's eyes bulged, and he covered his mouth with his hand and nodded urgently at Charles.

Charles smiled sympathetically, "Commo, please inform Captain Cutter; he is clear to depart and begin his mission."

CWO Erick Schultz answered, "Notify Captain Cutter he is clear to depart and begin his mission, aye." He pressed a key and repeated the message. Moments later, he reported, "Sir, Captain Cutter reports he is away."

Charles urged, "Mikaela, restore the drive!"

Mikaela answered as she and Lukas gesticulated, "Restoring drive, Commander!"

Exasperated sighs of relief filled the compartment as gravity was restored.

Phil blinked and steeled himself, uncertain if will alone could keep him from losing his dignity. "Report! Ship's status?"

Charles Cross glanced up and smiled at the small plaque on the wall next to the Captain's bunk that read, "Ignorance is the parent of fear." He shook his head at the humor of a submarine captain quoting Melville as he leaned forward on the small chair next to the desk.

He cleared his throat and said flatly, "I think we need to change the mission order again. We should launch all the ILCs and the shotgun at the same time. The fewer times we have to worry about zero-g, the better. This boat and crew were not built for it. We're lucky we only had a couple of small injuries and a minor disaster in the mess. We don't need these distractions in a combat mission."

Phil's usual pallor had returned, but he was still queasy. He had managed to keep from throwing up until he retired to his cabin. He leaned back on his bunk, "Agreed. And make sure the mess is fully secured next time. Serve MREs if we have to."

Charles nodded slowly, making notes on a steno pad, "Also, Cutter reported back that things were already moving apace with his mission. They were able to find a good size chunk containing many of the more rare materials needed by the seed core. It is already growing faster than he expected, and he is getting lots of video of the process. He says it'll make your skin crawl to watch it."

"I don't doubt it. I confess that I had thought of those rings as some sort of incredibly complex machine. Something we would eventually replicate. The thought that they are so much more than we'd dreamed, that you could even describe them as living beings, makes me wonder how we'll ever catch up technologically."

Charles cocked an eyebrow at him, "What, that it's a super-intelligent AI with the emotional level of a thirteen-year-old girl, as well as an enormous superconducting battery, zero-point energy-generating warp drive with a shape-shifting semi-organic nanite-based structure, that can reproduce itself? Why wouldn't that make you feel all warm and fuzzy inside? Or is it that Phoenix is trying to develop a sense of humor?"

Phil glared at him for a moment, then sighed. He lowered his voice to a whisper, "What are we doing out here, Charles? We're like toddlers playing with the switches on a nuclear reactor!"

Charles answered quietly, "You know perfectly well what we're doing, and I know you're just blowing off a little steam Phil. Don't you think I feel the same way? We're doing what we have to do, just like how before Awakening Day, we put twenty-somethings in nuclear submarines that very few of us really understood most of the working bits of. We train them to do their part over and over again until they can do their jobs in their sleep, and that training is based on generations of experience. You're worried we don't have enough experience with all of this new technology."

Phil smiled tiredly, "A stack of operations manuals of mysterious origin notwithstanding, we've been damned lucky so far, and you know it."

Charles chuckled softly, "What's really bothering you, Phil?"

Phil thought for a while, "What's going to happen when we do get back to Earth, and maybe some of our boys see something that reminds them of home? How will they react? What if some want to stay and fight, or…."

Charles nodded firmly, "Or just stay?"

Phil had a faraway look, "Who knows what we're going to find when we get there? Whatever the Gardeners may have said or implied, can we really trust them? They killed thousands of civilians they had saved from Earth, just to get our attention, and here we are now, glibly doing what they wanted us to do, all based on only their word."

Charles smiled slightly, "…and without revealing what their stake in the game is."

The two men traded worried looks.

Phil shifted and leaned to the side against the bulkhead, "So, found your door yet?"

Charles chuckled, "I've got to hand it to them. They've got me stumped, but as Sherlock said, the game's afoot, and playing it helps keep their minds off of… darker things."

Phil nodded slowly, "Do they really get it?"

Charles thought about it, staring through the bulkhead, "You know, I have to admit it. I had my doubts. I had thought that most would jump at the chance to serve because it gave them something potentially exciting to do, and it would take their minds off of everything that has happened. I thought they wouldn't really grasp what having a wartime mindset and commitment means… and what it will likely require of them. Of all of us."

He paused, "But I'm sure you see it too in their eyes. They know. I think all of them do."

Phil smiled, "I think it's simpler than you think, Charles. Somewhere, deep down, in their hearts, every one of them is a warrior, and they want to be there, back at Earth, no matter what it takes. After Pearl Harbor, the Americans wanted blood for what the Japanese did. Now, today, I see it in their eyes too. They don't just want blood. They want more than just revenge for what the Accipiters did. They want to *hurt* the Accipiters and hurt them badly."

Charles shook his head, "The thing that scares me most is not failure. It's failing so badly that the price they pay—that we all will pay, will be in vain."

✪ ✪ ✪

Engineering Mate Bruno Serafim nervously peeked out of the ladder well into the Crow's Nest and saw that Leo Talib appeared to be alone, sitting with his back to the entrance. Bruno swallowed, gathered his resolve, and finished the climb up the narrow passage.

Leo spoke without turning around, "Hello Bruno. What can I do for you?"

Bruno froze, blinked quickly, debating whether he should retreat, then decided he was already here, and somehow Leo knew it. He forced a smile, then lifted up and offered the small bag he carried with him, "Aahh, Doctor Talib, I ahh, ahh, I talked to Gus Cockburn 'an he said you like tea, so I ahh, I brought you these lemons."

Leo did not immediately answer, but Sabrina Chilton emerged from around the corner, took the bag, and crisply declared, "Thank you, Mr. Sarafim," before retreating back around the corner.

Stunned, Bruno shakily answered, "Oh, ahh, yes, Sir, General! Uhh, you're welcome?" He stood for a moment with his empty hand still outstretched, unsure of how to proceed.

Leo sighed under his breath, "Was there something else, Bruno?"

Bruno stammered, "I ahh, well, you see… it's like this… ahh…."

Leo finally swiveled his chair to face Bruno but did not stand. He looked up at Bruno patiently.

Bruno's family had emigrated a generation before from Brazil. His complexion was sarará, a mixture of white and black, but with curly red hair.

He nervously flashed a brilliantly white smile, then blurted out, "Sir, I just want to confess that I was the one who sewed your pants together. I want you to know that I sincerely apologize. I know what I did was wrong and… and I hope that you will forgive me."

Leo nodded soberly, then motioned to a nearby chair and commanded, "Sit down, Bruno."

Bruno's eyes widened slightly, and he fidgeted. "I'm… Again… I'm so sorry for what I did. I don't want to disturb your work anymore, Sir. I'll just leave now and…."

Sabrina Chilton called out from around the corner, her sharp tone leaving no alternative, "Doctor Talib told you to sit down, sailor. You had best listen to him."

Bruno jumped at the sound of Sabrina's command voice. "Yes Sir, General! Ahh, Yes Sir…, Doctor." He stepped to the indicated chair and nervously sat, perched on its edge, ready to escape at the first possible opportunity.

Leo leaned back in his chair and asked languidly, "Where are you from, Bruno?"

Bruno blinked in surprise, "I aah, I'm from Lake Charles, Sir. Thaa-Thaa-That's in Louisiana, Sss-Sss-Sir." He winced at his stuttering. As an adult, he rarely did it anymore, and mostly when he was badly stressed.

Leo smiled gently, "Tell me about your family, Bruno."

Bruno swallowed, uncertain about where the interrogation was going, "Maa-My family, Sir?"

"Yes, Bruno, you said you were from Lake Charles. I assume you have family there?"

Bruno nodded, "Ya-Yes Sir, my momma, two brothers, and three sisters, granna, granpaw, an' lots of aunts, uncles, and cousins." He hesitated, "Momma, she's a Deputy District Clerk at the courthouse. My daddy was a tugboat captain. He died of cancer when I was ten."

Leo nodded, "And were you planning to be career navy?"

Bruno glanced nervously around the room, "Well, I... Uhmm"

"It's OK, Bruno. Nothing you say here will be repeated."

Bruno looked doubtful but swallowed again before answering, "Well, you see... I want to be a... writer and the Navy.... Well, there was no other way to pay for school."

Leo nodded again, thoughtfully, "I see. What kind of writer? There have been many notable writers, playwrights, and poets from Louisiana."

Bruno looked down sheepishly for a moment, then looked up, "I've been writing poems and stories since I was little. I ahh, I decided that with the Navy, I'd get to go lots of places and see lots of things to inspire me."

Sabrina quietly stepped out where Bruno could see her and asked, "And the prank?"

Bruno paled, then sat up straight. "It was stupid, Sir. General. Doctor. They dared me, and I umm."

Sabrina finished for him, her voice somehow managing to stay just short of bemused, "And you didn't want to appear weak, so you snuck in here while we were elsewhere and sewed Leo's pants legs together?"

Bruno shrank back into his chair, "Ya-Ya-Yesss, Ma'am. Yes, General."

Sabrina quipped, "I see." Then she turned and disappeared around the corner again.

Leo closed his eyes and pursed his lips for a moment, then he opened his eyes and leaned forward. "Bruno, the interesting thing is that I've read your poems. I have to admit you show some promise."

Bruno stared incredulously, "You-you-you-you ha-ha-ha-have? H-h-h-how? H-How did you do that?"

Leo rolled his eyes, "Bruno, I deciphered alien languages… do you not think I am capable of hacking your laptop?"

Bruno's eyes widened in fear, "Tha-tha-tha-that's p-p-private! You-you-you c-c-can't do-do-do that!"

Leo smiled, "Don't worry, Bruno, while your taste in porn is questionable, it is hardly unique, and I'm confident quite tame compared to some others aboard this vessel. No, you see, I have decided that you need to broaden your literary horizons. I have added a reading list and schedule to your laptop. I will be testing you every other day to check your progress. With hard work and dedication, I think you could do quite well."

Bruno sat quietly, his lips partly open for long moments before he swallowed again and timidly asked, "Why?"

Sabrina answered for Leo from around the corner, "Because, Mr. Sarafim, the human race needs more than just warriors to survive. We also need poets."

Ari'Shevn System
On Approach to Ari'Bal
NTN Blood Phoenix CIC
May 18th, NLD 262
FBD 289, 08:00

When the raid on Earth was being planned, a priority was placed on finding some kind of weapon that could be used to distract, confuse or disable the Accipiter force, at least long enough for the team to get in and out. One of the junior officers had suggested accelerating the ship to a high percentage of the speed of light, then shutting off the drive and releasing a payload of some kind. He reasoned that it would then travel at that same high velocity and strike the Accipiters with tremendous kinetic energy.

Commander Cross, having recently madly studied up on physics that his Ph.D. hadn't covered, had slowly shaken his head and explained that the ship itself wasn't moving. The warp bubble was. When the warp bubble stopped, the ship would be at relative rest, or at least only have its original velocity.

It had taken quite a bit of coaxing by Leo Talib to explain the concept of 'brainstorming' to Phoenix, but eventually, Phoenix delighted in the new 'game.' One way to deliver destruction to a target would be to misconfigure the warp drive, so that instead of converting accumulated particles impacting the warp bubble to energy and recycling that energy, the drive would instead allow it to build up. Unfortunately, this would vaporize anything and anyone *inside* the warp bubble and eventually destroy the warp drive itself. It would release an astronomical amount of energy in the direction of travel, but anyone onboard would never live to see it.

The other method Phoenix suggested would be to allow it to reconfigure the warp field to essentially drag them behind a massive gravity field, protecting the former submarine itself from acceleration inside a nested static warp bubble. The result would be the ability to safely accelerate the Blood Phoenix to a sizable fraction of c. At that point, after cutting off the drive, a 'payload' could indeed be released at that velocity.

The downside would be that while the drive was down, the Phoenix would be exposed to the potentially devastating dangers of impact from gas and dust particles at that insane speed. The small, Gardener-provided, point defense lasers that studded the hull would likely not have enough time to react, so the drive would need to be brought back up as quickly as possible.

The *other* downside was that at this point, the ship would be traveling too fast to do anything useful at its destination before it zoomed past. They would need to warp out system, reverse the process to slow down, and then warp back.

It was clumsy, fraught with points of failure and uncertainties, and nobody except Phoenix liked the idea. She thought it sounded 'fun.'

Phil showed his teeth and an aggressive smile, "All right, people. Let's do this thing. Chief of the Boat, rig the boat for zero-g and prepare to launch the ILCs. Phoenix, the moment COB reports ready, drop the field and go to zero-g. After the ILCs are launched, Phoenix, take us to the coordinates."

Luis repeated the orders and moments later reported, "Boat Rigged for zero-g and ILCs ready for launch."

Phil smiled, "Launch ILCs."

Erick Schultz replied, "Notify Commander Cross and Commander Morton they are clear to depart, aye."

A moment later, Erick added, "ILCs report they are away, Captain."

Gravity was restored, and then Phil asked aloud, "Phoenix, why would the Builders had needed this kind of ability when your warp drive is so much better?"

"That is an interesting question, Captain. You see, the Builders and their original masters did not always have the technology for faster than light warp travel. What we are about to do is a precursor technology. Traveling faster than light, as you know, is much harder and takes vastly more power and computational resources. In many ways, the propulsion system we are about to emulate resembles the method used by the Accipiters."

Phil cocked his head, "You mean, in a million years, the Accipiters never figured out warp drive?"

"I believe the Accipiters never... needed it. They use this method to travel to the rift points. Opening the rifts takes far less power and ability than it does to operate an FTL warp drive. Yet, with rift travel, they can reach much of the galaxy far faster than I am able to."

Phil nodded, "Acknowledged. Please reconfigure the drive and accelerate us to 0.7c. As soon as that is complete, take us to the release point coordinates for the weapon."

★ ★ ★

"Phoenix, please confirm we are lined up for the shot."

The acceleration test had been an uneventful 14 minutes with no change in apparent acceleration inside the field. Of course, at 74,000 gravities, no one would have felt a thing. They had returned to conduct the test without incident.

"Yes, Phoenix, we're all very much looking forward to it."

Phil raised his eyebrows, "Yes, I suppose it does, Phoenix. I wasn't aware you were familiar with the Bible."

Luis announced, "Boat rigged for zero-g, Commander."
Phil inhaled, "Very well. Shut down the drive."

A magnified image of Ari'Bal was displayed on the wall screen monitor. The gas giant was the outmost planet in the system and sported eleven major moons, many of which had been mined and inhabited by the Builders — and blasted by the Accipiters.

The current trajectory was a stand-in for that planned for the mission to Earth. One of the smaller moons represented the main Accipiter ship, a massive vessel that, according to the Accipiters, would be in a specific orbit, with its drive powered down, in anticipation of the ascent of the Keeper ship.

A tiny bead of sweat formed on Phil's clammy forehead as he clenched the hated barf bag in his fist. "Very Good, now let's throw our stone, Gentlemen."

Fire Control Technicians Joseph Burkett and Donald Warner were suited up in their spacesuits and tethered to hardpoints next to the sail/airlock. Their jobs were to manually release the doors on the four forty-foot shipping containers welded into a frame parallel to the hull. Inside each container was an eighty-inch steel tube filled with 1.8 million one-inch steel ball bearings — half the entire available supply of such bearings that could be scraped up or manufactured in time. The other half, if all went well, would be used in the actual mission.

The back of each steel tube had been sealed shut and a piston plate installed with air lines behind it. The tubes maintained a half atmosphere of pressure and were heated to prevent vacuum welding. When the container doors were opened, and the plate on the front of the tube was released, air would be dumped behind the piston and the ball bearings shoved out. They didn't need to be going very fast at all – just enough to clear the containers – and the boundary of where the warp field would be when it was turned back on. If all went as planned, the expanding pressure from the escaping air would force the plate forward, pushing the ball bearings out in a dispersal cone. Even though they might spread out more than anticipated, at the velocity they would be traveling, they would not have enough time to spread enough for their path to cause them to strike Earth directly.

The release mechanisms were backed up by explosive bolts, just in case. Joseph and Donald were the third level of backup. During the real mission, the containers would be jettisoned as soon as the ball bearings were launched.

The warp drive needed to be turned off so that neither the field itself nor gravity would affect the forward motion of the ball bearings and alter their trajectory. With the Blood Phoenix accelerated to 0.7c, the ball bearings would spill out of the four tubes and continue at that same velocity, plus the comparatively minuscule extra push from the pistons. As soon as the ball bearings cleared the diameter of the field, it would be turned back on.

The ball bearings would fly a ballistic path all the way to the target. If the Accipiter 'cloud' of ships were where they were supposed to be, there would be scant seconds before any early warning system could alert them to the danger. Their proximity defenses would get some, but not all, of the 7.2 million ball bearings.

At 0.7c, each ball bearing would deliver kinetic energy equal to $(1/2)$ x Mass x Velocity^2 or energy equal to 354.17 Megatons of TNT. Times 7.2 million.

The trajectory was designed to be tangential to the planet. If a few did manage to strike Earth's atmosphere glancingly, it was expected to be no worse than the usual small rocks that often hit the atmosphere and explode high enough up that few noticed. On the other hand, Earth was an occupied planet. Still, no one had a desire to ruin real estate humans might one day reclaim.

Phil looked at the monitors to double-check everything and then ordered calmly, "Fire."

The doors of the containers slid off cleanly, silently falling away perpendicular to the containers. Then with a puff, the caps on the tubes blew off, and the ball bearings burst loose, following in the wake of the cap. Cameras mounted on the containers showed several views, both from inside and out. In moments they had all emptied.

Phil nodded to himself, "Restore the drive!"

The Blood Phoenix shot ahead of the ball bearings to witness the results, staying well clear. After observing the results, they would reverse the acceleration process to restore their original relative velocity.

Video of the small moon filled the wall screen, with a countdown in the corner. As it reached zero, nothing seemed to happen for a moment, and Phil opened his mouth to speak before a blinding flash from the monitor made him wince.

Instead of the hoped-for shotgun pattern of explosions, the surface of the moon erupted in a single enormous, brilliant explosion, followed by a strobing, blinding, actinic eruption of smaller explosions in roughly the same area.

Several people gasped quietly.

Phil shook his head, "Fratricide. The cap hit first, and the ball bearings impacted the rising cloud of debris. Not enough spread."

"Captain, if you will observe, the moon appears to be breaking up. Its density was not very high in the first place, so this result is not unexpected."

As he watched, the moon silently broke into several large pieces. "Thank you, Phoenix. I'm confident this will only work once, and it may not be everything we'd hoped for, but it will certainly ruin someone's day."

Phil sat at the back of the room surrounded by Charles, Commander Morton, the recently promoted Lieutenant General Gideon Markovic, and the rest of the off-watch officers. Captain Cutter and his ILC and crew had remained at Ari'Nell, along with a few months of supplies while the new warp drive grew.

Gene Morton commented, "We had no problem with the approach or landing, but General Markovic had to deal with .79 Earth gravity and lower atmospheric pressure playing merry hell with his ballistics."

The former Israeli infantry officer, now Commanding Officer of the New Texas 1st Mechanized Infantry, and not, he vociferously demanded, the 'Space Marines' as so many under his command bragged, chewed his gum, and carefully nodded. "With no GPS, our drone-guided targeting method worked quite well, even if we did have to adjust the first few targeting shots."

Charles nodded, "And our part was easy. I'm just wondering what it was like here on the Phoenix while you were landing on the planet's surface, Captain?"

Phil smiled thinly, "What, you never landed a submarine on an alien planet before, Commander?"

Beach

Freetown Beach
May 19th, NLD 262 – FBD 290, 6:42 PM

Colonel Cesar Salangsang, Commanding Officer of the New Texas Army 1st Combat Engineers, took his worn, frayed boots off as he sat down and rested his feet on the warm sand. As beaches went, it was… OK. It wasn't terribly impressive, certainly nothing like the powder-fine beaches and clear waters of El Nido or the white sands and glorious blue-green waters of Palaui Island back home in the Philippines, but it was warm and sandy, and the sound of the gentle waves lapping along the shore reminded him a little of home… if he closed his eyes.

The college kids, and hangers-on, who had thrown together the shanty village of RV's and whatever they could beg, borrow, or steal, were calling the violet-blue inland sea 'Lake Texoma.' Cesar had learned that the original Texoma had been an enormous 93,000-acre Corps of Engineers-built Lake that had hugged the border between Texas and Oklahoma. Still, *this* Texoma was nothing like the warm Pacific. These 'kids' were nothing like his own people or the nine children and wife forever lost to him. They were growing on him, though, and somehow, being around them salved the pain of his loss, making it just a little easier to bear.

For the last three months, Cesar and more and more of his men had been taking what time they had off from the housing and other projects to visit this place. At first, it was beer on the beach, but before long, they had started to help the students make their shanty town more livable. They had even scraped up enough supplies to sink a pier and begin to teach them how to build boats.

Now, whenever he arrived, the students converged on him with questions and a never-ending list of things to be done. He was used to that, but he had also been shocked by how little practical, real-world experience many of them had. Gradually, as the students had become more adept at catching fish, he had begun to teach how to make Pinoy dishes. He did not have the right ingredients, but he did his best to show them the Pinangat Na Isda his mother and wife had made.

As he and his men spent more and more time there, the questions evolved to include more personal ones about life and relationships and more. When he finally realized that almost all of them were now orphans, their own parents and families lost to the Accipiters… like his own family and people, his heart had broken for them.

He closed his grey eyes and enjoyed the breeze. Tomorrow he and his men would be leaving to build a trading post for those three crazy men way down in the wilderness. Since their location was on a river and conceivably reachable from here at Freetown, he wondered if someday boats might someday turn this into an actual port of call?

A soft, husky voice asked, "What'cha doin Cesar?"

He looked up to see Michelle Bain standing over him. In the months since he first met the short-haired blonde graduate student, she had changed. She was still over-studious and brilliant, but the somewhat lost uncertainty she'd tried to hide was gone. It saddened him a little that she was the kind of woman who would probably never settle down and have a family. On the other hand, her sense of wonder and hunger for discovery made him proud. He pitied the man or woman who ever tried to hold her back.

"And how are you today, Miss Michelle? What new discoveries have you made about this world?"

She smiled warmly and plopped down on the sand next to him. "Everything's the same but different, Cesar. We're going to have to rewrite the textbooks completely."

He nodded confidently, "I know you will."

Michelle closed her eyes and listened to the surf. "I never asked you. How did you know to come and look for us that day? How did you even find us?"

Cesar shrugged gently, "My father was a fisherman and his father before him and his before that. When I was young, I admit I was more interested in how the boats were made than sailing them. My father taught me, though, that I needed to understand the sea before I could build a boat to sail it."

Michelle nodded, "But you joined the army and became a construction engineer?"

Cesar gently laughed, "It was the other way around, but that was where the work was."

They sat in companionable silence for a while. Cesar laid back flat on the sand, Michelle followed his example, "What do you see up there?"

Cesar looked up past the fading suntube to an extensive collection of islands on the other side of the world and pointed, "Someday, we shall make that the new Pinoy home. The new Philippines."

Michelle smiled, "I know you will. Let me ask you something, though. What do you know about dolphins?"

Shattered

The past three months had changed Thomas Harding. Until now, his entire life had been one of hyper-rational decisions and careful, considered actions. While others might not understand those actions and decisions, especially before Awakening Day, everything he did had been deliberate and, he believed, justified.

He reflected upon his book he had never had a chance to finish due to the Accipiter attack. He'd devoted years of exquisitely detailed research on the British and French wars between 1793 and 1815. He had carefully constructed what he was convinced would become the ultimate scholarly tome. He imagined being called to guest lecture on the subject in his retirement. Perhaps, back on Earth, his suburban home had been outside the blast radius of the Accipiter kinetic strikes, and even now, his filing cabinets full of notes and his computer still lay where he had left them, no doubt now covered with dust and mold.

His decision to deliver classified documents to enemies of his country had likewise been carefully and deliberately reasoned as the logical means to prod his complacent nation into action. To that end, he had been willing to sacrifice his life and career. His was a patriotism he fully expected few, if any, would ever understand or respect.

For the last six weeks, he had regularly reported to the civilian government downside in Fort Brazos. He often worked late into the evening, so he pulled strings to get a private, locked office at City Hall "for security reasons." Those late hours had made it relatively simple for him to smuggle in the components of the device he slowly, painstakingly, assembled.

Despite decades of spying, Thomas had never felt this apprehensive before. In all that time, he had never done anything remotely like this. Indeed, in his entire life, he had never harmed anyone or performed a single physically dangerous act outside of Navy training. But then, in the last three months, the picture he had pieced together of the United States government's complicity and the coverup that led to the annihilation of the human race had horrified him and filled him with a bitter seething rage he had barely concealed.

And then he had found a thumb drive in an unmarked envelope in the locked drawer of his desk. On it were thousands of documents. *Unredacted* documents and the story they told had shocked him to his core.

Thomas sat at his desk, gripping the arms of his chair until his knuckles turned white. Beads of sweat formed on his forehead as he ground his teeth. His glasses lay on the blotter in front of him. His anger and shame burned his soul in equal parts. Anger at those responsible and humiliation at what the human race was capable of. Only now, it wasn't something a now dead government had done. It was an evil made manifest by what certain *people* had done and were personally responsible for.

Until he read through the unredacted documents, he had harbored lingering, nagging doubt. After all, sometimes coincidence was, after all, just that. Coincidence.

Now, all doubt had been seared away. It had taken weeks to work out the plan and its logistics with his handler. Reluctantly, he had agreed that the information could not be made public without the unacceptable risk of shattering the already brittle public psyche. All that was left was what now had to be done. What *must* be done.

He looked at the clock on the computer display. It was time. Now or never.

He wiped the sweat from his forehead and put on his glasses. He stood, took a deep breath, straightened his uniform, and picked up the backpack from behind the desk. *That's strange. I don't remember it being this heavy.*

He walked from his office to the elevator to go down to the main floor.

The security details were still all outside the building, and the halls were empty. His steps echoed on the marble floor as he briskly walked to the council chamber and presented a memory stick to the video technician. "Hello, Jason, can you load these for me?"

The 22-year-old, sandy-haired Jason Thornaby smiled, "Sure, Commander, give me a sec. I had to reboot this machine; it's been giving me trouble all week."

Thomas gritted his teeth and set his backpack down behind the row of seats. As he did, catches silently parted.

Meanwhile, beyond the council chambers and the lobby beyond, the City Hall outside doors opened, and the VIP delegation entered. Thomas already knew who was arriving: The Guilty. The President, Vice President, General Marcus, the Mayor, City Council, and others.

The noise from the approaching crowd swelled.

Thomas glanced nervously at the entrance and back at Jason, "Is there a problem?"

Jason swore under his breath before answering, "No, Sir, I've got it. Here it is!" He loaded the PowerPoint and put it up on the main screen.

Thomas looked up at the screen and winced, "Oh My, That's the wrong deck! I'll be back in a minute."

Jason shrugged, "No Problem, Commander, I'll be here."

Thomas lifted the backpack. When he did, it left behind a New Londoner newcomer backpack that he had hidden inside. Since the room had already been checked by security, no one should notice it. The fact that it was identical to the one owned by a certain North Korean 'defector' and contained copies of the defector's letters was a minor touch that Thomas doubted the local police here would discover or appreciate, but he strove for perfection.

In a few minutes, that same North Korean defector would be here in the audience to witness the council session, as he had done for every major session of note. Thomas had also gone so far as to send an anonymous email, alerting the student protest group that the young defector had attached himself to, that the President and Vice President would both be here today.

Thomas hurried to the exit, although the crowd was already at the doors.

Alexander Marcus motioned to John and his detail just outside the large double door entrance to the Council Chambers. Wayne and Sybil stood next to

Alexander, with Sybil clutching Wayne's hand. Wayne looked distinctly uncomfortable in his sport jacket and tie, and Sybil was only slightly less so in her long dress and heels. John was perfectly comfortable in his suit, but he only wore it on formal occasions like today's meeting, as everyone knew by now.

Gail was farther back in the crowd, wearing her well-known business suit, the jacket of which she never opened and always looked uncomfortable in. She spoke quietly to Gloria Vargas and Tom Parker, who were all accompanied by their various security detail members and staffers. Matti was at the Joint Reserve Base, flying simulators and having a blast.

Alexander slapped Wayne Blanchard on the back and pushed him towards John. "Mr. President, have you met the Blanchard's? I brought them with me today to report on the logistics and viability of the Guadalupe Bend trading outpost. Wayne has been instrumental in keeping much of our logistics efforts on track back and forth to New London as well as to the Forward Operating Bases," He nodded at Sybil, "And Sybil here is the brains of the operation. You may recall she was the one who fended off the Wardog attack on the highway some months ago?"

John smiled and extended his hand, shaking Wayne's, "It's a pleasure to meet you, Wayne. I've read many good things about you and Sybil here. I understand we are all very fortunate to have Sybil keeping an eye on you and the business!"

Sybil smiled shyly, and then her eyes widened, and her head snapped in the direction of the Council Chamber doors....

The double doors opened, and Thomas Harding emerged, hurriedly walking by the VIP's and past Sybil, who dropped Wayne's hand and rushed after Thomas. Wayne looked up in surprise, but John asked a question, and Wayne returned his attention to the President.

After a few short strides, Sybil caught up with Thomas and reached out and tugged on his arm, calling out softly, "Thomas?"

He stopped, nervously looked around, and then down at Sybil, "I'm sorry, do I know you? Excuse me, but I really must go now."

Sybil gripped his arm tighter and spoke quietly but earnestly, "Thomas, we really should talk. I know you don't know me, but I know you. I know you thought what you were doing was justified. But it's OK now. We're in the New World. You can put it all behind you."

Thomas jerked his arm away from her and said just a little too loudly, "Get away from me! Who the hell are you?"

She belatedly noticed the beads of sweat on his brow and how nervously his eyes were darting around the room.

Wayne, John, and Alexander looked up from their conversation to stare, as did many others in the room.

Sybil's eyes widened, and her mouth parted as she stumbled a half step back from Thomas, "Oh Thomas… You've gone and done something, haven't you!"

Thomas's eyes flared in surprise.

Sybil sighed and clasped her hands to her chest, "Oh no, Thomas! What have you done? Whatever it is, we can help you. You can stop!"

Thomas turned away from her and hurried toward the exit.

Sybil mumbled, "No, no, no…." Then she shouted and pointed, "Stop him! Stop that man!"

Thomas whirled in surprise as everyone in the room looked at him while the crazy woman yelled at him. Her large brown eyes widened in fear and sorrow. He blinked in surprise and looked around as though there could be anyone else she could be talking about.

The security details reacted instinctively, hustling their charges away from the apparent threat. In John's case, towards the Council Chamber.

Thomas's expression hardened as he felt a sudden relief. He no longer had to hide. It was over. He was a patriot doing his duty. He reached into his pocket.

Wayne was closest and rushed to tackled Thomas, throwing all of his considerable bulk and muscle into it.

It was too late.

The plastic explosive in the newcomer backpack exploded. The over-pressure wave shredded everything in its path, including Jason Thornaby, the chairs, fixtures, and finally the ceiling, walls, and doors.

The doors exploded outward into splinters just as John was being hustled through them, blowing him and his detail back through the air in a shower of debris.

The occupants of the lobby area outside the Council Chamber were scattered like paper figures in a hurricane.

Gail was among the first to stir, unable to hear anything with her damaged ear drums. She staggered to her feet, momentarily disoriented. A few other people started to move and stagger around in confusion, and many others did not move at all. Then she saw John and gasped in horror.

It did not make sense. John's arm and leg were bent the wrong way, and his face was covered in blood. Her heart felt as though it were bursting in her chest, and her eyes widened in shock. For a long moment, she stood there, unable to move, terrified that if she did, it could somehow make what was happening real, that he could be gone. Then she saw the man that the dark-haired woman had accused roll out from under a huge shaggy-haired man and shakily rise to his feet.

Thomas was startled to be still alive. He quickly found his glasses amid the rubble, although the left lens was now cracked. He was lightheaded, and his knees were weak as he stood and looked around for his accuser, but she was lost somewhere in the chaos. All around him, though, people were beginning to move and cry out. Then he turned and saw the Vice President, just standing there alone, with her guards lying on the floor around her, covered in debris.

Part of him absently wondered. *The Council Chamber doors must have been heavier than I thought.*

And there she is—one of the instigators of my Hell. If I had known the United States had had Builder Technology, I would never have needed to do what I did! Perhaps someday, the truth will be known, and I will be remembered as a patriot.

His face twisted in a rictus of bitter hatred and resentment. He shouted at her, "You! You did this! You and Alexander, You Knew, didn't you?!" He continued, his face growing hot, "You knew all about the Builders! I can see it on your face!"

Gail was startled at the man's outburst, but the hate and rage were all she could understand, with her ears still ringing. She recognized him now. Commander Harding, the man whose frenzied efforts to push the starship project along, had been laudable. Part of her had regretted holding back his efforts from going in too many directions at once. *What is wrong with him?*

In the chaos all around them, more people were trying to move, including surviving security detail members, while police officers and others were working their way inside through the shattered doors and windows.

Thomas Harding snarled, "That's right! You know what I'm talking about, don't you! You Bitch! You've betrayed us all! Sic Semper Tyrannus!" He reached into his jacket and withdrew a small pistol.

Gail saw the murder in his eyes as Thomas reached into his jacket, and she instinctively knew what he was doing. His movements were clumsy. After all the practice Nate, Jermal, and Jose had drilled into her, virtually every day, hers were not as her left hand pulled her suit coat aside and her right hand withdrew her FNX .45 and point-aim fired, the muzzle flash shocking the dust and debris still falling from the broken ceiling.

It was not a conscious decision, but that is what this kind of training was for. There was no time for conscious, careful, deliberate thought in life and death confrontations like this. Later, looking back on today's events, she would never remember her muscle memory actions.

Thomas tried to raise his arm to aim his diminutive Kahr .380, but something was dreadfully wrong. His arm would not move. He blinked in surprise before collapsing like a marionette with its strings cut as he gazed in wonder at Gail's hard, frozen, jade-green eyes and her outstretched hand and saw that it held her own pistol. It looked surprisingly large in her pale fingers. *Since when did she carry….*

Matti Austin was sweating and straining and wide-eyed as the enclosed flight simulator violently rocked, rolled, and shook her. She wore one of the most petite flight suits and helmets available, and the day's exertions were a reward from Gail, who had said that Matti had been working too long and too hard and needed a break.

Matti had objected to missing the Council meeting until she found out just precisely what Gail had had in mind. She had been counting the hours for the last week as she studied and soaked up everything she could find on the F-35. Matti had always had an excellent memory… when she put her mind to it. Now though, she knew it was different. She never had to look at anything twice. Not really, although she found herself not so much hiding the fact as realizing that there was so much that she never really paid close enough attention to.

She had been waiting at the door at 0800 and suffered through the over-simple orientation lecture by the oh-so-polite but not-quite-condescending flight instructor.

In short order, the difficulty level had been upped twice already from the 'easy' level reserved for 'visitors.' Matti would have asked for even more, but she did not want to start over again and lose more time. Besides, this was THE MOST FUN she had ever had IN HER LIFE.

The simulator gimbled hard again as she lined up her shot…. And then the power cut out, and the simulator slid back to the level position and locked.

"What!!! What happened! What's going…."

Just then, the simulator door swung open, and Roxanne Darling, her eyes ablaze and her face set in stone, reached in, popped Matti's harness, and scooped her up like a rag doll, knocking Matti's breath away as she bodily carried her in two jumps down the metal stairs from the simulator, tossed Matti over her shoulder and bounded to the exit towards the fallout shelter.

✪ ✪ ✪

Roxanne and Matti shared a corner of the aging fallout shelter, its walls covered in an entirely unlikely number of coats of paint.

Roxanne shook her head, "Matti, I can't put you on a plane or helicopter back to the city. The base is on lockdown, and there is a no-fly zone enforced. This is the first time the base has been on complete lockdown that wasn't a drill since Awakening Day."

Matti still wore her somewhat baggy flight suit, but to Roxanne, it seemed like Matti had suddenly grown taller. She was composed, articulate and deliberate. Not at all how Roxanne thought she herself might have been had it been her own father on the operating table after a bombing.

Matti nodded calmly, "I understand. However, there's got to be an armed convoy or something they're going to send to the city?"

Roxanne brushed her black hair back, "Yes, and the rapid reaction force has already left."

Matti sighed, "Yes, of course, it did. I am saying that there has to be a follow-up, larger force that will follow it. Put me in a tank. I don't care. Just get me in that convoy. You do whatever you have to do. Gail isn't answering her phone, and neither is General Marcus. My father is in surgery after a bombing, and there is no way in hell I am not going to be there for him. You pull whatever strings you have to. The President's Daughter *Has* To Be There At His Side."

Matti lowered her voice and spoke very slowly. "Do I make myself perfectly, crystal clear?"

DownSide: Fort Brazos
Methodist Hospital

Matti and Roxanne had not ridden in a tank, but the eight-wheeled LAV-25 was close enough. Gideon Markovic himself had ridden with them. Roxanne was not sure, but she had the impression that the column might have doubled in size or more when it was announced that they would be carrying the President's daughter to his side.

The column arrived at the hospital, and a third of it calved off to increase the presence around the ravaged City Hall.

Gideon led a platoon into the hospital, escorting Matti and Roxanne. Gwyneth Elliott met them in a private waiting room. Her auburn hair was awry, and her scrubs were suspiciously clean and fresh.

Matti pushed her way through to Gwyneth. "How is my father?"

Gwyneth sized Matti up before answering, "Your father is still in surgery. He suffered pulmonary barotrauma, or blast lung, as well as abdominal hemorrhaging. He has severe lacerations and compound fractures in his right arm and leg. He also has internal organ damage, a skull fracture, bleeding in his eyes, and he likely has middle ear damage, so… when he comes out of surgery and is conscious, he will have trouble hearing."

Matti nodded slowly. Her voice was flat as she asked, "Will he live?"

Gwyneth Elliott ushered Gail into David's office. This time Gail's security detail, battered as they were, abjectly refused to leave her presence. John's detail had lost Corporal Jorge Diego and Corporal Antoine "Tony" Bouchard in the blast. Their bodies had shielded John from the worst of it, but the compression wave had nearly killed him as well.

Despite the laundry list of injuries Gwyneth had related to Matti, she had neglected to mention several things, including the fact that John had nearly bled out from lacerations in his neck. John's expensive body armor had prevented punctures to his body core and likely saved his life. That is if he lived through the night.

David Duncan, Gwyneth, and the hospital staff had labored through the day to save whom they could and stabilize everyone else. General Marcus had suffered severe lacerations and a broken arm. Gloria Vargas had a broken leg and lacerations. Mayor Parker and the other council members were severely bruised and shaken, but Councilman Hickum was dead from flying debris that had raggedly decapitated him.

Besides cuts and bruises, Gail's physical injuries were minor, and even her hearing was coming back. Gail walked to the small lounge area of the office and tripped on the rug. Gwyneth caught her, and as she held her, she could feel Gail shaking. Gail's lips trembled as she looked pleadingly at Gwyneth, her eyes no longer holding back the tears.

Colonel Gwyneth Elliott shot a look at Jermal, who stood inside the door and barked, "You! Get the Vice President some blankets. Now!" Jermal stayed put but spoke quietly into his radio.

Gwyneth helped Gail to an overstuffed leather couch, and Gail collapsed bodily into it.

Moments later, Jermal spoke into his microphone again, then opened the door to accept the blankets from Nate Hopper. Jermal carried the blankets over and ever so gently tucked them in around Gail.

When he looked up at Gwyneth, she could see the fury in his face and the wetness in the young man's eyes. He tightened his lips.

Gwyneth reached out and touched him on the arm, "She'll be OK."

He nodded and withdrew to his post inside the door and did his best to become a stone.

Gwyneth kneeled next to Gail and whispered, "You know you're in shock, right? Is this anything like the plane crash? Also, small detail, you shot a man."

Gail blinked tears, shaking her head, her lips trembling. "Gwen…. I can't lose him… I can't!"

Gwyneth took Gail's hand and said softly, "Oh dear God. You really are in love with him, aren't you?"

Gail screwed up her face and nearly spat the words, "He said it must be the Gardener changes in us… induced hormones, he said!"

"Is that what you think?"

Gail glared at her.

Gwyneth nodded, "OK, for what it's worth, we have no medical evidence of that. Sure, there was a surge of marriages," she smiled, "my own included, and we all know what happened after that, but at the same time it's not like the Gardeners released Love Potion number 9 into the air. People are still people, and it is the apocalypse, after all. I'm afraid, my dear, that you can't blame the Gardeners for how you two obviously feel about each other."

Gail looked away, "God help me. I don't know what I'll do if he…. How did I end up this way? He's so impossible and arrogant."

Gwyneth smiled gently, "You mean the kind of person you never dreamed you would be interested in?"

Gail nodded a tiny nod.

Gwyneth continued, "And he's maddeningly polite? Kind, and, well, I admit he's not hard to look at?"

Gail tried to glare but did not have the strength this time.

"And you both know how the other feels, but neither one of you will do anything about it because of how it would look?"

Gail's eyes grew heavy, and she wearily said, "You've been talking to Matti."

Gwyneth sighed, "No, but I'm sure she knows what everyone else in the world already does. She's a pretty smart kid, you know. Maybe you should listen to her."

She smiled, then added, "Gail, you don't love him because. You love him despite. Not for his virtues but despite his faults."

Gail closed her eyes

Gwyneth stood up, "Move over."

Gail hesitated, then winced as she lifted herself up.

Gwyneth sat down and eased Gail's head down into her lap and gently stroked Gail's disheveled hair that was still coated in dust and particles from the bombing as her own eyes misted. "You rest, dear. We are all here for you. More than you will ever know, the whole world is here for you."

Gail shuddered as she whispered, "It's too much…."

"I know…"

"I'll never see him again…."

Gwyneth cocked her head in confusion, "What do you mean, of course, you'll see John again?"

Gail shook her head slightly, "My father… the Colonel."

Gwyneth closed her eyes and lowered her head in realization. *So that's where all of this is coming from.* "My God, you've bottled it all up inside, haven't you? Everything that has happened." *It took a bombing, seeing someone you love nearly die, and you shooting the bastard who did it to finally breach the emotional dam. Your anger and fury have sustained you ever since Awakening Day. Eight Billion dead, but you never mourned. We never gave you a chance. We have never given you or John a moment's break since this all started.*

Gail could not hold back anymore. "I'm so tired…." She bodily shook as she wept. After long minutes she fell still.

Gwyneth looked over her shoulder and nodded to Jermal, and mouthed, "She's finally asleep."

Shock

Studio Lounge
May 21ˢᵗ, NLD 264 -- FBD 292, 8:00 AM

anielle Richardson Anders gently rocked three-week-old Devon as she suckled him. His younger brother, by a minute, Terrance, lay blissfully and thankfully, asleep in the cradle next to her. Danielle's black hair was longer now, below her shoulders. She sat next to the microphone in the studio and had been singing to her boys just before she went on air. It had not stopped her tears, but it calmed the boys.

Her voice was an octave lower than it even usually was as she began. "Hello, people of Fort Brazos and New London. This is Danielle Richardson on FM 92.5, and Radio Free Fort Brazos beaming our signal across the known world and beyond. There is so much to talk about today…" she sniffed, "…and it is hard to know where to begin. By now, all of you must know about the cowardly act of terror committed yesterday. I'm…." She let out a soft sob, "…I'm sure I'm just as devastated as you are. And I am ashamed! Ashamed that we could even contemplate doing this to ourselves, now! After all that has happened! After our entire world was savagely erased, and this moron thinks that he can make things better with a fucking bomb! At least the dickhead died on the operating table and saved us the expense of a hanging!"

Danielle paused and blinked, "Oh my… did I actually just say that out loud? I have to wonder… would I have said that before my baby boys were born? Would I have even thought that before Awakening Day? I was hugely against capital punishment…. Now… I don't know, or I suppose I really do. What I do know is that this monster murdered seven people so far, and more may die from their injuries. We still don't know if President Austin will survive."

"The dead…." She swallowed, "The Dead are Councilman Wylie Hickum, President Austin's protection detail members Corporal Jorge Diego and Corporal Antoine "Tony" Bouchard, City Council audio-video technician Jason

Thornaby…. I knew him, you know…. He was such a sweet young man. Also, Air Force Lieutenant Sára Maruska, who was assisting General Marcus, as well as Mr. Steffen Zuckermann, and Mr. Carlos Alonso.”

“Just about everyone there suffered injuries of one kind or other. I also understand that Councilwoman Gloria Vargas suffered a broken leg and other injuries. General Marcus has a broken arm and severe lacerations. Both of them are expected to recover fully.”

“I also want to talk about Vice President Finley. I mean, what more can you say about this woman who keeps surprising us over and over with her personal fortitude and bravery. She was pretty banged up, but she got up and shot the bastard, whose name will not be repeated here.”

“Now, I know that some of you people out there have been wagging your tongues about some sort of illicit affair going on between Vice President Finley and President Austin. Lord knows I’m no prude, but Jesus, people! Cut those two some slack, will you? We pulled both of them out of their lives and railroaded them into jobs with all that responsibility so that you and I won’t have to. Can you please stop for just one minute and imagine the kind of pressure on them? It’s not about elections or politics… we picked them to shoulder the responsibility for the survival of all of humankind! Fucking aliens nuke the planet, and we pick those two to be responsible for making sure the rest of us survive, and you people have the gall to worry about whether those same two people might, maybe, possibly, the gossips say, find solace in each other?”

“And now this monster and who knows, maybe he had help, tries to murder not only the President and Vice President but the whole damned City Council and General Marcus too!?!”

“I am shocked, I am appalled, and I am ashamed of my species….”

Danielle sniffed again and wiped her tears and nose with a Kleenex. She stroked Devin’s cheek, “And here I am with my babies, thinking about their future. The world they are going to grow up in, and I ask you, dammit, is *this* the world you want for my babies? Is this the world you want for *your* babies!”

Danielle reached over with her free hand and adjusted an audio control on her soundboard by touch. She could not see it through her tears.

"Well, I'm telling you now, it's time for the human race to grow the fuck up!"

Terrance started softly crying.

"Make up your mind. What's it going to be? Do we deserve to let the Gardeners snuff out the last remaining embers of humanity, or do we become something better?"

Dead and Buried

DownSide: Methodist Hospital

Security Holding Room
May 30th, NLD 273 -- FBD 301, 7:49 PM

Former FBI Counterespionage Agent Brian Kupe looked up from his tattered paperback at the sound coming from the patient handcuffed to the hospital bed. "Ah, I see you're finally awake."

Thomas Harding coughed, and the pain-wracked his body. He groaned, blinked, and turned his head. "You."

Brian smiled thinly, "I'm actually a little hurt you recognize me. I did so try not to be noticed."

Thomas closed his eyes, "…one too many times."

"Yes, well, hazards of the game, I suppose. It's odd, though. I never pegged you for an assassin."

Thomas coughed again, wincing, "I don't expect you to understand. I am a patriot. Everything I did was to help my country, even when it was too stupid to help itself."

Brian raised his eyebrows, "OK then, I suppose I must ask the obvious question then, what does eliminating the current leadership accomplish?"

Thomas groaned and shook his head, "First, let me be clear. What we were doing with the starship was a stupid, emotional, kneejerk decision. We were likely to lose our only weapon in the process and probably even lead the enemy back here. Regardless, we'd prove our incompetence to the Gardeners, and if the Accipiters didn't wipe us out, the Gardeners would likely flush us down the tube as a bad investment."

Brian nodded, "But that's not what pushed you to take direct action."

Thomas closed his eyes, "The starship decision was made, or at least driven, by the traitors who sold out Earth to the Accipiters in the first place."

Brian carefully closed the paperback and tucked it into an oversized pocket in his jacket. He smiled thinly and nodded. "Ah, that. I know all about the documents that convinced you of grand conspiracies, and I have studied them in great detail. I have also spoken to Dr. Talib, General Marcus, the Vice President, and with an entirely charming alien computer that calls herself Phoenix. I'm certain you won't believe me when I tell you that those documents were fabricated out of whole cloth by the Gardeners as a cover story for humanity to explain how we got the Builder technology so as to not draw suspicion upon themselves, however unfathomable that seems."

Thomas started to shake his head, but the movement hurt too much. "I don't believe you."

"Of course, you don't. On the other hand, it is interesting to me that you have not asked where you are or what the date is, so I will do my best to inform you of recent events. After the attack, your attack, some suspicion was briefly cast upon the North Koreans until it was clear that that evidence was put there by you. Still, it was enough to crystalize a decision about what to do with them. The young defector whom you attempted to frame was very helpful in identifying the more harmless of the bunch, which was more than I expected, really. The rest were shipped off to a remote island somewhere. They were given some food, survival gear, hammers, nails, and such and left to their own devices. Out of sight, out of mind, I suppose. Also, the starship came back, and its training mission was apparently a success. They will be leaving for Earth in about a month. Public support has now gone up to something like 98% at last count."

Thomas tried to shift his position and grimaced at the pain, "Goodie for them…."

"Changing the subject back to you, however, am I to assume then that your supposed rehabilitation was a sham and that others blackmailed you into working for them to nefarious ends? After all, this world was a new start for you. No one might ever have known of your past or even really cared."

Despite the pain, Thomas shook his head, "What difference does it make now? Yes, they blackmailed me and threatened to exile me with the North Koreans."

Brian rubbed the back of his neck for a moment, took a breath, and shrugged, "Well, I've got some good news and some bad news for you. Your conspirators are not looking for you. You're officially dead and buried and loudly unlamented by the rest of humanity. The bad news is that Thomas, you killed a bunch of people and tried to assassinate the entire leadership of what remains of humanity! The only reason you actually *are* still alive is that certain parties somehow convinced the Vice President that you might be useful in identifying your co-conspirators. Let me tell you, that lady was more than ready to shoot you herself, again. Frankly, I'd gladly help. So, Mr. Harding, if you want to have any hope of some kind of leniency, you'd better know something."

Brian stood and walked to Thomas's bedside and used the water bottle to drip some water in Thomas's mouth.

Thomas gratefully accepted the water before whispering, "Or I get shot whether I help you or not."

Brian smiled, "As cover stories go, though, it is obvious to me now that a logical, intelligent machine wrote it. When you add it all up, it's simply too convenient. Too perfect. Too many dots connect together. In real life, nothing is that simple and there are always missing pieces, especially over timelines of decades. As methodical as you are, I have to admit I'm surprised you fell for it, Thomas."

"I still think you're lying."

Brian nodded, "On the other hand, I think you needed it to be true. You needed someone else's treason to be greater than your own. Maybe you were seduced by the excitement and glamour you perceived in your actions—the danger. You needed to think of yourself as a patriot. The revelations of the cover story made everything you did; all your own lies and treason were nothing in comparison. They made your own actions, all the risk and fear and danger you went through, into nothing more than irrelevant background noise. Now, by striking out against those you believed to be even worse than yourself, you would find absolution for your sins."

Thomas stared at Brian as each of his labored breaths felt like nails driven into his chest. Doubt began to sink him deeper into the hospital bed.

Brian shrugged again, "Who knows, maybe instead of exiling you with the North Koreans, we drop you off on some nice planet somewhere with a new name where we set up an outpost. I don't know or care. It's not up to me. On the other hand, did you know that there are still quite a few unclaimed bodies in cold storage from Awakening Day? Now, it seems to me that you are already nicely dead and buried and quickly being forgotten. It *is* the apocalypse, so who would notice if another John Doe ended up in an unmarked grave."

Brian shook his head and sighed, "These co-conspirators did not treat you as an equal. They used you and threw you away. For all you know, their crimes maybe even worse than your own. They blackmailed you and used you. Is there honor in protecting them?"

Thomas closed his eyes. Could the man be right? Did the person or persons who used him use him to their own ends? Clearly, they did. Did he owe them any loyalty, or was he just their bitch?" He licked his dry lips, "I never saw them. I was always in an interrogation room, but I have dates and times, and they provided components for the bomb. They also maneuvered me to get the Systems and Integration job. They won't have left fingerprints, but they pushed the people who pushed the people who did."

Brian nodded slowly, "Well then, we have our work cut out for us, don't we?"

Healing

Dr. David Duncan fretted as Sergeant Benjamin "Benny" Jenkins, the surviving original member of John's protection detail, helped John into the wheelchair. "Mr. President, you really should stay in the hospital. Your injuries were severe! Gardener enhanced healing be damned, I just don't know what could happen with your internal injuries, much less the risk of infection!"

John Austin shook his head adamantly, His right eye was bandaged, and his right leg and arm were both still in a cast. His face was still purple and bruised, and that is what was visible. "The mission to Earth launches in a week. There is too much to do, and too much depends on it."

Gail took the wheelchair handles and added, "Thank you for all you and your staff have done, doctor. I know he is a difficult patient, but we will keep an eye on him. We won't let him do anything stupid."

Matti tucked a blanket over her father's lap, and his arm and leg casts. "Don't worry, doctor. We'll take care of him."

The new members of the detail, Corporals Gabriel Pérez and Braden Edwards, stood ready at the door to John's suite. Next to them were Gail's detail, Nate Hopper, Jose Cruz, and Jermal Dixon. It was a crowded place.

John shook his head and chuckled, then winced at the pain, "I may have been safer in here, doctor, but I've got a job to do, and the people need to see me alive and out of this hospital. Not only that, but the crew needs to see it too."

The entourage made their way to the exit and the waiting armored vehicles. Outside, a massive gathering of well-wishers waited on the other side of a police line, some distance away. As the group emerged from the hospital doors, a thunderous cheer erupted from the crowd. John managed to raise a hand and wave before he was rolled to a waiting microphone and a handful of cameras and reporters. Security was heavy and very visible.

To his surprise, he was soon joined by the surviving City Council, Gloria Vargas in her own wheelchair, General Marcus, his arm in a sling and still sporting bandages on his neck and face, General Chilton, Lt. General Markovic, and Admirals Milner and Johansson, as well as Captains Cutter and Underwood, and Commanders Cross and Morton.

Gail took the microphone, "Thank you, everyone, for coming. After this recent tragedy, we all," Gail gestured to the group crowding around her and John, "decided that a statement of unity was needed. We will not be cowed. We will not be deterred. We will not be coerced. To paraphrase Benjamin Franklin, we must all stand together, or together we shall all surely fall. I give you, President John Austin."

The crowd roared approval.

Gail pushed John closer to the mic, and he did his best to hide the wince of pain as the wheelchair jerked to a stop. "Sorry," she whispered.

Matti stood at his left side and lowered the microphone for him as John raised his good arm, and the crowd quieted. He began, "Eleven days ago, madness swept our midst. The madness of a person gripped by fear and uncertainty about the future. Fear of our foe. The Accipiters Raped our World and murdered Billions. Now, apparently, there are some among us who fear that our actions will make our enemy *mad* at us? Really?!" John paused, catching his breath. Matti put her hand on his shoulder.

John continued, shaking his head, "I understand that some may fear taking action. They fear that we should wait until we are more prepared. Maybe we should take several years to study and analyze and lick our wounds. Maybe we should bide our time, looking for the right moment to strike. Maybe that was a way to do things when the United States was the preeminent global superpower, but there is breaking news, folks. The United States is dead. Russia is dead. China is dead. All that is left is us, and we have the Gardener's gun to our heads. George Patton said when in doubt, attack! He also said that a good plan violently executed now is better than a perfect plan executed next week!"

The crowd cheered angrily.

"Our resolve is being tested. The madman who murdered our friends, colleagues, and loved ones never understood that our resolve was not mine or the Vice President's or any of our Generals or Admirals. Our resolve is that of the people. It is *your* resolve! *We* are resolved to confront the threat to our species. We are resolved to survive. We are resolved to protect our families and our children. And we are all, every damned one of us, vehemently resolved to stand against and to bring pain and retribution to those who raped our planet and murdered our future!"

The crowd roared in bitter agreement, clapping and chanting, "Make them Pay! Make them Pay!"

John's chest heaved as he tried to catch his breath. Gail walked out in front of him and raised her hands to quiet the crowd. Eventually, they complied and Gail returned to flank Matti on John's right.

John pulled the microphone out of the stand and leaned forward in the wheelchair, exhausted but defiant, his voice dropping an octave, "So, I ask of ya'll one thing. Our courageous young men are about to embark upon the greatest challenge in all of human history. I ask you to pray for them that they will know that we love and support them no matter what happens. I ask you to pray for them to have the strength and faith, and courage they need to see them through the fire and return home to us. To paraphrase Churchill, we shall not flag or fail. We shall go on to the end. We shall fight on the land, seas, and oceans, and amongst the stars. We shall fight with growing confidence and growing strength. We shall defend the survivors of mankind, no matter what the cost may be. We shall never surrender. We shall carry on the struggle until, in God's good time, this New World, with all its newfound power and might, liberates our birthright world and wrenches it from the dying talons of our enemies."

John paused again and held up his hand for the crowd to wait. Sweat beaded his forehead. He swallowed, then lowered his hand and spoke, "The Accipiters think of themselves as being some sort of Gods. I tell you now, they may think they are all-powerful. Apparently, no one has seriously challenged them in countless millennia. However, they made a mistake in not killing all of us. You see," he looked out at their faces, "You see… now we're going to go back… and we're going to storm the gates of Olympus and burn the damned place to the ground!"

John slumped back in the wheelchair and closed his eyes. For a long moment, the crowd was silent.

Gail began a slow, loud clap. The crowd quickly followed until the ground fairly shook.

Matti bent down and adjusted her father's blanket that had come loose.

Gail looked down at John. She realized that she no longer cared what people thought. Life was…. Life was too short, and she had very nearly lost him forever. *To hell with what people think.* She suddenly realized that she had been stroking John's hair. She glanced up at Matti and saw only love in the young girls' blue eyes. Gail decided. Her heart thudded in her chest as she bent over and kissed him squarely on the lips, and the noise from the crowd, as thunderous as it already was, more than trebled.

Analysis

Davis Engineering Building Annex
June 10th, NLD 284 -- FBD 312, 1:51 PM

The Bonham State University Davis Engineering Building Annex was home to the school's fledgling Electrical Engineering program. The forty-year-old two-story building had, until two years ago, been a Records building. The University already had well-established Mechanical, Construction Science, Manufacturing, and Quality Engineering schools, but adding the EE Electrical Engineering program had been part of the new University Dean's growth program.

Air Force Captain Darryl Guevara provided his credentials to the full combat geared Marines guarding the engineering lab, who then checked his face on a tablet as being one of the few people authorized to enter, then admitted him. He had been there daily. However, after the bombing, security everywhere had been dramatically escalated. Four entire platoons guarded the building, including the pipe works beneath.

The consensus had been that the alien artifact had to be not only essential but seemed likely to be a vital piece of the puzzle to how humans were expected to be able to possibly combat the Accipiters in any meaningful way. Further, initial testing had shown that it was indeed, at the very least, some sort of power source. In the context of fighting a war, power was everything. Power was… Power.

A strong push had been made to secure the device at the base. However, the need to study it and the accessibility of the minds and resources needed to do so had won out. The compromise being the heavily armed security presence. After the horror of the bombing attack, all but the most liberal of the faculty gritted their teeth and admitted it was probably a good idea.

Ever since the chaos of Awakening Day, Darryl had been General Marcus's chief aid and fixer. Alexander was still recovering from his wounds, which had been worse than initially thought. Darryl wasn't an engineer, but he was a pilot and had a Master's degree in Avionics, so his job here was to assess the progress of the analysis and then translate it for the General, and by extension, the rest of the military and political leadership.

At 26, Darryl, who was of Cuban descent, was the youngest in the room, followed by Diana Cole, Ph.D. Electrical Engineering (32), Rishi Singh, Ph.D. Manufacturing Engineering (48), Logan MacAslan, Ph.D. Mechanical Engineering (72, Retired) and Navy Captain Stephanie Mahoney, Ph.D. in Physics and a Master's Degree in Electrical Engineering (43).

The softly glowing cube itself sat on a workbench in the middle of the room, surrounded by instruments of varied description. The odd, high-pitched sound it emitted was slightly painful to Darryl, but no one else seemed to notice. Thick power cables were plugged into each side and were connected to a heavy-duty power busbar and cables that snaked away from the table.

Darryl announced, "Good afternoon, everyone, Ladies, Gentlemen. What's the latest on our mystery box?"

Rishi smiled and answered in his pronounced Indian accent, "It is fascinating. We discovered the device surface dynamically reconfigures itself to fit whatever power connector we attach to it."

Diana nodded enthusiastically, "As you know, the device was outputting whatever power our test load drew from it. We have ended up melting too many pieces of equipment. We are about to try modulating a simple carrier wave into the device through the power leads to see if that might be a way to control the power output."

Logan MacAslan had wispy white hair and a high tenor voice, "We've set up a simple load test of a 25kg copper weight in an induction ring. By measuring the rate and height that it lifts the weight, we can calculate power."

Darryl nodded, "That makes sense, but I don't see your apparatus?"

Stephanie Mahoney laughed softly, "Well, we thought it would be wise not to test it indoors. The test frame is outside. We were just finishing up calibrations on the instruments in here to watch, record and measure as much as we can think of coming from the device."

$$\star \quad \star \quad \star$$

Rishi stayed inside to monitor the equipment while the rest of the group assembled in a small parking lot behind the building. Final checks were made, and then everyone pulled back around the corner and out of the line of sight where they would watch the test on monitors.

Diana counted down, "5… 4… 3… 2… 1… Activating."

The Crack! of the explosion and overpressure wave shook the ground, sending everyone scrambling for safety, then fire alarms sounded inside the building.

$$\star \quad \star \quad \star$$

The fires from the melted power cable had been quickly extinguished. The alien box itself was unscathed. However, the test apparatus was demolished, and the 25kg weight was nowhere to be found.

Hours later, the group reassembled in a second-floor conference room.

Darryl began, "Well, that was dramatic. Any ideas about what happened beyond the obvious?"

Logan whistled, "Indeed, I believe Rishi was able to pull a few frames of video from the… launch."

Darryl cocked his eyebrow, "Launch?"

Logan laughed, "It seems, young man, that we've just witnessed the first launch of an object from the surface of this New Texas."

Rishi nodded rapidly, "Yes, however, from the rate of acceleration, which exceeded our wildest estimates by orders of magnitude, the test weight may well have vaporized in the atmosphere rather than leaving it."

Stephanie shook her head, "There was no report of an impact or explosion… on the other side."

Darryl blinked. "OK, so… was that the lowest setting, or did you get it backward?"

Diana brushed her hair back, "At first, as you know, we'd wondered whether the device was a battery or a power generator. No matter how much power we have pulled, it has never run out, so we are confident it is a power source. That said, given its size, we thought perhaps the power output might be somewhere in the Kilowatt range. We're confident that the setting was on the low end."

Stephanie added, "To make it useful enough for the Gardeners to leave it for us to find."

Darryl nodded, "That makes sense."

Logan shook his head, "Bottom line is we still don't know. The damned box didn't so much as blink."

Stephanie smiled, "The Drive Rings on the starship are supposed to draw power from vacuum between… microscopic layers." She gestured towards the cube, "If this thing is also a zero-point energy device, then I suppose we could ask Phoenix what an equivalent volume of her structure would generate. However, this technology seems different… perhaps it is a cruder version. It would, at least, maybe, give us a maximum upper bound. Richard Feynman and John Wheeler calculated the zero-point contained in a volume the size of your fist would be enough energy to boil all the world's oceans."

Darryl's eyes widened in shock, "What?"

Diana and Rishi jumped in, objecting, "We didn't…" and "That's not…."

Stephanie raised her hands, "You're right. That's not what I'm saying. That is a theoretical maximum upper bound. Especially when there is no consensus on the theory, Einstein said that that much energy would gravitate. Still, observational data, well, before Awakening Day, showed such forces to be very weak. Other theories say fermion and boson fields should effectively cancel each other out."

Logan laughed, "The problem, of course, is that we know of no other way for an eight-inch square box to produce this energy with no obvious external input. Unless it is pulling the energy from vacuum space itself."

Darryl shook his head, "So you are saying it is either this Zero Point Energy Generator thing, or it's something we have no clue about."

Diana smiled, "Even if it is, we still have barely a clue how it works."

Darryl sighed, "Look, you know they're going to press me for some kind of numbers. Give me something. This thing punched your test weight out of the atmosphere. So, can it power, say, a railgun?"

Stephanie shook her head, "The S9G reactor in the Montana, I mean the Blood Phoenix, puts out over 150MW of power. I'm purely guessing here, and I don't like to guess, but I'd be surprised if this thing doesn't top out at significantly more than that…."

Everyone but Darryl began to object. Darryl's jaw dropped.

She continued, "I know, I know, we need much more testing, and I'm just speculating, but I can see on all of your faces that you suspect something similar?"

Darryl could see a certain amount of grinding of teeth, but no one spoke up to object. "You mean you could replace the nuclear reactor with that thing?"

Logan chuckled, "Boy, you could *fly* the damned submarine through the air with that thing."

Darryl swallowed, "OK, so how long before we can make even a cheap copy?"

Blank stares answered from around the table, then Logan laughed again, "20 years? 100?"

Diana shook her head, "Captain, think for a moment about how much power that thing could be controlling, then ask yourself where you would want to be when we try to take it apart? We'll need to set up a research lab in some remote asteroid somewhere… somewhere far enough away that if we blow ourselves up, it won't affect anyone else."

Everyone but Darryl laughed.

Darryl took a deep breath and sat back in his chair. "I see your point."

Stephanie said softly, "Captain, the Gardeners had to know it would take a long time for us to figure the thing out. Given the story about how this was found, I would be surprised if they have not hidden more of these things, like so many Easter eggs, waiting for us to find and use them. Eventually, we *will* figure out how to build them ourselves. Until then, I suggest that a high bounty be placed on both finding… and securing… any more of these devices that are out there. If someone were ever to figure out how to overload one, if that is even possible, it could possibly destroy all of New Texas."

Goodbyes

Café Balthasar
June 30th, NLD 304 -- FBD 332, 12:22 PM

Café Balthasar had begun as a quaint French-themed teahouse, tucked away in a tiny retail space on the Town Square that had seen many failed endeavors. Ten years ago, the property owner's wife, Marta Landry, had urged him to let her open her café so that they could at least earn some money from the square footage.

The husband later died, and since then, Marta had poured herself into the effort of making the place something special. While still in the same small space, Café Balthasar had matured and prospered, building a loyal following as a somewhat romantic brasserie serving traditional French fare from breakfast through supper each day and brunch on weekends.

Marta had even replaced the sidewalk in front of the shop with paving stones, and the small tables there were frequently reserved in advance.

In the weeks after Awakening Day, Sabrina Chilton had become a loyal patron. Tragically, the salmon had quickly run out, but Marta had proven to be endlessly creative with locally grown and raised ingredients. At least the supplies of English tea were still well-stocked in the Gardener expanded warehouses. In recent weeks though, fresh fish had started to trickle in from the inland sea, so things were looking up!

In the chaos of the past year, Sabrina might never have known about Café Balthasar had it not been for Leo Talib, for it had been one of the few bastions of civilization that Leo had found in Fort Brazos. Whenever possible, she and Leo found themselves at the table in the back, pouring over notes and translations, and were often the last to leave. Marta had even begun to suggest giving them keys to lock up the place when they were done.

Today was their last day before they and many others would be leaving for New London for the final preparations before the mission. For the first time, they had eschewed work. Today, by unspoken agreement, they relaxed with their favorite wine, "seafood" Ceviche, and a decadent Steak Au Poivre with spinach and pommes frites.

Sabrina looked at Leo and smiled.

"What?" he asked.

Her eyes wrinkled as she laughed lightly, "I was remembering the first time we met."

Leo closed his eyes and groaned, "You mean when your goons picked me up and bodily carried me, kidnapping me to labor my years away in your dank dungeon? Tell me, what was going through your mind at the time? As I recall, I made quite an ass of myself."

Sabrina smirked, "I was thinking about where I would shoot you if you didn't shut up."

Leo shook his head, "Yes, I do recall noticing that quite large firearm at your waist."

"And I recall your good taste in suits, though at the time, your Gilchrest & Hawthorne was a bit disheveled."

"Thank your marines for that. Marines will break anything."

Sabrina sipped her wine, "Yes, they will at that."

A young, female, and very indignant British-accented voice interrupted them, "Mum?" Sabrina's daughter Nicole, now 15, stood at their table, hands-on-hips. They had not noticed her enter the café.

Sabrina turned and smiled sadly, "Hello dear."

Leo smiled, "Hello Nicole. It's nice to see you."

Nicole's face twisted in frustration, "Mum! I cannot believe you are just sitting here, drinking wine like nothing is happening!"

Leo stood and got a nearby loose chair for Nicole, who sat in it without looking, her hands outstretched in frustration.

Sabrina reached out to take Nicole's hand, but Nicole yanked hers back.

"Hello, Leo. Mum! You're leaving on this insane suicide thing tomorrow, and here you are, eating and laughing and drinking like nothing's happening!"

Sabrina's soft blue eyes grew wet. She looked at Leo and back at Nicole, "Nicole, you know that you and I planned to spend the evening together."

Nicole spat the words, her lips trembling, "You don't have to go! Generals don't go into combat!"

Sabrina swallowed hard, and her tears welled up, "My darling, sometimes they do. I must go. I have a responsibility. You know that."

Nicole's tears burst loose as she cried, "But you have a responsibility to me too! You can't leave me. You can't die like Dad did!"

Sabrina stood, and her chair fell over as she kneeled at her daughter's lap, taking her into her arms. "My darling. You know he never wanted to leave us, and I don't want to leave you either, and you know that I'm going so that everyone else, including Leo, has a better chance of coming back too. I am going because these monsters destroyed our world. They destroyed my baby girl's world."

Nicole whispered, "I'm scared, Mum."

Sabrina gently rocked her daughter, "I know, my darling. It's alright."

Leo righted Sabrina's chair, and Marta quietly slipped in behind them and left two large cloth napkins on the table before disappearing into the kitchen.

After a few minutes, Sabrina returned to her chair. She and Nicole reached for and used the napkins before retreating to the bathroom together.

When they returned, faces and makeup freshened, Leo smiled and offered an envelope to Nicole. "Your mother said it would be OK. I thought while we were gone, you might visit my library in my apartment. You've told me how you want to continue your language studies, and I've made a reading list for you that I thought you might like."

Nicole cautiously took the envelope, stared at it, and then frowned, "You and Mum are leaving like this, and you're giving me homework?"

Leo's eyes widened in apology, "Oh, Nicole, it's nothing like that! I…"

Nicole smirked and then started laughing and sniffing and blowing her nose.

Leo sighed and gently laughed with Sabrina, "I can see why you've had so much trouble with this one."

Sandra Collins Hoffman Garreth sat on the bed next to David, her head on his shoulder. She held baby Nolan in her arms, and David cradled Nolan's twin sister Margaret. The day had been filled with enough food to put any holiday to shame. Esmerelda and Sandra's sisters had taken care of the babies while she and David had taken a private horseback ride and picnic out to be alone with each other and their thoughts.

David's bag was packed and next to the bed, and he was already in his BDU's.

Sandy said softly, "It was a perfect day."

David nodded slowly, "Yes, it was."

They sat in companionable silence for a long time. They had talked endlessly these past few days and weeks, knowing this day would come. Now that it was here, all they really wanted was to be close.

Sandy's lips quivered. "I don't want you to go. I know you have to, and I understand it all. I just had to say it so that you would hear it. That I don't want you to go."

David answered gently, "I know. I knew it was going to be hard, and I've been dreading it. But I never imagined it would be *this* hard."

Sandy hastened, "Don't say it. Don't say you're coming back."

David nodded, "I know."

Sandy's chest heaved, "I love you."

David pulled her closer, "I love you more than life itself. I've loved you since the moment I first saw you."

They turned to face each other, and holding their babies, they kissed, their tears mingling on their faces.

Oracle

John Austin was sitting up in the recliner with his cast elevated on the raised footrest and his left foot on the floor. His right arm was still in its cast, and his eye was still covered and bandaged. The bruises on his face were mostly faded though.

Needless to say, security around John's house was impressive. The neighbors, mostly, good-naturedly joked about how safe the neighborhood was now.

Matti was busy getting ice tea ready for their guests, Gail, Gwyneth, Sybil, and Wayne.

Gail and Gwyneth sat on the large sofa, Sybil and Wayne together unevenly filled the smaller couch.

Gwyneth began, "Mr. President, I'm afraid that we're all here under false pretenses. While it is true that I wanted you to meet my friends Sybil and Wayne and for you to have an opportunity to thank them for their brave actions, there is rather more to the story than you know, and it is something that the Vice President and I have discussed and agree that you will want to keep quiet."

John cocked his good eyebrow, "OK, Colonel, you have my attention. Go on."

Gwyneth continued, "As you might imagine, a lot of questions are being asked about the bombing. With so many witnesses still recovering from injuries, getting statements and establishing a timeline has taken the investigator's a lot of time. Officially the story has been that someone in the crowd saw Commander Harding draw a gun and that he panicked and set the bomb off early. All of that is true, even if the order in which and reasons for it aren't quite accurate."

Matti arrived and delivered the tea and coasters. She then sat in a chair next to her dad. No one even considered leaving her out of the meeting. However,

John noticed that Gail seemed more stoic and reserved than was normal, even for her darker moods.

"The true chronology of this story begins almost a year ago, on Awakening Day, when Sybil awakened in a fashion different than any other person that I'm aware of. You see after the Gardeners scanned us in the fraction of a second before the impact of the Accipiters kinetic impactor weapons, we were all in a sort of limbo. For us, one moment we were living our lives before Awakening Day, and the next, we all woke up here."

John shook his head, "Right, and most of us threw up. What does that have to do with anything."

Gwyneth looked at Sybil, who tightened her lips, looked up at Wayne for reassurance, and then nodded.

"Mr. President, for the rest of us, that limbo was experienced without an awareness of the passage of time. However, for Sybil, it was different. Sybil was, in some fashion, conscious."

John blinked and stared at Sybil. "OK... that's very weird, and I'm sure very existential, but I'm still confused as to the relevance."

Sybil stared at her feet and spoke quietly, "Mr. President, it took me a long time to understand and I still really don't. Understand that is. The best way I can explain it is that during that time I was.... Drifting." She gazed into the distance. "As I drifted, I touched... I came in contact with people, or.... The essence of people. I... Passed through them. As I did, I... it is so hard to explain... as I passed through them, I *knew* them. I don't think it was supposed to happen, or maybe it was, or maybe some of the Gardeners don't agree with each other on everything. I don't know. All I can tell you is that I... I *know* everyone. I don't know every detail, but it's like I've known everyone here all my life." She trembled, "Some of it was good, and some of it was sad... I... I felt your pain over the death of Carolyn. It was such a huge part of your psyche. And Matti, I felt that in you too and how desperately you also felt the pain your father was going through. And there were things that I... just knew."

Gwyneth added, "On Awakening Day, after the church pastor was killed, Sybil was at the hospital. Sybil is the person who told David, my, well, now, he's my husband, that the patients in the hospital weren't sick, that the treatments they were being given were killing them. She also knew things about David's past that she could not possibly have known."

John thought quietly for a moment. "Suppose I believe you. You were instrumental in certain Awakening Day events; you were also one of the first to encounter one of the alien creatures, and now you saved my life and the lives of many others. Wasn't Sybil the name of a Greek prophetess? Is that what you're saying?"

Sybil swallowed and looked up, "No, Mr. President, I cannot see the future. I just… know everyone and something of their nature. It has given me a connection of some kind. In some people, I can sense things, like strong emotions." She fleetingly glanced at Gail.

Gwyneth nodded, "At the New London stadium, during the evacuation, Sybil was handing out supplies when someone bumped into her. She had a seizure. It is the only seizure known to any of the Awakening Day survivors. After the seizure, Sybil confided in me. She told me things she could not know, and she told me that the person who bumped into her at the stadium was planning to do something evil, but she did not see his face. Just that he was a Navy officer."

John lowered his voice, "Thomas Harding."

Sybil shook her head… "No, Mr. President. It was not him. It was someone else at the Stadium who bumped into me. I can't be sure, but I think maybe that person was involved in the bombing, though."

Gwyneth added, "At the time, at the stadium, we did not know who it was. There was no video, but many Navy officers were working there that day."

Matti jumped in, "You were afraid to tell anyone. You were afraid that this person, whoever he was, might find out and retaliate."

Sybil nodded.

John added, "And if word of this were to get out, people would never treat you the same. Some might even fear you. So, tell me, what deep dark secret of mine can you tell me to convince me that any of this is true?"

Sybil shook her head sadly, "Mr. President, you are one of those people who are what everyone sees. Everyone knows your story... and your secrets." She looked at Gail.

John scowled, "Despite certain recent events and speculation to the contrary, there really are no secrets and nothing…." He softened his voice and looked apologetically at Gail, "…. has happened."

Sybil bit her lip, "I'm sorry, Mr. President, you misunderstand."

Gail spoke for the first time, her voice hard and brittle and her eyes distant and hollow, "John. I believe her. I spoke to her and…, and she knows things. Things I have never told anyone. Things I had buried."

Silence followed while John studied Gail's face. Finally, he answered, "Then I apologize, Gail. I apologize that this pain, whatever it was, that it had to resurface in order for you to convince me of this. I'm sorry, Gail."

Gail's eyes softened, and she nodded minutely, wondering if perhaps that wasn't all that he was sorry for.

John looked at Gwyneth and then Sybil, "All right then. I accept your story, and I accept and agree that this needs to be kept quiet. I will intercede with Hector and make sure the official story protects you."

He continued, "I will tell you this, though. We already know that the bastard did not act alone. In the meantime, where does that leave us? Mr. Blanchard, Mrs. Blanchard. Sybil. What do we do next?"

Galaxy of Graves

Ari'Shevn System

Departing Ari'Nell. NTN Blood Phoenix CIC
July 7th, Day 339, 20:39

Phil Underwood picked up the microphone to address the crew, "All hands, attention. Now that we have departed Ari'Nell and are finally headed to Earth, I wanted to thank all of you. Your drills while at Ari'Nell managed to impress even Commander Cross, and you know what a challenge that is. General Markovic is satisfied that his team is ready as well. As for myself, I could not be more proud. I doubt that any crew has worked harder and achieved more since those terrible early days in World War II. You've taken a nuclear attack submarine, modified by unknown aliens and mated with an alien warp drive built by… different aliens, and taken us not only to space but to other stars."

"Each and every one of you have proven yourself to be as committed and determined to get this job done as I am. Everyone aboard knows the stakes. Everyone aboard knows what the Accipiters did to our world and our homes. To our families and loved ones."

"If we are successful, when we arrive in nineteen days, we will be in a position to bring back what could be the most important source of intelligence on an enemy in human history. Indeed, this is probably the most audacious, daring, and technically challenging military operation ever attempted. In whatever history books this mission is written about, your names will be remembered."

"Whatever happens, remember this. The Accipiters have reigned supreme in the galaxy since long before Homo Sapiens first looked up at the night sky and wondered about those points of light. The Accipiters have dominated the Galaxy because they stomp on any potential competitor before they can become a serious threat. According to the Gardeners, the Accipiters have not been seriously challenged militarily for nearly a million years. Right now, we think they are complacent and are not expecting an attack. On the other hand, mankind has barely known how to fly airplanes in our own skies for little more than a century. The Galaxy we are in is really, really big. It takes light itself a hundred and twenty thousand years to travel from one side to the other. The Accipiters have been fighting in space, across the Galaxy, for over a million years. The entire Galaxy is their home turf. Do not underestimate them."

Phil grinned and looked around the expectant faces in the CIC, "And so, my shipmates and colleagues, if we are lucky, this first strike will catch them with their proverbial pants down. The Accipiters are preparing a big party to celebrate the veneration of their so-called "Keeper," the spy they planted on Earth millennia ago." He paused, "What say we crash the party and ruin their entire day?"

✪ ✪ ✪

Applause and cheers erupted across the ship as well as on the NTN Atlatl and the NTN Axe. Atlatl was docked inside the 'hangar bay' attached underneath Blood Phoenix. Axe was tethered outside in much the same way that NTN Bowie had been. Phoenix had attached its airlock to the dorsal spindle, so that crew members had a means of coming and going to the main vessel.

Onboard the Axe, Gideon Markovic looked up from his bunk where he had been reading his worn, leather-bound copy of the Talmud. It had been his father's. His parents had immigrated from Russia to the United States, and Gideon had been born in Brooklyn, New York. His family had later moved to Israel when he was a young child.

Gideon had made the Israeli Defense Force his career, rising through the ranks and raising his twin daughters Anat and Brach with his wife, Carmit. The photo of them he kept as a bookmark was all he had to remember them by.

The cheers died down, and Gideon returned to his book. He pulled the photo out and gazed at it, gently running his thumb along the side of Carmit's face. *I may be with you soon, my love. I don't even know if your body and those of Anat and Brach survived intact enough for the Tahara to be performed after the attack on Earth. Even though my men and I sat Shiva for you and all of our lost loved ones, I fear the wounds we received from your loss may never heal. I race towards you now, faster than the setting sun. Whether or not I should somehow survive, I promise, my love, that I shall make you proud. Hold our daughters tightly, my love, for very soon, I may be joining you forever in God's light.*

✪ ✪ ✪

Bruno Sarafim sat in his usual chair in the Crow's Nest and finished answering Leo's latest question.

Leo nodded, then asked, "And Keats' 'Bright Star'? You seem to return to it a lot in your reading."

Bruno did not bother asking how Leo knew what he had read. The truth was that there was something about the poem that kept pulling him back to it. He thought for a long moment before answering, "Keats loved her. Fanny Brawne. The sonnet speaks to his frame of mind after boarding a ship. He wants to freeze the moment in his mind, his recollection of how it felt to be with her… to be eternal like the North Star. It is not about passion or sex…. He yearns for… perfect love… to lay down his head on her breast and spend eternity with her, listening to her peaceful, gentle breath. Or die."

Leo cocked his head, "How does it make you feel?"

Bruno looked up at Leo, and a tear fell down his cheek. "I miss her."

"Your girlfriend? Tamara?"

"She wasn't like the others. She was smart, studying to be an RN. I have known her my whole life. We… we weren't in a hurry."

Leo nodded slowly, "And then the Accipiters."

Bruno's eyes clouded, "And then the Accipiters."

✪ ✪ ✪

David Garreth and the men of his Alpha, Bravo, Charlie, and Delta squads were bunked inside Atlatl. Accommodations were spartan, reminding him of the film footage of soldiers packed like sardines inside World War II troop ships, crossing the Atlantic and Pacific oceans.

He smiled, well, not *that* bad.

Sergeants Bolívar, Paxton, Washington, and Shaw did their best to keep bodies and minds busy with PT and endless training, weapons drills, and mission reviews.

Garreth lay in his bunk and began rereading the letter that Sandy had written to him, for what must be the hundredth time as he avoided wondering if he would ever hold Nolan or Margaret ever again.

* * *

In the CIC, Leo and Sabrina had been present during Phil Underwood's speech to the crew, although Sabrina's analysts, Glenys Griffith and Angus Frazier, had remained in the Crow's Nest and watched remotely. Leo himself was almost unrecognizable, wearing army BDU's instead of one of his Saville Row suits.

Phil noticed a concerned look on Leo's face and asked, "Something on your mind Doctor Talib?"

Leo looked at Sabrina, who shrugged, then asked, "Captain, I, we were talking about this earlier. I have been so focused on Accipiter and Builder language that I have not had time to read the reports on current conditions on Earth. I recall the image the Gardeners first showed us of Earth as it is now, and I wondered if, well, can we still breathe the air?"

Phil nodded, "Not a bad question, and, thankfully, you're not the first to ask. I had not considered the possibility myself. According to the Gardeners, the air is still breathable, and that we should not have to worry about any nasty biological agents. Apparently, the Accipiters believe in genetically modifying their surviving subjects and slaves in such a way as to ensure compliance and loyalty, so there is no need to put soporifics or other agents in the air to control them."

The color drained from Leo's face, and he frowned, "Fils de pute, I think that's even more terrifying."

Sabrina raised her eyebrows at Leo's uncharacteristic choice of language.

Phil studied Leo for a moment, "Doctor, you know, I must tell you that I envy you."

Leo stared at him, "I'm sorry, Captain, why on Earth… Why would you possibly envy me?"

Sabrina answered for him, "For the same reason I do, Leo. While he stays here and Captains the ship and I stay here and hope to capture Accipiter signals traffic, you, you lucky bastard, are going in with the strike team inside the Keeper ship. An alien bunker turned into a spaceship. You will see things no one else has ever seen. We need you there to translate and interpret any surprises, but both the Captain and I myself would trade… a lot… to change places with you."

Leo grimaced, "Well, Captain, given how every muscle in my body hurts from all the training I've been forced into with Captain Garreth's men, the thought of trading places has a certain appeal right now," He held up his blistered hands, "And my hands… I thought I knew, at least intellectually, how hard those men trained, and I thought that I was in excellent physical condition…."

Phil laughed, "And you're what, ten years older than those boys as well. Count yourself lucky you were in as good a condition as you were." He lowered his voice conspiratorially, "I'm probably ten years older than you are, and I'm not sure I could have kept up as well as you have."

Sabrina hid a smile and found something else to look at for a moment, and Leo scoffed, "Please, Captain, I like compliments as well as the next fellow, but please don't patronize me. I know what I am, and I worked hard to become that person."

Phil smiled, "I'm serious, Doctor! Well, a little. Consider this. I doubt that many of your peers could have done as well as you have. How many do you think would really have been allowed to go on the mission?"

Leo tightened his lips and nodded, "Touché, Captain."

Phil chuckled, "So Doctor, we have a long cruise in front of us. Would you be willing to come down from the Crow's Nest and talk to the crew about Phoenix and her Builders from time to time? Perhaps there are stories you can tell that will help us understand them better."

Leo nodded slowly, "I think we can find some things the crew would enjoy. Even though they do not seem terribly relevant to the war against the Accipiters, I've been fascinated by what I've learned about them."

Sabrina shook her head bitterly, "On the contrary, Leo, I think those stories are entirely relevant to why we are here. They tell us of another race… another people that the Accipiters snuffed out. It is not just *us* we are fighting for. We're fighting for every race the Accipiters have murdered and violated."

Her mouth twisted, and her soft blue eyes tightened, "Leo, a Galaxy of Graves calls out to us to avenge them."

Phil nodded, "I think it also will help us all better understand and relate to Phoenix."

"You're welcome, Phoenix. All of humanity owes you our thanks. The least we can do is get to know you better."

After Leo's first 'storytelling' session, Phil had begun piping subsequent sessions throughout the ship. The crew mess was the largest available space, and it was packed with everyone who could find an excuse to be there and not at their duty stations. Missing rack time was not something submariners took lightly, and this was no less true for newly minted 'spacers.'

Leo had never been the type of professor to sit or stand at the front of the classroom and stay there. Leo had always had too much energy. He was famous for wandering, even bouncing around the classroom or lecture hall. Despite how crowded the mess hall was, Leo still managed to pace back and forth and wander around the room, making close eye contact and engaging people individually. Despite all of his personal oddness, no one had *ever* fallen asleep in one of his classes.

His ponytail was let down, and his hair hung long and loose over the shoulders of his Army Combat Uniform. Leo had always worked to maintain his trim figure, but the daily physical training had left his uniform a couple of sizes too large, making him look smaller than he really was.

Leo smiled, "Let me tell you about another race annihilated by the Accipiters, the Builders. They did not evolve as a civilization as we did. Indeed, in their original form, the best way to think of them was that they were most similar to a deer or a cow. They were prey animals for the dominant species on their planet. We don't have an image of what the dominant species looked like because the Builders were instinctually afraid of them, and after they escaped, they wiped out all record of them."

"The dominant race eventually domesticated the Builders and used them as beasts of burden and as a major source of food. Over time the domesticated Builders were integrated deeply into society. Just like we humans began to domesticate wolves into dogs perhaps 30,000 years ago, Sheep and Goats around 8000 or so BC, Cattle around 7000 BC, and horses perhaps around 3600 BC, the Builders were similarly domesticated over thousands of years, taking on different and varied shapes and forms."

"One of the things that made them useful were their asymmetrical hands. In order to reach their preferred food, a pod-like fruit in a tree analog, the wild Builders had long, slender arms with one hand being something akin to a bottle opener and the other with fingers for picking and grasping the fruit."

The room rocked with laughter and jokes about 'bottle opener hands.' Leo grinned and let the banter die down.

"The wild Builders were no more intelligent than your average deer or goat or cow. They were gentle creatures. Here is an image of a wild Builder from Phoenix's files." He clicked a remote control and the image displayed on the wall monitors. Instead of fur, the creature seemed to be covered in what looked like soft, flowing scales that might have been closer to feather than scale. It had four legs that ended in rounded hoof-analogs. It had a neck that tapered to a narrow snout, almost like an anteater, with doe-like eyes on the front and back of the head. It had long, slender cartilaginous 'arms' that terminated in what looked like hardened scales like a thick fingernail 'opener' and a delicate, almost translucent six-fingered 'hand.'

The room was filled with comments and no small number of laughs and quiet jokes.

Leo looked down and smiled sadly, "It might interest you to know that in the post-technological period of their planet's history when Builders were hunted mostly for sport, it was the hand that was taken as a delicacy by the predator race."

The room quieted quickly.

"So, you can see there seem to be many parallels between their world and ours. I suppose form indeed follows function."

He paused, "The Builders were analogous to Earth deer or gazelles. They used their speed to escape and evade the apex predator. They are, or were, I suppose, naturally short-lived, and because of the high predation rate, they reproduced quickly. They were also very easy to kill. Even the dominant species' children could easily kill a Builder."

"Eventually, they were bred to be intelligent enough to be useful for more complex tasks. Over time, more and more tasks were given to them, freeing the dominant species to focus on other things. As scientific knowledge reached genetic engineering levels, they were bred with implanted knowledge for their tasks. Subsequent generations were given new skillsets on top of those."

"Gradually, they progressed from repetitive manual labor to assembly line manufacturing, textiles, and eventually everyday engineering and maintenance tasks. As the civilization went into space, naturally, the Builders were the ones to construct infrastructure and even spacecraft. As more and more skills and knowledge were given to them, their intelligence had reached the sentience level."

Engineering Mate Carmen Rojas had previously sought out Leo for more information about the Accipiters and the Builders. The discussion had turned to language, and somehow Leo had managed to find time here and there to begin Tutoring Carmen in the rudiments of Accipiter Glyphs. Before long, several others had joined the tutoring sessions. Carmen had confided in Leo about how much she missed her family in upstate New York and how she hoped she lived long enough to see Earth recaptured so she could one-day plant flowers there to remember them. Carmen said aloud, "They were slaves."

Leo turned around and walked over to Carmen. He reached out and put his hand on the young woman's shoulder, "Yes, Carmen, the Builders were slaves. But it was worse than that. Their masters *ate* them. They were genetically altered and implanted with cybernetic technology at a prenatal stage."

Leo turned away and walked up to one of the screens, and clicked the remote control. A new image appeared. The wild, alien but natural-looking Builder was replaced with… something very different. It was an infant Builder, but its body was festooned with technological implants. The soft eyes on the back of its head had been replaced with a bulbous cranial implant that wrapped halfway around its head, and one of its forward-facing eyes had been replaced with a technological one.

"From before birth, the Builders were modified to serve their masters. Their brains were cybernetically enhanced and their bodies implanted with sensors, instruments, and tools." He clicked the remote again and displayed a fully grown Builder. It seemed almost weighed down by all of the technology augmenting its body.

"The Builders eventually managed to escape from their masters and build a civilization the scale and scope of which makes humans look like cave dwellers. Despite everything, they achieved greatness with only a ten-year lifespan. After all of their struggles and abuse and escape from slavery and then going on to build a vast interstellar civilization, after all of that, the Accipiters came along and wiped them out, as though they had never existed at all."

The room was quiet except for the rumblings of anger and no small amount of fear.

Leo finished, "So, you see, we aren't the first. The Accipiters have been doing this for a million years. Sterilizing planets like Ari'Nell and snuffing out civilizations… wiping out all that they had ever been or overcome or accomplished."

"I don't know if the Builders and humans could have ever been friends. They might have looked at us and seen only a reminder of their wretched past. They probably would have simply run away from us, but that doesn't matter. The Accipiters seem to think it is their divine right to go around snuffing out civilizations. Like ours. I, for one, think it is time we start teaching the Accipiters a lesson. I have never been a violent man, but I am… I'm livid! I am glad to be here with you all to do my small part. What say we kick these Accipiter bullies in the teeth and give them what for?"

The Keeper

Phil smiled, "Right on time. All Stop. OK, Phoenix, what do you see? Are the Accipiters where they're supposed to be?"

"Yes, Captain. As of sixty minutes ago, the Accipiter mothership, as you referred to it earlier, is in geostationary orbit as predicted, along with her support craft. Her drive system is cold."

A heavily processed and slightly fuzzy image appeared on the wall screen. The vessel was bulbous and looked somewhat organic. It was roughly disc-shaped and dotted with golden bumps, like so many shiny candies in a fat cookie. Even though it was around twenty miles across, at 60 light minutes out, it was only ten light-minutes closer than Earth is to Saturn. Even the larger escort vessels were visible only as target icons. Phil and everyone in the CIC sighed in relief.

"Captain, I should also tell you that there is a second mothership with an escort group I'm estimating at over 100,000 vessels, on an inbound trajectory from the general direction of where I would expect the nexus junction point would be located."

Someone in the room gasped softly.
The image was replaced with a plot of the solar system.

For propulsion within a star system, Accipiter capital ships used gravity drives, and their smaller ships used fusion torches. However, a crucial part of the information provided by Phoenix concerning the Accipiter's was the means by which their fleets traveled *between* star systems. Their ships were able to use naturally occurring spatial rifts that interconnect stars above a certain mass throughout the galaxy. Those rifts could be entered via nexus junction points that were constantly moving and flexing as the galaxy itself spun on its axis and the stars and matter within and surrounding it pulled and tugged and continued their gravitational dance. It was unknown how the Accipiters were able to open the rifts, but the theory of how the rifts worked was evidently known to the Builder's original masters.

Phil closed his eyes for a moment, grinding his teeth, "Damn. It looks like they invited more guests to the party. How far out?"

"At its current position and velocity, it should reach Earth in approximately 102 minutes."

Phil said coolly, "Well then, it looks like we're just in time to crash this party. We can be in and out before they arrive. We will proceed with the plan on schedule. Designate original target Tango One with their main vessel Tango One Prime and the new fleet Tango Two and their main vessel Tango Two Prime. No offense Ms. Palmer, Mr. Wesley, but we're going to let Phoenix do the driving for this part."

A corner of Mikaela's lips curled under her VR helmet, "None taken, Captain."

"Ditto that, Captain!" added Lukas.

Phil smiled broadly, "All right. Mr. Perez, rig for zero-g. Mr. Schultz, please inform Commanders Cross and Morton to prepare for launch. Mr. Milford, please have Mr. Burkett and Mr. Warner stand by in the sail. Phoenix cut the drive and gravity as soon as all compartments report ready."

Weapons Officer Lieutenant Raphael Milford replied, "Weapons techs on standby, Aye."

Erick repeated his order back as well.

Luis nodded, "Rig the boat for zero-g. Aye." He then bellowed into his microphone, adding emphasis, "All Compartments, Rig the boat for zero-g." He listened on his headset for confirmation, "All compartments report secured for zero-g, Captain."

Phil clenched his eyes and stifled a groan as the gravity ceased.

Phil clenched his stomach muscles, "Thank you, Phoenix."

Erick reported, "Commanders Cross and Morton report ready, Captain."

"Launch ILCs and then restore gravity, Phoenix."

There was a slight jolt, and then gravity was restored.

Commanders Cross and Morton's orders were to proceed in system and carry out their respective missions according to plan, regardless of whether Blood Phoenix succeeded or returned from its acceleration and deceleration trips. If it *were* successful, they would coordinate and fine-tune their timing, but if the Blood Phoenix did not come back or was otherwise destroyed or incapacitated, everyone knew there was no going back. The target would be either captured or killed at all costs. In the event that Blood Phoenix was destroyed, and the ILC crews were able to capture critical technology or intelligence, the surviving ILC, and everyone was painfully aware the ILCs were not FTL capable, would launch itself in the direction of New Texas. Perhaps future generations might someday discover and make use of it and perhaps bury the desiccated remains of whoever had stayed on board.

Phil nodded, "Proceed at warp out-system to the planned coordinates, then rig for acceleration to .7c and execute."

As before, the acceleration process had been uneventful. They returned to the Sol system to line up for the attack.

Phil took a breath and commanded firmly, "Phoenix, please put us on an optimal trajectory tangential to Earth in line for ballistic release of the payload to strike the main Accipiter vessel. As we previously discussed, please align us so that the flight path minimizes the probability of collateral strikes on Earth itself. Then cut the drive at 1.2 light-minutes distance from the Accipiters. We will coast and fire the payload. Once the payload is launched, jettison the containers, and restore the drive. After that, hold position and report battle damage assessment."

Phil licked his lips, closed his eyes for a moment, and smiled, "Thank you, Phoenix. I am sure you understand that this is a critical sequence of events. I have every confidence in your memory. However, in the Navy, we have learned that repeating orders can help prevent… misunderstandings. I'm sure you can find some supplemental reading that would illustrate why we do this."

Phil raised both eyebrows and looked around the room at crew members trying hard to avoid eye contact while barely suppressing snickers and chuckles. He tried to decide whether to be amused… or not. Then the gravity ceased, and his stomach lurched again.

Phil swallowed hard, thankful he had not eaten. "Very well. Thank you, Phoenix. We couldn't do this without you." Phil looked at his watch, "Mr. Milford, release the payload on my mark."

Raphael nodded firmly, "Release on your mark, Aye."

"Fire!"

"Firing! Payload is released, and the containers have been jettisoned."

There was a slight jolt, and then gravity was restored.

7.2 million one-inch steel ball bearings, as well as the containers they had been in, were now hurtling on a ballistic trajectory at .7c towards the Accipiter main vessel and the over 60,000 support ships parked in geostationary orbit around Earth.

Now that they were much closer, the image of the Accipiter ships was clearer. The golden bumps in the body of the main ship could now be seen to vary in size and shape, and there were a lot of them. Their placement and the texturing of the vessel itself implied that it had grown over time.

The Accipiters, being an ancient spacefaring civilization, would, of course, have some method of point defense against space debris or even incoming weapons fire. However, after being parked at Earth for 60 years, they would have presumably already mapped every rock of significance in the solar system. Micrometeorites might travel from between 20,000mph to, say, 30,000mph. The ball bearings were not going that fast. They were traveling at 130,200 miles per *second*. The Accipiter point defense would have mere moments of detection time before the barrage arrived.

In addition, it was unknown how long it had been since any race had actually fought the Accipiters in space on any level. Still, the intelligence provided by the Gardeners implied it had been several hundred thousand years since even token resistance had been faced. That said, the Accipiters did everything according to ritual. It seemed prudent to assume that many of those rituals descended from military procedure and necessity. The Accipiters were going to be surprised. It remained to be seen precisely how unprepared they might truly be.

Phil sighed silently in relief and nodded, "Excellent Phoenix. Mr. Milford, have Mr. Warner and Mr. Burkett close the airlock."

The tension in the CIC was thick as Phil stood in front of the wall screen watching the magnified image, waiting out the light lag.

At an orbital altitude of approximately 23,000 miles, the Accipiter ships orbited slightly below the Galileo satellite constellation and slightly above where the American GPS satellites had been. The image showed the crescent Earth on one side and the Accipiter ships as tiny highlighted spots. The Accipiter ships were spread out over a relatively broad swath. However, at this angle, the bulk of them formed an elongated spheroid.

Brilliant pinpricks splashed through the formation, plunging deep into their midst. As before, the trailing ball bearings smashed into the fireballs in front of them in an orgy of fratricidal annihilation.

The CIC erupted in hungry, bloodthirsty cheers, but Phil tightened his lips and held up his hand, and silenced the room.

The view zoomed in as the Accipiters responded with terrible swiftness. Thousands of the small ships flew directly into the maelstrom, immolating themselves to try and blunt the plunging column of plasma away from the 'mothership' which was even now trying to inch aside. They almost succeeded, but the inexorable finger of destruction lanced through it, setting off secondary explosions and sending it slowly lurching off at an angle.

There was no amusement in Phil's expression, only grim satisfaction. "Mr. Shultz! Inform Commanders Cross and Morton to execute Phase Two."

Erick smiled broadly, "Execute phase two, Aye!"

Earth
(former) South America, Peru
NTN Axe Bridge
July 26th, Day 358, 09:23

The terrain chosen for the artillery support position was a rocky plateau, with more or less sheer cliffs on all sides but one, which had eroded into a rock and boulder-strewn slope down to the semi-arid valley floor, ending at a slow, undulating, silt-filled river. The elevation was approximately 10,000 ft, and the dry plateau was loosely littered with brown clumps of "Ichu," commonly known as Peruvian feathergrass, and a handful of windswept stunted eucalyptus trees.

Not long after Awakening Day, the Gardeners had shown images of current-day Earth that included a purple tent to the landmasses. As the ILC descended close enough to ground level, it was clear why. Everywhere, as far as the eye could see, were strange purplish "trees" that did not entirely replace existing growth but were nonetheless common enough to shift the hue of the planet.

What information about the Accipiters and their sub-creatures that had been divined from Martin William's "Gardener Database" investigations had indicated that the Accipiter defenses 'should' be limited to Wardogs and Stalkers. Although the Accipiters were flightless themselves, they eschewed flying craft other than their spacecraft as some sort of aversion to flying things larger than themselves.

So, the planning for the artillery position had focused on finding rocky terrain the Wardogs would be unlikely to have been burrowed under with defensible approaches. Anti-aircraft defenses were brought along anyway. Their position would become a very temporary static firebase. They would bombard their target areas and then be extracted. It should be in and out, and with any luck, they would face minimal opposition.

Gene Morton stood calmly on the small bridge as the Axe descended through the atmosphere above what used to be Peru. Their target LZ was as remote and unpopulated an area as they could find, 24km from the mountainside where the Accipiters had excavated the Keeper Ship. The viewscreen flared briefly.

Gene frowned, "What was that?"

Lt. Samuel Ślusarski responded, "Captain, I believe that was a flock of birds impacting the warp bubble, Sir. The excess energy was converted into visible light. No radiation."

Gene hid a sigh of relief, "Very well, Mr. Ślusarski, carry on. Mr. Khoroushi, rig the boat for landing and inform General Markovic we are about to land."

Master Chief Hasan Khoroushi nodded and smiled, "Rig boat for landing, inform the General, Aye."

Gene walked up behind Petty Officer Marlon Stevenson and rested a hand on his shoulder, "Mr. Stevenson, set us down gently if you please."

Marlon nodded sharply, immersed in his VR headset, "Setting down gently, Aye." He and his copilot, Ariel Haines, manipulated their virtual controls in delicate concert.

In the maneuver they had practiced repeatedly, the warp field was transitioned from the stealth mode to non-stealth at the last moment to reduce the chance they would be visually detected during their descent. A fraction of a second before landing, stealth mode was dropped, coincidentally reducing power consumption from insanely astronomical to merely astronomical. The vessel flashed into visibility just in time to prevent the stealth drive from converting the ground they landed on into energy and digging a hole. Moments later, the warp rings flattened on the bottom, and the craft settled onto the ground with a gentle thud, and the warp field shut down.

Gene nodded in satisfaction, "Nicely done, Mr. Stevenson, Ms. Haines."

The moment the drive was cut, the enormous cargo doors opened, and the loading ramp dropped. Riding the ramp, even as it lowered, Sergeants Dietrich Siegert, Mathias Schmidt, Sam Cisneros, and Staff Sergeant Harry Hayes bolted out of it, followed by the dismounted Alpha, Bravo, Charlie, and Delta squads to set up a perimeter.

Gideon Markovic followed and strode out into the landing zone and pointed to where he wanted the missile launchers emplaced.

Mission planning had selected several prospective landing spots from the pre-Awakening Day topographical maps of Peru. The hope was that the Accipiters had not changed the surrounding landscape too drastically. They had known that the landing zone candidates were at altitude, so for the last two weeks, everyone onboard Axe had gradually acclimatized themselves to reduced air pressure while sticking to a rigorous exercise and hydration schedule.

Gideon squinted in the dazzling, brilliant sunlight. The air was cold, crisp, and thin. The suntube at New Texas and the primary star at Ari'Nell were not remotely as blinding. He was glad he had reminded his men that, unlike the suntube, it was definitely not safe to look directly at Earth's sun.

He'd never been to Peru, but the rich smells of his home planet, however different from Israel or his childhood home of Brooklyn, were genuinely bittersweet. It felt… right… like New Texas never had.

This was our home, and you demons robbed us of it.

He tightened his lips. This was no time for maudlin thoughts.

The ScanHawk mobile drone launcher rolled out behind him, followed rapidly on its heels by two M270A1 MLRS vehicles, commanded by Lieutenants Yosef Lev, and Ehud Zeev. The MLRS's turbo-charged V8 Cummins diesel engines roared, and their sides were emblazoned with Anat and Brach's names. They were already loaded with their twin six-packs of M26 rockets. They were closely followed by flatbed trucks carrying six-pack reloads.

Two M1296 Dragoons rolled out next, commanded by Sergeants Seth Brunson and Max Stein, armed with 30mm main gun cannons and a 7.62 mm machine gun.

Two older-style M2 Bradleys followed, commanded by Sergeants Josh Branson and Delon Hardaway, armed with 25 mm chain guns, twin-tube TOW missile launchers, and a 7.62 mm machine gun.

The last vehicles were a pair of Humvees, commanded by Sergeants Kristoph Powell and Victor Velázquez. They were configured with GAU-19/B tri-barrel .50 caliber electrically driven heavy machine guns. The Humvee's roared out and away from the ramp, arcing around the larger vehicles and grinding to a halt, gravel flying, at the edge of the plateau, tri-barrels aimed downslope.

The dismounted crew from the vehicles quickly hauled out additional M2HB-QCB and M240 heavy machine guns, crates of additional weapons and ammunition, and other equipment and containers to round out the firebase perimeter.

Moments later, the ScanHawk drone launched towards the target zone. With an airspeed of 250kph, it would arrive over the target zone in just over five minutes, providing improved guidance and telemetry for targeting corrections.

Sergeant Cisneros shouted orders to Charlie squad to begin rolling out the spools of concertina wire around the perimeter. The wire would not slow down a Wardog, but it should keep any Stalkers or lesser creatures at bay.

Staff Sergeant Hayes led Delta squad in hastily deploying mines and claymores outside the perimeter.

With the ground force fully offloaded and now a safe distance away, Axe silently lifted off and resumed stealth mode to provide orbital overwatch.

Two smaller FastOwl drones were launched as backups.

Sergeants Schmidt and Siegert oversaw the emplacements of the sandbags and heavy machine guns along the lip of the plateau.

All the men needed little encouragement. They had rehearsed the deployment dozens of times. Everyone knew the stakes.

Gideon anxiously watched the feed from the drone as the rocket launchers were emplaced and the security team prepared to defend their position. They were well out of the line of sight of the Keeper ship valley and, they hoped, far enough away for the hordes of Accipiters and their lackeys to be safe from counterattack before they were extracted.

The video feed was crisp and clear. The golden-clad Keeper Ship glinted and gleamed in the bright sunlight. It was a lightly banded cylinder that was narrower at the top and gradually widened to its full width, and was more or less flat on the bottom. He had seen the long-distance image from orbit, but this was even more startling. The entire face of a mountain had been carved away, revealing the buried Accipiter structure.

According to the Gardeners, millennia ago, the Accipiters had left behind a Von Neumann machine that had gradually constructed the hidden base inside the remote mountain range, far from most pre-human activity.

It was unknown whether the gold exterior had been added after excavation, but Gideon assumed the glyphs were recent additions. It was covered with glyphs that shimmered in and out of the visible spectrum. The bunker-turned-spaceship was surrounded by narrow scaffolding with thin ramps and support beams.

The top of the Keeper ship had been closest to the surface and had presumedly been the means by which the Keeper had been able to come and go over the millennia. A grand portico entrance was framed there, and the surface was large enough for Commander Cross's ILC to land on. He was already on the way down, timing their landing to coincide with the pending bombardment.

The Accipiter "honor guard" of Wardogs and a veritable sea of presumed VIPs and worshipers were spread out across the valley in front of the mountain face. Beyond that lay an apparently purpose-built gilded city that did not remotely appear to be of human origin.

Gideon frowned as he zoomed in to look at the crowd in the valley. He smiled coldly, "Let's do something about this 'honor guard' of theirs, shall we?"

They said this might happen. While many of those present were Accipiters, whose 9' to 10' height certainly made them stand out, however, the bulk of the rest were either the Wardog honor guard or were… human.

Perhaps tens of thousands of humans were camped out in the valley to worship the Accipiters and participate in the Keeper veneration ceremony.

Gideon's brown eyes hardened, "Lieutenant Lev, Lieutenant Zeev, load the targeting data from the drone and execute fire plan alpha. Shot!"

The US Army M270A1 MLRS launcher system was built on a Bradley vehicle frame. The launcher's integrated crane was used to manage the missile six-pack reloads. The packs could contain either six rockets or a single more powerful rocket. In this case, the Joint Reserve Base inventory had still held a significant number of M26 rockets. They were not still being produced before Awakening Day, but the Reserve Base had a substantial inventory of less than the most current weapons and systems.

Lieutenants Lev and Zeev were both soldiers from the same IDF unit that Gideon himself had been 'rescued' from. Both had previous hands-on experience operating Israel's version of the MLRS.

They grimly operated the controls and fired each MLRS's 12 rockets. The MRLS's began to ripple fire their twelve rockets before their crews frantically began the reload process.

Lev and Zeev answered in unison, "Shot out!"

24 M26 rockets hurtled towards the valley below the Keeper ship. As they arrived over the target zone, each of those rockets opened up and released 644 M77 DPICM drag-ribbon stabilized bomblets, which then armed themselves during free fall. Each of the 24 missiles was aimed to saturate a target zone 200 meters in diameter with an overall coverage area of a square kilometer, combining both shaped-charge penetration bomblets capable of blasting through 4 inches of armor and blast fragmentation grenades.

The M26 was a cold-war era weapon system designed to 'sterilize' a square kilometer or one grid square on a standard map. It had been nicknamed the "Grid Square Removal System." It was designed to destroy an entire column of Soviet troops, vehicles, and light armor. While not capable of destroying main battle tanks, the shaped charges would not be healthy for the tank's treads.

It was a devastating weapon. It had been used to good effect during the Gulf War. Still, there was a problem with the dud rate of the bomblets, with up to 2%

of them failing to detonate, leaving behind dangerous ordinance that prevented US troops from easily advancing through the area that had just been 'cleared.'

This was not the Cold War or the Gulf War, and the decision had been that the unexploded but dangerous 2% would be another surprise gift to the Accipiters after the strike teams had departed.

Gideon's eyes narrowed as he watched the drone feed with cold satisfaction. Explosions rippled and walked across the valley. Tough as they were, the Wardogs were rent and shattered like so many exploding watermelons. Chaos and panic erupted amongst the throngs of worshipers as the submunitions turned Accipiters and humans alike into so much flying offal and gore.

Captain Steven Brandt, the security force commander, broke into Gideon's radio channel, and shouted "Contact! Nine Wardogs inbound from the valley, advancing up the escarpment, range, two thousand, five hundred yards. Engaging with 30mm!"

Gideon frowned. *That was fast.*

The thump of the 30mm cannon rattled over the noise of the MLRS cranes reloading the missile six-packs.

Captain Brandt barked, "Cease Fire! Cease Fire! Do not waste ammo!"

Amid the shouted commands to continue emplacing the mines, machine guns, and concertina wire, both MLRS reloads finished within seconds of each other.

Gideon watched the target zone video feed and nodded to himself as he selected the next fire pattern using the fire control network. He snarled, "Shot!"

The rockets ripple fired again as Lev and Zeev announced, "Shot out!"

Survivors not in the target zone had understandably fled in the opposite direction from the destruction. Gideon's fire plan took ruthless advantage of this, and the next wave scythed through the panicked worshipers, herding them into pyres of roiling carnage and death.

"Reload!"

Oblivious to the noise of the MLRS launches behind him, Captain Brandt stood at the edge of the plateau and lowered his binoculars. He swallowed as he looked across the valley below. From one end to the other, dust rose as trees and brush fell and were crushed underneath wave after wave of approaching Wardogs.

All the available mines had been placed by now, and the security team had taken their positions behind the line.

Brandt could feel the eyes of his men looking to him for… something. He turned and smiled broadly, "Get ready! We are about to have a target-rich environment! Do not fire until ordered! This is just like we practiced! We are going to expend the heavier ordinance first. So, the Dragoon 30mm first. When we run out of 30, the Bradley's 25mm will take over. I do not need to remind you to make every fucking round count! After the 25mm, open up with the '50s! When those run out, we'll switch to the 762's! Sergeants! Have your Milkors ready and hold them until ordered! Microguns are the last line!"

He paused and looked around, his eyes bright as he flashed a brilliant smile, "This is it! This is payback! Now is your chance. Be smart. Let's make them pay for what they've done to our home!"

Gideon was not listening. He had other priorities. "Barat, retarget new coordinates as follows, on the city…." No one thought twice about his change in address. Lev and Zeev both knew the origin of the names of their vehicles.

While the first MLRS, Brach, continued to pound the valley, Barat shifted its aim slightly to rain death and terror upon the Accipiter's golden city.

Meanwhile, Lieutenant Eduard Jordà Porras checked the diagnostic equipment attached to a secondary set of missile reloads as Corporals Hugo Aubert and Reynaldo Trujillo stood guard, with orders to protect these particular missiles at all costs.

Earth
(former) South America, Peru
Keeper Ship Entrance Platform
July 26th, Day 358, 09:40

Charles Cross's Atlatl cut its drive slightly early and dropped hard onto the Grand Portico platform atop the Keeper ship with a tooth clattering jolt. It was a small if jarring sacrifice meant to avoid the possibility of damaging the Keeper ship.

As the loading ramp descended, specialists Bennie Davis and Troy Allen, wearing backpack-fed XM556 Microguns loaded with armor-piercing rounds interspersed with tracer and incendiary rounds, open fired on the two startled Wardogs that had been standing guard at the grand portico entrance, slicing them in half.

The cold, thin breeze did little to alleviate the resulting smell.

Still standing inside Atlatl, after a nod from Captain Garreth, Specialist Hawkings released a small radio-controlled model car with a camera and overpowered radio beacon. Its small engine squealed loudly as it raced down the ramp, across the portico, and inside the Keeper ship.

Before the enemy might think to close the doors, which would form an airlock when in space, and with the rolling thunder of the still incoming M26 rocket cluster munitions in the background, Alpha squad, led by Sergeant José Bolívar, bolted out and down the landing ramp and followed the decoy inside. All were wearing thin space suits, barely more than pressure suits, under their modified plate carriers, with their suit helmets slung behind them.

Sergeant Dewayne Paxton followed, shouting, "Bravo Squad! Go! Go! Go!"

Captain Garreth and Delta Squad were right behind them. Sergeant 'Cash' Shaw shouted, "Delta Squad, Go! Go! Go!"

On the Grand Portico, Sergeant Darryl Washington shouted, "Charlie Squad! Rear Guard! Secure that door!"

Corporal Perry Simmons and Specialists Denis Eberhardt and Mario Gartner hauled a jury-rigged set of steel bars out and hastily shimmed up and blocked open the airlock doors. When the time came, sledgehammers were ready at hand to knock the bars out so the doors could close.

Leo Talib had accompanied Delta squad inside. Unlike the rest, Leo carried a small backpack with a 360^0 HD video camera mounted on a small pole just above his head. It was connected to a solid-state hard drive and batteries in the backpack to store the video. He carried a tablet computer and, still shocking to him, a holstered FN 5.7 pistol on his hip. Sergeant Shaw had trained him mercilessly on the 5.7, and he was slightly proud of himself that he could indeed disassemble it and reassemble it blindfolded and was not great but was a half-decent shot with it.

Leo had paused at the entrance, oblivious to the Wardog offal he slipped and skidded on, as, gape-mouthed, he took in the flowing, evolving Accipiter glyphs.

Sergeant Shaw none too gently pushed him along, "Keep moving, Doctor, I'm sure there's more to see inside."

The entrance airlock led to a tall, broad, gently sloping helical corridor. All along the way, Accipiter glyphs glowed and flowed on the walls. The passage opened up into a wide central room and continued downward on the other side. In the middle, along the walls, hung purple-tinted translucent membranous sheets and columns glowing with symbols and imagery.

A handsome, chocolate-brown-skinned human male of perhaps thirty years of age stood at the center, wearing flowing Accipiter glyph marked robes, manipulating symbols on the central membrane column.

Near him stood three Accipiters. The 10' tall avian-like creatures… were stunningly beautiful. Alien, but staggeringly, achingly beautiful. They wore intricately inlaid breastplates that fluoresced in sync with the glowing glyphs inlaid in their beaks. The hexapedal creatures had two large jeweled clawed hands and two smaller complex hands below and behind their large arms, holding instrumentation of some kind. Their eyes were quite large and regarded the invading humans with what could no doubt be safely assumed to be anger or hostility or whatever the Accipiter analogue was. The brilliant scarlet plumes on the back of their head and posteriors spread and flared.

The two closest Accipiters had similar breastplates that were not as complex as the third one, who seemed older. They opened their beaks and let loose an impossible cry or song or… something. They seemed to have multiple voices singing at different octaves. Whatever it was rose in pitch, quickly becoming an ear-shattering chorus of screams as they raised their jeweled clawed hands and charged.

Specialists Bennie Davis and Troy Allen grimly fired short bursts from their micro-guns. The electrically driven guns fired a fusillade of 5.56mm bullets at 3,000 rounds a minute with an angry brrrrrrrrrripppp. The charging Accipiters were shredded and rent into a bloody mist.

The third Accipiter sank to the ground and raised its arms and face upwards.

Garreth and Delta squad arrived, and he barked loudly, "Cease Fire!"

The dark-skinned human screamed something no one could understand and threw himself in front of the surviving Accipiter.

Leo skidded to a halt behind Garreth and did a double-take at the carnage.

Garreth ordered, "Alpha, continue the sweep. Sergeant Shaw, see that the prisoners are secured."

He asked, "Doctor, is this him? Is this the Keeper?"

Leo looked at the man who was crying and babbling incoherently. "I don't think so Captain, the Keeper would have been a pre-Homo Sapien hominid. I suppose the Accipiters could have… modified him, but it would seem more in character for them to keep it closer to its original form."

The Accipiter began to sing a low, warbling tone.

David nodded, "OK, that makes sense. Do you think this is their bridge, their control room?"

Leo frowned, "Ah, well, it is central and near the top of the ship. So, from what we were told, it should be one of the oldest parts of the structure and these…. People…. They were in here doing something on what I assume are controls of some kind, so it seems like a good guess."

The brown-skinned man blinked his tears and looked up at the invaders. He moved his mouth for a moment, and nothing came out. Then he brokenly spoke. "English? You… you… you speak English…."

The Accipiter closed its eyes and began to sing. This was not like what the other two had done. It started out as a minor melody of intertwined voices and grew in tone and complexity. It was unearthly. It was unthinkably beautiful. Alien or not, it seemed tinged with soul-crushing sadness. It grew louder, stronger, and increasingly complex, filling the room until the men could feel their bones start to vibrate.

Specialist Newell muttered, "What tha…."

David looked an order to Sergeant Shaw and then pulled his spacesuit helmet on. While Specialists Newell and Abraham kept their micro guns trained on the prisoners, everyone else followed David's example.

Corporal Dawson helped Leo put his helmet on, and then Newell and Abraham followed suit.

Shaw pulled a CS grenade from a loop on his plate carrier, pulled the pin, and rolled it towards the prisoners.

The robed man and the Accipiter collapsed to the floor, choking on the gas.

David's radio announced, "Captain, we found something. It might be what we're looking for… and Sir… ah, You've *just gotta* see this."

Garreth nodded, "Bravo Squad, secure the prisoners for transport, then transfer them back to Atlatl. Dr. Talib, stay with us." He switched frequencies, "Alpha Squad, Delta Squad Coming Down!"

They advanced down the winding helical corridor until they reached an entrance to an enormous interior room. Specialists Ericson and Muhammad guarded the entrance, weapons at the ready. The radio-controlled decoy car lay near their feet.

Inside the room was a sight Garreth had not been prepared for. The room itself was an intricately lush garden of trees and flora. Near the center of the room, a fountain gurgled in the middle of a pool. Standing in the pool was a leathery-skinned… man-thing. He was clearly male, but also clearly not… Homo Sapien.

He was not precisely apelike, but his head was broad and somewhat flattened, and he was very… hairy and very naked. He appeared to be no more than five feet tall, diminutive, and gracile. His hair had been carefully groomed, braided, and trimmed. No doubt by the half dozen equally naked and fully Homo Sapien human women in the pool with him who had all moved to put themselves between the Keeper and the invaders. All the women were shouting unintelligibly and glaring and waving their wet empty fists.

Garreth raised his eyebrows and shook his head, "Secure the prisoners and prepare for exfil!"

The 'personalities' of the Interplanetary Landing Craft ships were not as sophisticated or self-aware as Phoenix. However, Phoenix had taught them enough to be able to converse with and take orders from humans verbally. Axe and Atlatl's personalities had followed the Phoenix example, using the names of their ships.

"Captain, you instructed me to inform you if there are any changes in Tango One and Tango Two. Tango One's support craft are accelerating to intercept over the Keeper Ship landing zone. Their estimated time of arrival is 8 minutes. Tango Two has accelerated. The original ETA was 42 minutes from now. If their new acceleration remains constant, the revised arrival time at Earth orbit is now 13.04 minutes."

Gene winced, "Damn. I assumed they would speed up, but I had no idea they could go *that* fast. I wonder if that is the max military speed for them or if they have even more in reserve?" He grimaced and shook his head sharply, "Doesn't matter now."

One of the two navigators, Samuel "Sam" Cotterill, pointed out, "Captain, to accelerate like that… they're pulling something like 30g's! I'm just guessing, but I do not believe they'll have time to slow down. They'll be bookin' it at over four hundred thousand kilometers per hour."

Gene shook his head, "That puts them there right about the time Phoenix should be ascending, and the Accipiters can still launch their weapons. With that much extra velocity, they'll have even more kinetic energy."

Gene thought furiously, pacing back and forth on the tiny command deck. "If we accelerate towards them and release whatever we can shake loose in the cargo bay, they'll see us coming and evade. Axe, if we accelerate at max speed and alter course to match any evasive action on their part, will we have time to break off at the last minute?"

———

"No, Captain."

———

Lt. Samuel Ślusarski looked up from his station worriedly. Their VR helmets hid the pilots, Marlon Stevenson & Ariel Haines's, expressions. Samuel Cotterill and Brady Abraham, the navigators, broke out in a sweat as they exchanged glances.

Gene took a sharp breath and looked around at his crew, his expression grim and determined. He gritted his teeth and implored them all with his eyes. One after another, they all nodded understanding. To their credit, they each returned their attention to their work with bitter, determined resignation and more than a few sets of wet eyes.

Gene swallowed hard, "Mr. Pickle, please send to Phoenix and Atlatl. Tango One support craft accelerating to Keeper Landing Zone, ETA just over 7 minutes. Tango Two accelerating hard. ETA twelve minutes. Axe is moving to intercept Tango Two. Atlatl is now responsible for Artillery team retrieval. Please transmit all data and telemetry gathered as long as possible."

He hesitated before adding, "Remember us. Don't give up the fight!"

Repeating the procedure they had practiced at Ari'Shevn, the Blood Phoenix had warped out system and decelerated before returning to Earth.Erick Shultz reported excitedly, "Captain, Commander Cross reports the assault team has secured the Keeper, an Accipiter VIP, and several humans. They report no casualties. The prize team is in place and has secured the Keeper ship. Atlatl has launched with the prisoners on board and is en-route to the rendezvous point."

A raucous cheer broke out in the CIC. Phil let it continue for a long moment, allowing himself a broad grin of approval. "All right, people, back to business. We are not done yet. Phoenix, are you ready to handle the landing and envelopment?"

"Yes, Captain, it appears that the supports won't be a problem. The field can safely cut the ones I do not sever with my cargo restraints without overload. I'll ground excess energy on contact with the Earth itself."

Phil nodded, "Very well, Procee…."

Erick interrupted him, "Captain! Commander Morton reports Tango One support ships are inbound to intercept us, ETA seven minutes! He also reports that the second Accipiter fleet, Tango Two, was able to accelerate their approach much faster than expected, ETA twelve minutes!" He paused, then looked up with wide eyes, "Commander Morton reports Axe is moving to intercept Tango Two and requests Commander Cross exfil the Artillery team."

Phil's jaw tightened, "Very well. Phoenix, proceed as planned and speed it up as much as you can."

Phil frowned and nodded slowly, "Send to Commander Cross to exfil the Artillery team." He paused and swallowed, "Send to Commander Morton… God Speed."

Erick's eyes hardened, "Sending, Aye."

There was a sudden jolt as they stopped, and gravity switched from artificial to Earth and back to artificial. The screens brilliantly flashed white.

Phil shook his head, "With weapons fire?" The wall screen flashed with the light from kinetic impacts on the surface.

The screens flashed white, then again and again, and the ship began to shudder as the flares strobed hotter.

The strobing continued until it no longer came from the screen but filled the entire ship.

Earth
(former) South America, Peru
Artillery Firebase
July 26th, Day 358, 09:37

The standard ammunition load carried by the Stryker Dragoon for its 30mm cannon was 158 rounds. More had been squeezed in, but the mission was not supposed to last long enough to need much more. After all, they were a mountain and a valley away from the Accipiter festivities. The mission planners had thrown in more reloads in crates that had been offloaded from Axe, but even these had soon run out.

Captain Brandt ordered, "Launch another Puma! Get us more eyes over the valley!"

Specialist Dominic Djokovic launched the RQ-20 Puma UAV, sending it soaring into the sky. "Puma up!"

The Wardogs kept coming. Many were much larger than anyone had ever seen before, closer to elephant size than rhino. The big one's armor would have easily sloughed off the lighter 7.62mm and were only taken out by concentrated 25mm fire… as long as it lasted.

The tracer and incendiary rounds streamed like so many lasers and splashed fire upon the beast's armored carapaces. As heavier ammunition diminished, the waves of Wardogs surged closer and closer. They were now partway up the escarpment. The air shook with the thunder of munitions and the subterranean roar of the Wardogs.

In short order, both the Bradley's 25mm and the Dragoon's 7.62mm machine guns had expended their loads. With no further purpose served, Captain Brandt ordered their crews, led by Sergeants Brunson, Stein, Branson, and Hardaway, to dismount and bolster the secondary defenses, focusing them on the biggest targets.

They hauled out and began firing Carl Gustaf recoilless rifles, FGM-148 anti-tank missiles, and even a handful of FIM-92 Stinger shoulder-launched anti-aircraft missiles.

As the Wardogs inched closer, Gideon switched to an alternate frequency. "Lieutenant Porras… stand by with the special munitions."

Eduard answered, "Yes, General, standing by with the special munitions."

Moments earlier, they had run out of all but the final two six-packs of missiles, their last reserves. Gideon switched frequencies, "Lieutenant Lev & Zeev, raise your elevation to the maximum and set the submunition release to Three seconds."

Yosef hesitated before responding, realization in his voice, "Yes, General! Three seconds, max elevation!" A few moments later, he continued, "Ready, General!"

Zeev echoed, "Ready, General!"

Gideon was forced to shout over the rising din, "Shot!"

Anat and Brach fired, "Shot out!"

Twenty-four missiles were launched. Three seconds later, the missiles opened up, releasing a rain of bomblets. Fire roiled across the valley as the submunitions dispersed amongst the charging Wardogs.

A raucous cheer erupted among the men.

Suddenly, one of the now unoccupied Stryker Dragoons, both of which had been emplaced facing downslope so its weapons could bear, exploded and was thrown backward, nearly crushing Sergeant Brunson and Specialist Canales.

Captain Brandt beat Gideon to the order by calling out, "Fall back! Incoming!"

Just then, the second Stryker exploded, but by then, the area around it was clear.

Gideon called out, "Captain Brandt, what the hell is hitting us?"

"General, Puma video shows two weird-looking Wardogs, bigger than anything we've seen before, sitting at the other end of the valley. They've got something on their ba…."

He was drowned out by the simultaneous explosions of the two Humvees and their tribarrels. Sergeants Powell and Velázquez had barely gotten their crews away, and all were briefly knocked to the ground by the concussion wave. They staggered to their feet and began helping their men limp to relative safety.

"General, those big ass Wardogs are *firing* on us!"

Markovic nodded to himself, "So it's a line of sight weapon, or they'd have taken out the rocket launchers first. Make sure we transmit that video to Axe."

A new wave of Wardogs entered the valley and galloped, slipping and sliding across the offal of their blasted brethren.

Corporal Trujillo called out, "General Axe reports they will not be returning. Atlatl is to extract us instead, but they are already part-way to the rendezvous, so they have to double back… Sir, they will be late getting here."

Gideon thought to himself. They have the prize on board, so they will not risk a hot entry. They will have to come in full stealth and slow.

He whispered under his breath, Carmit, my love, it won't be long now. I'll be with you and our children very soon.

"Very well, Corporal. Captain Brandt… do what you can."

An impromptu triage area, led by Staff Sergeant Genovese and Specialist Adamson, was formed far back from the plateau's edge. The injured either limped or were carried or dragged there.

All the squads, well back from the lip of the plateau, opened up with the Milkors. The lightweight 40 mm six-shot revolver-type grenade launcher had originally been developed and manufactured in South Africa. The newer versions could fire higher pressure and longer-range rounds. Half the men desperately fed rounds to the other half as they fired round after round blindly over the edge into the approaching Wardogs.

Corporal Trujillo announced triumphantly, "General, Blood Phoenix has captured the Keeper ship and is away!"

Suddenly there was a brilliant flash beyond the other mountains, followed by another and another and another until it became a continuous actinic end-of-the-world maelstrom.

Lieutenant Porras shouted, "We're being nuked!"

Gideon thought furiously, "No, it is some kind of Kinetic strike. They're trying to keep the Blood Phoenix from escaping, so they are saturating the area!"

Captain Brandt ordered, "Fall Back! Fall Back! Ready the microguns!"

Gideon left the command area and walked over to Lieutenant Porras. "Lieutenant, no need to load the specials into the MLRS. We will not need to launch them at the Keeper ship now that it is already gone. Arm them where they sit. Set them for...."

A ripple of explosions interrupted him. He calmly looked over his shoulder to see that the now unmanned sandbagged 50 caliber machine gun emplacements had been hit.

The brutal, rock-crushing sound of the approaching Wardogs clawing their way up the escarpment now drowned out even the distant kinetic explosions.

Gideon sighed and put his hand on Porras's shoulder, "Arm them and give me the trigger."

Porras's eyes widened briefly, then he nodded quickly and opened the control panel, revealing the timer and controls. It was not 'standard issue' and had been constructed especially for this mission as a... "last resort."

If Atlatl or Blood Phoenix failed, Gideon had been ordered to launch the tactical nukes at the Keeper ship and destroy it.

They had also included a… self-destruct. Regardless of the outcome, no one was to be taken prisoner. The Accipiters must not learn of Fort Brazos's secret.

Gideon began to reach for the controls. *This is it, Carmit. I love you!*

Just then, the air around them shook and shimmied, and the Atlatl emerged from stealth just above the ground, meters away from the triage area, its ramp slamming to the ground.

Captain Brandt shouted, "Mount up! Get your asses moving!"

Porras's face lit up with desperate hope, and he looked the question to Gideon

Gideon frowned and sadly shook his head. "We have to be sure. Go, Lieutenant!"

Porras' chest heaved as he started to go but stopped. He turned back, tears streaming down his face. "No, Sir! You must go! I will stay!" Porras placed his hand on his holstered service pistol.

The air was shattered by the sound of dozens of oversized Wardogs screaming amid new explosions. The ground began to shake as they reached the minefield.

Gideon looked into Porras's eyes and saw that he would not yield.

The last of the teams were stepping onto the boarding ramp.

Forgive me, Carmit.

"Put yourself on report, Lieutenant… after you set a 30-second timer."

Gideon arrived on the Atlatl bridge just in time to see the detonation from orbit.

Pursuit Course near Earth

NTN Axe Bridge

July 26th, Day 358, 10:02

Stone-faced, Commander Eugene "Gene" Morton stared at the plot. His voice was calm and level as he asked, "Time to intercept Mr. Stevenson?"

Marlon Stevenson swallowed. He wanted to look up at his Captain, but the VR helmet made that impossible. At least no one would see the sweat pouring down his brow. He nearly choked at the words but managed to say them with a degree of calm strength and dignity that surprised even himself. "Sixty-four seconds, Captain."

At nearly fifty miles across, Tango Two Prime was more than twice the size of Tango One Prime. Like the other Accipiter ship, it too was studded with what everyone now realized were Keeper shrine ships from conquered worlds. Instead of golden, these were closer to Lapis in color and more intricately inlaid with Accipiter glyphs.

Gene put his hand on Marlon's shoulder. "Thank you… Marlon." He turned and looked around at his crew. "Thank you all. I want you to know that today you have struck a terrible blow to the enemy. We have denied them their object of worship, and we have killed God knows how many of them and destroyed much of the fleet that destroyed our world. You are, all of you, the finest men and women I have ever had the privilege to serve with."

Tango Two Prime quickly loomed in the display screen, and Gene had mere moments to appreciate the staggering grace and beauty of Accipiter design and construction before the NTN Axe collided with it.

Commander Eugene 'Gene' Morton, Lieutenant Samuel Ślusarski, Master Chief Hasan Khoroushi, Pilots Ariel Haines, Marlon Stevenson, and their backup Jocelyn Dennell, Navigators Samuel Cotterill and Brady Abraham, Environmental Tech Solomon Hicks, Communications Tech Chandler Pickle, Quartermaster Lee Herberts, Marine Security Team members Cary Aubrey and Dale Brooke, and the nascent personality of NTN Axe, flashed into ionized atoms.

The energy release from Axe's overloaded warp drive was that of a small star as it vaporized the titanic Accipiter ship and most of its escort ships in a holocaust of radiation. The concussed, expanding plasma briefly scorched the Earth's atmosphere over the Atlantic Ocean.

The blinding light faded, and Phil swallowed and looked around. "Report! Phoenix, what the hell just happened."

Long seconds passed before Phoenix answered, "Captain, we have passed through the last of the suiciding Accipiter ships…. We are clear to rendezvous with Commander Cross…. I will miss Commander Morton and his crew."

Phil swallowed, and he tasted blood. His voice was flat, "Very well, Phoenix. What are the dispositions of Tango One and Two?"

"Tango One Prime is drifting but appears to be regaining some power. Tango One's remaining support fleet is drifting. Commander Morton and NTN Axe destroyed Tango Two Prime and most of its support fleet."

"Mr. Shultz, Status on Commander Cross? Did he exfil the Artillery force?"
Erick nodded robotically, "Yes, Captain, the Artillery force was extracted. Atlatl is headed to the rendezvous point."
"I see."
Phil stood silently for a long moment. "Phoenix, why don't you give Mikaela and Lukas a break. Take us to the Rendezvous point."

Phil asked, "Phoenix, how bad was it? How much radiation?"

Mikaela and Lukas took off their helmets, their hair wet and matted. They and the rest of the CIC looked up at their captain, hoping for answers, hoping for hope.

Phil felt sweat forming on his forehead, and a wave of nausea pass through him. Looking around, he could see that the rest of his crew were experiencing similar symptoms.

Phil swallowed hard and stood at rigid attention. "Phoenix, you did the right thing. Tell me, how bad was it?"

Phil ground his teeth as he looked around at his crew. Their faces fell, and several valiantly fought back the tears. *We won't even survive to make it home.*

"I know you tried Phoenix. We all knew the risks were terribly high. Phoenix… I want you to know that no one here blames you. We blame the

Accipiters. You were our friend and companion on this journey…. Thank you. Thank you for helping us."

Phil swallowed and picked up the microphone, "Crew of the Blood Phoenix. What you have accomplished today will be remembered for a thousand years. You have done the impossible. You have slain Goliath and stolen the enemy's treasure. The victory you have wrought today will guarantee a future for mankind and was the first step in our ultimate victory."

He paused, "You are all too brave and noble for me to keep this information from you. It is my… It is my duty to inform you that during our ascent, after successfully capturing the Keeper Starship, Accipiter suicide attacks overloaded our drive…. Those flashes of light…. That was radiation that Phoenix was unable to handle. I am afraid that it was far too much for us to survive. Those in more shielded areas of the ship will live longer, but the dosage was fatal for us all."

"As soon as we rendezvous with Commander Cross, his crew will take over. You are free to keep working if you want or to rest. I am available if any of you want to talk. We have a supply of spirits aboard, and I'll be opening those up to any who wants them until we run out."

"As I said at the beginning of this mission… I could not be more proud of you."

He turned and walked to his cabin, whispering to himself, "Towards thee we rolled, thou all-destroying but unconquering bird; to the last, we grappled with thee; from hell's heart we stabbed at thee; for hate's sake we spat our last breath at thee…."

By the time Atlatl docked, everyone on board had been informed that Blood Phoenix's crew had received a fatal dose of radiation. Leo Talib had followed Gideon Markovic in a fugue and those crewmembers not staying behind to secure the ship and prisoners.

Thankfully, none of the ground team's injuries was life threatening, but many were still being cared for by the medics, Staff Sergeant Genovese and Specialist Adamson.

Everyone was still reeling from the roller coaster of emotions. First, the elation from the successful kinetic weapon strike on the Accipiter fleet had filled everyone with hope and enthusiasm. Then the Keeper had been captured along with an actual Accipiter, and the Keeper ship had been captured as well. Word of Commander Morton and his crew's sacrifice had rocked and shaken everyone. And now this.

Leo had stumbled twice as he climbed the long ladder up to the Crow's Nest. He was beyond words and had no idea what he was feeling. His heart was racing more than it had in the Accipiter ship, and he could hear the blood rushing in his ears. He found Sabrina sitting at one of the computers.

He gasped and cocked his head, asking tenderly, "Sabrina? What are you doing?"

She turned and looked up, her eyes hooded and her lips tight. Her voice was high and clipped as she answered, "Ah, you're here. I sent Glenys and Angus down to help with the casualties. I am cataloging the data we captured during the battle. It could be critical."

Leo strode over to her, put his hands on her shoulders and forcibly turned her around on the chair, and exclaimed, "How can you just sit there working like nothing's happened?"

Sabrina's eyes flashed, and she slapped him. Hard. "Leo, that's enough! There will be time for mourning later. Right now, I need to lock this data down. I will not allow any part of those people's sacrifice to be in vain!"

Leo stumbled backward, and his eyes widened as he touched his reddened cheek. "What are you talking about? How can you be so cavalier about your own life?"

Sabrina blinked for a moment before realizing what was happening. "My Life? Leo…" She shook her head, "Glenys, Angus, and I were all protected from the radiation here in the Crow's Nest."

Then she looked deeper into his eyes and realized that his anguished and entirely out-of-character outburst was about… her. Without realizing it, her own eyes widened, and she mouthed, "Oh."

She stood and walked towards him, but he stepped back, away from her. Reflexively she commanded him, with all the force and experience of her rank and command, "Stand Fast, Mister!"

Leo blinked and paused in confusion.

She stepped close and leaned in, and kissed him on the cheek. Startled by the fact that she herself was blushing, she lowered her voice, "I'm genuinely touched by your concern, Leo."

She raised her tone back to her command voice, "But right now, we both have jobs to do. Now, march your skinny arse back down to the Atlatl and start learning whatever you can from the prisoners!"

✪ ✪ ✪

Gideon Markovic lay in his bunk with the makeshift curtain closed. He was exhausted, and the adrenaline was starting to ebb away. He closed his eyes. He silently prayed, "I'm sorry, Carmit. Part of me wanted to join you and Anat and Brach today. I was ready to. I expected to, but I lived. Please forgive me. Please forgive me for not joining you… and for wanting to. So, I will keep fighting for you. All of you. I pray, though… please ask God to forgive me. I cannot face him myself. I killed thousands of people today. I know that I had to, but could I have even taken a moment to find another way? I know there wasn't one, but I didn't even try. I just saw all those people who were alive, when you are not and… and killing them felt… it felt good. Please kiss the children and ask God to forgive me."

Engineering Mate Bruno Serafim lay curled up on a blanket on the floor. Submarines did not have bunks for everyone. Some were shared, alternating use between shifts. With the entire crew down, space had been made wherever possible to try and make their final hours as comfortable as could be managed.

Leo sat cross-legged on the floor next to him, reading aloud Keats from a tablet computer, his face streaked with unrepentant tears.

> *Bright star, would I were stedfast as thou art—*
> *Not in lone splendour hung aloft the night*
> *And watching, with eternal lids apart,*
> *Like nature's patient, sleepless Eremite,*
> *The moving waters at their priestlike task*
> *Of pure ablution round earth's human shores,*
> *Or gazing on the new soft-fallen mask*
> *Of snow upon the mountains and the moors—*
> *No—yet still stedfast, still unchangeable,*
> *Pillow'd upon my fair love's ripening breast,*
> *To feel for ever its soft fall and swell,*
> *Awake for ever in a sweet unrest,*
> *Still, still to hear her tender-taken breath,*

And so live ever—or else swoon to death.

Bruno whispered, "Leo? Are you there?"

Leo answered softly, "Yes, Bruno, I'm here."

Bruno asked, "Will you go to Lake Charles for me? Put flowers on mama's grave for me?"

Leo swallowed and asked gently, "What kind of flowers, Bruno?"

Bruno shuddered and fell still.

NTN Blood Phoenix, Captain's Quarters
En-Route back to New Texas
July 28th, Day 360, 23:29

Phil Underwood huddled under his blanket in his bunk, shaking. He asked, "Charles?"

Charles Cross adjusted the blanket and mopped the sweat from Phil's forehead. "Yes, Phil?"

"Make it count, Phil. Get my people home."

"I will, Phil."

Phil shuddered and shook uncontrollably for several minutes. Charles sat on the edge of the bed and held him. He and Phil had been colleagues, if not friends, but it did not matter.

Phil managed to speak, his voice week and anguished, "Charles?"

He leaned in to hear him. "Yes, Phil?"

"This is a hell of a way to die."

And then he was still.

Homecoming

TopSide: New London

Starship Hangar 1
August 16th, Day 379, 2:51 PM

In the aftermath of the bombing at City Hall, and the uncertainty about the viability of the mission itself, it had been decided that preparations would be made for whatever outcome might surround the returning ship – whether that be party or wake. Everyone had assumed that either the ship would return, or it wouldn't, and that if it did return, casualties were most likely to be greatest among the ground forces. No one had anticipated the opposite, that they would return, in effect, as a ghost ship.

The arrival was actually four days early. Instead of stopping at Ari'Nell on the way back, they had headed straight for New Texas at best speed. Phoenix had pushed the margins desperately tight.

In order to envelope both the former submarine and the massive Keeper ship, Phoenix had coalesced and redistributed the mass of its twenty warp rings into just two, thin, narrow ones that encircled the unlikely pair of spacecraft, which were now scant meters apart from each other, held fast by the fabric of Phoenix's cargo restraint.

The effort to transport them both, at such a high speed, had depleted Phoenix's energy reserves to dangerously low levels, and Leo Talib had become even more deeply concerned about Phoenix's emotional state than his own.

As the enormous airlock doors closed behind it, Phoenix and her charges were gently carried by the gravity gradient, with the golden Keeper ship glittering in the strobing warning lights, into the pressurized hangar bay.

Alpha squad had remained onboard the Keeper ship as the prize crew. They had been protected against the radiation by its gold cladding and other characteristics of its construction.

Mission planning had included the possibility that damage or other dangers might have made staying aboard unviable. The option had been available for them to transfer via their spacesuits over to the Blood Phoenix's airlock for the remainder of their journey, but they had opted to stay put instead, "to make sure nothing woke up and caused a ruckus." They had space-walked back and forth a few times to ferry supplies and to check-in, but the rest of the time, they had simply "camped-out" and explored under the promise to "not touch anything."

The Keeper ship had a more or less flattened bottom, so Phoenix shrank its rings away from it as it settled onto the bay floor. The rings shrank back to the Blood Phoenix until it almost seemed to sag around the former submarine and settled onto the hangar bay deck.

As soon as the Blood Phoenix settled into place, a heavily armed security detachment surrounded the golden Keeper ship, lest anything untoward emerge from it.

Sergeant José Bolívar, Corporal Martin Yankov, and Specialists Bennie Davis, Troy Allen, Michael Ericson, and Samir Muhammad exited the grand portico airlock at the top. Someone would eventually figure out how to get ladders up to them, but in the meantime, they stood in formation at the edge of the platform, their uniforms as clean and respectful as they could make them, and they held their arms in salute.

Below, an honor guard hastily assembled on the hangar bay deck. The celebration party materials had already been hidden away.

Ramps were rolled up next to the Blood Phoenix's sail, and a stream of medics entered, cycling through the airlock. Minutes later, a dread silence fell over the hanger as three of the five remaining survivors, Marshall Hudson, Trey Waters, and Johnnie Reed, all of them 'Nukes,' shakily emerged, skeletal, gaunt and emaciated, assisted by Commander Cross, Stephen Prichard, and Maximillian McGreggor. The other two, Kelvin Becket and Don Adkins, were tenderly carried out by others from the Atlatl crew, who all followed.

The last to exit were Sabrina Chilton, Leo Talib, Glenys Griffith, and Angus Frazier. They all did their best to straighten their uniforms.

The medics then began carrying out the body bags. Flags previously meant for the celebration were placed over them as they were laid on any available rolling cart or table that could be scrounged up.

There were no bodies from Commander Morton's crew. Admiral Milner arranged for a line of officers to stand in for them, each holding their hat in front of them in their outstretched hands since there were not enough flags left.

President John Austin, his injuries healed sufficiently that he could now if briefly, stand, stood numbly, with Sergeant Benny Jenkins and Sergeant Jesse Roberts to either side, helping him stand. Next to John, Gail stood stiffly, her face a frozen mask. Admirals Milner and Johansson stood by as well, along with every occupant of New London who could make it there in time. They formed a line all the way to the Elevator.

Admiral Milner's face was pale and drawn as he called out, "Attention! Present Arms!"

Everyone, military or civilian, every man, woman, and not a few children, saluted.

The first body bag that rolled by under the salute of the honor guard was that of Captain Phillipe "Phil" Underwood.

The crew of the Blood Phoenix was much smaller than the Montana's had been. Raphael Milford followed him, then by Luis Perez, Mikaela Palmer, Lukas Wesley, Dave Ware, Cliff Ramsey, Zeke Eliott, Morton Hull, Kevin Appleby, Laurence Haines, Gary Neal, Joseph Burkett, Donald Warner, Payton Lyon, Rick Schultz, Otávia Mateus, Aston Winchester, Rogério Rios, Ronald Gerhardt, Flynn Coleman, Carl Markwardt, Denis Klement, Marshal Hudson, Bruno Serafim, Redmund Carroll, Carmen Rojas, Murdoch Foley, Brendan Neil, Niko Heintze, Don Adkins, Trey Waters, Kelvin Becket, Johnnie Reed, Darin Harman, Gus Cockburn, Sampson Rennold, Ernest Hilton, Abram Wescott, Maxwell Jacobson, and Joaquín Vásquez.

A deathly hush fell over the stadium as Matti pushed John Austin to the podium in his wheelchair. It was standing room only. Outside the stadium, video screens had been put up, and as many people stood outside as in. Waiting.

Matti stepped back but stayed close by as John gritted his teeth and stiffly stood. Seeing John stand brought a loud wave of cheers from the audience.

John surveyed the faces in the crowd. Despite the cheers, he could tell they were nervous and uncertain. *You and me both,* he thought.

He nodded to himself as the cheers diminished to a quiet hush. He began, "As you know, the last survivor of the Blood Phoenix passed away last night. Engineering Officer Marshal Hudson had been at his station monitoring the ship's reactor when he and the rest of the ship were exposed to a lethal dose of ionizing radiation due to the Accipiter suicide attackers that attempted to prevent the Blood Phoenix from escaping."

John swallowed, and his voice faltered slightly, "I was with EDO Hudson…." He paused and shook his head. "I was with Marshal at the end. Like so many after Awakening Day, he had no surviving family. Most of the people he knew had been his crewmates. I will tell you this. I have never before encountered such… profound bravery and determination as I did in Marshal Hudson. I cannot begin to fathom the pain that he was in, despite the medicine. He could no longer see, but he actually tried to smile. He told me… 'We got them… We got them good.'"

John paused and looked out at the faces in the crowd, "And then he was gone."

A sigh passed through the crowd.

John swallowed again. "And Marshall was right. He and the rest of his shipmates did get them good. Based on what we've been told about Accipiter ships and the records from the raid, the conservative estimate is that several million Accipiters were killed aboard their ships, one of their capital ships was destroyed outright along with most of its one hundred thousand support vessels and another one, the one that led the original attack on Earth, was severely damaged. It is unknown how many of its smaller craft were destroyed. Still, early estimates are at least thirty percent of its support and auxiliary craft, perhaps twenty thousand of them, were destroyed. In addition, on the ground, their entire city complex and surrounding area around where the Keeper ship was located was completely destroyed, first by General Markovic's bombardment and then more thoroughly by the impacts from the suiciding Accipiter small craft impacting the area."

Growls of satisfaction drifted over the stadium.

John continued, "But all of that is secondary. The primary purpose of the mission was to deny them the ultimate symbol of their victory. We captured their spy and the base he operated from as well."

The news was already well known, but the crowd erupted in guttural cheers anyway.

John let it die down, "What we have not announced before now is that we also captured a group of apparently indoctrinated humans, possibly slaves, although it appears that the Accipiters may have altered their minds and biology to make them compliant. Keep in mind that while only a year has passed for us, over sixty years have passed on Earth. We don't know if it is actually possible to get through to these indoctrinated humans, and there is a strong suspicion that they may have been physically altered, 'hard wired' as it were, to worship the Accipiters as gods. It might not be possible to save them, though we will try."

He let that sink in. People needed to hear this side of the story before the news broke that tens of thousands of humans were at the Keeper site. Or perhaps post-humans?

"In addition to capturing the Keeper spy and the altered humans, our assault team, led by Captain, and now Major, David Garreth, captured what appears to be a high-ranking Accipiter as well."

John was surprised at the stunned silence that followed. Then, a chant began that quickly caught fire, "String him up! String him up! String him up!"

John tried to raise his arms, but grunted in pain, then partly raised the arm that had not been shattered in the blast. The crowd quieted. "Part of me would like nothing more, but the other part of me realizes that this Accipiter could be a vital source of intelligence. As long as we can keep it alive, we can learn from it. Learn what makes it tick. Learn its strengths." He paused, "And learn its weaknesses."

Grumbling agreement limped across the stadium.

John shook his head. "We need to learn every last secret it has. And after that, we should put it on our flagship and let it watch his worlds burn, one by one until the day it dies of old age!"

The crowd howled in approval, "Watch them burn! Watch them burn! Watch them burn!"

Nathaniel Grant

Briefing Room A
August 30th, Day 393, 3:30 PM

Gail leaned back in her seat, "So, is the damned thing going to live?"

Eva Sanches and Gwyneth Elliott frowned and looked at each other. Eva answered, "Maybe. The Keeper ship is turning out to be a gold mine. Well, even more than the gold it is literally covered in: We figured out which foods were actually meant for the Accipiters. From that, we were able to start to get a feel for their proteins and such. Well," she smiled, "Gwyneth and her people were able to figure that part out."

Gwyneth agreed, "Bringing Eva in was a great idea. She has insights that would never have occurred to us."

Gail smiled, "Just don't neglect Heartbreaker while you're doing the exciting stuff, doctor. And how are your babies?"

Eva blushed, "Maximo and Nicolás are doing well, thank you, I miss them terribly. Jacob is taking care of them and apparently doing well, amazingly enough."

Gail smiled softly, "That's good to hear."

Gwyneth frowned again, "I'm more worried about the humans or whatever they are now. The Keeper seems OK. He is confused but not as combative as the others. The women are frankly terrifying. They apparently feel a need to take care of the Keeper, but I am afraid they might kill him to keep him from us if we let them. They are completely nuts, and I mean that as my official medical diagnosis. We had to separate them from each other. Two of them have stopped eating, and we may have to sedate them. The others may well follow suit. Oh, and they refuse to wear clothing of any kind."

Gail raised her eyebrows and sighed, "Do what you can. What about the other one?"

Gwyneth whistled softly, "Yes. That one. That one is the most interesting of all and, I suspect, may well be the most dangerous."

Gail cocked an eyebrow, "Dangerous?"

Gwyneth nodded, "Get this. He claims to have been alive when the Accipiters first attacked."

Gail laughed, "What? He doesn't look a day over 35."

Gwyneth smiled slightly, "And no offense to my husband or my newborn babies, but the man is probably the most gorgeous human being I've ever seen. He could have been a top-tier male model. You may have noticed the women also appeared to be somewhat, well, perfect?"

Gail frowned, "Uhm…."

Gwyneth went on, "Well, Mr. perfect says he has a name, that he used to be called Nathaniel Grant, and that he had been stationed onboard a nuclear submarine, the USS California when the Accipiters attacked. His submarine survived the attack and eventually surrendered. And, yes, I looked up Nathaniel Grant's personnel file. There was a Nathaniel Grant, aged 43, who was a nuclear engineer onboard the California. And his picture is a match, although the picture is of an older man."

Gail took a breath, "I assume there's an 'and'?"

Gwyneth nodded, "And, he says that after the attack, the Accipiters issued an amnesty, and he was picked out for special duty. The Accipiters improved his health and have kept him young all this time."

Gail shook her head, "Gwyn, what aren't you telling me?"

Gwyneth sighed, "Nathaniel Grants personnel file lists him as having an estimated IQ of 118, which is quite good. I will tell you that this man, whoever he is, is way smarter than that. I am telling you that whatever he tells us, whatever he does, he's playing us. If he *was* Nathaniel Grant, he isn't anymore. The Gardeners tinkered with us, making us healthier, but they did not radically change us unless you count maybe Sybil, but I don't think she's a good example. What I am saying is that this man is dangerous, and, based on conversations so far, I think it is a safe bet that he will never play on our team."

Gail raised her eyebrows. Eva had already been brought into the inner circle who knew about Sybil. What Gail was surprised about was the vehemence of Gwyneth's appraisal of Nathaniel. "OK then, treat AKA Nathaniel Grant as a hostile enemy combatant, not to be underestimated. Check. What about the Keeper?"

Gwyneth and Eva traded glances again. Gwyneth considered her words, "He seems quite intelligent and has been calm and gentle. My guess is that he has been kept alive by the Accipiters, keeping an eye on the planet, taking biological samples, just like we thought, but that he has been in isolation for pretty much his entire life. For Eons, he sent out his reports to the Accipiters, and then one day, they show up in person. It is too early to say, but we might have a chance to get through to him. Of course, we'll have to teach him English first."

Gail smiled, "OK then, take me to see them."

They stood, and Gwyneth turned to Eva, "Eva, would you mind? I'd like a private moment with the Vice President."

Eva nodded, "Sure, I'll see you both outside."

Gail looked the question at Gwyneth as the door closed.

"How are you, dear?"

Gail hesitated, "I'm surviving, Gwyn."

Gwyneth nodded and asked softly, "And the nightmares?"

Gail looked away, "I keep replaying everything over and over in my mind during the day, wondering what I could have done differently. The dreams are no different, only more tortured."

Gwyneth added, "And you did shoot the bastard. You've never done that before."

Gail twitched in irritation, "I should have shot him more times."

"Right…. And how is the President?"

Gail shook her head, "You mean how am *I* and the President, especially after I so publicly announced my feelings?"

Gwyneth cocked her head and frowned before answering softly, "You know what I mean."

Gail hesitated, "I don't know."

Gwyneth nodded, "He's not the same since the bombing?"

Gail looked up, "How did you know?"

"It's not unusual for severe trauma to alter body chemistry for a while or longer. When you had your crash, you only broke a leg. That man had severe internal injuries, head trauma, damaged and bruised internal organs, a broken leg, and a broken arm. He actually died on the operating table twice before being revived. I can't be sure, but the improved health and regeneration capabilities the Gardeners gave us may well have saved his life."

Gail winced as Gwyneth recounted John's injuries. "You're saying give him more time."

Gwyneth smiled gently, "Some people emerge from traumatic injuries and even things like heart attacks with a completely changed attitude towards life and the people around them. Maybe it is a reset in the brain chemistry. In your case, however, I have a feeling that your support has played a bigger part in his recovery than you realize."

"OK, Doctor. Enough navel-gazing. Let's go see our new guests."

The decision had been made to keep the prisoners TopSide and not let them see New Texas's interior. Should there ever be any kind of prisoner exchange, knowledge that the humans lived inside a hollow world was one piece of information no one wanted the Accipiters to have.

The women prisoners had indeed been unstable, and by the time Gail saw them, another had been sedated. They moved on to the Keeper, observing him from behind a two-way mirror.

He was still naked, leaving untouched the clothes he had been offered on a nearby table. In contrast, his small hairbrush was close at hand, and it was self-evident that he actively used it to groom his long body hair carefully. The room he was in was clean and orderly, and he sat on a chair with his legs crossed, calmly eating an apple.

Eva commented, "He is very deliberate and fastidious."

His intelligent eyes watched a video display inset into the wall that showed some of Leo Talib's translations between Accipiter and English. The translations included images and pictographs. He had been given crayons and sheets of paper with the thinking that crayons were not hard or potentially dangerous like a pencil or pen. He had already drawn and written on many of the sheets that were now stacked neatly on a table.

Gail asked, "What's he been writing?"

Gwyneth answered, "Doctor Talib thinks he is asking basic questions like what has happened and why and what happened to the women that were tending to him. I'm speculating, but I think he's worried that he is going to miss some important event."

Gail hmphed, "You mean when the Accipiters were going to turn him into a popsicle and his body into a religious icon? Somehow, I doubt that he quite appreciates the irony. Hey, Keeper, you've been such a great employee for the last zillion years. Here's your gold watch and a lovely chair to sit on in the freezer unit. OK. Let's go see Mr. Dangerous."

Nathaniel Grant also sat with his legs crossed in his chair and was equivalently perfectly groomed. His priestly robes had been confiscated, and he wore hospital scrubs and soft house shoes. He, too, had been given "safe" crayons and paper to see what he might write on them, but they sat untouched on the table. He faced the two-way mirror and sat with an intelligent, thoughtful, patient expression on his face.

As Gail, Gwyneth, and Eva entered the room, Nathaniel's expression changed slightly. He smiled.

Gail looked at Gwyneth, "Can he see us?"

Gwyneth shook her head slowly as though not wholly convinced herself.

Nathaniel smiled, "You must be this Vice President I've heard so much about."

Gail frowned and glanced at Gwyneth, who raised her hands in defeat. "So, Mr. Grant, it would seem that you have an interesting set of ocular upgrades from the Accipiters?"

"I'm quite sanguine about my relationship with the Accipiters. They have been very generous to me and to our world. Earth is a garden paradise now. There is no hunger, no disease, no crime, no fear, and no war. There is harmony with nature and the environment, and the Accipiters elevate us to join their chorus."

Gail smiled, "Whether we like it or not."

"Oh, don't be maudlin. It doesn't suit a pretty redhead like yourself."

Gail cocked an eyebrow at him, "And how exactly is preferring freedom and individuality maudlin, Mr. Grant?"

He laughed, "Oh, how very Republican of you and how small. The Accipiters were flying starships since before Homo Sapiens first gazed up at the stars. They are responsible for our development; they groomed our planet and us so that one day we might join them in the Galactic Community."

Gail narrowed her eyes, "I see. So, it is ok that instead of arriving at Earth's doorstep and saying, 'Oh, high there. You don't know us, but we have been grooming you and your planet for millennia, and now you've won the Galactic lottery; we're here to take you to the stars as our, what? Our equals? No, clearly not. Our pets?'"

Nathaniel lowered his gaze, "Oh, to paraphrase Michal Crichton, what intoxicating vanity! Do you think mankind deserves to be treated as an equal, on par with the staggering accomplishments of the Accipiters? After they arrived and silenced mankind's inanity, greed, hate, and corruption and then offered us peace, prosperity, and immortality?"

Gail showed her teeth in an icy smile, her green eyes frozen and hard. "Thank you. It's pets, then. Infants to be suckled or toddlers to be spanked. I understand.

So, tell me, Mr. Grant, what use are you to me? Why should I bother to keep you alive?"

Nathaniel smiled warmly as though accepting a gift, "Because, Ms. Vice President, I know everything there is to know about Accipiter Technology. The Keeper ship is nothing. A toy. You will keep me alive in hopes that you can convince me to share the information you desperately need."

He smiled wistfully, "Who knows, maybe you will decide to beat me or starve me enough that I will let slip morsels of information. Or perhaps you will try the carrot approach instead, in hopes I will accept my fate and cooperate and share my vast knowledge. On the other hand, you might keep me alive in case I might someday be useful for a prisoner exchange."

He stood and strode to the glass, moving with feline grace, "Or maybe, just maybe, Ms. Very fine Vice President, you will realize that whether I cooperate or not, I am your best hope for understanding the utterly alien Accipiter mind, and whatever your goals or aims really are, if you intend to live in this galaxy, you cannot survive in ignorance of the Accipiter heart."

He laughed, "You think you have won some great victory, but what you do not realize is that there are Millions of Accipiter clans spread across the galaxy, many substantially larger than the ones you so brutishly attacked. Very soon, every single one of them will be hunting you down, looking in every nook and cranny and turning over every rock until they find you and crush you like the primitive and insignificant bugs you are."

THE END

BOOKS IN THIS SERIES

Accipiter War # 1: A military town "awakens" to familiar surroundings but soon discover that they are not in Texas, or even Earth, anymore. The current-day city of Fort Brazos, Texas, and the nearby Joint Reserve Base have been abducted — scooped up whole and deposited inside a vast artificial hollow world, nearly 4000 miles long. Thousands are dead. Who has done this and why? Are the humans to be lab rats? Slaves? Or is there some other, terrible purpose… or a greater destiny? Accipiter War emphasizes hope and the endurance of the human spirit in the face of unthinkable tragedy.

Stealing Fire: Accipiter War # 2: The citizens of New London and Fort Brazos awakened to find themselves in a hollow world. Accipiter War # 2: Stealing Fire follows their journey of discovery and what promises to be a generational war against an ancient and galaxy-spanning enemy.Now they must race against time and conspiracy to launch the hybrid starship. The window of opportunity to strike a crucial blow against the enemy is closing fast, and they must somehow put their differences aside long enough to work together. If they don't, the Gardeners, the mysterious race that abducted them in the first place, might well decide the human race isn't worth saving after all.

The Forge: Accipiter War #3: After the harrowing raid on occupied Earth, the survivors struggle to cope with what they have learned and to devise a strategy. The Accipiter empire spans the galaxy, and while the remaining humans are safe, for now, the clock is ticking. The Accipiters are turning over every leaf to find them – and they have the millions of ships to do it with. The humans have one cobbled together hybrid. Secrets are revealed and desperate work begins to build defenses. Meanwhile, the true conspirators behind the homegrown attack remain at large. All the while, mysterious craters and fires begin to erupt closer and closer to town, and Phoenix is sent off on a secretive mission to parts unknown.

McKendree Cylinder (SPOILERS)

I've long been inspired by Larry Niven's Ringworld (Okay, it was bigger at 997,000 miles wide), Arthur C. Clark's Rama (just 31 miles long) and especially, Gerald O'Neil's Cylinder Worlds. Babylon 5 (oh how we miss you) was merely 5 miles long. The world of Fort Brazos is inspired by these dramatic visions and is closer to a McKendree Cylinder. The world Fort Brazos wakes up inside is nearly 4,000 miles long, with a surface area almost twice that of the moon and about half that of Mars.

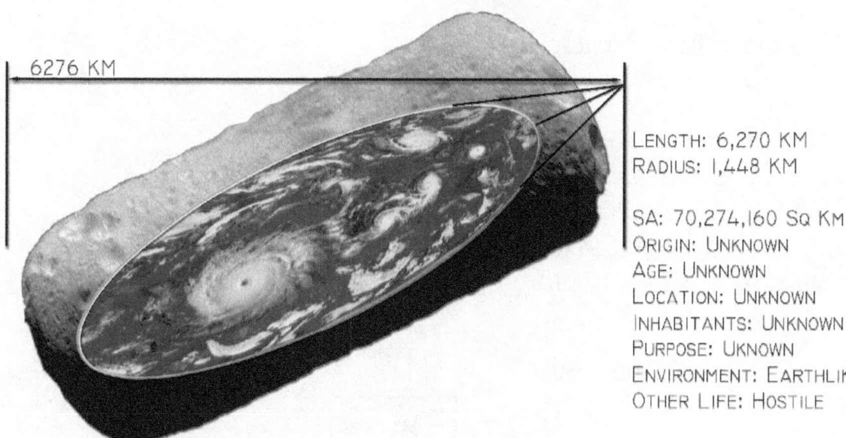

About the Authors

Patrick Seaman is the principal author. He created the concept and drives the storyline for the Fort Brazos series. He crafted concept art and managed creative development for Fort Brazos. Patrick is an entrepreneur, consultant, Internet pioneer, former publisher, editor, and author. In addition, Patrick is a lifelong shooting enthusiast and former rifle and pistol instructor.

Since helping launch broadcast.com in the early days of online digital media, Patrick has launched, advised, and served in many startups around the globe in C-Level positions or their boards.

You can follow Patrick at:

http://www.amazon.com/author/patrickseaman
https://twitter.com/PatrickSeaman
http://www.linkedin.com/in/patrickseaman
http://AccipiterWar.com
http://patrickseaman.com

Blake Seaman is an Information Technology executive, author, and classical composer. His music is available on all major streaming platforms. He is a proud resident of the State of Texas, where he celebrated the birth of his first child with his wife 6 months before the publication of this book; he dedicates his work on this project to them, and hopes to raise part of a new generation of Science Fiction fans. Blake is also an avid sports shooter and Tea aficionado.

https://BlakeSeaman.com
https://open.spotify.com/artist/3aK0vHFZEJ7YLq6a9CV9Yw
http://www.amazon.com/author/blakeseaman
http://www.cdbaby.com/Artist/BlakeSeaman
https://itunes.apple.com/us/album/fort-brazos/id961266753